Nina Blakeman

BLIND VISION

outskirts press

Blind Vision

v3.0r1.1

Outskirts Press, Inc.
http://www.outskirtspress.com

ISBN: 978-1-9772-3405-6

PRINTED IN THE UNITED STATES OF AMERICA

One

Wednesday, October 4, 2017 12:40 p.m.

He wasn't sure if it was a place for him—a town full of gumdrops and marigolds. She said it would do him good, curbing the cynicism he'd been nursing ever since he could remember. He'd heard them talk. Some drivel about the weather, corn prices, and the scratch-off. Often times, it would be followed with a full belly laugh, content in their own hillbilly minds. Before he knew it, he was sending them a disingenuous grin, conveying that he cared when, honestly, he didn't give a damn. But he'd bear it . . . *for her.*

They were in their early thirties when Callie and Richard came to Sperling to set-up their neurology practice, a small town just forty-five miles south of Fort Worth, Texas. It was just shy of twelve-thousand people and possessed a charm of a by-gone era. The fact that the bubbly Callie hailed from such a Rockwellesque burg was a surprise to no one.

Callie had just rounded on her patients at Lake Sperling Medical Center. She needed to get back to the office, appointments were scheduled to start in twenty minutes. Waiting for the elevator, she dug through her bag for her keys until the personalized key chain found her hand. It was a small rectangular block of wood with a pyro-graphic *Corky* etched into it. It had been her father's nickname for Callie, because of her buoyant personality—one that would make even the crotchetiest cur crack a smile.

The elevator doors opened. A laboratory technician was riding down, a supply tote in his hand. Callie turned from him to look straight ahead, hitting the lobby button. The doors closed only to reopen at the floor immediately below. The technician got off, but before he did, made a flippant inquiry. "You be going hobo Hollister, Doc?"

The remark confused her. She ignored the man as the doors slid closed with a soft *thump.*

The elevator stopped on the first floor and Callie stepped off, merging into the busy traffic of the hospital foyer. Various signs with arrows were suspended from the ceiling . . . Radiology, Surgery, Intensive Care, Cafeteria, Physician Parking. Staff and visitors were hurried, navigating their own predetermined course. Talk intermingled in the air with assorted conversations, varied in their degree of seriousness. But words such as *frayed*, *punk*, and *grunge* seemed to circle her.

A call came out. "Oh, Callie, I mean, Dr. Wallace, wait up. It's me, Marta. Hold up, will ya?"

Callie stopped in her tracks, hearing her name.

She looked over her shoulder to see Marta Gutierrez running after her, housekeeping cart in tow, using it to separate the crowd as if parting the Red Sea.

Marta put the brakes on, stopping just short of rolling over Callie's foot. She was out of breath. "Well, my goodness. Little Callie Wallace, all grown up. Your mother told me you were back in town—brought a handsome man with you, too!"

They shared a quick hug before Marta backed away sheepishly. The Gutierrez's and the Wallace's had been neighbors for years. Rose Wallace had remained in the family home, even after her husband's death. "His name is Dr. Richard Cortez, and we are just friends. I'm still with Zane. But home just isn't home without Daddy."

Her father's heart had failed him Callie's third year of medical school. If it hadn't been for Richard, she wondered if she would've even made it through. Richard had never wanted to take credit for the strength he knew she had within her all along. The death of her father had hit her hard, but when Richard had asked her what her father would say if he saw her crawling up into a ball and quitting, she knew the answer. Callie chuckled at the thought of her father using one of his many fishing metaphors. *Corky, I knew when I caught you, you were a keeper. But seeing you like this, maybe I ought to have just thrown you back.*

"You know if you come by and see your mother, I know she'd love it. And while you're there, I'm still pretty handy with a sewing machine. I mean, you're an important doctor now. No sense going around like a stray."

All of a sudden, Callie remembered how meddlesome Marta could be, and to make matters worse, she didn't have a clue what the woman was talking about. "Look, Marta, I'm really running late. Nice seeing you, but I need to get going. Appointments start in the office at one. Richard is a good friend, but I'm not going to take advantage of his good nature by sticking him with my patient load. I'll see you around, okay?"

Callie made her way to the automated doors that separated the hospital from the covered parking garage designated for physicians only. She stepped over the threshold and the doors slid closed behind her, shutting out the chaos of the hospital to echoing sounds of the advancing car, the screech of a brake, the occasional horn. She was oblivious to the alarm being sounded inside the facility, *code blue, code blue, room 501.*

Callie Wallace and Richard Cortez's friendship took root in medical school. They were both determined to be neurologists—their youthful fancy to be revered as Galileo to astronomy. Despite being separated during their one-year internship, the residency program put them right back into each other's orbit. And that's where they stayed, two dippers aligned in the sky. Now that Callie and Richard were in practice together, their relationship extended to colleagues. They took call for one another, shared administrative duties, and even gave each other a flu shot at the start of fall. Callie grimaced at the thought of the nagging ache that still lingered in her bum, even after a week. *Injections are definitely not Richard's forte*, she thought.

It was a little after one o'clock when Callie got to the office. Richard couldn't help himself. "Whoa, is that what they're wearing in Paris this year . . . or should I say Milan? Since when have you been into distressed fashion?"

Callie looked down at her ensemble, clueless to another baffling remark. She went into the bathroom to check in the mirror. At first, she didn't see it. But then she turned her back to the mirror and looked over her shoulder. There it was, where the sleeve met the bodice, the blouse was torn, revealing her bra strap, the color naughty noir, as it laid across the back of her bare shoulder. She walked back out with disgust plastered across her face. "I knew it would be just a matter of time before something like this happened. First, I over-slept and was rushed. Then, it was that tricky closet light. Sometimes it works, sometimes it doesn't. This morning it didn't. I've asked Zane to take a look at it, but he hasn't gotten to it yet. Do you know he had the nerve to ask me if the bulb was burned out? I've already made rounds at the hospital and no one said a word . . . or maybe they did: *hobo Hollister*, can you believe it? I'm sure this wardrobe malfunction is the joke of the hospital gossip-line. Do I have time to run home and change before we start seeing patients?"

Richard grabbed her lab jacket off the coat rack and fed her arms through the sleeves of the white lab coat. She obediently accommodated him. "There," Richard said, "no one else will know. Patients start any minute. Jamie already has the rooms filled. You know, this could be the start of a joke. How many neurologists does it take to screw in a light bulb?"

"Very funny," Callie pouted.

"Oh, come on," Richard said. "Where's your sense of humor? You, better than anyone, know the Atkins' ranch is about an hour's drive from Sperling. When Zane comes to see you on the weekends, I don't think home repairs are on his mind. You bought an older house. The problem could be a number of things. Sounds like a wiring issue to me. I'll tell you what. You make those chicken enchiladas of yours, and I'll come by tonight and see if I can't get to the bottom of the problem. Deal?"

"Deal," a grateful Callie replied.

It was then that Jamie Collins, the office nurse,

popped her head in. It struck Callie as strange as the nurse usually knocked. Callie half expected Jamie to tell them she was ready to get started on the afternoon appointments, but that wasn't what Jamie had on her mind. Her speech was pressured, anxious. "Dr. Wallace, the hospital just called. It's about Mr. Murphy . . . he's dead. The code-team tried unsuccessfully to revive him. Mrs. Murphy is on line two. She wants to know what happened to her husband . . . and she sounds mad as hell. I could feel the flames from her tongue licking through the receiver. I don't mind telling you, Dr. Wallace, she scares the shit out of me."

Two

Seventeen Months Earlier

Callie looked over the new patient's health history. The forty-six-year-old male, Clyde Murphy, reported with a history of relapsing-remitting multiple sclerosis since the age of thirty-nine, treated with the monoclonal antibody, natalizumab. She thumbed the patient's insurance information curiously as the drug was reported to cost over thirty-six thousand dollars a year. Her brows arched as she noted the man didn't carry insurance, but was self-pay. Last relapse was twenty months earlier. No known allergies. No children at home. Occupation: oil and gas. Purpose of today's visit: to establish himself with Sperling Neurology Group. Previous neurologist deceased, motor vehicle accident.

Callie knocked on the exam room door, simultaneously opening it as the words *come in* were muttered. "Hello, Mr. Murphy. I'm Dr. Wallace."

He stood briefly to shake her hand. "Nice to meet you, ma'am," the man said as he retook his seat on the exam table.

She'd seen it in the chart, but somehow, she

expected him to be taller. His presence exceeded his stature of five-eight. A weathered face and calloused hands spoke to a working man's ethic. A collared, long-sleeved, button-down shirt along with pressed jeans and cowboy boots could represent almost anyone who chose practicality over style. His cowboy hat sat on a chair in the corner beside his wife, who was a sharp contrast to his unpretentious spirit.

Mildred Murphy. Callie had seen her picture in the style section of the Sunday paper more times than she could remember. The rumors were that the woman had the temperament of a wild boar. There she sat, top-to-bottom in Coco Chanel, eyeing Callie like she was some country hick. "Well, you look barely old enough to enjoy a good martini," the woman huffed.

Callie knew taking on Mr. Murphy as a patient wasn't going to be easy because of the wife's reputation alone. But *he* was her patient, not the wife. "I can assure you, I'm old enough and duly qualified. Feel free to check my credentials, Mrs. Murphy."

A snide laugh came from the woman. "I can assure you, Dr. Wallace, I already have. Tell me, who are your people?"

Clyde intervened. "Now Mildred, don't be a snob."

The wife took offense at her husband's interference. "Clyde, I've spent countless hours with my charity work to support the medical community of this town. I feel I have a certain responsibility to the citizens of Sperling. I want to ensure we have as fine a medical staff that one would find at John Hopkin's, that's all. I mean, take her partner, for example. *Ick*, a scholarship boy, really? Is that someone we really want for Sperling?"

Callie noticed her patient staring up at the ceiling, an attempt to hold his temper. She didn't like the direction the visit was going. She knew Richard was just as qualified as she was, and how he afforded his education should be immaterial. Callie made a mental note to take that particular bit of information down from the website. She chose to ignore the question of her lineage and addressed her patient directly. "Mr. Murphy, I see from your chart you're in the oil and gas industry. Does your diagnosis interfere with your day-to-day activities, or your ability to make a living?"

"Heck, no. My grandfather was a wildcatter. I come from a long line of hearty stock. I have no problem getting my hands dirty, if you know what I mean. In fact, I prefer it to the paperwork, damn bureaucrats. I've been feeling pretty good on this medication. It's enough to break the bank, but it's worth it."

Mildred interjected. "Money is no object when it comes to your health, dear."

Clyde Murphy didn't mince words. "Mildred, my money is never an object when it comes to something you want. The bottom line is that you want me to make more money, is all."

Callie cleared her throat. "Excuse me, but I think we should get back to the matter at hand. Have you heard there is a new drug on the market, ocrelizumab? It's only given once every six months, but the cost is over sixty thousand dollars a year. I'll let you think on that and we can discuss it at your next visit, if you like."

"See, Mildred," Clyde said, "the woman is all business. I like that. You could learn a thing or two from her."

"Let's just hope she *actually* knows her business, dear," Mildred remarked flippantly.

Callie was losing patience. "I'm sorry, but I really need to examine my patient. Mrs. Murphy, perhaps it would be best if you went to the waiting room."

"Oh, let her stay," Mr. Murphy grumbled. "Trust me, Doc, what Mildred imagines happening can be far worse than what she actually sees. Mildred, keep that trap of yours shut and stop interrupting, okay?"

Annoyed, Mildred pressed her lips tight, and jerked her head to face the wall.

"That's more like it," the man said. "Doc, I suppose we ought to get on with this. Mildred can only stay this way for ten minutes or so before her personality splits. Now, do I need to put on one of those gowns, or what? To be honest, I'd rather not."

Callie bit her bottom lip to keep a laugh from escaping. “That won’t be necessary. I just need you to take off your boots, socks too.”

Callie donned a pair of gloves and rolled her chair over to the dangling pair of legs. “Mr. Murphy, close your eyes and keep them shut until I instruct you to open them.” Callie saw the man shut his eyes. She grabbed his big toe and pointed it upward. “Mr. Murphy, is your toe pointed up or down?”

“Up.”

Callie caught Mrs. Murphy leering at her, but when Callie met her gaze, the woman quickly turned away. “Okay, now, is it up or down?”

“Still up,” he replied.

“Now?”

“Down.”

Mildred was antagonized by the idea of *up down, up down* being a legitimate medical test. Their grandchild was capable of such rudimentary foolishness.

Callie picked up a blunted needle and a cotton ball. “Okay, sir, tell me if you feel something sharp or soft.” She went on to finish her sensory and proprioception assessment before moving on to examine her patient’s motor function, balance, and coordination. The exam ended with a screen of the man’s cranial nerve function.

“Well, am I going to live, Doc?”

Callie was preoccupied, going through the records that had been forwarded to her office. "How's your diet?"

"Appetite is fine," he replied. "There's nothing like a steak seared on the grill and a loaded baked potato."

"No fish?"

"I can't stand the smell. The taste is even worse."

"Any trouble with your prostate? Does prostate cancer run in your family?"

Mr. Murphy looked embarrassed as he firmly stated, "No cancer. And for your information, I can still knock the paint off the fence at six-feet."

Callie had her back to the man, still rooting through his record. She let a grin slip at his reference to the force of his urine stream. She came across the man's prostate-specific antigen test that was within normal limits. "I see that you had a PSA less than a year ago and it was normal. I want you to supplement your diet with fish oil. It has been shown to reduce disability progression with fewer relapses. You told me that it's been almost two years since your last relapse, so let's do everything possible to maintain the status quo. In your record, it states your last infusion of natalizumab was two weeks ago. Is that correct?"

"That's right. Is the infusion still every twenty-eight days?"

"Yes, that means we need to set you up to get that

done in two weeks, here at the clinic. Jamie will help you with that on your way out. It hasn't been that long since you had an EKG and nothing today makes me think there's an issue on that front. But I do want you to get a complete blood count today so I have a benchmark for comparison before your next treatment. I'll call you only if there is a problem, but I don't expect one."

Mr. Murphy looked surprised. "So, is that it?"

"That's it. No need to worry, no prostate exam today, okay?"

His laugh was somewhere between joy and relief. "You know, you're all right, Doc. I have to admit, I felt a little reluctant coming here today, but you seem to know your shit . . . I mean stuff, pardon me, ma'am. You got a sense of humor too. I like that."

Callie saw the man's boots sitting up on the floor with the socks neatly rolled inside. She picked them up and handed them to her patient. "I think you're okay too, Mr. Murphy. I'll see you in a couple of weeks, but call if you need anything beforehand."

Mildred saw the physician preparing to leave, her husband digging his socks out of his boots. "Doctor, if you will, a word in the hall."

The wife followed Callie out of the room, shutting the door behind her. She obviously didn't want her husband to hear. "Look missy, you may have wound

Clyde around that little finger of yours, but you need to know, right now, I call the shots. When I say jump, you ask how high. You got that?"

Callie wasn't fazed. She half expected it. "Mrs. Murphy, I need you to understand something. No one dictates to me how to practice, or how I conduct myself with my patients. It should give you some solace that my powers of observation are quite keen. Right now, all I see before me is a woman whose roots are showing and has lipstick smeared on her teeth. Oh, and that lump on the side of your neck, you should really get that checked out."

Three

Wednesday, October 4, 2017 06:45 p.m.

It gave her some peace, Richard being there. Callie had meant to hire an electrician, but she couldn't seem to break away during normal business hours to meet a repairman. Richard swore he could fix that closet light. He was a champ. But because of her trying day, he politely asked if they should make it another time. Frankly, she was glad to have him nearby. He'd told her he felt guilty about asking her to cook, so he stopped and picked up a pizza. She was visibly upset about Mr. Murphy, her patient with multiple sclerosis whose condition had relapsed. The treatment with daily high-dose intravenous steroid had ended and the transition to a moderate dose every other day was proving uneventful. Callie had planned to discharge him the next day. A visiting nurse could oversee the rest of his treatment at home until she could transition him to oral prednisone. The wife had wanted answers, but Callie didn't have any.

A preoccupied Callie sat on the couch with her feet tucked beneath her. With one hand, she twisted her soft, brunette hair around her finger—a habit she picked up after constant chewing on her thumb nail finally drew blood. A partially eaten slice of pizza dangled limp from the other. She had no appetite, guilt burning in her gut. Overcome with worry, she brooded over what Mr. Murphy's autopsy would show. Only the occasional sound from Richard's cordless tools brought her from the mental library she'd been sourcing as to the possible cause of her patient's death.

Richard came out of the bedroom with his tool box and a couple of empty cartons in hand. "Callie, I think I got it. *Electrician*, ha! I told you I could do it. All I have to do is flip the breaker that feeds the bedroom, and you'll be able to witness the plethora of skills I possess."

Callie only managed a half-smile to Richard's attempt at self-deprecating humor.

He was gentle with her, wiping a single tear that had managed to escape the cusp of her eye. "Callie, you lost a patient—it happens. We knew going in we'd meet something like this."

Her self-confidence was shaken, embarrassed that Richard had picked up on it. She didn't want him to see her vulnerable, a quality her mother had told her was *unattractive*. "When you flip that switch, watch for sparks," Callie countered. "I don't want the house burning down before I make my second mortgage payment to the credit union."

Callie was relieved when Richard went out to the garage. It gave her a minute to pull herself together. On her way to the bedroom, she stopped by the kitchen to throw the remainder of her uneaten slice in the trash. The doorbell caught her off-guard.

She opened the door. The harsh early autumn sunset caught her in the face. Callie put her hand to her brow and narrowed her eyes.

There was Mildred Murphy on the doorstep, wearing designer shades and a Carolina Herrera pantsuit in winter white. No such thing as a fashion faux pas to be caught in traditional white after Labor Day . . . no, not for the socialite. But neither was she in mourning black. The woman's expression was one of disdain. A venomous disparagement began to flow from her mouth to slap the physician down to a mangled, belittled fragment.

"I . . . I'm so . . . sorry," stumbled from Callie's mouth.

The enraged woman took no solace from those words, only gasoline to the fire. Words like *squash*, *eradicate*, *eviscerate*, *maim*, *career castration* came at Callie like a hurricane's mighty wave to a dinghy.

"Get the hell away from her, now!" Richard asserted, coming from behind to put his hand to Callie's shoulder. "You don't belong here, Mrs. Murphy. This is highly inappropriate."

"And I suppose it is appropriate that my husband is being hacked away on by a forensic medical examiner?" the indignant woman sassed. "Maybe Dr. Wallace should have chosen *that* as her specialty! After all, what harm could she do to the dead, right?"

Richard slammed the door in the woman's face. He pulled a drape to the side to see the woman go off in a huff. That was quickly followed by the screech of tires peeling out.

"You shouldn't have done that," a beaten Callie muttered. "She's going to ruin me, you know."

"You need to put it out of your mind," he advised. "It does no one any good. We know nothing until the autopsy results are in. Come on, let's go check that closet light."

Callie reluctantly followed her friend to the bedroom to see a soft glow of light flood into the dimly lit room. Callie sat on the edge of the bed, staring blankly into the lit closet.

Richard sat down beside his grief-stricken partner. He didn't expect what came next . . . her lips on his. He gently pushed her back. "Callie, this can't happen. You're not feeling yourself."

"Richard, how can you understand? Nothing like this has ever happened to you."

He wanted to lighten her mood. Richard tapped her knee, "Come on, I'm hungry. Come with me to the kitchen and keep me company. You didn't eat all the pizza, did you?"

"I barely ate at all," she replied.

Richard didn't want it to come out like this, but he figured there wouldn't be a good time. "Well, I'll make you a deal. You eat another slice, and I mean the whole thing, and I'll tell you about a woman I've met. Our second date is this Saturday."

Callie wasn't sure how she felt about the news. She feigned excitement. "That's great. Tell me a little something about her."

"Well, like I said, it's just date number two. It's too soon to tell if she's *the one.*"

"Let's be fair. You know everything about Zane. He'd be here now if he didn't have to run the family ranch."

"I admire Zane, I really do. It's great how his whole family pitches in to help. It's my understanding that's what a family is supposed to do. I have to say, you are both from better stock than me."

Richard was envious of Callie's fond childhood memories. While enjoying her childhood in the sleepy, backwater town of Sperling, Richard grew up on the streets of southeast Fort Worth. Day-to-day, it was a struggle. Richard was the youngest of three boys. When he remembered his father, the man who'd run out on his wife and children, the memories were nothing but bad.

They lived in a two-bedroom apartment. The boys were latch-key kids, and while their mother worked, they had to fend for themselves. His older brothers would smoke grass and watch TV. That in itself didn't bother Richard because it mellowed them out. The worst thing that happened was their insatiable appetite—one that left Richard with a bellowing belly.

By the time Richard graduated high school, both of his brothers had been in trouble with the law. Richard saw they had no future and was determined to build a life for himself, hoping to leave behind the shudder he felt as the shrill of a siren screamed down the street. He wanted to provide his mother with a life that his dead-beat dad hadn't given her. Richard worked hard, graduated at the top of his class. Scholarships and top recommendations got him into Dallas's Southern Methodist University, then medical school followed. His only regret was that he hadn't befriended Callie earlier. He knew of her, but really didn't *know* her. *Wallace*, a familiar name stuck somewhere in a myriad of memories. A group project forced them together. He was captivated by her charisma and her upbringing. She was unlike any of the inner-city women he'd known. She was energetic, smart, and beautiful, inside and out, and she spoke with a slow drawl. But Callie made it clear from the start she had a beau back home, Zane Atkins. He was the son of a prominent rancher. The long and short of it, that guy was from money.

"Growing up, you had it pretty rough, but you grew up solid," Callie said. "No matter what you came from, you've been a good friend to me."

"That's it, Callie. A friend. I know how you feel about Zane and I don't like seeing this side of you. And another thing, I want you to stop beating yourself up. Besides, you've got call this weekend. How else am I supposed to go out on my date?"

Callie chuckled, feeling a little better. He always had that effect on her. "You're right, Richard. I just have to find a way to process what happened and move forward. And about earlier . . . it won't happen again, I promise."

Four

Twenty-three Years Earlier

Richard came barreling up the stairs to their third-floor apartment, as fast as his nine-year-old legs could take him, anyway. He stormed into the apartment to see his mother seated at the kitchen table. She was going through her coupons.

"Mamá, where are my brothers?" Richard asked, trying to catch his breath. "I can't find them."

"Ricardo, today is Saturday. Your brothers have two more Saturdays after this one before their community service assignment is complete. I won't be picking them up until five o'clock this afternoon."

"They're sure in a lot of trouble for just making a mess," the boy concluded.

His mother didn't look up from the task of trying to keep the weekly shopping list within budget. "It's called vandalism, Ricardo. It's a crime. At least I can depend on you not to disappoint me."

Richard appreciated his mother's vote of confidence. He went and sat in the chair next to her for a lack of anything better to do. After all, most of the good Saturday morning cartoons were over. "Mamá, I keep telling you I like to be called Richie. That's what my friends call me."

Teresa Cortez felt her muscles tense to her son's words. "Ricardo, keep your voice down. Your father is home. He doesn't like it that you snubbed your nose at your given name, Tohias Ricardo Cortez. He's very proud of his Hispanic heritage. Calling you Ricardo is his form of compromise, not Richie."

Richard was pragmatic for his age. "Nothing wrong with being Hispanic. Nothing wrong with being white, either. You're white. The only difference between you and Dad is that you're not an asshole. That's the real difference in people. Isn't it?"

Teresa pulled her son's chair close to hers. She bent down to be near his ear. "Keep your voice down, niño. That's no way to speak of your father. Besides, you know how he gets when he's upset." Suddenly, she felt self-conscious of the bruises to her arms, pulling down her sleeves to cover them.

But it was too late. Richard had already seen them, as he'd seen the others over the years. He glanced over at the calculator display which read $37.50. He knew his mother's grocery budget was forty-five dollars for the week to feed five people. He knew it because it was her reason to deny his countless requests to add whatever sugary snack or cereal to the basket. "I've got five dollars hidden in my room if you need it, Mamá."

Teresa felt as if her heart would melt. "Oh, Ricardo, no, no, no. That's your money. Besides, you have a birthday party this afternoon for that girl in your class. You plan on buying her a gift, don't you?"

"I thought maybe you might have a spare lipstick or something I could give her. Girls are hard to buy for . . . they're complicated."

Teresa couldn't help but laugh at the elementary analysis that came so close to the truth. "Oh, Ricardo, you're the brightest star in my sky, you know that? Tell me, why were you looking for your brothers?"

Richard was busying himself going through the coupons as a boy might look through baseball cards. "I want to ride the bike to the party—it's twelve blocks away. They told me I always have to ask, first, before I can use it." He held up two coupons. "This one expired a month ago. This one says you need to buy two to get one free. Sounds expensive."

Teresa picked the expired one out of her son's hand. "Oh darn, that's the one I was looking for. It was for a dollar-fifty off laundry detergent. Just once, just once, I'd like to buy the name-brand. I guess it's store-brand detergent again this week."

Richard sat there, offering no solution to his mother's ongoing problems. "So, what about the lipstick?"

"Ricardo, the lipstick mamás wear isn't meant for little girls. A gift like that might upset her parents.

Now, as far as the bike, you can tell your brothers *I* said you could use it, okay?"

He smiled at the thought of having that issue solved. Richard didn't foresee a problem getting there, but when it came time to leave, the other parents would come to pick up their kid and see him starting to walk home. Someone would insist on giving him a ride—one that would inevitably end outside their run-down apartment building. At least with the bike, he'd be able to hold on to some of his dignity. "But what am I going to take as a gift? What about a package of cookies? Here's fifty-cents off Keebler's."

Teresa knew her boy saw the practicality of the idea. What little boy wouldn't like his own package of cookies? What little boy wouldn't like his own party? These were things her children were often denied. "Hijo, you know that if I came home with a package of cookies, and your father got wind of it, he'd take them for himself."

"But what if we kept them in the car?" Richard countered.

"What if your father takes the car? If that happens, the cookies won't be there when he comes home. You know that."

"But what if I put my name on it?"

Teresa was close to tears. It was easier with the older boys . . . they understood. "Ricardo, your father has had a difficult life. He works hard. He gets grumpy sometimes."

"It's not an excuse to eat a kid's cookies. I hate him."

"Ricardo, don't say such a thing!" Teresa exclaimed, looking around to make sure Tomas wasn't within earshot. It tired her, always on the defense and trying to keep the peace.

"You work hard too, Mamá. I've seen him stealing from your purse."

Teresa knew that they all did, except her Ricardo. "Hijo, I don't know what makes some people so selfish. It's best not to hate him, but pray for him."

"Whatever," Richard muttered under his breath.

The mother knew she was going down a bad road. She needed to change the subject. "I'll tell you what. Go to your room and get that five dollars of yours. You can go to the store with me. I bet we can find a package of flavored lip glosses, fruit or ice cream. I think your friend will like that and it's something meant for a girl her age."

That excited the boy. Richard liked the idea of going with his mother. She didn't make his stomach hurt . . . not like his father did. "Okay, but let's get the ice cream flavored. Kids don't like fruit." He ran off to his room—the one that he shared with his brothers.

It didn't take long before Teresa heard her son, a

mix of anger and tears. "What are you doing in here? Hey, that's mine. You give that back!"

"Shut up, you damn brat," Tomas grunted. The man put his hand on the boy's forehead and pushed. Richard fell backward to land on his ass, knowing better than to cry. He watched as his father pocketed the five.

Teresa came rushing in, not knowing the extent of the latest Tomas crisis she was walking into. "What's going on, Tomas? Why is Ricardo on the floor?"

"He's got my five dollars, Mamá."

Tomas had been regarded as the most handsome boy at school. He'd been a smooth-talker, always saying the right thing. He'd talk-up her parents —yes, sir, this . . . no, ma'am, that—her friends envious, wanting every detail in which to compare their lives to hers. But when she'd gotten pregnant, no friend could be found. Tomas had done what was expected of him, but as each child came, he got meaner and meaner. Teresa lost count how many times Tomas had told her that she'd ruined his life. "Tomas, he's just a boy. Give him his money back. If it's for beer, I'm about to go shopping. I'll pick you up a six-pack. We'll just go without meat one night."

Her husband looked down at the boy with contempt. "Damn little shit. You and your tattle-telling. Everything under this roof is mine. You understand that?"

His father loomed over him. Richard was anticipating his father to take a shot at him, so when his father swung his foot to kick him, Richard scurried with his feet and hands to take his keister in reverse. The man missed, which pissed him off even more.

Teresa knew the look on her husband's face, the scowl with spittle seeping from the corner of his mouth, jaw clenched. It was the 'I want to hit someone' look. She cautioned her son. "Ricardo, go to Mrs. Martinez's apartment. Stay there until I come to get you."

Mrs. Martinez. It was code that Richard needed to get to a safe place right away. She was a gruff, widow woman who lived down the hall. But her real name was Martin, not Martinez. When Richard would arrive, the woman would call the police about a disturbance at the boy's apartment, no details. When the police arrived, that would end the abusive encounter. Tomas would apologize for being so loud and reassure them that everything was fine, just a little spat. He'd tell the authorities that it wouldn't happen again . . . until it did.

Normally Richard was quick to obey his mother, especially when his father got that way. But today, it was different. "I'm not going to leave you, Mamá. We can call the cops," he said through the tears.

The father was furious at the boy's insolence. "You

a big man now, cry-baby?" A nefarious laugh was followed by Tomas grabbing his son by the back of his shirt and a belt loop of his jeans. Richard was physically thrown from the room, hitting a leg of the table as a few coupons drifted to the floor. The bedroom door slammed shut and Richard heard the lock engage.

Richard heard his mother's pleas from the other side of the door. "Ricardo, please, just go to Mrs. Martinez's. Don't make trouble—be a good boy."

Stupid bitch! Stupid kids! Then they came—his mother's excruciating cries.

Time and time again, Richard heard his father's hand hit his mother. A resonating sound meant the hand was open, a thud meant it was closed. A fist. Richard felt his bravery shrinking to nothing. His mother had told him that fighting back would only make things worse. He remained on the floor, covering his ears to muffle the sounds. But Richard soon realized that his paralysis wasn't doing his mother any good. He got up and ran out the door, headed for 'Mrs. Martinez's'. She knew the drill—they all knew the drill. He confessed to the woman that it was all his fault. His mother was being beat-up over five dollars. His five dollars.

Five

Wednesday, October 4, 2017 11:20 p.m.

Callie hated the idea of taking a sleeping pill, but she'd done it anyway. She had gone to bed a little after ten and had been tossing and turning ever since. Her mind was still reeling from the day's events. Within only minutes she felt the effect, her eyes getting heavy. Just when she was about to doze off, she felt a presence in the room. She leaned over and turned on the lamp.

Her heart shook in its sac. A phantasmal vacuum sucked at her life-giving breath, solely, purposely, lobe-by-lobe. Bile rose in her throat. Hands and feet went cold, plebes in the hierarchy of circulatory need. Eyes became keen, targeting each dust mote daring to show itself in the murky light.

"Corky, don't looked so surprised," the man said. "I told you I'd be there for you if you ever needed me."

Callie just stared at the man wearing a fishing vest and a wide brimmed bucket hat, hooks dangling.

"What's the matter, Corky? Cat got your tongue?"

Callie's response was no more than a whisper into the night. "Daddy? It can't be."

"Corky, you were always so stubborn. Open your mind, will ya. I only died, I'm not dead."

Callie looked to where the man sat on the edge of the bed. The mattress gave to his weight and the bed covers creased to accommodate him. The presence had mass. "But it's impossible."

"Is that what that high-dollar education got you—that I'm impossible? I thought I taught you that anything is possible. Why do you think I spent all that time chasing that thirty-pound bass? I never broke any records, but I got you. I'm so proud of you, Corky."

"Are you real?"

"Well, of course I am." The apparition rolled up his sleeve and there was the tattoo of a rose on his forearm. Rose was the name of her mother. "How is your mother doing, Corky? I don't know how well she'd tolerate me 'popping in' like this—her blood pressure and all. Oh, never mind that, let's stay on topic. I understand from a Mr. Murphy that you had a bad day."

Heavy were those words from her father, a specter or a dream, that sent tears spilling from her eyes. "Oh, Daddy, I lost a patient today, a Mr. Clyde Murphy. I've been over it again and again in my mind. I can't understand what made him die so suddenly. I suppose it could have been a clot, but it wasn't like he was inactive. I had ordered physical therapy throughout his stay, solely to prevent such a thing. Or maybe . . ."

"Easy now, Corky. You could let your mind run wild, or you could just accept that it was his time. You know when God calls you home, you go home. I ought to know. I've been on the receiving end of that order."

"Daddy, were you . . . were you scared?"

"Scared of what, Corky?"

"Of dying," she said softly, as if she said it too loudly, the Grim Reaper himself would surely darken her door.

"Oh, heck no. It was like the end of a fine day of fishing, once you've bagged your limit. I was content to head on home."

"Mom and I have missed you, especially Mom. To this day, your rod and tackle box sit right where you left them. Aunt Clare mentioned her son might like to have them, and well, let's just say they haven't been welcomed since."

The man laughed so hard he clutched his side. It felt like old times. "That's Rose, all right. She's always been such a spitfire. I guess that's what gets her blood pressure up. I told her the best remedy for that was a day of fishing, but she never took to it . . . called it *boring*."

Callie gave a smile.

"That's my girl. Now, lay back down and go to sleep. I've got to get going. I was told to be back by midnight or they'd lock the pearly gates. You don't want your dad locked out, do ya?"

"No, Daddy," she said as she started to close her eyes. "Daddy, will you be back?"

"You can bet on it, Corky."

"I'm glad," she said, her voice trailing.

Six

Friday, October 6, 2017 12:20 p.m.

It was the breakroom, otherwise known as the nurses' lounge. It was anything but aesthetically pleasing or relaxing. Practical was the word, he thought. The walls were eggshell-white with spotty scuffs so apparent, they stood out like type to a page. A card table with a few fold-out chairs served a utilitarian need, but little else. A dated refrigerator and a microwave that hadn't worked since he'd been hired three months ago showed the disregard of the place. Marcus stooped low, grabbing his earbuds from his locker. It was number fourteen of fifteen, the last of three rows of five—the one that ran along the floor.

Marcus Davis was a skinny African American man in his mid-thirties. He worked on the neuro intensive care unit; nothing so dignified as a nurse, but an orderly. The work was menial, but it was what his job called for . . . his *real* job. Personally, he didn't care for its duties or the collateral damage that came with it. But Dr. Callie Wallace had no right to talk to him that way. She'd laid into him like he wasn't even human.

He only had a half-hour for lunch. He hadn't even

eaten. He wasn't hungry, and that in itself was odd. Despite having a voracious appetite, and no other symptoms, his mother had once dragged him, and embarrassingly so, to the doctor to test him for worms. When the physician had informed his mother that Marcus was completely healthy, the thought should've eased her mind. But instead, she continued to peruse her folk medicine books as to why her baby boy wasn't gaining weight like the other children. To that day, he hadn't got over the humiliation.

Marcus put his earbuds in. He wanted to try and relax with some music while he waited for Jamie Collins to get there. Marcus wanted to know why her boss had gone all postal on him late Wednesday afternoon. He'd tried to shake it off, but it wore on him like a splinter festering under the skin. He leaned back on what passed for a couch. With his eyes closed and his long, lanky legs stretched out in front of him, Marcus started to relax. But it was short-lived. It wasn't long before Jamie was shaking Marcus's knee. He opened his eyes and pulled out the earphones. He was relieved to see that no one else was in the lounge.

It took Marcus a minute to get his thoughts together. "Hey, Jamie, thanks for coming over. You know I don't have much of a lunch break, too short for me to meet you over at the Neurology Group offices."

Jamie replied, "I have to tell you, I was a little

surprised to get your call. The incident you described that afternoon just doesn't sound like the Dr. Wallace I know."

"Well, I'm telling you it happened. She freaked me out, Jamie. Dr. Wallace became unglued, yelling at me like I'm some piece of nothing. Dang, I'm the one who found Mr. Murphy, but I didn't kill him."

Jamie inquired, "Just tell me exactly what she said."

"Well, first she wanted to know the *exact* time I found Mr. Murphy's body, where it was, and how it was positioned. She wanted to know the last time I checked on him. She also wanted to know how long it was before I found Mr. Murphy's body and the time it took for me to call a code."

Jamie looked puzzled. "Perhaps she just wanted to know what the hell happened?"

Marcus thought about it, and that only made him more anxious. He got up from the couch and started to pace. He was frustrated that Jamie didn't seem to be *hearing* him. There was a whine to his voice. "Jamie, girl, you ain't getting it. She was all kind of disrespectful to me. She wasn't asking me, more like interrogating me. Trust me, I know the difference. She was writing down everything I said. I felt like she was trying to catch me in a lie. She was asking about Mr. Murphy's chart. She told me she was going to go through it with a fine-toothed comb and if she found any discrepancy between what I said and the written record, she would take the issue to administration."

Jamie was sympathetic. It was apparent the encounter had left him shaken. "Marcus, I'm sorry the situation went down like that, but try and understand her position. I think this is the first patient she's lost *unexpectedly*."

Marcus felt exasperated. "Jamie, I ain't nobody's dog. She had no right . . . no right."

"Look Marcus, if I were you, I wouldn't take it personally. Both Dr. Wallace and Dr. Cortez are seeing patients in the office this afternoon. Let me feel the situation out. If she's still smoldering, Dr. Cortez always has a way of putting it out. I'll talk to her if I can."

Marcus didn't seem to appreciate Jamie's *don't worry* advice. "Man, Jamie! You got to help me. I need this job. I got a wife and a kid. Then there's the bills, man, the bills."

"I'll do my best, Marcus. Call me later tonight, okay? I'm not trying to say the incident wasn't hard on you, I can see that it was, but the Dr. Wallace I know isn't one to threaten anyone's job."

Marcus was adamant. "Well, you got that wrong, because she did. You weren't there. You didn't hear her, I did."

It was then that Jane Timmons popped her head in the lounge. She was the head nurse of the neuro intensive care unit. Her words were sharp and to the point. "Davis, lunch is over. Mr. Campbell's bathroom light is going off. He needs help getting back to bed. And this time, do a better job cleaning his ass."

Seven

Friday, October 6, 2017 12:30 p.m.

Piped Italian music flowed from above. Synthetic ivy climbed the Tuscan sun-colored walls, reaching for imitative windows, complete with shutters and flower boxes. An artificial braided ficus intermingled with twinkling bulbs accented the room. Strategically placed antiquated wood burning stoves and casks brought forth a bygone era. Softly lit, it was a place for lovers, but that Friday afternoon, Callie sat across the table from her mother, Rose Wallace. It was Callie's idea for the impromptu lunch at *Olea's Kitchen*. Her first appointment for the afternoon wasn't until two. The waitress came and sat two glasses of iced water in front of them.

"Good afternoon, ladies. My name is Mia. I'll be taking care of you, today. Are there any questions about the menu?"

Rose barely acknowledged the woman's presence, and Callie followed suit.

"Okay . . . fine," the waitress mumbled. "Our special today is an autumn squash, pear, and pecan salad with a cup of roasted red pepper bisque. Can I bring either one of you something else to drink while you continue to look at the menu?"

Rose was quick to respond. "Callie, I'm going to have a glass of wine. Care to join me?"

"Mother, it's a little early, don't you think?"

"No, I don't," Rose spat. "I'll take the house cabernet, and make it a large pour. I have a feeling I'm going to need it."

Annoyed, Callie did her best not to let it show. "I'll take iced tea, unsweetened."

Mia scribbled the drink orders down and left.

Callie made sure the waitress was out of ear-shot. "Mother, what was that dig about?"

"What are you talking about, Callie?"

"The one about you *needing* a drink."

Rose thought her daughter would have observed the obvious. "I just happen to know what this little lunch is about, that's all."

Callie's response was curt. "Oh, you do?"

"Callie, it's like I told you when you called the other night, or should I say in the middle of the night, your father has been dead years now. There's no way he materialized in your room. You're a woman of science, for Pete's sake. It was just a dream. You said it yourself, it didn't happen last night. What did you do, not sleep? I'm only asking because you look like shit. And before you ask, no, he's 'never come to visit me.'"

"Thank you, Mother. Thank you for making your daughter feel like some hungover hag. But maybe, just maybe, you never needed him as desperately as I did. It was so real. Why can't you believe me, or at least pretend to?"

Rose bit back, but kept her voice low, stern. "I have never believed in supporting false narratives. What you're purposing simply isn't realistic. But primarily, I just don't believe in ghosts!"

Mia approached their table with the drink order. The word *ghosts* still lingered in the air. The waitress wondered why all the nuts got seated in her section. She managed a smile as she set the drinks down. "Are you two ladies ready to order?"

Callie watched her mother out of the corner of her eye. She was hungrily going after her wine, so Callie decided to tell Mia her selection. "I'll take the special, the soup and the salad. Mother?"

Rose set her wine glass down. "I'll have the spinach and feta quiche."

Mia made note of the order then collected their menus. She wondered if the haunting tale would continue to be spun once she left their table.

Again, Rose went for her wine glass. Before she drank, she grumbled, "I can't believe I came out with you only to be lectured on how I don't support you enough."

Callie didn't want to be so hard on her. Her father's death had been especially difficult for her mother. "I just wish you could be a little more like Daddy, that's all."

Rose shot back. "Well, I'm not your father . . . and I'm not dead." She sipped. "*But I'm beginning to think that might be preferable at this point*," she mumbled under her breath.

Callie took offense, pointing her finger at the woman. "See? *See*? That's what I mean. Instead of trying to ease my anxiety, you're turning my fears against me. This is like Tinker all over again."

"That yippy dachshund?"

"I loved that dog," Callie recalled. "You let me believe he'd run away. I looked for him for hours. I went to bed crying. And then what did you do to make me feel better? You told me you found him and had him put to sleep."

"Well, I had," Rose replied.

"Mother, that's not all you said. You said we needed to get a good night's sleep, so we could go wake him up in the morning. I was eight. I believed you. Apparently, my grief was keeping you up."

"Callie, that was twenty-four years ago. And don't underestimate the importance of a good night's sleep. Besides, parents lie to their kids all the time. It's part of the job. You were a child. Now, you're grown. You need to learn to cope with the unpleasantries of life. And unfortunately, death is one of those."

"Mother, I saw the rose tattoo on his forearm. The colors were so vivid; the green leaves emerging from the delicate stem, the soft, red petals perfectly nudged, one inside the other."

The wine wasn't numbing Rose fast enough. She took a gulp and swallowed hard. "Callie, it's not like I didn't love your father. I can assure you I did—and still do. But that eyesore on his arm did nothing for me. Despite that, over the years, as his skin lost its tone, the flower seemed to wilt and the colors fade. Not to mention the sun spots from all those years on the lake. Your memory of it was manifested through a drug-induced dream."

Mia approached the table with their orders as *drug-induced dream* left the older woman's tongue. The wine glass was almost empty. The waitress noted the small port-wine smudges that stained the corners of the customer's mouth. Mia put the food down in front of them and asked if they needed anything else. A *no thank you* look sent her on her way, so the two could continue their ominous conversation of spooks and pharmaceutical trips.

Callie took a bite of her salad. She closed her eyes as the fall flavors left a smile on her face. She relished the balance of savory and sweet. "Oh, Mother, you should try this. It's delicious."

Rose wiped her mouth and repositioned the napkin in her lap. "Callie, if I wanted to try the salad, I would've ordered it. Now, tell me what really has you so upset. Is it the ugly business surrounding Mr. Murphy?"

Callie dropped her fork at the mere mention of the man's name. Diners in close proximity heard it hit the floor with a clatter, then a diminishing metallic pulse until it sat still in the aisle. "Mother, Dad knew about Mr. Murphy, too. The man is the one who told Dad to come see me, that I needed him. What if Dad somehow relayed that bit of information to you?"

"Like extrasensory perception?"

Mia had arrived with a clean fork and placed it near Callie's plate. She bent over to pick the dirty fork out of the walkway. *ESP*, she thought, giving a cheesy grin as she walked off.

"Why not?" Callie responded. "I can't seem to convey to you how *real* this experience was for me."

Rose was becoming exasperated by her daughter's illogical rationalizing. She drained her glass before explaining. "I'll tell you why not," Rose spouted. "Sperling is a small town, Callie. I ran into my neighbor, Marta Gutierrez, at the market yesterday morning. She works in housekeeping at the Medical Center. She told me. Frankly, Callie, ESP? Are you losing it?"

Callie hung her head at the notion. "I'm sorry,

Mother. I know I must sound so foolish. You're right, I'm not dealing with the root cause of my anxiety. Richard came over Wednesday night to fix my closet light. It was great having him there, but after he left, I guess I let my worst fears get the better of me. When I was young, Dad always made my troubles seem to disappear. And no one knows better than me about those awful side-effects associated with sleeping pills. I feel so ridiculous. I guess there might be something else, I suppose."

Rose lifted her glass, but sat it back down, genuinely surprised it was empty. "And what would that be?"

"Well, Richard told me the other night that he'd met someone. In fact, he's got a date with her this weekend. What if I'm feeling a bit insecure about that? I mean, since we met, I've pretty much had him all to myself. It's going to be more difficult to spend time with him alone if he has someone special in his life."

Rose was feeling the wine. She giggled. "I guess so . . . unless the woman is into sharing."

Mia was unfortunate enough to hear the reference to a swinging lifestyle. She wondered *why me*, and if her whole day was going to be inundated with freaks. She smiled in spite of her thoughts. "If there's not going to be anything else, I'll be your cashier when

you're ready." She went off, leaving the check behind on the table.

This time it was Callie that chuckled. "Mother, you don't think she heard you, do you?"

Rose reached in her purse for her wallet. "I've got this, Callie." She grabbed the check. She took the pen that accompanied it and jotted something on the bill. That was before putting it to the table's edge with the credit card atop.

Curiosity got the best of Callie. She picked up the check and read what her mother had written. *For a good time call 555-0162.* Callie had to put her hand to her mouth to muffle the laugh. "Mother, you're incorrigible. Whose number is that, anyway? It looks familiar, but I can't quite place it."

"Oh, it is, dear," Rose snickered. "It's your Aunt Clare's."

Eight

Twenty-two Years Earlier

Clare came home from work, two sacks of groceries cradled in her arms. She sat them on the kitchen counter and hurriedly began to unpack them.

Rose watched her harried sister scurry around the kitchen, and looked at the items that were placed on the counter. "Clare, what's going on? Spaghetti? Salad? I thought we were eating out tonight."

"Change of plans," Clare said.

"But I've been cooped up in this tiny apartment of yours all day. I told you dinner was going to be my treat," Rose explained.

Clare turned the tap on full blast. She began to fill a large pot with water, not stopping to consider what her sister was proposing. "We can go out anytime."

"Clare, I'm going home to Sperling the day after tomorrow. You're the one who asked me to come visit you here in Dallas. During my stay, you haven't taken any time off work to spend with me, and then when I think we're going to have a night out, you tell me we're staying in."

Clare didn't even look at her sister. "Look, can you

give me a hand here? I need these vegetables chopped for the salad. I also need this bottle of wine opened so it can breathe. We're having a guest for dinner. He's going to be here in twenty minutes."

Rose realized the issue of going out was a dead one. She started to wash off the tomatoes. "So, when did you become an expert on aerating wine, and by-the-way, who's the guy?"

"The man from across the hall, Tomas Cortez."

Rose couldn't believe her ears. She shut off the faucet, demanding Clare's attention. "Clare, stop. Look at me."

Clare was perturbed, one hand on her hip, the other holding a jar of ready-made sauce. "What is it, Rose?"

"You know good and well what's the matter. I told you about that man my second day here. He gives me the creeps. I've caught him watching me when I go downstairs to get your mail and I think he followed me when I went out for a walk the day before yesterday. That's why I've avoided going out until we're able to go out together. How is it he's coming to dinner?"

Clare saw the water starting to boil, adding three handfuls of pasta. "I ran into him in the lobby this morning on my way out to work. He suggested we get together. He said he would bring dessert."

"I can't believe you, Clare. Did it ever occur to you to ask me if I was okay with it?"

Clare had the spaghetti sauce jar turned upside down over a pan on the stove. Years of resentment and jealousy were taken out on the remnants that clung to the side of the glass jar with each jerk of her arm. "Ask you? Ask you? You with your husband, the little girl, the beautiful home, the perfect figure. Hell, you don't even have to work. Some guy takes an interest in me and you somehow turn the whole thing into something about you. Can't you do this one thing for me?"

Rose knew her sister always had a way of turning on the guilt. "Clare, what do you really know about this guy? If he's home during the day and available for dinner in the evening, does he even have a job?"

Clare moved over to crowd her sister, bumping her hip against Rose's. "Here, get out of the way! I'll make the salad myself. Tomas will be here any minute. And for your information, he works construction, and it's been a rainy spring."

Ding-dong

"Damn it," Clare spouted. "That's him. I haven't even had a chance to check my hair or make-up. I'm going to freshen-up. Let him in, will you? Fix him a drink."

Rose couldn't believe how the evening was

unfolding. Briefly, she entertained the idea of packing-up and going home, but Clare would never forgive her for not being her wingman, woman, or whatever. The spaghetti sauce had already started to boil with bits of it erupting and spattering the stovetop. Rose turned the burner down, took a deep breath, and went to answer the door.

He was handsome, no doubt. Rose had a fleeting thought, *what does this guy see in Clare?*

"Can I come in?" Tomas asked.

"Yes, of course. Excuse my manners," Rose said, stepping aside to let him pass.

He handed her a discounted store-bought apple pie as he came in. The pasta water could be heard boiling over. Rose hurried to the kitchen to take care of the latest problem—one of many she felt would follow that evening.

"Anything I can do to help?" he asked.

Rose turned off all the burners to the stove. Her resentment was growing. Why is this my headache, she wondered. She felt the man's eyes on her, as she had before. He'd followed her to the kitchen.

"I see you're wearing a wedding ring. Married?" he inquired.

"Yes. You? Children?"

The man's conflicting response struck Rose as odd. He nodded an affirmation, but spoke a denial.

"Nay, the whole family thing isn't for me. Tell me, does your husband tell you how beautiful you are?"

Rose wasn't sure what to say. That's when Clare sashayed out of the bedroom, beelining it for her guest. Rose couldn't remember a time when she'd been so glad to see her sister. Clare emerged from the bedroom in a low-cut, skin-tight number, and high heels. Her sister had trouble pulling off the look, being only five-foot-two and stocky. Rose had once heard a classmate of hers refer to Clare as corn-fed.

"Oh, Tomas, I think the idea for a dinner party was a grand concept," Clare emoted. "Oh, and look, you don't have a drink. You must forgive my sister, Rose. She doesn't understand the fine art of entertaining, bless her heart. She's here visiting me from a quaint little town called Sperling. Is scotch, neat, okay?"

Tomas ignored the woman, but extended his hand to Rose. "Tomas Cortez, nice to meet you."

Rose reluctantly shook the man's hand. "Rose Wallace," she said.

In the last minute, Tomas had learned the enticing woman's first and last name and where she lived. As far as he was concerned, the evening was going splendidly.

"Tomas, that drink?" Clare reminded him.

"Oh, yes. Scotch will be fine, but on the rocks, please."

"I'll get that for him, Clare," Rose said. "I think you two should go into the living room and relax. It's much more comfortable in there."

"Good idea," Clare said. "Tomas, let me show you my selection of movies. Perhaps we could watch one after dinner. I do have to warn you, though. Some of them can be a bit racy, but we're all adults here, right?"

Tomas took the drink Rose handed him. His hand on hers lingered longer than it should. "Clare, you go ahead. I'll be there in a minute. I see some soda there on the counter. I think I'll add a bit to my drink."

Rose saw her sister reluctantly walk to the living room. She didn't like the feeling of being alone in the kitchen with this man. She busied herself, straining the pasta. She was about to transfer it to a serving bowl, but he was behind her, tight behind her. Her body was pinned between him and the sink. She smelled the liquor on his breath, heard the clacking of ice in the tumbler as he continuously swirled his drink. A rhythmic rocking of his hips was a repetitious reminder of his growing erection. "Clare," Rose urgently called out. "Can you come in here and give me a hand?"

The pressure on Rose was released. She could still smell it, the man's carnal stench that hung in the air like a rank musk. She felt sick. Clare was in the doorway to the kitchen, annoyed. "Some sous-chef you are, Rose. Do I have to do everything myself? Tomas, go on into the living room. I have some movies picked out. They're on the coffee table. Maybe there'll be something that interests you. I have to help Rose get this dinner on the table. Give us five minutes."

Clare watched as Tomas went off into the other room. "Rose, is it too much for me to ask that you give me a few minutes alone with this guy? Do you really need help, or are you just trying to sabotage my life?"

"Clare, I really don't feel well. Maybe you should ask him to leave," Rose pleaded.

"Well, isn't that convenient. Do you want me to be alone the rest of my life?"

"Of course not."

"Well then, if you're not really feeling good, just sit at the table and pick at your food, sip some water."

"Okay, but after dinner I'm going to excuse myself to go pack," Rose told her sister. "I think I'm going to drive home in the morning. I miss my family. Besides, you'll be at work all day tomorrow, anyway."

"Last I knew, I was your family too, but all right. I think I have things handled from here."

The three sat at the table, making small talk. Tomas's wine remained untouched, but he'd drained his scotch glass. "Clare, honey, can you go fix me another drink? Just a splash of soda, okay?"

Clare was all too eager to please her handsome

neighbor, but Rose didn't want to be left alone with the man again. "Maybe I could get it," Rose offered. "Clare, stay put."

"Nonsense," Clare said. "I'll get it."

Rose watched Clare disappear into the kitchen, Tomas watching too. He turned back to face her. His stare on her was so intense, it was as if he wanted to control her, own her. No sound was emitted from him, his lips forming the words to mouth, *I want to fuck you.*

Rose was in shock, paralyzed by the man's mute assault.

Clare suddenly reappeared, full scotch glass in hand. "Rose, maybe you should go lie down," she suggested. "You're awfully pale."

Rose thought she'd have trouble finding her words, but she was wrong. "Clare, you need to excuse me, but I have to pack. I'm going to be driving back to Sperling tonight."

Nine

Friday, October 6, 2017 2:05 p.m.

Gus was sixty-two years old and feeling every bit of it. The afternoon sky was darkening, thunderheads forming, explaining why his joints were aching like they were. He wasn't due to get off until five, and he still needed to replace the thermostat in the physician dictation room on the neuro floor. He planned to do it after his break.

Gus took a drag of his cigarette. He'd picked up the nasty habit back in the army. Most of his smoking buddies had quit. . . or died. Gus preferred if he could be a member of the former and not the latter. Maybe after the first of the year, he thought. He recalled when he'd tried before, using the gum. But the cravings were too much, and he started up again. He figured he'd have to get a prescription for the pill he saw on the television and go that route. But he wasn't ready to give it a go just yet. It was what he'd witnessed a day ago that still had him unnerved.

Gus Ferguson was a maintenance electrician with the Medical Center. He'd received his ten-year pin at the employee appreciation dinner two months ago.

He got that and a twenty-five-dollar gift certificate to *Barbeque Bucks* downtown. To him, the certificate was worthless. As a kid, he'd gotten sick from a bad brisket. To Gus, the aroma of tobacco was much preferable to the stench of smoked meat.

He heard his name from a distance, breaking his chain of thought. "Hey, Gus," Marta called. She was busy taking the cellophane off a new pack of menthols. She had no more gotten to the Butt Hut with a cigarette between her lips, when Gus had the lighter ready for her. She took a deep breath in. She wanted to get the nicotine's full effect to the pleasure center of her brain. Once she exhaled, Marta pulled her sweater tight around her chest. "I guess a cold front is blowing in . . . burr."

"Yep," Gus agreed. "I remember a time when we could smoke in the lounge with a cup of coffee. Now, we've been cast-out to this smoking station. It's like the frontier. Could it be any further away from the hospital?"

Gus realized something was off. "Hey, what are you doing working today? It's Friday. You work the first part of the week, right?"

"Someone called in sick. They called me to see if I could fill in. It's just for eight hours, not twelve. I get off in an hour, but I wasn't going to let them cut me short a break." Marta looked up at the corrugated covering overhead. "Well, it isn't much, but it's got a roof to keep the rain off of us," Marta reasoned. "Would this be considered a poor man's pergola?"

Gus exhaled. The rising gray plume began to dissipate before his eyes. "No, I think it's more like a bus stop with a smoker's outpost stuck in the middle of it."

Marta eyed the simple roofed structure and its wooden bench. "I suppose you're right. What do you have going on this afternoon, Gus?"

"Oh, I need to replace a thermostat in the dictation room up on neuro, dreading it, too. Did you know the voice recognition tool of the patient's electronic medical record that the physicians use is powered by artificial intelligence? Hell, that shit is going to take all our jobs."

Marta thought of the incident on the neuro unit the other day. Codes were always *messy*. "I cleaned up in the room Mr. Murphy coded in, *after*. I'd like to see AI clean a room like that . . . a real train wreck. Too bad the guy had to die. I hate it when we lose one. You know, I ran into Dr. Wallace's mother yesterday morning at the store. She didn't seem to know a thing about it. Now, in my culture, a family member's business is the whole family's business. It's how we do things."

Gus had finished his cigarette and looked at his watch. "I guess I have time for another." He lit it up and took in a deep breath.

Marta noticed the man's troubled look. "Something bothering you, Gus?"

"It's just. . . it's just, I think there's a whole lot Mrs. Wallace doesn't know about her daughter."

Smoke rushed out of Marta's mouth and nose. "Gus, what are you talking about?" she asked before taking another drag.

"Oh, it's that finicky thermostat. That's where it started."

Marta's brow furrowed. "I'm not getting where you're coming from."

Gus took a puff before he continued. "Yesterday, I got a work order for that dictation room. It was freezing in there. The thermostat was set to heat, but it didn't. The blower was working, though. I had the cover off. I was about to cut the power to the unit to mess with the wiring when Dr. Wallace came in. I was going to tell her good morning, but something about her didn't seem quite right."

"What do you mean by *not right*?"

"Well, she came into the room and it was like she didn't see me, but I was clearly in her line of sight. It seemed like, to her, I wasn't there. Marta, I know in my gut, she just didn't see me. Then, she started talking to herself."

The gossip fascinated her. "Well, don't keep me in suspense. What did she say?"

"It was like she was having a fight with someone who was not there. It seemed personal. . . some guy named Zane. She said she'd been waiting for him her whole life, and she was still waiting. She said he wasn't enough man for her. Real cold stuff to say to a guy . . . real cold. She said half the time he smelled. Oh, and then there's the matter of kissing. She said his kisses disgusted her."

Marta's curiosity was piqued, a familiar name. "Zane, you say?"

"Weird, right? I thought the gentlemanly thing to do was to clear my throat, so she'd have to acknowledge me."

"Then what did she do?"

"She was looking straight at me, but I'm telling you, she didn't *see* me. Then, she said 'how dare you' and slapped the air. After that, she turned and left. That, on top of the thing with the Murphy patient, I don't know if the two things are connected or not."

"Maybe she just needed a place she could blow off some steam. You know, practicing what she was going to say. Are you sure you were in her direct line of sight?"

"I'm positive plus there was the clearing of my throat. It just didn't register to her that someone else was in the room except this Zane guy. . . who wasn't."

"Well, you know her mother is a neighbor of mine,

and I happen to know that Dr. Wallace is a good woman. Have you told anybody else what you just told me?"

"Heck, no. She would just turn it around on me, making me sound like the crazy one. After all, she's a physician, and I'm in maintenance. I'm too old to be finding another job. That's one of the reasons I dread changing out that thermostat. What if it happens again?"

"No, no, she only comes to the hospital in the mornings to make rounds, unless there's an emergency. In the afternoon, she sees patients in the office."

Gus put the remainder of his cigarette out. His break was over. A tapping was heard overhead, light rain hitting the tin roof. "I guess it's starting to rain. We better get going before it starts to pour."

Marta abruptly stopped him. "Oh, Gus, I'm making tamales this weekend. Can I put you down for a dozen?"

"Make it two, Marta," Gus replied. "You make the best in town, but I have a proposition for you. At eight dollars a dozen, the total would be sixteen dollars. What, instead of paying cash, I give you a twenty-five-dollar certificate to *Barbeque Bucks*? You'd come out ahead nine dollars on the deal."

"Nice try, Gus, but I still have my certificate from two years ago. It'll be strictly cash."

Gus started to laugh, but the rain was coming

harder. "I guess we better make a run for it, or we'll get soaked." They dashed towards the hospital, but they were only able to run half-way before they both broke out in an atonal symphony of emphysemic hacks.

Ten

Saturday, October 7, 2017 10:20 p.m.

Jane was in the last stall of the staff restroom. Most of the patients had gone to sleep, and she depended on the ancillary staff to keep things quiet. She fastened the tourniquet around her left arm, and put the end of the band between her teeth. Once a flash-back of blood streamed into the syringe, Jane yanked her head sharply to the right to release the band's restriction. She slowly pushed the morphine into her system. She planned to sit on the toilet until the initial rush of the high plateaued to a steady-state of euphoria—one in which she would finish her shift. Habits like Jane's were best carried out on the night-shift. That's why she *volunteered* to work the Saturday 7P-7A shift that was often so difficult to staff.

Jane Timmons had been in her position at the hospital for the last six years. During this time, she'd endured multiple trials. One of which included her husband of twenty years, running off like he did. She went to work one morning, like she had so many times before. When Jane came home, she'd found he'd moved out and left her nothing more than a *Dear*

Jane letter. The irony of it still stung. She had quickly checked the bank account, and it was empty with the rent due in two days. Her husband had run-off with a dental hygienist thirty years his junior. She was only five years older than their son, but she had perky breasts and porcelain veneers. The other woman insisted their son call her mommy. . . the bitch.

Jane wasn't sure at what point after her husband had left that things started to spin out of control. One day, she looked in the mirror and an old woman was staring back. Her hair was streaked with gray, her eyes were dulled with saggy bags beneath them, and puppet lines framed her chin. There wasn't much about her life she wanted to remember. The drinking began with just a glass of red wine a night. . . *for her health.* But then came the headaches, and then the pain pills, the ones taken with another glass of wine. When three glasses weren't sufficient to take the edge off the day, a bottle would have to suffice. It was about that time that her son started to get in trouble with the law. First, it was truancy, and then minor-in-possession. But it was motor vehicle theft that landed her boy in the juvenile unit. Last she knew, he was studying for his high school equivalency exam.

Jane heard the door to the women's room open. Someone went into the stall next to hers. She didn't want to appear suspicious by lingering long after another woman had come and gone. Nor did she want to come face-to-face with this woman and risk appearing impaired. Jane took a deep breath before leaving the stall, but it was too late. There she was, right next to Dr. Callie Wallace.

Jane was careful to keep her sentences short and not to slur her words. "Evening, Dr. Wallace."

"Good evening, Jane. I bet I'm the last person you'd expected to see here. There's a sign on the doctor's restroom that it is closed for repairs. I'm a little surprised to see you, though. When did you start working evenings?"

"Need extra money."

"Oh, I see. Well, I've admitted a Mary Scott. I saw her down in the emergency room. She's had a stroke—a complication of uncontrolled atrial fibrillation. Her heart rate is irregular and running one-hundred-forties. She's pretty unstable, so I put in an arterial line. There's a cardiologist consulting. I've put her orders in the computer. One of your staff members is doing the admission paperwork with her family now."

For a moment, Jane thought she was seeing double. She blinked her eyes several times, shaking her head back and forth until the physician came into focus. The doctor was washing her hands at the sink. Although in a drug-induced stupor, Jane knew she couldn't leave the restroom without herself practicing the hygienic ritual.

As the two stood at the sinks, Callie looked up at the nurse through the mirror. "Jane, are you feeling all right?"

"Just tired."

Callie turned towards her with concern. "Jane, you're sweating. There's perspiration running down your brow. You're flushed. Do you have a fever?"

Jane watched as Dr. Wallace dried her hands, crumpled the towel, then threw it away. What came next was unexpected. The physician was coming for her forehead. Abruptly, Jane swiped at the oncoming hand, knocking it out of the way. The woman looked shocked by her sudden reaction. Jane knew she should try to explain her defensiveness. "I'm sorry about that, but I'm wine."

Callie didn't know what to make of Jane's reaction. "You just said you were wine."

Jane was beginning to lose control with an underlying anger seeping toward the surface. Her words were cutting. "I'm fine. I'm fine. That's what I said. Maybe you just need to get your hearing checked. I just don't like to be touched, that's all."

Jane needed to get out of there. She rudely brushed past the doctor, going out into the hall. It was then that Jane felt something wet on her sleeve. At first, she thought she had splashed water on it. But the bright crimson stain told her otherwise. Jane was wearing a standard scrub uniform of elastic waisted pants and a short-sleeved tunic top. Beneath the tunic, she wore a long-sleeved pristine white t-shirt. "Oh, no," Jane mumbled as she snuck into a nearby stairwell. Blood had oozed from the injection site and stained the tee. She began to pace, wondering if the stain had been there when she'd raised her arm to block the physician's reach. Suddenly, Jane's panic rose a notch. She reached into the pockets sewn to the front of her tunic top. The tourniquet wasn't there. She figured she must have dropped it on the bathroom floor. Paranoia began to overtake her. She couldn't afford to lose one more thing in her life. If Dr. Wallace reported to administration that she was working while using, it could ruin what was left of her life. She put her back against the wall, slid towards the floor and cried.

Jane had lost her husband, her son was incarcerated, and if terminated, she'd become homeless. In recent months, she'd distanced herself from her family so as to not be lectured on her substance abuse. She felt alone. Dr. Wallace was the only one who stood between her current situation, pathetic as it was, and destitution.

The tears dried, but the anger rose up. Jane wasn't about to let this happen. She got up and started to pace. I hate that woman, Jane thought. The woman could ruin her life just like she ruined a perfectly good high. As she saw it, delusional as it was, the whole situation was that doctor's fault.

There was the problem of the shirt. Jane needed to get rid of it. In short-sleeves, she planned to apply a simple adhesive bandage over the injection site, hoping there wasn't bruising. Jane pulled the tunic top up over her head, followed by the stained tee. Except for her bra, she was essentially topless. That's when the door to the stairwell opened, sending an echoing sound that bounced from wall to wall and down the steps. There Jane stood, in all her glory, face-to-face with Dr. Callie Wallace again. The physician eyed her up and down, before proceeding down the stairs.

Callie took the first few steps down, slowly and purposefully, mulling around what she should do. There was a lilt in her voice. "You have a *good* evening, Nurse Timmons," she said before continuing her descent.

Eleven

Saturday, October 7, 2017 11:55 p.m.

Zane leaned back on the couch with a beer in one hand, the remote in the other. He channel-surfed with his feet up on the coffee table, waiting for Callie to get home from her late-night call. His full-quill ostrich boots sat in the corner. He wore his best boots and jeans when he came to see Callie. His work boots and weathered denims were for the ranch. He'd learned that lesson the hard way when he hadn't bothered to change or shower before coming to see her once, and once was all it took. She'd read him the riot act over that one.

Zane knew Callie wouldn't appreciate his feet up on the table like they were, but his socks were clean. Swaddled in cotton, the toes wiggled as if they had a mind of their own. He was thinking how good it felt to be off his feet. But when he heard the garage door open, he realized Callie was home. That bit of knowledge sent him to sit straight up and put his feet flat on the floor.

Callie came in exhausted. Zane jumped up to welcome her home. "Rough night?" he asked.

No matter how wore-out she was, Callie never tired of looking at Zane. Six-foot-one, his muscular lean frame was highlighted by chiseled facial features and stunning blue-eyes that reminded Callie of a tropical lagoon. The fact that he'd stood by her all these years, even when she was at medical school, showed his loyalty and devotion. Callie had seemed to hit the jackpot when it came to Zane, but despite this, when he leaned in to kiss her, she quickly turned her head. She told herself that it was the beer on his breath.

Zane noticed the cool reaction. "Anything wrong?"

She flat-out lied. "No, I'm just tired, that's all. Plus, I ate some pretty spicy fast-food earlier. I'm still dealing with the after-shocks of that experience. In fact, I feel pretty gritty all over. I'm going to get cleaned up and hope that I don't get called out again. You can go on to bed, if you like."

Zane wanted to take Callie's explanation at face value. "No, I'll wait up for you. Maybe when you get out, I could give you a back rub."

Callie seemed to snap. "I'm not really in the mood, if *that's* what's on your mind."

Zane became defensive. "If *that* to which you are referring is messing around, no, that's not what I had in mind. You've been acting strange ever since I got here last night. What is going on with you, Callie?"

"Nothing is going on with me, Zane. Look, I told

you before, you don't have to come on the weekends I have call, because I never know how much time I'll have to spend with you."

Zane was defiant. "That's a line of bullshit and you know it! You used to say that if we could just spend ten minutes together, you could get through the next week without a complaint. Now, it's like, 'Meh, come if you want; otherwise, not.'"

Callie sighed as if Zane complaints were just one more thing to contend with. She felt compelled to further explain her mood. "Look, Zane, I don't want to fight. I'm just having a hard time keeping it together this week."

He tried to empathize. "You told me about the patient you lost this week. Now, I know you're a professional and all, but everyone needs someone to lean on sometimes. That's why I'm here. . . nothing else."

Callie wanted to defuse the situation. "Zane, I appreciate you, I really do, but it's more than that."

Zane had his suspicions. "Does this behavior of yours have anything to do with the fact that Richard is out with another woman tonight?"

The remark caught Callie off guard, but she didn't want Zane to know it. She didn't want him to know he'd hit the nail on the head. She didn't want to be jealous. Callie wanted Richard to be happy. . . she really did. It seemed like everything she'd gone through lately had her feeling out of sorts. “Zane, Richard is like a brother to me, you know that. I want him to find someone special. . . to have what we have.”

Zane seemed skeptical. “Are you sure?”

Callie was quick to respond, an overcorrection. “Of course, I'm sure. On top of everything else, I came across a nurse on the neuro ICU floor tonight and she was stoned out of her gourd. I don't know exactly how I'm going to handle it.”

To Zane, it was as if Callie's problem was a relief to him. “Is that all? You have to turn this person in and you know it. That person needs help.”

“Things are not always so cut-and-dry. You don't understand, she's been going through some things. I need to think on it.”

“Callie, this type of indecision isn't like you. There are the patients to consider. You need to get them out of the impaired nurse's reach. Call the house supervisor at the Medical Center. The nurse needs to be drug-tested now, before she hurts herself or someone else.”

“You don't know Kyle Anderson.”

“The administrator?”

“Yes, he's such a jerk. What if I'm wrong? Just implying that the nurse is using, whether it's true or not, that would end her career, not just at the Medical Center, but period. With him, the matter would be about punitive measures, not treatment.”

"But what you described, it seemed so apparent."

Callie was exhausted. "Look, Zane, I just want to get some sleep. You go on to bed. I really need to shower first."

It was if a vengeful fate had heard her need for rest. It was the tone of the text that Callie recognized as a message from the hospital. Zane patiently waited to gauge the nature of the message—would she be going out again or would a simple phone call suffice?

Callie noticed Zane lingering. "Honey, there's no need for both of us being kept up. You go get some sleep."

Zane reluctantly went off to the bedroom, but ran back into the living room only moments later to the sound of Callie's scream. He found her shaking in her skin; but otherwise, frozen in place. "Callie, Callie, what is it?"

But she didn't speak. Her eyes huge and round as if she visualized a horrible scene. Her fingers gripped the phone like a vice. Zane pried it loose, but the screen had gone black. He hit the home button and the message reappeared.

Mary Scott pronounced dead at 12:15 a.m., October 8, 2017

Zane couldn't believe Callie had frozen like that. He grabbed her by the arms and gently shook her. "Callie, Callie, come on girl. Get a grip. I know you've been trained to deal with this kind of thing. Don't fall apart on me now. This woman's family is going to need you."

Zane slipped on his boots, grabbing his keys and Callie's coat. He was coaxing her out the door. "Callie, I'm going to drive you to the hospital. We'll pick you up a coffee on the way. I'll be there with you, right by your side. We can handle anything as long as we have each other. And with what you told me about that nurse, we need to get a handle on that situation right now."

Callie was still in shock, but moved in accordance to Zane's lead.

Zane kept his cool. He was Callie's rock. "You need to text the hospital and tell them you are on your way. Let's go."

Callie followed his instructions, but somewhere, deep inside, felt robotic, disconnected. She did manage to say, "Thank you, Richard. I don't know what I'd do without you."

He shook his head, wondering if he heard her right. "What did you say? Did you just call me Richard?"

The accusation was sobering. "Of course not!"

"Callie, I don't know what's going on with you, but you need to get your shit together. We've known each other a long time, since high school. But right now, you're like a stranger to me."

Twelve

Fourteen Years Earlier

The two romped around under the covers like two pups caught up under the sheets, a mix of an eager appetite and careless regard. The flirtatious back and forth went on between Zane and Callie until the two eighteen-year-olds finally settled into a united embrace—laughs replaced with sensual cries and sighs.

Callie was the first to surface, throwing back the covers. "I'm going to hop in the shower. My folks are due back in about an hour. Are we going out tonight?"

Zane sat up in bed. He couldn't take his eyes off her . . . firm body, supple breasts. He was going to miss Callie, but he wasn't going to stand in her way. The summer had gone by fast. She was leaving for the university in two weeks. He just hoped there'd be a place for him in her new life. He was determined to wait, but would she, he wondered. It was the reality of things that concerned him. "Hurry up. I'll clean up after you."

She turned on the shower to let the water warm. She stood in the doorway, teasing him. "You could join me, if you like."

He seriously considered her offer, but laughed it off instead. "If I come in there, your folks will catch us for sure. Now, go on . . . hurry up. I thought we'd get a burger and fries at *Dickerson's Drug* and catch *Catwoman* at the movies."

Four minutes later, Callie emerged. Her water-drenched hair laid flat, but started to spring to life as she towel-dried it. "Your turn. I left the water running for you."

Zane hopped out of bed and scurried into the shower. Callie got a kick out of his modesty. He was in-and-out in half his usual time, a towel wrapped around his waist. He'd go to where he left his underwear and pants, turn his back to her, and put them on. She knew him . . . he knew her.

They made Callie's bed and moved into the living room for fear one of her parents would come home early. "Where's your mother, anyway?" Zane asked.

"She volunteers at the mission downtown one day a week, washing sheets and making up beds for the homeless. But I was told I couldn't go out for the evening without checking in with one of them first—house rules. So, it's going to be a bit before we can head out. But tell me, do you really want to see *Catwoman*? Isn't that a tad juvenile?"

Zane raised his eyebrows, smirked. "Nothing

juvenile about Halle Berry. Hey, do you have anything around here to eat?"

"You can't wait an hour?" Callie asked him.

"I'm just a growing boy. At least that's what my mom tells me. Just a sandwich or something to hold me over."

"I'll tell you what. I'll fix you a sandwich, but instead of *Catwoman*, we go see *The Manchurian Candidate*," she said as she walked into the kitchen.

The disappointment on his face said it all, but Zane was relieved she wasn't in the room to see it. "A political thriller? Really, Callie? Sounds a little dry to me . . . a bit too serious."

"Post-war era, sleeper agent, intrigue, it all sounds like guy-stuff to me," she said from the other room.

"Callie," he said, followed by a brief pause, "are you changing on me?"

Callie popped her head out of the kitchen. She was holding a couple of bread slices and a package of shaven turkey breast. She knew Zane, and the question wasn't playful banter. Concerned, she went and sat down on the couch next to him. "What's that supposed to mean?"

Zane regretted having opened the can of worms the minute he'd asked the question. He tried to change the subject. "That for me?" he asked, looking at what she held in her hands. He quickly grabbed the items and started to throw together a dry sandwich.

But it was too late. Callie was adamant. "Zane, I asked you a question."

He took a bite, hoping a full mouth would delay the inevitable, but she was staring him down. His tongue managed to shove the food up inside his cheek. "Callie, you leave in a couple of weeks. Can't we just enjoy the time we have left?"

"Zane, me going off to school, it has to be on your mind. I think we should talk about it, *really* talk about it."

The topic was making him nervous. He took another bite, but practically swallowed it whole. "Look, a month ago when you went off to orientation with your folks, I didn't think anything of it. But when you came back with that schedule of yours, I about freaked . . . inorganic chemistry, physics, calculus. What are you going to have in common with a cowboy who runs cattle?"

Callie knew she needed to tread lightly. "Zane, have I ever made you feel less than my equal? We're partners, right?"

"Callie, be realistic. You want to be a doctor and I'm just a cowhand."

She didn't want the discussion to become heated, but Zane was pushing her buttons. "Zane, I love you, but you're full of shit. Are you testing me? Is this what *I'm just a cowhand* crap is all about? That ranch of your father's is a family business and it's about one of the most lucrative in the state."

Zane sat upright, amazed. He tried not to laugh, but he couldn't help himself. "Callie, you just cursed. I don't think I've ever heard you use foul language before. It's cute, right?"

Callie wasn't laughing.

"Oh, come on, Callie," he teased. "This isn't about your ten-year plan, is it?"

She wasn't in a joking mood. "I think it's about you referring to yourself as a cowhand, you making fun of my frustration and word choice, and you making light of my strategies to obtain my goals."

It was time. Zane knew it. There were things that needed to be addressed. "Sounds to me like you're trying to pick a fight so we don't have to face what we need to face. Life is messy, Callie. You can't always control it."

Callie was angry. "Well, you sure can't with that *whatever* attitude of yours. Right now, you're sounding like we won't make it, just because I want to get an education. That, or you want to go ahead and call it quits. Is that what today was, one last roll in the hay for old times' sake?"

Zane got up from the couch and started to pace. He pointed his finger at her. "You are putting words in my mouth."

Callie got up to face him—game on. "I'm trying to find a way for us to make it through this!"

He knew he needed to take it down a notch. Zane relaxed his aggressive stance, allowed his arms to fall to his side. "Callie, your school is in south Texas. Even with weekends, the time it would take to drive there, when all is said and done, there'd be very little time for us to be together. And that doesn't even take into account the weekends my dad needs me on the ranch, and you needing to study for exams. You're going to be meeting new people, having new experiences."

From fury to tears in seconds, Callie plopped down on the couch. She grabbed a throw pillow and hugged it tight. "I just thought if we even had ten minutes together, I could make it through the week," she managed through the sobs. "What good is my plan, my charts, if you're not willing to go through this with me? I even made an algorithm for us to follow given any particular obstacle."

Caught up in their own drama, the couple didn't hear the garage door or Callie's mother as she came in through the kitchen.

Rose wasn't comfortable with what she'd walked into. "Zane, I didn't expect you to be here so early. Have you and Callie been here alone?"

Callie felt the need to explain. "Mother, Zane and I were just . . ."

But Zane wanted to make his position clear. "Mrs. Wallace, Callie and I were just discussing some of the challenges we're going to face when she leaves for school. I wanted to reassure her that, if she has what it takes to tackle undergraduate and medical school, I've got what it takes to stand by her. Callie can count on me."

What Zane had said didn't fully resonate with Rose, a conclusion without first knowing there'd been a problem. "But Callie, you look as if you've been crying."

But what Zane had said didn't escape Callie. "Oh Mother, I'm so lucky to have a guy like Zane in my life. I guess I was overcome, reduced to tears, but I'm okay now."

"All right," Rose said. "But you both should consider yourself lucky I'm the one that got home first. If it would've been Callie's father, I don't think he would've been so understanding at finding you two alone in the house this way."

Callie was afraid her mother knew more than she was letting on. "What way?"

Rose pointed at the package of turkey. "With his lunch meat on the coffee table and crumbs all over the couch. What in the hell has been going on here? Was this you, Zane?"

Callie jumped in. "That was me, Mother. I guess I forgot, no eating in the living room, house rules."

"Well, young lady, I think at your age, you'd know better. You're not going out tonight until you clean-up this mess. Do you want us to get ants? Now, if you two will excuse me, I'm going to soak in a hot tub. My back is killing me."

When Callie's mother left, Zane spoke up. "Why did you take the blame for me? I would've owned up to it. For a minute there, I thought she knew we'd been in the sack."

Callie stood up and embraced him. As they held each other, she whispered in his ear. "Zane, I knew you'd be there for me. Running interference for you with my mother was the least I could do. See? We can weather it, no matter what the problem."

Zane felt the tight hold Callie had on him. His chin rested on her shoulder as he stared at a collage of family photos on the far wall . . . seeing nothing in particular. Zane didn't think deciding what movie to see or a few crumbs on the sofa constituted a true problem. He wanted to be supportive, but there was underlying doubt in his voice that anything had really been resolved. "You're right, Callie. We'll just stick to your ten-year plan, follow the algorithm."

Thirteen

Sunday, October 8, 2017, 11:15 p.m.

Her head was pounding, but thankfully, Callie had a little less than eight hours left of call, before Richard would take over, tomorrow morning. Despite that, she dreaded what Monday would bring. She'd already received a text from Kyle Anderson to be at his office at ten the next morning, regarding certain situations that had unfolded over the weekend, but he'd failed to provide any specifics.

It had gotten late. Zane hadn't wanted to leave, but Callie had insisted. His family ranch was a business and it needed to be run as one. It's not like she didn't appreciate Zane taking her to the hospital last night, but Callie felt the situation was far from over. She'd been dealing with the deceased patient's family when Zane told the house supervisor of her comment regarding an impaired staff member. She later learned each member of the night shift on the neuro ICU floor was subjected to a drug screen right then and there. Callie was concerned over Jane's future, but felt there'd be enough fallout from the situation to go around.

Callie stood at the bathroom sink and spat what was left of her toothpaste in the sink, rinsed her mouth, and mindlessly watched as the water took the foam down the drain. She simultaneously turned off the spout and looked in the mirror to see a tired form of herself, one she barely recognized. She dabbed her mouth dry and was ready to head to bed. She climbed in, turning off the bedside lamp. She fell into a hard sleep just minutes after her head hit the pillow.

"Corky, Corky, wake up. We need to talk," the voice said.

Callie switched on the light. She blinked her eyes a few times in an attempt to rouse herself. She wondered how long she'd actually been asleep. It seemed like only minutes, but the possibility it could be morning was plausible. She glanced at the clock—it was 11:23 p.m.

She looked over in the corner of the bedroom to see her father sitting in a chair. The images and the colors were as sharp and vivid as before. "Oh, no, not again," she mumbled.

"Hey, that's no way to greet your old man."

Callie rationalized she was dreaming, and she thought if she just went along with it, the quality of the sleep would be better than if she fought the situation. "I'm sorry, Dad. What's up?"

"Now, that's more like it. Hey, do you remember

the story I told you of the mysterious fish die-off that occurred shortly before you were born? It was 1982 when hundreds of dead fish were found on the Lake Sperling shore."

"Dad, I really need to get some sleep. Dead fish washing up on shore some thirty-five years ago isn't my idea of a bed-time story that would facilitate sweet dreams."

"Well, Corky, this story is not a fairy tale and neither is what I have to tell you. You see, there was a parasite in the water that year, forcing the fish to shallow water. Ultimately, the fish were oxygen deprived and died."

"Besides the year being a really bad fishing season for you, Dad, is there supposed to be a moral to this story?"

"Corky, it seems you're not taking what I'm trying to tell you seriously, and you should be."

"Dad, what exactly are you trying to tell me?"

"I'm trying to tell you that you have a parasite in your waters."

"What do you mean by that?" Callie asked. "Are you speaking literally or figuratively?"

"Both."

Her cell phone rang.

It took Callie a moment to orient herself before she answered, praying it wasn't the hospital. It wasn't.

It was from Richard. She answered her phone while looking towards the chair in the corner. The image of her father was gone. That, in itself, was disheartening.

"Hi, Richard. How was your weekend?"

"Callie, you sound a little funny. Is everything okay?"

"Oh, I'm fine. What's up?"

"Well, I was wondering if everything went okay for you this weekend?"

"Why do you ask? I was going to report off to you in the morning, as usual."

"Well, we just got back into town and I've heard a few things."

Richard caught Callie off guard. Her free hand went to cover her gaping mouth. "What . . . wait, you went out-of-town with this girl. . . on a second date?"

"I know it sounds like we're going a little fast," he tried to explain.

"You think? Yeah!"

"It started out innocently enough. We were just going to a place she knew where the color change of the leaves is evidently spectacular. It wasn't supposed to be like *that*."

A punch to the gut. The thought of Richard in an intimate relationship made Callie's stomach turn. She was determined to hide the jealousy that had washed over her. She needed to know. "But you just said it wasn't supposed to be like *that*, but it was, wasn't it?"

"Callie, I'm not going to kiss and tell, but this woman, I mean, she's amazing. I'm telling you she might be the one."

Callie made a passive-aggressive stab. "Boy, that Sandy must really be something to get you this riled-up."

"Her name is Sara, but I told you that. You're deflecting."

Callie wanted more details, but realized she wasn't going to get any. "I don't know what you mean," she denied.

Richard wanted to get to the point of the call. "The reason I called is that I went up to the hospital tonight after I got back in town. I'd made a bet with one of the night security guards on the Cowboys Packers game, and I just wanted to go ahead and pay up. It hurts enough that the Boys let me down, again, but to have it hurt in the pocketbook, too, is painful. I just wanted to pay what I owed, and get it over with. Well, it so happened, he had a few interesting things to tell me. Your torn blouse is not what's on the hospital gossip line. Rumors have it is that you're losing your edge. . . and your grip on reality. He mentioned another death, too. Do you have anything you need to tell me?"

The thought of Mary Scott's death nauseated Callie, but she didn't want Richard to know it. She was going to try and play it down. "Talk about exaggerating. I just feel a little stressed. Nothing to worry about, I assure you. There was a Mrs. Scott that died shortly after her admission to the intensive care unit with a stroke, among other things. There is going to be an autopsy, but I spoke with her cardiologist, and we came to the consensus that she threw another clot, despite being on an anticoagulant."

He needed her to reassure him. "Are you sure there's nothing to the rumors about your frame of mind?"

"I have no idea what these gossip-mongers mean. I have had some issues with a couple of staff members this last week, but they should not take these things personally. But I guess they did and they're exacting their revenge by tarnishing my reputation and stability. I assure you, there's nothing to worry about. I have a meeting with Kyle Anderson tomorrow at ten. I'll address the issue there."

The idea of an impromptu meeting concerned him. "What's the meeting supposed to be about?"

"He didn't exactly say, but I have a feeling that Mrs. Murphy is making waves. Perhaps she is threatening a law suit, concerning her husband's death. But until the final autopsy report comes in, it all seems a bit premature. There was no negligence in the matter."

"Callie, I don't think you should go to that meeting alone," Richard cautioned. "I want to go with you."

She didn't want to worry about the meeting, but with Richard this upset, Callie wondered if she was underestimating the seriousness of it all. Lately, she'd been thinking thoughts she wouldn't ordinarily think and saying things she wouldn't ordinarily say. Part of her was wondering if she was really going crazy. But was it possible that other people thought so too? Not to mention two dead patients within a four-day period. "Don't you think you're overreacting . . . just a little? Look, we both know Anderson is a real pinhead, but I think I can handle him. You told me yourself that things like this happen. I'm sure the autopsies will reveal that every precaution was taken regarding their treatment plans, and despite that, sentinel events occurred."

"Callie, I don't trust Anderson and you shouldn't either. He's a jackal. I'm really concerned about the rumors concerning your frame of mind. The security guard, we've been friends for some time now, and he's not one to blow smoke. I won't accept no for an answer. I'm going with you to that meeting tomorrow morning—no argument."

With that, all Callie heard on the other line was

dead air. He'd hung up. Callie was left holding her phone, wondering why Richard had been so adamant, and what in the world were people actually saying about her. She put her phone down, turned off the light. It was probably sometime after three before she was able to get back to sleep.

Fourteen

Monday, October 9, 2017 10:10 a.m.

Callie and Richard sat next to each other in the reception area of the administrator's office. Callie was uneasy, nervous, her right leg a jackhammer with its jumpy twitch. The security guard sitting across the room didn't help. Kyle Anderson's secretary pretended to be busy with her own duties, but Callie knew the woman was aware of everything and everyone in that office reception area. Richard reached out and patted her hand, but then removed it, each of them keeping to themselves in a professional manner. After a few minutes, it was Richard that was becoming inpatient. He got up and approached the secretary's desk.

Richard put his fists on the edge of her desk and leaned in, speaking low, but in an authoritative manner. "How much longer is this going to take?"

"I wasn't aware that you had an appointment with Mr. Anderson, Dr. Cortez," the woman coolly responded.

"Dr. Wallace does and she's my partner. If there's an issue with her, then it's an issue for our practice. If I don't get in on that meeting, there will be no meeting. Understand?"

The receptionist took off her glasses. Holding them in her hand, she began shaking them at the physician as she spoke. "Look, Dr. Cortez, just because you're leaning on my desk, bullying me, and making threats doesn't mean you're going to get your way. Mr. Anderson has been in meetings with various staff members since eight o'clock this morning. Some meetings take longer than others. Dr. Wallace is just going to have to wait her turn."

Richard was protective of Callie. He wanted to know who the administrator had been with, but before he could ask, he was interrupted.

The security guard who was in the office stood up, responding to the rising tension of the two at the desk. "Is there a problem, ma'am?"

"No, but thank you," she responded. "I'm used to his egotistical kind."

That's when the administrator's door opened and Jane Timmons emerged. She'd been crying—her eyes swollen and red—her cheeks flushed and streaked from streaming tears. The security guard stood ready. He'd been called to escort Jane Timmons from the building. She was terminated. He approached the woman who'd stopped right in front of where Dr. Wallace was seated.

Jane made no attempt to hide her disdain for the physician. "Look at you sitting there, *Dr. Wallace*. Do you feel important, taking a person's livelihood away. . . taking someone's life away from them? I've lost my job because of you and my nursing license will most likely be suspended. I'm barely keeping the utilities on as it is, but now I won't have to worry. That's because I won't be able to keep a roof over my head. You think you're something, don't you? I'll tell you what you are. You sit there so sanctimonious, but you're a killer just the same."

Kyle Anderson emerged from his office, interrupting Jane's rant. "Guard, please escort Ms. Timmons to her locker to collect her belongings and then make sure she leaves the grounds without further incident."

The guard grabbed the woman by the arm and started to pull her towards the door, but not before she was heard threatening Callie Wallace. "You cost me my life, now it's going to be your turn."

Kyle Anderson yelled, "Guard, get her out of here, now!"

Jane Timmons yanked her arm away from the guard's grasp. "I'm going. I'm going." She brought her finger up, pointing it at Callie. "You should have minded your own business. You watch your back, because when you least expect it, pay-back's a bitch."

Richard interjected. "Everyone here just heard you threaten her."

"So what?" Jane responded. "What else do I have to lose? At least in prison, I'll have a roof over my head, three squares a day to fill my belly."

The guard retook his grip on the woman and forced her from the area as Kyle Anderson and the rest of the room watched. "Good riddance," Anderson muttered.

Fifteen

Monday, October 9, 2017 10:35 a.m.

Callie had been shaken up by the encounter with Jane Timmons. . . and mortified. This is why she hadn't initially reported the nurse. She wanted a little time to think about how to handle the situation. She tried to avoid acting impulsively whenever possible. She knew administration would see it as a violation of policy, and she began to wonder if this was the purpose of the meeting.

Kyle Anderson poked his head out the office. "Dr. Wallace, I'll see you now. Come on in."

Richard spoke up. "Mr. Anderson, I want to be included in the meeting."

"This doesn't concern you, Cortez," the administrator rebuked.

"We're in medical practice together," Richard explained. "Her concerns are my concerns."

Kyle Anderson eyed Callie Wallace. "Dr. Wallace, are you sure this is in your best interest? Information discussed in these meetings are confidential, and there will be certain specifics you might not want disclosed."

What the administrator said raised Callie's

concerns about the real purpose of the meeting. But Richard was her friend and partner. She believed his presence would work in her favor. "I believe Dr. Cortez has the best interest of our practice in mind."

With that, Dr. Wallace and Dr. Cortez went into the office. Kyle Anderson followed and closed the door behind them. He motioned for the physicians to take a seat at the conference table. Callie felt like her life would never be the same after this meeting. She remembered her father's words . . . *There's a parasite in your waters.*

After everyone was seated, Mr. Anderson began. "Dr. Wallace, several issues have come to light since last week that I'd like to cover in this meeting and I want you to have the opportunity to respond to the accusations being made against you."

"Okay," Callie flatly responded. "If this is about Mrs. Murphy, I can assure you. . ."

Kyle put his hand up, interrupting. "*I can assure you*, Dr. Wallace, that this doesn't concern Mrs. Murphy. Now, if I can continue."

Callie bit her lip to hide her frustration. She felt like a little girl being chastised for her behavior, but didn't understand what she'd done wrong.

"Now, while this has nothing to do with the spouse of the deceased patient, it does have to do with subsequent actions taken since Mr. Murphy's death," the administrator explained. "The first issue I'd like to discuss is an orderly on the neurological ICU floor, a Mr. Marcus Davis. He's made a complaint against you with Human Resources, claiming you treated him in a hostile manner that he feels was racially motivated."

The accusation shocked Callie. "That's absolutely ridiculous!"

Her reaction didn't faze the administrator. "Let me finish, Dr. Wallace. The issue in question occurred when you came to the floor after you were notified of Mr. Murphy's death. He claims you interrogated him and repeatedly looked for fault in the actions he took and threatened his job. He felt you were holding him accountable for the outcome despite the role he works under is supervised by licensed staff that are ultimately held responsible."

What Kyle Anderson said next was a lie, but he wanted to see Callie Wallace squirm. "He stated that you even called him 'boy.'"

Richard's jaw dropped. He looked over at Callie who had a confused look on her face. "Callie, is there anything to this?"

"No, no," Callie muttered. "That's not what happened. I know Marcus. Our relationship has always been cordial. When I first came to the floor, I saw Marcus sitting at the nurse's station. I was agitated, I admit that, but it was over the event—not him. I asked to see the incident report and inquired if the electronic record had been up-dated to reflect what led to the patient's condition being discovered, actions taken, pronouncement of death, and physician notification."

Richard inquired, "Callie, do you recall if anyone else was around?"

Callie shook her head. "I don't remember seeing anyone else. I suppose they were tending to patient care. I can't tell you for sure. What I can be certain of is that I would never use such a derogatory term. I'm a professional and would hope Mr. Anderson would give me some credit."

"You see," Richard said. "Mr. Anderson, this is probably nothing more than a simple misunderstanding. If you give Callie a chance to speak with Mr. Davis, I'm sure they could clear the air and the matter would be resolved."

Callie jumped in enthusiastically, "Of course, I would be happy to talk with Marcus. I don't want something like this to exist between us."

"I knew there was a simple solution to this," Richard explained. "I know for certain Callie isn't racist. So, if that's all, I guess we'll be going."

Kyle Anderson noticed the physicians getting up and preparing to leave. He cautioned them. "Not so fast. We're not done here. I'll consider your proposed resolution, but I don't want you confronting Mr. Davis with the issue until I can ascertain that he's agreeable to meeting with you. Now, with that being said, things are far from being over."

The administrator watched as the two physicians retook their seats. "Now, there's the issue of Ms. Timmons. Her drug screen showed opiate and alcohol use. It's my understanding that it was your *boyfriend* who notified the house supervisor of an impaired staff member on the floor. . . not you. So, you were aware of the possible harm this person could inflict, and yet, you left vulnerable patients in her care, including your patient that is now deceased, Mary Scott."

Callie tried to explain. "Well, that's not technically correct. Mary Scott was assigned another registered nurse to care for her, not Jane Timmons."

The comment angered Kyle Anderson. "Don't be glib with me, Dr. Wallace! That doesn't mean anything. Anyone that could possibly have had an interaction with an impaired staff member was at risk. I happen to know that Ms. Timmons covered for Scott's nurse when she took her thirty-minute supper break and one of her fifteen-minute shift breaks."

Callie regretted that she had treated the situation in so blasé a manner. It hadn't spoken to her professionalism. "I apologize. . . you're right. I should have reported the incident to the house supervisor right away. And it was inappropriate for me to speak of hospital issues outside of the facility."

Richard wanted to be supportive of Callie. "There you go. Her judgment was a little off. It was late. She was tired. One incident is not indicative of her overall abilities."

The administrator responded to Richard's comments. "You seem quite confident in your partner. But I happen to know that a staff member observed her talking to herself, having one-sided conversations."

"That's a lie," Callie blurted out. "Who is saying such things?"

"A long-time employee," was all that Mr. Anderson disclosed. "It seems that the said conversation involved someone named Zane. I also understand that's the name of your boyfriend who reported that an impaired staff member was on the floor that night. A coincidence? I don't think so."

Richard's supportive nature turned to concern. "Callie, can you explain this?"

Callie was at a loss. "Richard, I don't know what to say. I have no explanation. . . I don't remember any of this."

Richard tried to cover for his partner . . . his friend. "Look, Mr. Anderson, what if Callie goes to see an internist and a psychiatrist, of your choosing, of course, and has a complete work-up. She'll sign a disclosure that all results be made available to you."

Richard turned to Callie. "You would be willing to do that, wouldn't you, Callie?"

By this time Callie was feeling lost. "I suppose so," she vacantly uttered.

Kyle Anderson was quick to respond. "That would be a good start, speaking to your physical and mental wellbeing. But there is still another issue."

Callie had been secretly glad there was no mention of her seeing and speaking to her dead father, but when she heard *still another issue*, she just dropped her head. It was as if she was expecting Richard to lead her charge. . . and he did.

"Go ahead, just spell it out," Richard demanded.

The administrator was happy to oblige in his own sadistic manner. He grabbed his laptop and pulled up Mr. Murphy's electronic medical record. "I understand that Mr. Murphy's admitting diagnosis was multiple sclerosis, and that you were treating him with high-dose steroid therapy. Is that correct?"

Callie just nodded.

"Well," Mr. Anderson continued, "per protocol, you were to use 160 mg of intravenous methyl-prednisolone administered daily for a week, and you were in the process of reducing the dose to 64 mg, tapering to every other day for a period of 1 month. Tell me,

Dr. Wallace, what type of signs and symptoms would a patient exhibit if the dose tapering was not done appropriately and a sudden decrease in dose was given instead?"

Richard was adamant his partner kept quiet. "Don't answer that, Callie! Anderson, get to the point. I feel like you're trying to set her up."

"All right, Dr. Cortez. Preliminary autopsy results showed extremely high levels of excitatory neurotransmitters and their metabolites in Mr. Murphy's blood and urine."

Richard again stepped in. "That could be the result from the trauma of death and subsequent rescue attempt, using adrenaline. Another possible explanation is that the patient had a pheochromocytoma. That's an adrenaline-producing adrenal tumor."

"Thank you for the pathology lesson, Dr. Cortez," Mr. Anderson sarcastically responded. "On physical examination it was determined that the patient did not exhibit any cancerous lesions, and the adrenal glands were not hypertrophic, anything but." He took a moment to turn the computer screen to where both physicians had a view of Mr. Murphy's physician's order screen. He continued, "If you look here, Dr. Wallace, you didn't enter an order for the reduction of methylprednisolone from 160 mg to 64 mg. Instead, you entered the reduction of the drug to 6 mg. He received

10X less of the drug than he should have received. And in case you were wondering, yes it was you who logged in to place the order—the IT man confirmed this for me."

Callie looked at the screen in disbelief. "That's impossible," Callie mumbled. "I always try to be so careful."

Mr. Anderson smirked at the painful look on her face. "Not only is it possible, but the nurse's medication administration record confirmed that Mr. Murphy was underdosed. It is also possible that the medical examiner may rule Mr. Murphy's death was attributed to adrenal crisis. Tell me physicians, can this be explained?"

Richard was tense, burrowing his stare at the screen. "This can't be right. Tell him, Callie. Tell him there's a logical explanation."

But Callie couldn't. She just mumbled, "It's all my fault. . . it's all my fault."

Richard put his hand up in an attempt to stop the assault on Callie's character. "No, no, no, this isn't going down like this. Callie wouldn't make such an egregious error. There has to be a logical explanation here. Mr. Anderson, Kyle, why don't you stop trying to assassinate her character and career? Why don't you keep an open mind? What might you be willing to do to work with us to get this figured out?"

Mr. Anderson felt the power of his position. He sighed. "Well, Dr. Cortez, it was my intention to suspend Dr. Wallace's privileges until the official report comes in on the cause of Mr. Murphy's death. If it's what I suspect, and with all these other troubling issues, her privileges at this facility will be revoked. However, because of her willingness to apologize to Mr. Davis, and agreeing to a complete medical and psychological evaluation, I would consider a probationary period under your supervision, Dr. Cortez, of course. But if Mr. Murphy's death is ruled as a complication of adrenal crisis, and one of these other issues are proved without a doubt, Dr. Wallace, your services will no longer be desired at Lake Sperling Medical Center. Are we clear?"

Callie just nodded, but other than that, she felt numb. . . paralyzed. Her life was falling apart. She felt Richard help her up from her chair, encouraging her to leave. They were just out of earshot from the administrator's secretary when she heard Richard tell her, "Callie, I think we need to get you a lawyer."

Sixteen

Tuesday, October 10, 2017 1:20 a.m.

Gus lit up a cigarette at the kitchen table, inhaling deeply. He couldn't sleep and didn't want to wake his wife, Delores, with his tossing and turning. He looked up at the clock on the wall, disgusted by the hour, and also by the time piece itself. It was one of those old black and white plastic clocks fashioned as a cat with the tail functioning as a pendulum and the eyes moving in tandem with it. Even the table he sat at was out of the 1950's. It was a chrome kitchen table with six chairs of red and gray vinyl. It wasn't the couple's intention to be retro. . . they just were.

Gus sensed a pair of eyes on him. He looked over his shoulder to see Delores donning a housecoat while simultaneously rolling her eyes. He knew all-too-well what the passive-aggressive response was aimed at—it was the Jack Daniel's bottle sitting in front of him. If the man was misreading his wife's signals, it was her grabbing the bottle by its neck and returning it to the cupboard, high above the sink, that told him he knew her, and all too well. Gus tapped his cigarette on the ashtray as he watched Delores grab the milk from the refrigerator and pour it into a saucepan she had on the stove.

"You could warm that milk faster in the microwave, you know," Gus advised.

"What are you saying, Gus? Do you want us to get the cancer?"

Now it was Gus's turn to roll his eyes. Luckily for him, Delores was at the stove with her back to him. "Delores, how many times have we been over this? The microwave won't give you cancer."

"Oh my," she sarcastically replied. "I thought you worked in maintenance at that hospital. Are you a doctor now?"

Gus took a puff, watching Delores continually stir the milk to prevent it from scorching the pan. She tapped the wooden spoon on its edge and then turned off the heat. She had two cups out and carefully poured the warmed milk into them.

Ugh, Gus thought. One of them was for him. Nothing like warm milk to chase down your whiskey. "Make sure mine doesn't have any skin on it."

"I used the spoon to keep it out," she said as she placed the cups on the table. She took a seat next to her husband, reaching to grab one of his cigarettes from the pack that sat on the table between them. Delores took a few quick puffs to set the flame.

Gus eyed his wife. He had no right to throw stones

as he saw the irony of the situation. "Really, Delores? Research has shown a positive correlation between tobacco and cancer, and you're worried about the microwave."

Delores shrugged her shoulders. "Gus, drink your milk. You need your rest. The alarm is going to go off in a few hours. Besides, how many times have we had this discussion? The campaign to get people to stop smoking is a government-led conspiracy concocted by the democrats. Who are these scientists anyway? I'll tell you who they are. . . they're Democrats. But tell me this. Where does brain cancer afflicting the young people come from that never smoked a day in their life? I'll tell you where it comes from—it's from the microwaves, cell phones, and electrical substations."

Gus blew out a big sigh, accompanied by a plume of smoke. "Delores, I'm not going to hash this out with you again."

Delores couldn't believe her ears. "Then why do you keep bringing it up? Never mind that, what's got you up? You usually sleep like a log."

"Oh, it was work today, or should I say yesterday? You know I'm not a snitch, but I think I got someone in trouble."

Delores was concerned. "What kind of trouble? Have you got yourself mixed up in something?"

"No, no, nothing like that. Don't worry. I just feel

bad is all. When all was said and done, I thought someone was going to get fired. But from what I heard, there was a temporary stay. I'm just afraid the person will inevitably be terminated."

Delores listened intently, hugging her cup of milk in her hands while her cigarette burned in the ashtray. But she wasn't going to let her husband get away with such vague details. "But I want you to stop with this *someone* business. Is it one of the guys in your department?"

"No, that wouldn't bother me, especially if the person was a douche that made the rest of us look bad. It was a doctor."

"No foolin'?" Delores exclaimed.

"Yeah," he reluctantly admitted. "I was called into the big-shot's office first thing yesterday morning. I didn't even know anyone knew what I'd seen except Marta Gutierrez."

"Really, you told Marta, but not me? Anybody who's anybody knows what a blabber-mouth that woman is. She makes a great tamale, but she wags that tongue of hers just about every chance she gets."

"Well, in hindsight, I probably shouldn't have said anything."

Delores was frustrated. She took a drag of her cigarette. "Well, now that you have, and half the world knows about it, can you tell your wife?"

With his wife already irritated, Gus decided he'd

better down his milk. He really didn't want to speak of the situation again. He didn't even want to think about it. But he knew Delores, and there was no getting around it. "I was called to check on a thermostat on one of those specialized floors—this one specializes on disorders of the nervous system and such. One of the doctors, a lady doctor, came into the dictation room where the thermostat was located. She started having a fight, well, with no one. It would've been a real knock-down-drag-out if someone else would've been involved. But there she was. . . babbling on like there was no tomorrow."

Delores was caught up in the tale. "Were you scared? Was she like one of those escaped patients from a psychiatric hospital? What if she was . . . posing as a doctor?"

Gus struggled to explain. "Delores, this isn't one of your daytime soaps. It's real life. Now, I wouldn't exactly say I was scared, just weirded-out. I tried to talk to her, but she didn't even acknowledge me."

"Oh Gus, that's supposed to be dangerous. I've heard you shouldn't even approach someone when they're in that condition."

"That's a sleepwalker, Delores. She wasn't asleep."

"Oh, I see. Tell me, do I know this lady doctor?"

"Yeah, you know her. Her name is Dr. Callie Wallace."

"Hmm," Delores muttered. "I don't recognize the name."

Gus reassured her. "Yeah, you do. I introduced you to her at the Fourth of July Parade—the one on the square."

Delores searched her memory. "You mean that delightful girl, early thirties? I remember now. She was so lovely with that soft brown, curly hair, and those bright eyes. Well, she practically just beamed. I can't believe it—I simply can't believe it."

It came to Gus that Delores wasn't one to be up in the night either. "Sorry if I woke you up, hun. Then I dump my problems on you. I'll try to make it up to you, take you out for dinner tonight after I get off."

Delores shook her head. "You didn't wake me up, Gus. You see, I have some guilt of my own. I should've told you when you came home from work, but the timing never seemed right."

Gus didn't like the sound of where the discussion was going. "Go ahead and tell me, Delores. What did you do?"

She knew she'd feel better if she just got it out. "I loaned Fergus two-hundred-dollars."

Gus slammed his hand on the table. "Damn it, Delores. We've talked about this. You might as well say you gave Fergus two-hundred-dollars."

"I know we agreed not to give him any more

money, but you should have seen him," she said. "Our grandson is really having trouble finding steady work because of his epilepsy. He said he'd pay us back as soon as he can."

Annoyed, Gus couldn't help himself. "Let me guess, Delores, he's in between jobs right now. What happened to his job at the cell phone place?"

"Well, he said he accidentally overslept one morning, and they let him go. He said the manager didn't give him a chance to explain or anything."

Gus shook his head in disgust. He'd heard them all . . . one excuse after another. "So, nothing about his epilepsy. I didn't think so. Our boy told me Fergus's epilepsy has been well controlled. He's twenty-four. There's no reason for this. If he's having trouble finding work, maybe he needs to get his ass in school and learn a trade. All we're doing by giving him money is enabling him, understand?"

"I get it, Gus, I do . . . but it's hard," Delores admitted. "You should've seen him, really pathetic."

She'd always had a soft spot for Fergus, but she knew she'd have to toughen up. Delores felt the guilt lift off her chest. She didn't like keeping things from Gus. It didn't make for a good marriage, she reasoned.

Gus eyed the feline clock on the wall. He snuffed out his cigarette. He pushed his chair back from the table. Time had gotten away from him. In a few hours, the sun would be up. "Well, we just need to stick together on this, okay? Can you believe that ridiculous clock still works? Hard to believe it's still hanging on the wall. . . but it is. I'm going to bed, you coming?"

She smiled at the man she'd loved all these years. That was his way of saying, *all was forgiven*. "I'm coming, dear."

Seventeen

Thursday, October 12, 2017 2:40 a.m.

Jane Timmons was getting nervous. It had been only a few days since she'd been fired and her withdrawal symptoms were getting worse. She sat in a back booth of the *Flap 'n Jack*, a 24-hour diner, just like she'd been instructed to do. She'd wait five more minutes, no more. Those that frequented the establishment at that hour made her uncomfortable. No one out at that hour was up to anything good, she reasoned, including herself. It was then that Marcus Davis grabbed the edges of the table and slid into the booth opposite her.

"You're late," she snapped.

"I do it on purpose," Marcus admitted. "I just don't like to be the first to show. A black guy sitting by his self this time of night is trouble, so the customer gets here first, then I meet up. Understand?"

Jane was sadly offended. "I'd like to think I was more to you than just a customer."

A waitress appeared. She looked to be over sixty, but fatigue could have masked her true age. She wore tight fitting brown polyester pants with a brown cotton top that had eyelet lace trimming its round collar.

Her badge said Marge. “What can I get you two folks tonight?”

“Just two black coffees,” Marcus said.

The waitress didn’t bother to write the order down. She doubted the two would even drink the coffee.

After Marge was out of earshot, Marcus picked the conversation back up. “I don’t think we got much in common, at least not any more. Only difference is now our business happens outside of the hospital instead of in it.”

“I know something we have in common,” Jane smugly replied.

“Oh?”

“Really, you don’t know? Go ahead and tell me you don’t hate Dr. Callie Wallace as much as I do. Go ahead and tell me you’re not happy about how things are turning out for her.”

The waitress appeared with two mugs of black coffee and sat one in front of each of the customers. “Here ya go, big spenders. Don’t forget to leave my quarter tip, ya hear?”

Marcus took a sip. He half expected it to taste like tar, but it was fresh. “I’m not entirely unhappy about it, but she’ll probably just get a slap on the wrist like most white folks do. Anyway, I know, she be a racist, through and through. I even asked her nurse for help, but I didn't get any. It made me look like a real fool. She's no different than any other white, protecting their own kind. I got this call from Kyle Anderson. He says she wants to 'clear the air' and apologize for any misunderstanding. I say she can stuff her apology up where the sun ain't shinin'."

Jane was suddenly conscious of the fact she was white. But she wasn't about to go down that road. "Oh, come on. You didn't really tell him that. . . did you?"

"No, I suppose not, but it's what I meant. I just told him, in not so many words, I wasn't interested in what she had to say on the matter. I tells him I heard what I heard."

Jane was ready to endorse his efforts. "Good for you. These doctors have been getting away with treating people like you and me like peasants for years. They hit on us. They keep their jobs, but we get fired. They kill somebody, it gets swept under the rug. I self-medicate to try and handle my awful life, and I lose everything. Other people get *treated* for their PTSD, but I'm told to clean out my locker and not let the door hit me in the backside on the way out."

"What do you mean *people* like us?" Marcus asked with a hint of sarcasm in his voice.

"Well, working people," Jane explained.

Marcus was feeling somewhere between

frustration and anger. "You don't know my story, lady. I doubt you'd even ask. I doubt I'd even tell you. You don't know me."

Jane was taken aback. . . afraid she might've offended him. "Look, all I meant is that, at the end of the day, we want the same thing—to keep a roof over our head, feed our families, pay the bills, and if we're lucky, have enough left over to go to a movie or out to eat. We weren't born with a silver spoon in our mouth, like *them*. For us, it's paycheck to paycheck."

Marcus accepted the explanation. "Well, when you put it like that, I guess you're right. But I have my own plans for Dr. Wallace."

Jane smiled, a wicked smile. She leaned into the table so as to not miss one detail. "Oh? This sounds intriguing. . . do tell."

Marcus shifted his eyes around. He wanted to make sure no one could hear him or observe his actions. When he was sure the coast was clear, he opened his jacket, ever so slightly, to reveal the gun he was carrying.

Jane gasped. "Holy smoke! You're joking, right? Is that a 9 mm?"

Marcus was trying to be discreet, but the woman's reaction wasn't. Despite his edgy affect, he kept his voice low and deep. "What the heck, Jane? Keep it down, will ya? Why not tell everyone in the joint I'm packing? Keep it together, woman."

Jane felt self-conscious. She took a quick look around to make sure she hadn't drawn unwarranted attention. No one even seemed interested in the biracial couple, ages apart, that sat huddled together in the corner booth. She matched her tone to his, but the devious smile from before remained glued to her face. "Jeez, Marcus, I'm sorry about that. It's just that you caught me a little off guard. Are you going to kill her or just scare her?"

"You are a crazy bitch, if you think I'd tell you anything."

"I wouldn't tell anyone," Jane countered. "I promise, my lips are sealed."

"Woman, you just a junkie. Your promises don't mean nothin'. You'd sell out your own momma for your next fix."

Jane didn't care for the man's opinion of her, but it didn't last long. The thought of the high was more deliriously appealing than the disparaging remark, concerning her or her mother. She asked, "You got the stuff?"

"You got the money?"

"I only got one-twenty of it," Jane confessed.

Marcus started to get up. He didn't have the time or the patience for Jane's games.

"Marcus wait. . . wait. Sit back down. I can explain. Just give me a minute, will ya?"

Reluctantly, Marcus slid back in the booth. He knew he'd regret it, but he did it anyway. "We've been over this before. You tell me you want an eight-ball of coke. I tell you it will set you back a C-note plus forty. You acting like this is some kind of handout, a free.99."

Jane looked confused, but she was determined to explain. "I had to pawn my wedding band and that's all the guy gave me for it. It was the last valuable thing that I owned. It's not like it had any sentimental value—my ex is such a dip wad. I'd like to be a fly on the wall when that twenty-one-year-old dental hygienist learns what he's really about. I know I'm a little short, but I'll get you next time."

Marcus wasn't buying her reasoning. "Ain't you got child support comin' your way?"

Jane shook her head. "That boy of mine is at the juvenile unit. The greedy state is charging us for the boy's incarceration, so the child support isn't coming to me anymore. They're garnishing my ex-husband's wages."

"No way?" he said in disbelief. "So, you're spending your last dime to get high and not get by?"

Jane was desperate. "Please, Marcus, I'll make-up the difference next time. You have my word."

There was a half-hearted laugh. "I learned long ago the word of a junkie don't mean nothin'," Marcus asserted.

"I'm not a junkie," Jane snapped. "Stop calling me that. I just need a little something to get over this rough patch. After this, I probably won't even need it anymore. I plan to put out some résumés, fill out some applications, and I'm sure to be working in a couple of weeks. I'll sell my plasma if I have to."

"Show me what you got," Marcus demanded.

Jane pushed the envelope across the table. Marcus counted the cash. The woman had been on the up-and-up regarding that; otherwise, Marcus thought she sounded delusional about her employment options.

Marcus pushed his own envelope across the table that contained the plastic bag of cocaine. He left two dollars on the table for the coffee. Before he left, he had some final words for the woman. "You is a junkie, Jane. You talk just like one. And don't forget to leave a quarter tip for the waitress, okay?"

Eighteen

Tuesday, October 17, 2017 9:35 a.m.

The law firm of Peterson, Deutch and Deutch had been established fifteen years ago and their reputation was beyond reproach. The firm's claim to fame was medical malpractice. Whether representing a plaintiff, or a defendant, it didn't really matter. The partners considered the direction of the suit to be immaterial. What mattered was the knowledge of the law and the skill of the argument. . . and money, of course, money.

It had taken Callie two weeks to get an appointment. She'd been escorted to the empty office of Hayden Deutch. His secretary told her that he'd been detained, but he would be in soon. The woman offered Callie a cup of coffee, but she declined, knowing her nerves were already shot. She'd had another restless night of the surreal apparition of her father. She awoke to a fitful fight with the covers that she misconstrued as a boatful of nightcrawlers slithering across her skin. Callie's sleeves were long to cover the claw marks she'd made to rid herself of the muculent worms. She had already made up her mind, that under no circumstances, would she tell anyone else about the angling-themed dreams of her dad. When Callie thought back to how she must've sounded recounting the one dream she'd had with her mother, she just felt ridiculous.

Callie's anxious state was compounded by the fact that she'd been instructed to come to the appointment alone. The reason given was that outside interference, although well meaning, could adulterate strategies meant to offer the defendant the best possible defense. Callie took that to mean what she'd say in front of a friend or family member might be glossed over, so the companion wouldn't think so negatively of her. The attorney needed the truth and nothing but the ugly truth. She came alone and she felt alone.

Guilt was another factor that heightened her tension. Richard was now taking call 24/7 until Callie's issues with the hospital could be resolved. She was allowed to admit and round on her patients, but Richard had to sign off on her charts. Administration had made its position clear—no emergent or intensive care permitted. Because of Richard's extra workload, Callie had offered to cover his office patients, but he'd declined. She'd also learned that Marcus Davis had refused her offer to reconcile any misunderstanding that might have taken place. She'd heard that Marcus's opinion was that *no misunderstanding had occurred.* She planned to discuss the matter with the attorney, wondering if drafting a letter to Mr. Davis was a plausible solution to abating an otherwise contentious situation.

It seemed to her that one day she'd had the ideal life, and now, it seemed to be coming apart at the seams. Her appointment to see the internist and the psychiatrist had been set by Kyle Anderson's office for next week. She dreaded what the results might show, because right now, she felt like she was teetering on the edge of a world grounded by reasonable thought and the abyss of insanity.

Callie welcomed the thoughts of the past weekend that drifted into her head. She'd spent it with Zane at the Atkins' ranch. Zane had suggested the idea, saying that the fresh air and a change of pace would do her a world of good. . . and he'd been right. The one *inconvenience* Callie still faced when she visited Zane at his parents' ranch was the fact that he still lived with his folks. His parents were elderly and Zane was their primary caregiver, with his sister helping out on the weekends. Callie knew the Atkins were good people, but their conservative views often clashed with her own. The biggest one was *our house, our rules.* Callie and Zane weren't married, and therefore, they would not share a bed. But it was on one of Callie's first visits out to the ranch that Zane showed her what it really meant to live and work together. . . a genuine bonding. It seemed strange to Callie that on the previous weekend, being with Zane was about the last thing she wanted. The thought of it almost sickened her. But over the weekend, the time with him had been bliss. No wonder people talked as if she was confused, she thought. She *felt* confused! In Callie's opinion, the visit to the ranch had ended all too soon. This time, she'd found the traditional norms of the Atkins safe and comforting. She'd slept solid, no bizarre dreams with ethereal visitors. She'd woken up rested with a home-cooked breakfast and fresh perked coffee awaiting her. The lifestyle had been deemed clean living long ago, and Callie had felt clean. . . clean and refreshed. But it didn't last long. The weekend was over and her dirty problems were right in front of her.

Callie eyed the office. It was beautiful, and no doubt, expensively decorated. The mahogany-paneled walls set the stage for the Telluride executive desk with wood panels, accompanied by the leather chairs and sofa of deep, rich burgundy and blue tones. An entire wall, from floor to ceiling, shelved books dedicated to what seemed to be casebooks. They were accessible by a sliding ladder. Raised bands on flawless spines added stability and structure to the classic old tomes. Navigational antiques accented the room. Callie particularly noted the sextant, vintage naval ship lights, and a compass binnacle. These, and the framed nautical charts on the wall, told Callie the attorney had a mariner's interests.

A man's voice came from behind where Callie was seated. "Dr. Wallace, I'm so sorry to have kept you waiting. There was an unforeseen issue with one of my clients. The prosecutor's office threw us a curveball, last minute. But it wasn't anything I couldn't handle. I hope you understand."

Callie noted the man as he first entered her peripheral vision, following him to where he stood in front of her to shake her hand. He was about six-foot, give or take, with the beginnings of a middle-aged paunch around the waist. His dark suit, with contrasting pristine white shirt, was elegant. His tie had a knot with a pedigree, the Full Windsor knot. The tie itself pictured a vague background map of Texas, and to the forefront, a Texas flag with bluebonnets beneath it. Callie was not yet convinced on the man's skill as a litigator, but she was convinced he was a man of style and charm. She noted he was staring at her, as well.

He took a seat behind the large desk. "Dr. Wallace, is your foot fitted with a battery?"

The question confused Callie. "I'm sorry. I don't get your meaning."

"It's your leg," he explained. "It's jumping like a toad on amphetamines. There's no need to be nervous."

Callie consciously quieted the nervous habit,

stilling the leg's erratic movement. "I guess I'm a bit on edge. I never had to see a lawyer before."

"Well, despite what you may have heard, we don't bite. And besides that, there hasn't been any actual legal action taken against you, as of yet. But you are concerned that such action may be imminent. Do I have that right?"

Callie was uncomfortable. "It appears so. . . a man is dead. I filled out the questionnaire you emailed me and sent it back. I laid out the difficulties I've been having at Lake Sperling Medical Center. Mr. Murphy's death is just one of the concerns the administrator has with me."

"Dr. Wallace, I did get the questionnaire back and have reviewed it. I do have to wonder what exactly you want from me at this juncture. It hasn't yet been established that you were negligent in Mr. Murphy's death, and even if you were, it doesn't necessarily mean a malpractice suit will be filed. Now, the issues you outlined regarding Jane Timmons, Mr. Davis, and the supposed incident where you, let's just say, argued with yourself, could easily be dismissed. We merely explain these instances were a result of stress and fatigue, and propose a plan of action on how you intend to address these circumstances in the future. With regards to Mr. Murphy, if your actions are not found negligent, I could represent you in a slander suit against the Medical Center. It would state that its premature action resulted in harm to your reputation with excessive disciplinary action taken against you. When do you expect Mr. Murphy's final autopsy report?"

"I don't expect it to be more than two weeks," Callie replied. She managed a smile. "You make it sound like I have choices. I definitely didn't feel that way when I came in here today."

"You always have choices, Dr. Wallace. What matters is if the court agrees with the choices you've made. Tell me, have you ever made a dosage mistake like the one you've described with the methylprednisolone?"

"No, never, I swear. And if I had to swear to it today, I would say that I ordered 64 mg, not 6 mg. But. . ."

"But what, Dr. Wallace?"

"There is something else. I doubt it is even relevant. It's just that, in the matter of Jane Timmons, it's not only the fact that I found her impaired. I found her impaired and didn't report it right away, and in the meantime, another one of my patients died in the neuro's ICU, a Mrs. Scott. Do you think that could present a problem?"

Hayden Deutch leaned back in his chair. He stroked the length his neck, followed by a long-exasperated sigh. "Yes, Dr. Wallace, I do think that is relevant, and speaks to your judgment, or lack thereof. Is there anything else you have forgotten to tell me?"

"No, I don't think so," Callie replied. "Why would you ask?"

"Because, whenever a client says *there's one other thing* that means there's usually more than just one thing. So, I have to ask you again, is there anything else you need to tell me?"

"Well, technically, I'm not the one who reported Jane Timmons as impaired. . . it was my boyfriend."

"I see," the attorney said as he tried to contemplate the repercussions of the matter.

"I was going to . . . I was," Callie tried to explain. "I just thought it was more important to deal with the Scott family first. I guess if I was to be perfectly honest, . . ."

The attorney cut her off. "That would be nice, Dr. Wallace," he chastised.

Callie felt like a scolded schoolgirl, again. "I just haven't been feeling myself, lately. My boyfriend suggested I spend the weekend with him at his parents' ranch. He said it would do me good, and he was right. I started to feel like myself again. But being back in Sperling, the old insecurities have resurfaced. Maybe, I'm not well."

Mr. Deutch placed his elbows on the desk and laced his fingers together. "It seems, Dr. Wallace, that your self-esteem has taken quite a hit. If I'm going to represent you, I need you to toughen up. Even if you don't feel confident, you need to fake it. Keep the appointments next week with the internist and the psychiatrist—you go in confident. You're a physician, not a mouse. Arrogance should come naturally to you. Get that head up and look them square in the eye—no bouncing the knee around, either. I know things seem bad now, but there is no indication that they actually are. The probation is only temporary until more concrete facts come to light. Understand?"

Callie wasn't one for theatrics, but she trusted the man. "You said something about the possibility of a slander case?"

"Well, in light of the new details you explained today, it appears that the Medical Center is just taking reasonable precautions to ensure patient safety. Like I said, it's just temporary."

"I guess I don't understand," Callie admitted. "Are you taking my case or not?"

"I think it's wise you sought legal counsel. I'm going to represent you, but we'll talk strategy when the actual facts are in. Your father was a good friend of mine. I don't know if you knew that."

Callie shook her head.

The lawyer affectionately chuckled at the memory of Mr. Wallace. "Yeah, we both loved fishing. He was more of a fresh-water type of guy, where I prefer salt-water, deep sea fishing. In these parts, it was a lot easier for him to get to his favorite fishing hole than it ever has been for me. He could tell the wildest, most outlandish fishing stories I ever heard. Did he ever tell you any of those?"

Callie lied. "No, no, I can't say that he ever did."

Nineteen

Thursday, October 19, 2017 10:15 a.m.

Marta was just finishing up the breakfast dishes that mid-October morning. Gazing out the kitchen window, she saw a lawn littered in leaves. A job for Raul, she thought. Normally, the dishes would have been done, but the phone wasn't giving her any peace. It wasn't just the number of calls, but the nature of them, as well. Her aunt, on her mother's side, was close to death down in the Houston area. Six months ago, her aunt lived in the desolate nowhere of the Oklahoma panhandle, Boise City. But when the woman learned she had breast cancer that had metastasized to the brain, she wasn't about to take any chances . . . she was going to Houston. She'd watched her sister, Marta's mother, suffer terrible pain and decline until the end, and she was determined to get the best, cutting-edge therapy—the type offered at MD Anderson Cancer Center. Marta had a cousin that lived in a Houston suburb, Cinco Ranch, who took their aunt in. Despite aggressive therapy, the aunt was losing the battle. Family members in the Houston area were keeping vigil and calling with hourly updates.

Marta knew she was one ring away from the news that her aunt had passed. The only comfort for her was that, when the time came, her mother would be waiting for her sister, angel wings in hand.

The ring caused Marta to jump. She quickly dried her hands and braced herself for the possibility that her aunt had taken her last breath. But when she picked up her phone, she was taken aback to discover no call. The ring came again and Marta realized that she'd become oversensitive to such sounds. . . *get a grip,* she told herself. *It's just the doorbell.* She went to the window and looked out, surprised to see Rose Wallace standing on the porch.

Marta instinctively fussed with her hair before answering the door. "Rose, how lovely to see you."

"Hello, Marta, I'm sorry to just stop by like this without calling. I guess it comes down to the fact that I didn't really know what to say regarding why I wanted to see you. Listen to me rattle on," she said as her voiced started to crack. "Do you have a minute? Can I come in?"

Marta could see that her neighbor was upset. "Oh certainly, Rose. Please excuse my manners. I guess I'm a little preoccupied today."

They stood, momentarily, in the living room. Marta offered, "We can sit in here, or in the kitchen. I still have some coffee."

“Coffee would be great,” Rose said.

The two made their way into the kitchen. Rose took a seat at the table while Marta poured the coffee. Marta asked, “Cream or sugar?”

Rose hated to be particular, but if the coffee had been made hours ago, it might be bitter. “Milk will be fine, thank you.”

Marta placed the cups on the table, grabbed the carton from the refrigerator, and took a seat next to her neighbor. “Rose, is everything okay?”

Rose poured a dab of it in the coffee and stirred mindlessly. The concern in Marta’s voice almost sent Rose crying, but she pushed the urge down. “I can’t imagine this is the best time for company. I mean, I know you work the Monday through Wednesday twelve-hour shifts at the hospital. Your first day off this week, your first morning off, and here I am. I’m sure you have a lot to do.”

Marta was convinced that something specific was troubling the woman. “Yes, that’s true, but that doesn’t mean I don’t have an hour for a friend.”

Rose forced a brief smile. Her mood was anything but happy. “Marta, tell me something. I guess I always wondered why you have a job in housekeeping at the hospital. Raul makes a good living with the city. You live in a nice neighborhood and you have a lovely home. I don’t mean to pry, but the pay-scale at the hospital for custodians can't be enough to make or break your family finances."

Marta took a sip of coffee before starting to explain. "I don't mind the question, really, I don't. Where you have it right, about the family finances, that's true. My husband's salary is more than sufficient. Raul makes a comfortable living for us. I guess what you don't understand is that I work at the Medical Center, not for the pay, but the *idea* of family."

"I guess I don't understand," Rose admitted.

"Well, it's been thirty-four years now since my mother died. I remember it like it was yesterday. She was way too young. It was breast cancer. It runs rampant in my family and treatment then isn't like what we have now. I've been genetically tested, and by the grace of God, I was negative for the gene variation that makes a woman susceptible to it. I was pregnant when she was diagnosed. I wanted to go to her, but my pregnancy was complicated by pre-eclampsia. My doctor prescribed bedrest for the remainder of my pregnancy and Raul held me to it. I felt helpless. I had to tell my mother goodbye over the phone. It was heart wrenching."

Rose listened intently, but she had questions. "I'm sorry to hear that, Marta, but what does that have to do with your job at the hospital?"

"I was depressed after my mother died, feeling in

some ways like I brought that diagnosis to her door. But following the birth of my son, it just got worse. One day, I decided I'd crawl out of my own grief. I started volunteering, but that wasn't what I was looking for in terms of gratification. I mean, fund raising and packing care packages wasn't doing it. It's been twelve years since I joined the Medical Center family. I know housekeeping isn't glamorous, but I have access to just about every room in that hospital. If I manage my duties just right, I have time to sit awhile with the dying patient. I tell the new mother how beautiful she looks. I bring a cool rag to the nauseated chemo patient. I listen to the old man's stories that he's told his family hundreds of times. It's about the people, I suppose. I learned that it's the small things in life that matter. . . that, and I'm a pretty good housekeeper, too."

Rose smiled, and this time, it was genuine. She took a quick look around the woman's house. It was immaculate. Rose knew her neighbor smoked, but there wasn't even a hint of it in the air. "I think that's wonderful—it's a beautiful story."

Rose paused, and took a deep breath. It was time to get to point. "Marta, what's happening at that hospital with my Callie? I heard things. There's whispering behind my back, pointing. I've tried to call my daughter, but when she answers the phone, she just shuts me down. She tells me she has everything under control, but I feel like she doesn't."

Marta held her hands around the coffee cup on the table and stared down at it. It was hard to look the desperate woman in the eye, especially since she regrettably might've told a *couple* of people what Gus had said. But Marta made herself do it anyway. She was sure her face said it all, but she was going to choose her words carefully. "I think a lot of Callie, you know that. I watched the girl grow-up, crawling all over her father's bass boat, and darting up and down the block with that bike of hers. But the truth of the matter is that she's on probation with limited privileges. Personally, I think the situation will be cleared up in no time. Rose, most of the people that work at the Medical Center are good people, but there are some that have a vindictive heart, and I'm afraid Callie might have crossed paths with a few of them. One of them is the administrator, Kyle Anderson. Some are trying to call her loco, but we know that's not true. Try to have faith. She'll come to you when she's ready."

Rose wanted to believe her. "Thank you, Marta. Thanks for being straight with me. I've counted on you all these years and you haven't let me down yet. I just wish Callie's father was still alive. He always had such a way with her. At least she has Richard. I only met him once, just briefly. But I have his number if I need it. He'll watch her back, just like you've watched mine."

Marta thought back to what Gus had told her. "What about her boyfriend, Zane is it? Everything going okay between those two?"

Marta caught her friend daydreaming. "Rose?"

"Oh, yeah, yeah, him. He's okay, I guess, but he's away so much of the time. Callie needs those close to home in her corner."

"Rose, where were you just now?"

"Oh, I was just thinking about when Callie was a girl. She was so driven, a meticulous planner. Hell, her contingency plan had contingency plans. And talk about determination, she had nerves of steel."

With that, Marta was in full agreement. "Yeah, remember the incident at the edge of our property development? What was the name of that gymnast Callie was trying to emulate?"

"How could I forget? Her name was Sheryl Madden. She was a world champion gymnast in the nineties, cute girl and really talented. Callie was obsessed with everything Sheryl. She even tried to wear her hair the same way, but Callie's brown curls would always find a way of escaping that gymnastic bun. Once I caught her with a box of blond hair dye. She didn't speak to me for a week after I dumped it down the drain. After you brought her home that day, it took everything I could muster not to strangle her. I was just so grateful she hadn't broken anything."

"I don't think I'll ever forget it," Marta said. "I was driving home from the market, and turned into the entrance of our housing development. It was a day just like any other day. There was that five-foot brick and mortar wall with the name of our development on it, River Fall Estates. There was Callie in a one-piece swimming suit. It had to be fifty degrees outside. She was jumping on an exercise trampoline and before I knew it, she'd leapt atop the concrete ledge of the wall like it was some sort of balance beam. I slammed on the brakes, demanded she get down, loaded her and that trampoline up, and drove her home. Talk about nerves of steel."

"Now that I think about it, sounds like plain recklessness to me," Rose grumbled.

"Yes, I see your point," Marta agreed. "I suppose every parent needs to be grateful that their child makes it to adulthood alive. But it doesn't mean we stop looking out for them. In fact, Tuesday is the administrator's afternoon to play golf. I'll just tell his secretary that his office didn't get cleaned the night before, and I've come to touch it up. If I see anything suspicious, I'll give you a call."

Rose was surprised how blunt Marta was being. "I would never ask you to do anything that could get you in trouble. Let's just see how things play out."

Not since the awful rumors about Callie had started to circulate had Rose felt more content, having had someone to confide in. She heard a phone ringing in the other room. “Marta, do you need to get that?”

“I’ll see to it in a minute,” she replied. “If God has made His mind up about something, there’s nothing I can do about it. Right now, I’m exactly where I need to be. More coffee?”

Twenty

Saturday, October 21, 2017 8:25 p.m.

Jamie picked at her banana split. She felt pathetic. Another Saturday night, and no one to share it with. The counter at the soda fountain had only two empty seats, one on either side of her. The rest of the stools were occupied with high school students. At least they have a life, Jamie concluded. In her eyes, the world was made for couples. They were the ones at the movies, eating in the fine restaurants, or going to enjoy the nightlife the big city provided, not drowning their sorrows in a sugar-high at *Dickerson's Drug*.

Jamie took a bite, rationalizing she was eating fruit. She'd lost ten pounds, but no one had noticed. If they had, they'd kept their comments to themselves. She knew she had forty more pounds to go, but she just couldn't spend another night in that tiny apartment of hers, watching re-runs. It was like the saying goes, she reasoned, that when you're alone, everywhere you look, there are couples in love.

At the age of thirty-seven, Jamie had never married . . . never been asked. She'd been a licensed practical nurse for eleven years. Her reason for pursuing the career hadn't been to help people, but because she thought it might help her meet a man. In Jamie's world, he'd be a little older with a chronic condition, like emphysema, something she could help him manage. It would be hard for him to get out, and he'd desire some female companionship. But things hadn't turned out that way. It was like she thought, everybody had somebody . . . even the emphysemic.

Another spoonful went to her mouth. Jamie had already paid for the dessert—no sense in just letting it melt. She eyed the high school girls at the counter. She saw how young and beautiful they were . . . and thin. Their figures were shapely and tight. Their tresses had luster and gently rolled over their shoulders. It made Jamie self-conscious of her own mousy brown hair with a bob-cut style that screamed frumpy, not sexy. Nor were the bouts of acne she experienced. She thought as she aged, this would disappear, but that was just another miscalculation on her part.

Jamie used the edge of her spoon to cut a piece of banana off. It had a trickle of fudge on it, and she quickly brought it to her mouth before she changed her mind. She wondered why she was so down on herself right now, but when the bell over the pharmacy door tinkled, she knew why. It was Callie Wallace, *Dr. Callie Wallace*, the darling of Sperling. And to top it off, she had that handsome boyfriend with her, the one whose mere presence made Jamie stutter. That's all she needed, her boss, on her night off. Marcus Davis came to Jamie's mind. He'd wanted her to intercede with Dr. Wallace on his behalf. But the more she'd thought about it, it wasn't her place to chastise the behavior of someone who signed her checks. It was that, and when Marcus mentioned that he had a wife, Jamie lost all incentive.

With a quick look over her shoulder, Jamie saw that Dr. Wallace and *friend* had taken a booth and were perusing the laminated menus. But she didn't want to be noticed, so she returned to facing forward. She thought back to when she first went to work for the two young neurologists. She really believed that Dr. Wallace had a thing for her partner, the way she doted on him and such. It was a thought that stuck with her, despite Dr. Wallace's ongoing relationship with her boyfriend, Zane. Then, there was also the fact that every time she'd seen Dr. Cortez and Zane together, they were chummy. No animosity there at all. It was just that *something* that Jamie couldn't shake. She wondered if she had thought this because of her own feelings. She couldn't believe that a man and a woman could have just a platonic relationship. To her, it seemed impossible. But she relished the idea of Dr. Cortez, Richard, taking a romantic interest in herself. He was handsome, as well, but not in Zane's rugged way . . . more in a scholastic way. With that thought, Jamie shoved the dessert boat away. Forty more pounds and a makeover, she told herself. Richard Cortez wouldn't be able to help himself. Maybe, she fantasized, they'd be madly in love by next spring, just in time for a June wedding.

Reality caught up with Jamie. There was the issue of the woman calling the office and asking to speak to *Richie*. Jamie was worried Dr. Cortez had started to date. The woman, Sara, would call the office several times a day. At first, Jamie thought it was just a drug company representative. But she'd overheard one of their telephone conversations. There'd been a lot of laughing, teasing, and plans being made for after dark. She wondered why such calls would be coming to the office, and not to the physician's cell phone. Jamie had taken a chance and tried it when she knew he was too busy to answer, and his mailbox was full. With how busy he'd been, she just figured that type of thing wasn't on top of his priority list.

Jamie felt a hand on her shoulder. She'd been so busy trying to figure out other people's lives, she'd almost forgotten an existence of her own.

Dr. Wallace was standing behind her. The physician had a friendly demeanor about her. "Jamie, I almost didn't see you sitting there. Zane and I have ordered a plate of fries. We'd love for you to join us."

"No thanks, Dr. Wallace. In fact, I'm just finishing up. Anyway, I'm supposed to meet a friend of mine for the ten o'clock movie—the one from DC Comics."

"Oh, yeah. Zane and I saw that last night. No worries. I won't send any spoilers your way. Monday, we can compare notes, okay?"

Jamie wanted to hate the doctor. It would be easier for her to accept her own short-comings that way. But she just couldn't hate the darling of Sperling. Callie Wallace had to be five years younger than her, take a year or so. Things seemed to come easier for people like Callie Wallace, Jamie reasoned. As for her life, she had to fight for every little scrap. Tonight, she lied about her plans, and now, she was committed to seeing a movie she had very little interest in. And to top it off, she didn't have the money in her budget for the price of a Saturday night ticket. She'd have to go to the half-price matinee tomorrow.

Jamie gave a slight grin, a false impression that she looked forward to Monday's critique of the sci-fi flick. "Dr. Wallace, I don't mean to overstep, but there's something I was wondering about."

"What's that, Jamie?"

"These calls to the office, the ones from the woman named Sara, is she with a pharmaceutical company?"

There was a grin on the physician's face. "Jamie, Dr. Cortez has a new lady friend. I'm afraid these ridiculous issues of mine at the Medical Center are putting somewhat of a damper on the spring of their relationship. The woman does appear resilient, though, don't you think?"

Jamie began to respond, but eyed Zane approaching over Dr. Wallace's shoulder. "Have you me-me-met her?"

Callie knew Zane must be nearby. She thought Jamie's nervousness was cute.

"Callie, the fries are here," Zane announced.

"Thanks, Zane. You go ahead, I'll be right there," Callie replied.

Zane took the hint and returned to their table. Callie wanted to convey to Jamie that she understood her uneasiness. "Zane is quite handsome, isn't he? But to answer your question, no, I haven't met Sara yet. Dr. Cortez will introduce her to us when he feels the time is right."

Jamie felt like the air had been taken out of her sail. Her shoulders fell. "Well, if Dr. Cortez thinks she's special, then I'm sure she is. I'll see you on Monday, okay?"

Callie watched as Jamie left the drugstore, head hung low. She knew the woman needed a friend, but she seriously doubted Jamie had one.

Twenty-one

Monday, October 23, 2017 12:10 p.m.

Business was hopping at the *Flap 'n Jack*. It was par for the course. The diner's *Meatloaf Monday* lunch special with a free cobbler for dessert was a Sperling favorite, especially at $5.99 a plate. Richard was in a booth by the window, waving Sara over. She appeared confused or irritated—Richard couldn't tell which.

As Sara approached, Richard stood. He gave her a peck on the cheek and they sat down. The menus were stacked between the napkin holder and the salt and pepper shakers. Richard grabbed two, handing one to Sara.

Richard already knew he was going to have the meatloaf, but perused the menu, just in case something else seemed to whet his appetite. "Everything go okay at the bank this morning?" he asked.

"Work is fine," she flatly replied.

Richard noticed the sour mood. "I recommend the special. I know meatloaf sounds like some Midwest staple, but it's really good here. And for the price, well, the crowd speaks for itself."

Sara had her lips pressed tight.

"Hun," Richard began. "Is anything wrong? You seem a bit . . . uptight."

Sara parted her lips, blowing out the breath she apparently had been holding. "Work is fine, Richie. I'm fine. But this, *this diner*, why are we eating here?"

Richard hadn't seen this side of Sara. "What's wrong with the *Flap 'n Jack*?"

"Okay, let's say this diner is nice, but *Olea's Kitchen* is much, much nicer. I have barely seen you. You don't have time to talk to me, and when you do, you ask me to meet you at this greasy spoon."

Richard was offended. "This place serves good, wholesome food. Have you ever tried the meatloaf? It practically melts in your mouth. Besides, *Olea's Kitchen* is over-priced, the servings are small, and the service is slow."

Sara's dismissive hand gesture didn't go unnoticed by Richard. He knew he needed to try and reason with her. "Sweetheart, I know I've been busy and haven't had the time I want to spend with you. I just need you to understand for a little bit longer. If I do happen to get called, I know I can get a to-go box here and settle up the check in less than five minutes. Callie's issues should be resolved next week, and things will be back to normal soon."

Sara was sharp with her question. "And what if they don't?"

Richard hadn't actually considered the alternative. "What?"

"What if she is deemed unfit to practice? What will you do then? What will it mean for us?"

"Sara, I really think you're getting ahead of yourself."

The waitress showed up with two waters. "What can I get for you two today?"

Richard didn't want to have the *us* conversation with Sara. He planned to give her something else to focus on. "We'll take three specials. There will be someone else joining us. She's just running a little late."

What Richard had said didn't get by Sara. She waited until after the waitress left before starting her gripe. "You know, I can order for myself. And who's supposed to be joining us? I was hoping to have a little alone time with you. It's not that Callie is it?"

Richard was beginning to notice little things that weren't so little. It was a side to Sara he hadn't seen before. There was a controlling, vindictive side veiled beneath the coiffed hair and bright red lipstick. It was a side that made him think she cared more about the status of being with a physician, instead of what it actually took to be with one. But she had to learn he was just a man, who happened to be a physician, who happened to eat at the *Flap 'n Jack*. "No, it's not Callie.

But if it was, what's your beef with her? You haven't even met her."

Sara knew she'd over-played her hand. "Richie, Richie, I don't have a problem with your little friend. I bet you think I'm some kind of shrew, but really, I'm not. I guess I'm a little jealous is all, the way you bring her up . . . *all the time*. Forgive me?"

The waitress suddenly appeared with three plates. Richard couldn't help but notice Sara's scowl as she looked down upon the slice of meatloaf, the rounded scoop of potatoes covered in brown gravy, and on the side, green beans.

He also noticed how she blamed her insecurities about Callie on him. Richard smiled at the waitress and thanked her before she left. "Something wrong with your food?" he asked Sara.

"No, no, it's fine," she disingenuously replied. "And that remark about Callie . . . it was uncalled for. I'm sorry, I jumped to conclusions. And when you think the time is right for Callie and me to meet, I'm sure we'll be the best of friends."

A young woman approached the table. "Dr. Cortez, I'm Haley. I'm sorry I'm late. Class went a little long."

Richard moved in closer to the wall, to make room for her in the booth. "Hello, Haley. I hope you like meatloaf."

"I do, thanks. I'm starved, and college students rarely pass up a free meal. I hope my age isn't a problem for you. I promise you, there isn't a better party planner in town."

Sara had been raking through her potatoes with her fork, but when she heard mention of a party, her ears perked up. Maybe, she'd judged Richard too harshly. She couldn't help but wonder if he was planning a party to introduce her to his family and friends. "I think I might have heard of you, Haley. Did you plan the Sorenson wedding?"

Haley felt uncomfortable at the stranger's question. "Uhm, no."

Richard sensed the awkwardness. "I'm sorry. Haley, this is my friend, Sara. I was just thinking she might have some refreshing and unique party ideas."

"Nice to meet you, Sara," the planner said.

Curiosity was getting the best of Sara. "Oh, Richie, are you going to let me in on this little plan of yours?"

Haley enthusiastically jumped in. "It's a surprise party."

Richard was hesitant to answer, considering how the earlier conversation went.

Sara was condescending. "Dear, how is it supposed to be a surprise when I already know about it?"

Puzzled, Haley glanced at Dr. Cortez. "I thought you said the party was for someone named Callie?"

Richard knew he couldn't put off the inevitable. "Sara, Haley is here to help me plan a surprise birthday party for Callie. Her birthday is the thirty-first, Halloween. We only have a week."

Haley went on long-winded and chatty with all the ideas she had for the event. Dr. Cortez explicitly told her—no grim or scary themes associated with the holiday. He wanted it to be a masquerade party. As she prattled on, she didn't notice Sara scowling at Richard.

Richard's phone went off. He reached for it and noticed it was the hospital. *Thank God*, he thought to himself. He signaled the waitress for a to-go box. He reached into his jacket for his wallet and a piece of paper. He put twenty-five dollars on the table, realizing Sara had not eaten a thing. The paper he handed to Haley. "Here's the guest list and their contact information. I'll make sure she's out of the house from, at least, four to seven. That should give you time to set-up and have the guests arrive. Let me know what you and Sara come up with. I can't wait to hear the ideas."

With that, Richard left with the Styrofoam container in hand. Haley sat there nervously as the woman across the table glared at her with an icy stare, jaws clenched. Haley took one last bite off her plate before reaching inside her portfolio. She slipped the guest list into a side pocket and grabbed a business card. "Look, if you have any ideas, here's my card. I forgot there's somewhere I need to be."

Haley stopped at the cashier to ask for her free cobbler. She looked back to see the Sara woman seething in the booth. A part of Haley felt the woman might spontaneously combust.

Twenty-two

Monday, October 23, 2017 10:25 p.m.

Callie knew what she was doing was the last thing she should do before going to sleep, but she had to tackle the issue. She was sitting up in bed, with textbooks open to various chapters on psychology and psychiatry, while she thumbed through her tablet computer. The appointments to evaluate her mental and physical health were next week. As an afterthought, agreeing to such an imperious demand felt like a mistake. Her health was her business, not that of Lake Sperling Medical Center. Another concern was what Kyle Anderson would do with the information once he had access to it. But Mr. Deutch hadn't seemed to take issue with it. Maybe he thought that if they didn't find anything wrong with her, it would pave an easy path to a slander suit. But that was not what bothered Callie. It was what they *might* find.

The physical exam was in three days, and Callie felt fairly confident that the objective aspects of the exam would show her in perfect health. She was almost thirty-three, and had enjoyed good health throughout most of her life without significant injury.

The question was, what was the origin of her problems? Her frustration stemmed from the fact that she was a neurologist, and she couldn't pinpoint anything specific. The episodes she'd experienced, or allegedly had experienced, some of which she remembered, some of which she did not, didn't follow any specific pattern that would lead to a definitive diagnosis. The prospect that she'd been experiencing seizures had entered her mind. She'd thought about asking Richard about it, as he was as equally qualified as her to make such a diagnosis. But she was resigned to the fact that Richard's role in her life, especially now, was more of a big-brother and protector. He wouldn't be able to remain objective, and she knew herself, that the episodes she'd experienced didn't follow any classic epileptic pattern. She remembered the Sunday night Richard had called, after he'd been out of town with Sara. Callie had been conversing with her deceased father just seconds before the call came in, and when it did, the apparition was gone from the corner chair. It was reality intermingled with non-reality.

While that was disconcerting enough, it was the mental health evaluation the day before the physical exam which really concerned her. That would be a tough one, and she knew it. It was the source for all the research she'd been doing throughout the evening. Callie needed to buckle down to the business at hand, beating the psychological tests. She suspected she would be administered the Minnesota Multiphasic Personality Inventory, specifically the MMPI-2-RF, a psychometric test focused on personality and psychopathology. The section which had Callie the most concerned was the section testing for Bizarre Mentation. Then there was the Validity Scales, once named the Fake Bad Scale, used to detect the legitimacy of the patient's answers. There are those who present with a negative response bias to detect malingering in cases such as personal injury. Then there are those people who want to down-play their psychological symptoms with acquiescence bias. Callie wanted to down-play her issues, but she didn't want to be accused of it. Her plan was to have a balance between the positive and negative key issues in her life, favoring the positive ones, but only slightly.

Callie's eyes were getting heavy. Hours of screen time and rooting through old textbooks were taking a toll. Her breathing was getting slower and deeper. Her arms were having trouble holding her tablet at eye level, and she felt her head sinking far into the billowy soft filling of her pillow. The room was getting darker and cooler. Or was it the storm clouds billowing and the cool air from the lake chilling her?

Before she knew it, Callie was sitting up in a fright. She saw her father on the shore, at the boat launch, waving goodbye. He was yelling something at her . . . something about being careful of the parasite. The fourteen-foot aluminum Jon boat was headed to the depths of the lake, and her without a lifejacket. Rising winds and increasing swells made Callie feel unsteady. There were two wooden benches, on one of which Callie was seated. She reached across the width of the boat, and white-knuckled her grip. The only time she would let go was to sweep her hand beneath the bench for a lifejacket. An electrical discharge lit the sky, a rumble of thunder soon followed. Rain began to fall. Callie knew this wasn't the boat for these types of waters. She called to the man operating the outboard motor, but he didn't acknowledge her. He wore a yellow slicker and matching hat, with a lifejacket secured to him. He sat perpendicular to her. She yelled at him that he needed to slow down and that they needed to head back to shore—the hull was beginning to fill with water. He turned to her. The wind and the rain beat his face, distorting his features, but Callie knew him. It was Kyle Anderson, laughing to mock her panic.

Kyle killed the motor, lowering the anchor. "I know what you're doing, Callie," he shouted over the storm. "You're looking for another lifejacket, but there isn't one. You see, you're going to have an accident on a night not meant for boating. Even if you don't drown, you won't be able to avoid the *Naegleria fowleri* in the water."

Callie sensed the vindictiveness in his voice. What she said next wasn't a stretch. "Let me guess, the organism is a parasite," she loudly proclaimed.

Kyle began to clap. "Very good, Dr. Wallace. Still first in your class, I see. But do you know how the parasite enters your body? I'll tell you, it's through the nose. Unpleasant, right? First, there's the headache, then the seizures, then the hallucinations, then coma, followed by death. Now, don't look at me that way. If you don't drown, the survival rate for this infection is only 2-3%. I say the odds are not in your favor. I say we get this nightmare underway."

Callie watched the man straddle the boat and began to erratically rock it. The boat was sitting low in the water from the weight of the rain, and this made it easy for lake water to spill in over the sides. Callie maintained her tight grip on the boat's edge. Her voice raspy, "How do you know you won't fall in the water, infecting yourself?"

"I'm too mean to die, Callie. Don't believe me, just ask your father."

The notion of such a thing infuriated her. Callie lunged at Anderson, knocking him off his feet. Although on top of him, she was stunned by their collapse into the water-filled hull with legs strung mid-air. His hands wrapped tightly around her throat, and she sensed what little light there was fading.

Cough, cough, cough

Callie jolted up in bed. The grip on her throat was firm, but it was her own. She quickly released the hold she had on herself. She was hyperventilating. As if the bed was a flooded death trap, she jumped from it, sending her tablet and textbooks tumbling to the floor.

She made her way to the master bath. Callie turned on the faucet, and thought, how ironic it was that all she wanted was to splash water on her face. She looked in the mirror over the sink. She blinked to shed the water from her eyelashes, to see drops falling from her jaw and chin. There they were, the red imprinted marks of fingers that had dug into her throat. It was the first time Callie really *felt* crazy, but she was determined to get to the bottom of it all. She felt like crying, but she choked the urge down.

Twenty-three

Tuesday, October 31, 2017 4:00 p.m.

The cynical thought came to Callie late that afternoon, *some birthday*. She sat with Richard by her side, anxiously waiting to be called back for her MRI. The two days of testing last week had started to take its toll. The only thing that gave her solace was the fact that the process was almost complete. What had surprised her most from the whole ordeal was the visit to the psychiatrist, Dr. Lambert. He'd discussed his conclusions with her, and the findings had actually made her feel *better*. But the conclusion to her was apparent . . . if it wasn't mental, the issue must be physical.

"You nervous?" Richard asked. "The test is routine, you know that. There's nothing to worry about."

Callie immediately looked down at her leg to see if it was shaking. She'd sworn to herself she was going to work on that nervous habit, and today her legs were still. Instead, Callie was chewing on her thumb nail, and that must've been what Richard picked up on. "Oh, I know. I just wish the Medical Center's MRI machine was open at both ends. It's the machine's confining tube, and my head will be in it. I have to admit, I'm embarrassed about having to call you. I requested sedation, but then I was told, after I have it, I can't drive until tomorrow. Now, I need a chauffeur."

"Callie, you know I don't mind. Besides, with it being your birthday, I'd already made arrangements to get off early, other than call. If I do get called, I'll just have your mother come get you. After all, we've celebrated your birthday together for years, and today is no exception. I've already made dinner reservations for us at that French bistro you like so much."

Callie was sarcastic. "Yeah, when you signed on to be my friend, I bet you didn't expect toting me around to the doctor. I'll probably be on senior care before we know it."

Richard dismissed her mordant mood. "Oh, come on now. Things are not as bad as that. Let's take your mind off the brain scan. You conveyed the visit with the psychiatrist went better than expected. Now, tell me about it. Any surprises? Are you a serial killer?"

Her friend always had a way of making her laugh. "No, silly. And if you don't believe me, you can check my freezer and the cellar when you take me home."

Richard let a chuckle slip. "Maybe I will. Remind me later, okay? Now, getting back to the appointment."

"Well, I guess I passed, or that was the impression I got. First, he told me that self-talk is not indicative of mental illness, but in fact can be a healthy way to support myself, especially when I'm stressed about something. Secondly, he encouraged me to draft a letter to Marcus Davis and send it certified through Hayden Deutch's office. He said I wasn't responsible for how Marcus feels, and if he chooses not to accept my apology for the misunderstanding, that's all on him. With the right intention, the letter will show goodwill on my part."

Richard nodded with approval. "Sounds solid. But what about the real issue?"

"According to the psychiatrist, he says it's not unusual for mothers and daughters to have contentious relationships. I used to think of her as emotionally distant but he pointed out that I returned to Sperling where she still lives, so there must be something nurturing about the situation that I sought out. He said that speaks to my commitment to family and community. He says those types of values extend to my long-term relationship with Zane. As for my father, I was a daddy's girl, I admit that. He told me he wouldn't be surprised if I have some unresolved guilt about not being able to help him with his health issues, especially with me being in the medical field."

"I didn't mean your relationship with your folks. I mean, look at mine. If that's what makes a person unstable, half the world would need to be committed. No, what I meant was the methylprednisolone dose."

It wasn't that Callie had misunderstood what Richard had asked her. She just didn't want to talk about it, especially not with him. She really valued her relationship with Richard, and admitting she had made a mistake—she just didn't want to look *less* in his eyes. "Richard, I have to ask you a question."

"Okay."

"What would be a better outcome to you, if I had emotional problems or if I was just a screw-up?"

"Now, Callie, what kind of talk is that? My first inclination was to ask you if that was some sort of trick question, but I can tell from the expression on your face, it's not. The truth is I don't think of you as either of those things. You're my friend . . . my best friend, warts and all."

"But I'm also your partner, someone you're supposed to be able to count on. How are you supposed to trust me when I've been so careless?"

"So, is this what all the fuss is about . . . you made a mistake?"

Callie hung her head, keeping her voice low. "Yeah, I guess it is. I mean, it has to be. There's no other explanation."

Richard gently lifted her drooping chin with his hand. "Callie, look at me."

She reluctantly looked up.

His voice was kind and soft. "Callie, how did you

feel about me when I made a gaffe? Remember some of my exams back in medical school? There was so much red ink, you'd think someone bled on it. But you never gave up on me, did you?"

Callie's voice remained timid. "Well, to answer your question, we tried to fix it . . .tried to figure out where your answer went wrong. Everyone makes mistakes. We're only human."

Richard gestured to shake her hand. "Nice to meet you, everyone."

Callie's eyes teared up. "Oh, Richard, it's not a time for joking. Someone's dead, maybe another."

"I'm not joking," he insisted. "But what *you are doing* is focusing on one bad situation that turned tragic that could have been nothing more than a slip of your finger off the keyboard. What *you are not doing* is thinking of the countless patients you have helped and will continue to do so after this is over. So, I'm going to ask you, again, what did the psychiatrist say about the dosing error?"

Before Callie could answer, a nurse suddenly appeared with a medication souffle cup and a glass of water. "Dr. Wallace, here is 10 mg of Valium. Please, take it with only a sip of water. You haven't had anything else to eat or drink in the last two hours, have you? The test we have you scheduled for today uses contrast dye, and you shouldn't have had anything by mouth."

Callie took the sedation with just a sip, as instructed. "No, I haven't had anything. Will it be much longer?"

"No," the nurse replied. "Let's give the pill twenty minutes or so, to work. I'll be back in a bit to escort you back to the imaging room. Do you need to empty your bladder before I go? I don't want you getting up by yourself."

"No, I'm okay," Callie replied. "I've got my friend here."

Richard watched the nurse walk away. "So, am I going to finally hear what the shrink's advice was?"

"Oh, yeah," Callie said. "He basically said what you did, that I'm human and I need to admit if I unintentionally made a mistake, and to learn from it. He said if a lawsuit is brought, I need to notify my malpractice carrier and let them negotiate a settlement . . . and then move on."

To Richard, Callie's answer seemed somewhat incomplete. "What did he mean by *learn from it*? Callie, what did you take from that message?"

"For starters, he told me to start with the HALT method before I react to a situation. I'm supposed to ask myself if I'm hungry, angry, lonely, or tired. To avoid acting impulsively, I'm supposed to evaluate how I feel."

Richard was skeptical. "Callie, we make hundreds

to thousands of decisions every day, especially on call. And during an emergency, when time is brain tissue, are you going to decide you're hungry and go have a snack before you act? If it's three-thirty in the morning, are you going to take a nap first?"

Richard had his doubts about the practicality of the psychiatrist's advice, but before he could continue his argument, he felt a thud. He looked down to see Callie's head resting on his shoulder. She'd nodded off. He stroked her hair and whispered, "Happy birthday, Callie. Happy birthday, girl."

Twenty-four

Tuesday, October 31, 2017 7:30 p.m.

The crowd screamed, "Surprise!!!"

Callie felt her heart skip a beat. Mouth open, hands crossed over her chest, she was genuinely delighted and bewildered at the group of Mardi Gras-like well-wishers masked in faux obscurity. She looked over at Richard who had already donned his carnival guise. In his hand, he held an intricate mask of golden swirls flared at the temples, framed in rhinestones; in its center, a crown to overlay the brow. Richard pulled back at its elastic band and slipped it over Callie's head, adjusting its fit over her eyes. This was followed by a peck on the cheek.

Callie beamed with excitement. To Richard's gesture, she said, "You're something else, you know that? You better not let Zane see you do that."

Zane snuck up on her, picked her up by the waist, and began twirling her around. "Too late," he teased. "Now, it's my turn to wish some love on the birthday girl."

She squealed with joy, not expecting Zane until Friday. But she was getting light-headed. "Put me down, lover boy. Put me down."

Zane released his grip on her, easing her back down. She laughed deliriously as Richard and Zane steadied her. The room spun a time or two before Callie started to feel solid on her feet. The sedation from earlier and the glass of wine at dinner did nothing to help her vertigo. Unbeknownst to the trio, other party goers questioned Callie's sobriety and looked on with a critical eye. One was Kyle Anderson, and the other, Sara.

The party planner approached Richard. "Dr. Cortez, I hoped things here are to your liking?"

Richard looked at the party girl. "Callie, this is Haley. She made tonight's festivities possible. I couldn't have done it without her."

Haley might've otherwise felt ill at ease with the compliment, but she knew she was good at her job. "Wait until you guys see the cake. Vanilla buttermilk with whipped strawberry icing, topped with a variety of berries and kiwi. Some of the guests are really eyeing it. I wouldn't wait too long before you cut into it."

Callie felt overwhelmed, but in a good way. "Haley, it's so nice to meet you. I don't know how you guys were able to pull this off, because honestly, I had no clue. The decorations, the hors d'oeuvres, the cocktails . . . everything is perfect. And look at the . . ."

Callie's chain of thought was broken as she saw a woman rapidly approaching her. Mask or no mask, the person was unmistakable and needed no introduction. She watched as the hand grabbed her upper arm, pulling her off to the side for a private tête-à-tête.

"Hello, Mother. So glad you could make it."

Rose wanted answers. "Callie, tell me the truth, have you been drinking?"

"Mother, relax. It's my birthday."

"I know perfectly well it's your birthday. I was there, remember?"

"Oh, yeah," Callie snorted.

Rose's warning was stern. "Take it down a notch, will you? People are staring."

"Why can't I have a little fun without you ruining it? If people are staring, it's because I'm the guest of honor. There's no need for you to make a federal case of it."

"Callie, you're being very loud and you're stumbling about. Even with the mask, I can see that your eyes are only half open and they're bloodshot. I want an answer, how much have you had to drink?"

"I swear, Mother, I only had one glass of wine with dinner, that's all. Oh . . ."

"Oh, what?"

"I took a sedative for my MRI earlier. I probably shouldn't have mixed the two. I am feeling a little loopy."

To Rose, her daughter was stating the obvious.

"You think? I'm glad your Aunt Clare isn't here tonight. With the spectacle you're making, it would be the topic of holiday dinners for years to come. I can only imagine what that Kyle Anderson must be thinking. He hasn't taken his eyes off you since you came in."

Callie watched as her mother pointed him out of the crowd. Her mood quickly fell flat. "What's he doing here?"

"Maybe you ought to take that up with the party planner," Rose advised before walking off.

Callie looked over to see Zane and Richard joking around in the kitchen, not far from where she and Richard had come in from the garage. She wasn't going to ask Haley about this situation. She'd just met the young woman, and the guest list wouldn't have been her responsibility anyway. She went to confront Richard. "Can you tell me why Anderson is at my party? That man has caused me nothing but grief these past weeks. How could you do this to me, Richard?"

Zane didn't give Richard a chance to respond. He immediately took on the role of protector. "Callie, point him out to me. I'm about to go give that guy a piece of my mind . . . that, or my fist."

Zane seemed so gallant and heroic. Callie thought the idea appealing. His black velvet mask trimmed with silver craft lace was embellished with a glittery fleur-de-lis pattern. It made her think of a dashing Zorro. But she came to her senses. "Zane, you know you can't do that. I'm really close to becoming fully reinstated. Threats and intimidation will only complicate things."

Richard wanted to explain himself. "Zane, Callie's right. I only invited the man as a strategic move. I really didn't think he would have the cojones to show up. The invitation was just a ploy to show him that his coercive tactics towards her weren't working. Frankly, I'm glad he came, so he can see all the people at the Medical Center and in Sperling who love and support her."

Zane nodded as if the man was making sense.

Richard continued, "Callie, look over there. There's old man Dickerson, from *Dickerson's Drug*. Since he retired and his son took over, he's been pretty much a recluse. But here he is at your party. Then, there's your dad's old buddy who runs the bait shop down at the marina. Over there, on the couch, is the cardiologist you consulted with on Mrs. Scott's case. He's not ghosting you. He's here to support you like so many of us are wanting to do. See the pregnant woman, heading down the hall to the bathroom. I'm guessing, but I think that's her second trip there since we arrived. She's the neurosurgeon's wife. She looks like she's about to pop at any minute, but the couple came out tonight to celebrate you."

Callie relented. "Okay, okay, I get it, I'm *loved* and *appreciated*. Point well taken. It was a pretty clever plan on your part, I'll give you that. But who's the guy in the corner with the cowboy hat, talking to Jamie? He looks familiar, but I can't quite place him."

"Oh, he's with me," Zane replied. "He's my plus-one. You know him. His name is Cody. He's one of hands at the ranch. I was hoping he and Jamie might hit it off."

Just when Callie thought she had Zane figured out, he did something more to amaze her. He's genuinely a good guy, she thought to herself. "Zane, that was really, really thoughtful. Jamie never has had much luck with men, and her self-esteem, well, it's pretty low. Thank you for thinking of her."

"Now, Callie, it's best to let nature take its course, here," Zane cautioned. "Cody's been burned before, and he's a bit gun-shy. He's been through a messy divorce, got a couple of kids."

A beautiful slender blonde came up on the conversation. She had on a slinky red number with flashy mask to match that sported a flamboyant plume at the temple. Her tone was flirty. "Richie, there you are. If I didn't know any better, I'd swear you were avoiding me. Aren't you going to introduce me to your friends?"

Callie and Zane looked at each other in disbelief.

No words were necessary, the look said it all . . . is she for real? *Richie*, really?

It was obvious the way Richard had tensed up. He cleared his throat before he spoke. “Guys, this is Sara. Sara, this is my partner, Callie Wallace and her boyfriend, Zane Atkins.”

Zane nodded in her direction. “Nice to meet you, ma’am.”

Sara seemed to take offense. “I think I’m a little young to be called ma’am, don’t you? Now, I’ll forgive you this time, big fella, but just because those eyes of yours are enough to melt butter.”

Callie saw how Sara was looking at Zane. It was like she might devour him right then and there. As far as she was concerned, Sara hadn’t even acknowledged her. Even though she was the guest of honor, Richard’s *friend* was treating her like a stick of furniture. Callie decided to intrude on the visual assault being made on her boyfriend. “Hi, I’m Callie. It’s nice to finally meet you. I’ve been ribbing Richard, trying to get him to open up about you. But you know him, getting information out of him is like trying to move a mountain with a shovel.”

Sara huffed. “Well, I guess I’ve never seen that side of him, because I’ve heard more about *you* than I ever cared to know. By the way, was that your mother you were talking to earlier? She’s quite the busy-body, isn’t she?”

Richard gave a nervous laugh, hoping to take the edge off the obvious insult. "Oh, Sara, you're hilarious. Always the kidder. Now, if you two will excuse us, I want to introduce Sara to Kyle Anderson."

Callie watched as Richard put his hand to Sara's back, prompting her to move away. They walked in the administrator's direction. "She's a real piece of work, don't you think, Zane?"

"Callie, you have to excuse me as I'm feeling a little violated right now from the visual groping that woman just gave me. I hope Richie knows what he's doing."

They both looked at each other and simultaneously said *Richie* before they busted out laughing. But the moment was cut short when Callie noticed Richard heading just shy of Kyle Anderson, to the left. Odder still, he was directing Sara right to the man's back. Then it came, the subtle push, knocking Sara into Kyle who subsequently landed into the three-layer cake. It took a minute for the crowd to fully absorb the incident, but once they did, a roar of laughter ensued. Then, they broke out in song,

Happy birthday to you. Happy birthday to you. Happy birthday, dear Callie. Happy birthday to you.

Kyle Anderson was livid, trying to wipe the cake

and fruit out of his hair. He took off his mask only to appear like some fluffy-faced, wide-eyed cat off Instagram. "Cortez!" he yelled. "Why doesn't your clumsy girlfriend watch where she's going? She's a damn idiot. Look at me! Look at my shirt! It's a Brunello Cucinelli."

Sara was speechless to the insult delivered in a room full of strangers. She looked down to see the spattering of cake to her outfit. Eyes leering, teeth clinched, and fists balled, she left the house in a rage.

Richard just shrugged his shoulders, lifting his hands to the air in wonder. He addressed the onlookers. "What can I say? She's a real looker, but I guess she can't hold her liquor. I suppose we're going to call it a night. Happy birthday, Callie."

Callie caught sight of the wink Richard sent her way before he went chasing after Sara. *Best birthday ever*, she said to herself.

Twenty-five

Wednesday, November 1, 2017 08:35 a.m.

November rolled in with a whisper. Normally, at that hour of the morning Callie would be at home, nursing a cup of coffee. But the Haley girl had a crew in to clean up. The living room carpet needed shampooing from the cake "mishap', but it was all worth it in Callie's mind. She desperately wanted to call Richard about how the rest of his evening went with Sara, but she knew she'd have to wait for him to bring it up. She didn't expect to see him in the office until that afternoon. Currently, she didn't have any patients in the hospital, but Richard did. She suspected he was busy making rounds.

Jamie buzzed in. "Dr. Wallace, I have Kyle Anderson on line three."

Panic rushed over her with the thought that Mr. Murphy's final autopsy result were in. She mumbled under her breath, "Please let it be about last night and the cake. Maybe he just wants me to pay for his dry cleaning."

She picked up the receiver and hit the blinking light. "Good morning, Mr. Anderson. What can I do for you this morning?"

"Dr. Wallace, I trust you enjoyed your party last night?"

"I did, thank you. And that issue with the cake, I'm sorry that happened to you. Dreadful accident."

"That is not an issue I have with you, Dr. Wallace. Listen, why I've called. Have you checked your e-mail this morning?"

"No, I've haven't got to it yet."

"Well, I forwarded four reports to you. One was from the internist, and one from the psychiatrist. As it turns out, there appears to be nothing wrong with you, Dr. Wallace."

Callie let out a sigh of relief. "And the MRI of the brain?"

"Let's see," he said, perusing the details of the study. "No altered signal intensity of the cerebrum, brainstem, or cerebellum. No indication of fixed lesion or shift to the midline. No vascular or ventricular abnormality. The conclusion is a normal study."

Callie was overcome with relief, but she wanted to contain her excitement. "That's it . . . a clean bill of health and it's over? But what are the other two documents?"

Mr. Anderson continued. "I see that you sought legal counsel regarding the matters we discussed the other day. There was a letter drafted to Marcus Davis from the law offices of Peterson, Deutch and Deutch, and the firm's stern challenge to hospital policies that could've contributed to Mr. Murphy's death. But I hope what I'm about to say will ease any animosities that might exist between Sperling Neurology Group and the Medical Center."

Callie asked, "And what would that be?"

"With these results, it is my consensus that your privileges at the Medical Center be fully reinstated. I can't very well withhold a physician's privileges when her physical and mental competence has been proven, can I? That was a good call Dr. Cortez made on your behalf."

Callie was wary. "What about Mr. Murphy's final autopsy results?"

"Not in yet. If it is determined that the cause of death was a result of adrenal crisis, then it will be in the family's court about what action to take. If a suit is brought against the hospital, we have policies in place to handle such things. If you are named, you will be solely responsible for handling the matter with your malpractice carrier. Let's face it, Dr. Wallace, if every negligent matter were grounds to deny a physician the right to practice in a hospital, most hospitals would be empty. It's unfortunate, but true."

Callie was reluctant to get her hopes up. "What about Mrs. Scott?"

"When the Scott family learned that insurance

wasn't going to pay for the autopsy, they refused to pay out-of-pocket. But erring on the side of caution, the hospital did absorb the cost of a post-mortem CT scan. It wasn't a blood clot that killed her as you first-believed. It was an air embolus. The hospital plans to open an event investigation and analysis to reflect a systems-based approach, including contributing factors. Scott's body has been released for burial."

She saw Richard pop his head in her office. Callie put her finger to her lips and motioned for him to come in and sit down.

Callie was curious. "Such as the woman's arterial line being mismanaged or the condition of Jane Timmons?"

"That remains to be seen, Dr. Wallace," the administrator said.

With that, Kyle Anderson hung up. Callie had won . . . at least that round.

Callie and Richard tried to contain their enthusiasm. They didn't want Jamie to hear how excited they were over Kyle Anderson's decision to fully reinstate Callie's privileges—they wanted to play it *cool.*

Richard was having trouble believing that the ordeal was over. "So, your MRI was normal?"

"Brain scan, lab work . . . all normal. I need to handle my stress better, like we discussed, but other than that, I'm ready to get back to work, full-time."

Behind closed doors, Richard reported off on the hospitalized patients, agreeing that Callie would assume call starting at ten that day until seven in the morning on Monday. Callie was absolutely overjoyed to take over the responsibility—her life was back on track. She shot a quick text to the hospital emergency room to notify them of the change in their schedule.

She reflected over the whole ordeal. “Richard, I can’t even fathom how things unfolded so quickly. But you handled Anderson perfectly.”

Richard appreciated the compliment, referring to his strategic prowess. “Well, I couldn’t let anything happen to my best girl.”

Callie knew they were just two friends kidding around. “I’m your best girl, huh? What about Sara?”

“I knew it wouldn’t be long before you said something.”

Callie feigned ignorance. “Did I say something? What something?”

Richard felt compelled to discuss Sara’s behavior from the night before. “Look, I know Sara can be *a bit much*, but I think it stems from her own insecurities. I told her there’s no need to be concerned, that my relationship with you is purely platonic. She just gets ideas in her head. Can you understand?”

“Well, if you go around saying I’m your best girl,

that ought to do it. I guess that explains her off-putting attitude towards me, but it really doesn't explain the dig she took at my mother. You know, you never told me how you two met."

Richard shrugged. "As for your mother, I can't say. But if you want to know how we met, I'll tell you. It was at the bank, seeing about a loan for a new electroencephalogram machine. The one we have now, some of the waveforms and spikes seem erratic, maybe interference. We got it used for a good price, and now I know why."

"First National Bank?" Callie asked.

"Yeah."

"Well, did you get it?"

"Get what?"

"The loan, silly?"

"Well, when the issues came up for you at the Medical Center, I asked Sara to put the process on hold until we knew the outcome. I guess I can tell her to go ahead and process the loan. I was thinking of an EEG/PSG model."

Callie interrupted him. "Wait, polysomnography? You want to start doing sleep studies?"

"Maybe."

"Just a minute, buddy. How did we get off the topic of Sara? You're good at that, diversion."

"I try."

Callie wanted the latest. "So, tell me, how did you get out of the cake debacle?"

"Well, to tell you the truth, I haven't yet. Last night, I tried to explain to her that she just tripped, but she insisted that I pushed her."

"You did . . . I saw you do it."

"Well, yeah, but I don't want her to think that. Besides, I didn't have time to pick you out a gift. I had to give you something."

Callie laughed, thinking of Anderson face-planting into her birthday cake. "It was great, but the party sufficed, really. So, what's your plan to get back in Sara's good graces?"

"How do you know that I want to?"

"Because of the way you look when you talk about her, that twinkle in your eye."

"That obvious?"

"Yeah."

Richard began to get cool in his stance and speech. "I can tell you don't like her. You don't approve."

Callie was defensive. "I didn't say that."

"You didn't have to. It's the way you sound when you talk about her, that cutting edge in your tone."

"*Touché*."

Richard thought he should just get this portion of the discussion over with. "Go ahead and ask."

"Ask what?"

"What do I see in her?"

Callie felt like she was going out on thin ice. "Am I that obvious?"

"Yeah, you are. Look, I know this kind of thing can cause a rift between friends. That side of her that you saw, she's not like that with me. I bet you think she's not good for me, but you're wrong—she's smart, funny."

Callie felt mischievous. "Well-built, blonde, trashy."

Richard suddenly tensed up. "Did you just call her trashy?"

Callie was adamant. "No, no, that's not what I said. I said flashy. You know, with the dress, matching mask with the feather."

He continued, not thoroughly convinced by her explanation. "I know the outfit she wore last night was a bit on the gaudy side, but she really wanted to make a good impression. I hope to teach her a thing or two about refinement and subtlety, and if you're patient, I know you could have a positive impact on her."

Callie felt like somehow their friendship was being tested. "The hope to change someone often leads to disappointment, Richard. The person we try and change often grows to resent it."

"Callie, you don't understand. You didn't grow up like I did. My mom was a single mother, my dad had run off, we lived in a bad neighborhood, money was tight. Back then, it was about survival. I wasn't the man I am now. I knew little of higher education or proper diction. I had to learn as I went along. Sara didn't have those opportunities to grow, like I did. She had to work her way up to the position she now has at the bank."

Callie was curious. "Is she from Sperling?"

"Yes, but from what I could gather, she's from a poor upbringing. She was raised by her father. She has a brother, but she rarely hears from him. He's in the metroplex somewhere. Her dad drinks and her mother, prison. There was really no one to teach her the social graces."

Callie wanted to be careful. "You know, Richard, you mentioning Sara's upbringing makes me think . . ."

Richard sensed Callie's hesitation. "What, Callie?"

"Look Richard, I don't mean to be presumptuous, but there are signs with Sara, her mannerisms, her word choices, her behavior. Those things, taken into account with the fact that she's from a low socioeconomic background, remind me of an adult suffering from a mild case of shaken baby syndrome as an infant."

He didn't like what she was insinuating. "That is presumptuous. Some might even call it profiling. I just said she came from a poor upbringing. You can't automatically assume she was from an abusive home."

Callie's phone went off. There was a patient for her to see in the emergency room. Time had flown-by. It was a quarter past ten. She was actually relieved to be called away from the conversation that left her feeling backed into a corner. In truth, she felt that the relationship Richard was in would only end in heart-ache. But those were words she'd never utter to her friend . . . never.

Twenty-six

Thursday, November 2, 2017 10:20 a.m.

Callie planned to wing-it . . . so unlike her. Grumbling skies overhead looked as if the clouds might open-up any minute. She brought her umbrella, just in case the rain started while she was in the bank. Rounds at the hospital started early, at six that morning, so she would have time for the errand. Callie was going to make an attempt to win over Sara even though she knew it wasn't going to be easy, like a pup to a feral cat.

Callie felt the eager stare of new account specialists as she walked past. She could almost imagine their disappointment, hopes of a commission dashed as she presented her back to them on the way to the elevators. An old-fashioned window box served as the directory, departments and corresponding floors outlined with plastic letters and numbers. The loan department was on the fourth floor. Callie pushed the up-button just as a boom of thunder sounded overhead.

As she waited for the elevator, a text came to her from Hayden Deutch. It said the certified letter to Marcus Davis came back as address unknown. Callie thought it odd, but when the elevator doors opened, she knew she had a bigger problem to tackle. For a moment, Callie thought of taking the stairs. It was the fear of being trapped in the elevator if the bank was to lose power in the storm. But she wasn't going to let her claustrophobia be an issue for her today. And as she reasoned, the ride to the fourth floor was uneventful. Her eyes scanned the room. The office walls were a third paneled wood and the remainder transparent glass. The office on the far left had Sara seated at a desk, busy with a customer. Callie took a seat in the reception area and mindlessly thumbed through a magazine. Her immediate plan was just to ask Sara to lunch tomorrow. Callie had thought to phone, but it would've been too easy for Sara to turn her down. The invitation had to be face-to-face.

It could have been two minutes, it could have been ten, that had passed before Callie realized Sara's office was empty. Marta Gutierrez had seemed to appear out of nowhere. The woman motioned for Callie to follow her. They landed up behind a corner office. "Dr. Wallace, what are you doing here?" Marta asked. "Are you crazy coming here?"

"I might ask you the same thing, Marta. Was that you in Sara's office?"

"Yes, but you shouldn't be here," Marta cautioned.

"Why on earth not? I'm only here to invite her to

lunch tomorrow. If the woman is going to be a mainstay in Richard's, I mean Dr. Cortez's, life, I think Sara and I should get to know each other better."

Marta's tone was sharp. "I don't mean any disrespect, Dr. Wallace, but Sara doesn't like you . . . *at all.* It seems like every time your name comes up, she gets ugly. If she gets her way, you're the one that's going to get pushed from Dr. Cortez's life. You've got to trust me on this as it isn't always what she says, it's how she says it."

"Not until you explain yourself. There's absolutely no reason that woman should have that type of animosity towards me."

Marta cautiously looked around. "Okay, but I only have a minute. Sara took a call, then excused herself. She apologized and said the matter was urgent, but wouldn't take long."

"Wait," Callie interrupted. "Are you actually here applying for a loan?"

"Yes, a home improvement loan. I reminded her that we spoke the other night, briefly, at your party. She called it a clown show, by the way, for a clown. When I learned this was where she worked, I took it upon myself to find out what her beef with you is really all about."

Callie was having trouble believing her mother's neighbor was really applying for a loan in order to run interference for her with her partner's new girlfriend. "So, so, what is the loan for?"

"I thought about redoing the bathroom, getting one of those whirling jet-tubes. But that's beside the point. How she feels about you, you're not going to get anywhere with her."

"Why not?" As an afterthought, Callie added, "She really called me a clown?"

Marta regrettably confirmed the insult. "She had some other choice words to say, but I don't think this is the place to go into it. That woman, she can be absolutely vile. Hey, did you happen to see Kyle Anderson on your way in? He'd been meeting with Sara before I had my appointment with her. He looked a little steamed. Weird, huh?"

The women's corner conversation was interrupted by the *ahem* to their back. They turned around to see Sara tight-lipped, leering at them with her arms frigidly folded across her chest. "I'm sorry to interrupt this Punchinello convention, but Mrs. Gutierrez, I have a decision on your loan. Let's return to the office, so we can finish conducting our business, shall we?"

Callie was fully aware that she, again, had been called a clown, but she didn't think Marta picked up on the reference. But the remark wasn't going to deter Callie from trying to forge a relationship with the woman. She bubbly chimed in, "Hi, Sara. I'm so glad you could come to the party the other night. It was fun, wasn't . . ."

Sara was stern when it came to Callie's niceties. "Dr. Wallace, this is a place of business. I would ask you not to interfere with the work being conducted here."

Marta felt compelled to stick-up for Rose's girl. "Sara, it's okay. Callie Wallace is a long-time family friend. In fact, the Wallace family have been our neighbors for about thirty years. And when Rose's husband died, Raul and I put several family members up in our home."

Sara's response was stone-hearted. "Mrs. Gutierrez, maybe you'll be so lucky to do that again when Rose Wallace dies, hopefully, sometime soon. Now, if we could return to the office so our business can be concluded, I would appreciate it."

Marta couldn't believe the brutal reply, and right in front of Rose's girl. Marta slipped her arm behind Callie, instinctively pulling her close. "That's an awful thing to say. I think our business here is done."

Sara wasn't about to let Marta Gutierrez have the last word. "I couldn't agree more. Mrs. Gutierrez, your loan has been denied. I'm sorry, but First National won't be able to help you."

Marta couldn't believe it. "But my credit score is

eight-ten. I've worked in the same place for over ten years. This can't be right."

"I'm sorry, Mrs. Gutierrez, but the decision is final," Sara snapped.

Infuriated, Marta said, "Callie, you're up. I'm out of here." Then she stormed off.

Callie and Sara stood there looking at each other. It was Sara that spoke first. "What did she mean by that?"

Lightning flashed and the lights blinked. A storm was looming. To Callie, it was foreboding. "I don't know, but she can be temperamental. The reason I'm here is to invite you to lunch tomorrow—*Olea's Kitchen*. I think it's time you and I get to know each other a little better . . . for Richard's sake."

Sara hadn't warmed at all. "I suppose I could go . . . for Richie's sake. But I can't guarantee I'll be able to eat, considering the company."

Twenty-seven

Thursday, November 2, 2017 Dusk

It rained throughout the day, booms cracking, gusts howling, bolts striking. Traffic that would've normally proceeded with rapid fluidity, crawled through the flooded streets. Tires peeled through the water as headlights forged the way for weary drivers, heading home after a hard day's work.

Marcus was no exception. His back was killing him. Two patients in the intensive unit were total care and morbidly obese, at that. The assignment was tedious and his patience was wearing thin. He was wondering if his lack of progress was the reason for his frustration or if it was the mundane day-to-day activities that were weighing on him. One thing he knew for certain is that he wanted to go home to see his wife and son.

But that wasn't in the cards for Marcus, at least not now. Not since he'd been assigned to the case in Sperling by the field office in Houston. He'd been staying in a Bureau rental, address unknown. Right now, all Marcus knew was that Sperling was a far cry from home.

He knew it was the joke he'd played on the Special Agent in Charge that landed him the assignment from hell. Now that Marcus thought about it, it'd been a real stupid thing to do. It was one of the first things taught to new recruits at the academy, you have to be smart to be a special agent, but you're not smarter than the FBI.

They'd pranked each other for years—friends since college. But when push came to shove, Marcus was out-ranked by his friend who had one pissed-off wife. The joke went like this: Marcus had five minutes, at the most. His friend was a real germophobe from way back. When the man went to the men's room, he left his cell phone in his office. He'd just ended a call before heading to the restroom and Marcus saw his chance. Marcus had on his phone a photoshopped picture of his boss's face on a baboon with an erection. He texted it to the man's phone and saved it to his photos. Marcus then cleared the thread of their text conversations. He found the message thread for the man's wife and texted her the photo with the caption, want some lovin' tonight. Then Marcus returned to his desk. It didn't take long before the SAC figured out who the culprit was. Maybe that was because his friend had always been a little smarter than Marcus, a lot more determined, and the man could kiss ass like no one else. That's what sent his friend up the ranks while Marcus was left behind to do grueling field work.

There was an accident ahead. Traffic was at a standstill. Marcus saw an officer out in the downpour, trying to manage the gridlock. The rain hitting the roof of his beater car and the swishing of its wipers started to lull Marcus to a place of contentment. It was that or fatigue inching up on him. His mind wondered off to the day he'd gotten the assignment. He'd never even heard of Sperling.

A young South Korean female, Ha-eun Hwang, was found dead at the bottom of a stairwell at Lake Sperling Medical Center. She was a forensic science student at the local community college doing a rotation in the morgue. At first, the case looked cut-and-dry. Either it was a horrible accident in which she fell to her death or a homicide in which she was pushed. In the case of the latter, no motive had been established. So why call in the FBI was what Marcus wanted to know.

It's what was discovered about three weeks prior to Ms. Hwang's death that caught the Bureau's attention. Two different funeral homes on two different occasions reported instances of the corpses having post-mortem bruising to the nose, one with a partial collapse of the eye's orbit, and both with significant drainage from the nares. A closer look revealed they both had a fracture to the sphenoid bone, one that separates the nasal cavity from the brain. Radiographic study concluded that the base of the brain had been compromised, an injury not related to their cause of death. One, a thirty-three-year-old black male who died from injuries sustained in a motor vehicle accident. The other, a twenty-seven-year-old female who succumbed to her stabbing injuries, a victim of domestic violence. The transsphenoidal approach was described as being crudely performed.

Both bodies had been picked up from the Lake Sperling Medical Center morgue. The question was whether the mutilations were in anyway related to the death of Ms. Hwang. His cover as an orderly who happened to be a two-bit drug pusher gave him access to the respectable aspects of the facility, as well as what went on in the shadows.

Marcus's initial meeting with the hospital's administrator went something like this . . .

The administrator struck Marcus as the nervous type, but a federal agent often had that effect on people. "I understand you've been briefed on my role here."

"Yes, Agent Davis, I have been. I'm hoping we can

get this ugly business cleared up as soon as possible. I can't afford a scandal. I had Human Resources pull the personnel files of those on the neurology floor, as you requested. Between the full-time employees and those part-time, there's twelve in all. You'll also find credentialing files for the physicians that routinely admit to that floor, but you must understand, other specialties also work that unit if patients develop complications that require their expertise. For instance, a stroke patient can develop an ileus and require a gastrointestinal consult, that sort of thing."

"I trust you had an employee badge made for me, one keyed to access every room in this hospital, even this one."

Anderson reluctantly handed it over to the man. "I just hope you'll be discreet. I don't know how I would explain to a busy-body nurse your snooping around the O.R. supply room. That's just not a place an orderly from neuro would be found."

"I understand how to do my job, Mr. Anderson, or should I say Dr. Anderson?"

Anderson was uncomfortable. He got up from his desk and went to stand by the window to look out. "I guess I shouldn't be so surprised that you know that about me. I try to come off as strictly a financial man. My brother-in-law got me put in this position, you know, after. He serves on the board of Care Corporation of

America. Lake Sperling Medical Center is just one of the hospitals under their umbrella."

"You mean after your stint in the federal pen for tax evasion?"

"It's not what you think. Things were just getting harder; the bills were piling up."

"How are the hands, Doctor?"

Anderson still couldn't face the man. He kept rolling his hands, one into the other. "Some days are better than others. The medication helps some, but it's still a problem."

Marcus needed to know. "Anderson, let me see. Turn around, hold out your arms in front of you."

Kyle knew what the exercise would show. He was slow to turn around. But it was inevitable. He faced Special Agent Davis and put his arms out in front of him, fingers extended. The tremors were obvious.

"It must've been difficult for a neurosurgeon to come to terms with . . . the shaking," Marcus said.

"I still haven't, Agent Davis, I still haven't."

Marcus was relieved to see the traffic moving, but was startled when the phone rang. Marcus recognized the number. It was the Sperling police captain and he knew he needed to take it. Before he left Houston, the SAC instructed him to fully cooperate with the

Sperling police. He didn't want to hear back that Marcus was making trouble.

The call was short and to the point. He'd been asked to assist in a call behind a tire shop on the east-side. Marcus knew the place. It was a couple of blocks from his rental. The officer waved him through the intersection, and Marcus figured, with the weather, he'd get to the scene in five minutes or so.

When Marcus pulled in behind the tire shop, the sun had gone down and it was dark. He left his car up beside the business for fear he'd get it stuck in the mud. Flashlight in hand, he ventured over to where officers were gathered. Marcus was getting drenched, but with the strong gusts, he knew an umbrella's ribs would fracture. With each step he took, he felt his foot being sucked into the earth. He had to physically draw each foot from the mud's pull, a burn to his back.

When Marcus reached the yellow-taped perimeter of the scene, the captain approached him. Marcus found himself trying to talk over the muffling weather. "You got something for me here?"

"Yeah, in fact, I think you might know the victim. His cell phone had your number in it. Funny thing, though, no wallet."

With his free hand, Marcus wiped clear the water dripping into his eyes. "You got a body, I guess? The perp must be an amateur, leaving a phone on him."

They took a few steps in, penetrating the select circle of those called to the scene. Marcus sent the flashlight's beam to the ground. A young man's body had been unearthed from a shallow grave by the storm. The body was bloated, face swollen. Even distorted, Marcus knew him. He'd sold him a gram of cocaine a few days ago. "He's done business with me before, but I don't have a legitimate name. The guy went by Fergus."

"Was he hard-core?"

Marcus shook his head. "Nay, I don't think so. I pegged him to be more of the weekend party type. Think he overdosed?"

"Hard to say whether he did or whether he didn't. Pretty safe to assume he didn't bury himself. I just wanted to give you heads up. I think you should get on out of here, though. Detective Monroe from homicide is coming. He was the one working the Hwang case before you took it over. I don't want him asking questions about why you're here. He's suspicious as it is."

Marcus was drenched, and cold. A sharp contrast to his back which was on fire. He blew out a frustrated sigh, thinking of the blow-hard, Monroe. "Somehow, someway, I need a damn break in this case."

Twenty-eight

Friday, November 3, 2017 2:05 a.m.

The storm had blown out. With the skies clearing, the temperature was falling and the stars stood out bright against a caliginous sky. Callie's eyes were feeling heavy as she eased her car into the garage after a late-night call to the hospital.

Callie didn't remember going to bed. She must've gone to sleep the minute her head hit the pillow. She did remember a chill and wadding the blanket beneath her chin.

The campfire crackled and popped. The light from it was reassuring, its warmth comforting, and the smell of the fish her father was cooking over it, well . . . fishy. Wrapped snuggly in the blanket, Callie sat quietly in the fold-out chair, swinging her legs up and down in a scissoring motion. In truth, she was having trouble sitting still, but she knew she had to be *good* as her daddy was in a mood. It struck her funny that her feet never touched the ground. That's when she noticed she was small, maybe only ten or eleven in age.

The smell of the fish did nothing for her appetite.

She craved cheese pizza. In a pinch, chicken nuggets would do. One thing for certain, Callie knew that when she grew up, she'd have fries for every meal. She doubted she'd ever eat fish . . . blah.

But she'd eat it tonight as she had so many times before, for her father's sake. It meant so much to him and Callie didn't have the heart to disappoint him. After all, he was the best dad ever. The girl only wished her mother would appreciate what a catch she had in him.

Her father spoke over his shoulder in her direction. "Corky, dinner is about ready. Go to the cooler and grab me a beer, will ya?"

Callie didn't have a full-on look at her father's face. His back was primarily to her while he focused on frying up his catch. But from what she could see, he was young, and his hair brown—not salt-n-pepper like she remembered.

Callie wanted a soda, but she was surprised at the sound of her own squeaky voice. "Can I have a pop, Pop?"

Her father laughed even though he'd heard the dumb joke a hundred times. "Sure."

The young Callie pulled the tab on her father's light beer and handed it to him. He'd let her take a sip before, but Callie thought it was bitter and left a bad taste in her mouth. "Uhm, Dad?"

"Yeah?"

Callie focused her attention towards the ground, nervously shuffling her feet in the dirt. "You and Mom been fighting, huh?"

"I'm sorry you had to hear that, Corky."

"But where did she go?"

"She went to the city."

Her father hadn't turned around to face her. Callie figured it was best the conversation took place this way.

"Did she go by herself?"

"She *said* she went to go see Aunt Clare."

"Oh."

Callie didn't want to ask the question, fearful that she might start crying. Daddy didn't like it when she cried. She wondered what would be worse, tears or her father's answer. "Dad, are you and Mom going to get a divorce? Because if you are, I want to live with you."

Her father tried to sound reassuring, but he was firm. "Corky, it was just a little fight, nothing more. I have nothing more to say about it and I don't want you bringing it up again. Do you understand?"

Callie always felt bad when her father scolded her. "Yes, sir."

"Okay, now get over here. Your fish is ready."

Callie felt like pouting. "I'm not hungry. Is it okay if I go to bed?"

"Yeah." *Pause* "Hey, Corky?"

"Yes, sir."

"Before you turn in, I want you to come over here and give your old dad a hug—one of your special ones."

Callie sat up, drenched. She was clutching a pillow. Her heart was racing, consciously having to focus on slowing her breathing down. She hadn't thought about the summer of 1995 in years. It was the summer her mother was gone *a lot*. Callie had spent most of her time with her father down at the lake. She remembered that once she'd asked her mother if she could go with her on one of her special trips to the city. Her mother's answer had been a definitive *no*.

Twenty-nine

Friday, November 3, 2018 12:25 p.m.

Callie had made the lunch reservation for 12:15, but she was running late, just arriving at the restaurant. Now wasn't the time for her to appear rushed or rattled. She had to be on her best game. Callie knew Sara was completely wrong for her friend, but she had to be careful. A situation like this could ruin her friendship with Richard. Once Callie settled down last night, she racked her brain over what could be Sara's angle. She doubted it was money. Richard didn't come from any, and anything they'd made with the practice, that was sunk back into the business. Despite that, Richard was a catch . . . no doubt, but something was off about Sara. She wondered why Richard was attracted to someone so crass. Callie knew the woman didn't like her, and for the life of her, she didn't know why. She was left with only one conclusion—Richard's relationship with the woman was based purely on physical attraction.

The hostess escorted Callie to the table and she was genuinely surprised to see Richard sitting next to Sara. Richard stood up when he saw her approaching. "I thought you might've had a change of heart," he said. "I'm glad you didn't, though. I heard you were picking up the tab."

Once everyone had taken their seat, Sara took it upon herself to explain Richard's presence. "Callie, I know you wanted this to be a girl's lunch, but I saw this as an opportunity for you to get to know us . . . as a couple."

Even though Richard being there was unexpected, Callie was relieved to have a go-between. "Oh, I see. Well, in that case, Richard, I'm glad you were able to join us."

Richard was just relieved his presence wasn't going to be a problem. "Now why would I miss an opportunity to have lunch with my two favorite girls. Since you invited her, Sara has done nothing but go on and on about how she was looking forward to today."

Callie had a hard time believing that. "Really?"

"Yes, really. Haven't you been looking forward to it?" Sara sarcastically inquired.

Callie saw an opportunity to tease Richard. "Well, actually, I was hoping we could bond over some of Richard's idiosyncrasies like how he squeezes the toothpaste from the middle of the tube or how he leaves his dirty socks on the kitchen floor."

Sara chimed in. "Or how he never cleans that

coffee mug of his—the one stained permanently brown inside."

The two women simultaneously busted out laughing while Richard grumbled to himself, trying to keep a sense of humor.

The waitress came up to the table. Callie recognized Mia, but hoped the server didn't remember her . . . or her mother. The three placed their orders. That's when Sara excused herself to go to the lady's room.

Once out of earshot, Callie leaned in and spoke with a sense of urgency. "Richard, what are you really doing here?"

"Look, it wasn't my idea. Sara suggested it. She said you don't like her and want to break us up. She said you were pretty rude to her at the bank yesterday."

Callie was astonished, but not in a good way. "Me? Oh, you've got to be kidding. She's the one that wished my mother dead and insinuated that I was enough to kill her appetite which is hilarious, by-the-way, since she has ordered the most expensive thing on the menu."

"Sounds like a case of she said, she said."

"Richard, don't make light of this. It's not funny. I'm the one really trying, not her."

Sara returned and noticed that the conversation at the table had suddenly turned quiet. "Don't stop on my account. Did I miss anything?"

Richard gave her a peck on the cheek. "The only one missed was you, dear."

Looking at the lovebirds, Callie felt like she was going to be sick, but feigned a smile at the gesture. "Sara, I was glad I was able to catch up with you at the bank yesterday. I can't remember the last time I was actually in a bank, with online services and such. Oh, and that Japanese Maple the bank has out front is a magnificent red. Is it a Bloodgood or a Crimson Queen?"

Sara shrugged her shoulders, disinterested. "Who cares? It's just a tree."

Callie thought the woman's interest in autumn foliage would break the tension between them, but that wasn't the case. "I just thought since you and Richard . . ."

Richard felt the need to run interference. "Sara, I think Callie might want your advice about something."

The woman seemed to be intrigued by what Richard said. Callie jumped on the opportunity. "Yes, Sara, I was hoping to bend your ear about something, with you being in banking and all."

Sara was sloppy sweet, coming across as being interested in helping. "If I can. What's the question?"

"Well, since Richard and I have opened our practice, it's been run as a partnership. But I was thinking there might be some benefit to restructuring it as a corporation or a limited liability company. What do you think?"

Sara looked at Callie, basically disinterested. She seemed puzzled by the nature of the question. "I thought this was going to be about loans. I work in the loan department. You know that, you were there."

Marta had been right. It wasn't so much what Sara said, it was how she said it. Callie didn't like Sara's tone either. She felt like Sara was talking down to her.

Richard picked-up on how uneasy the women were, so he joined the conversation. "Sara, *honey*, Callie knows you work in the loan department. It's just that she knows that a banking entity is the pulse for the financial needs of everyone, from the individual client to various business structures. Maybe you're the closest person she knows who she considers an expert."

Callie felt the bile rising, but she pushed it down as Sara seemed to be eating-up Richard's attempt at flattery. "Well, when you put it that way, okay," Sara said. "Basically, an LLC means unincorporated. An LLC and a corporation have different record keeping and reporting requirements. The business entity is either one or the other, not both. But that doesn't mean they can't share characteristics of each other. Think of an LLC as being the child between a corporation and a partnership. Is that clear enough for you?"

It took everything Callie had to hold her temper. "Yes, I think I understand, thank you." But something in Callie's armament broke. She mumbled under her breath, "Oh brother, I knew to Google it, but no, I had to ask."

Sara sneered. "I heard that," she snapped.

Mia appeared with the tray of food. For Callie, the server placed a plate of eggplant parmesan in front of her. Next served was Richard's *ossobuco*. Finally, was Sara's *strangozzi* with black truffle. Sara looked down on her plate with disgust. "This isn't what I ordered."

Mia frantically took her notebook out of her apron pocket. The dish was expensive, and if it was sent back, it would be coming out of her pocket.

Callie felt sorry for the waitress, seeing how flustered the woman looked. "Sara, just shut your yap and listen. You did too order that, and you're going to eat it."

Sara wasn't about to be humiliated like that in public . . . not again, anyway. She stood up, positioning herself to loom over the seated Callie. "You have some nerve, thinking you're something . . . thinking I'm trash."

Mia sensed the tension and hastily retreated to go find the manager.

Richard tried to intervene. "Sara, I don't think Callie meant to overstep."

This angered Callie. She took the napkin from her lap and threw it on the table. "Overstep, Richard, really? Is that all you have to say? I think if Sara has something to say, she should say it to my face."

Callie stood up, eye-to-eye with her blonde, 34- DD aggressor. If looks could kill, they say. That prompted Richard to get up and try to intervene, but it was too late.

The indignant Sara lashed out. "You've got balls calling me a gold-digging bitch, a stupid ass."

Callie stood there in disbelief. "I never called you any such thing."

Sara was seething. "You liar! We heard you!" And with that came the sucker-punch.

Callie didn't see it coming. She fell backward in what seemed like slow motion. Her arms flailed out, the right toward a nearby bussing station. A rubber dishpan took the hit with dirty dishes from a recently vacated table scattering. Utensils flew, plates shattered, a wine glass splintering into a bed of shards. It was there that the back of Callie's head came to rest, glass fragments embedding her scalp.

Dazed, Callie looked up to see a crowd of strangers forming around her. Voices echoed around her. *Is she breathing? Should someone call the police? I think she needs an ambulance. Is there a doctor here?*

Richard made his way through the on-lookers. He crouched down to help Callie sit upright, brushing away pasta and olives that clung to her curls. He spoke in a whisper. "Callie, are you all right? Why did you call her that, why?"

Callie instinctively reached toward the back of her head and brought back a blood-stained palm. "What happened?"

"You had an accident," Richard informed her. He looked up at the crowd. "Did anyone see a blonde, about five-seven, blue dress?"

The manager spoke up. "She ran out of here just when the lady fell. But this woman here, she's bleeding. Do I need to call an ambulance? Does she need to see a doctor?"

Richard quickly got to his feet. He spoke with urgency. "I am a doctor. She'll be fine, but she needs to be taken to the emergency room to have the glass fragments removed, wounds cleaned, gashes stitched. Can you give her a ride?"

The manager quickly scanned the crowd, wondering if the physician was actually talking to him. He was taken aback by the request. He hesitated before answering, not sure if the suggestion was actually a good idea. "Me? Sure . . . I guess."

Richard stepped over Callie and started to make his way through the crowd. He rushed out the door, thinking Sara couldn't have gone too far.

Thirty

Friday, November 3, 2017 8:10 p.m.

Zane held her tight, told her to let it all out. He softly chastised her for not telling him sooner what was going on in her life. At the shoulder, his shirt was soaked with tears. His tight embrace kept her steady against him while the sobbing and heaving ran its course. He ran his hand softly over the back of her head, feeling the ends of the nylon sutures prickling through her hair.

Zane eased Callie down on the sofa. He brushed her hair from her face. He gently placed his hands of either side of her temples and ran his thumbs under her eyes to clear the tears. "There, there, Callie, chin up. That's my girl. Everything is going to be okay. I know how much Richard means to you. You two will work this out. I thought you should know that I called him, and he's just as upset."

Sniffling, she snatched the tissue Zane was handing her. "Oh, I just bet he told you everything that happened was my fault. You guys have a way of sticking together in situations like this. I mean nothing is Sara's fault, is it?"

"He said you called Sara a gold-digging bitch, a stupid ass, and chastised her when she wanted to send her order back to the kitchen."

"As far as what Sara ordered, she was trying to blame the waitress. It wasn't the server's fault that Sara was just trying to stick it to me, ordering the most expensive thing on the menu when I'm paying. That thing about calling Sara a gold-digger, I don't know where he's coming up with that idea . . . it didn't happen. As far as being a stupid ass, that kind of back-alley vernacular isn't like me. You know that."

"Well Callie, you tell me how the afternoon went. What exactly went on at the office and don't just say it was 'awful'. Tell me exactly what that means."

Callie sniffed. "As I told you, I was lying there in filth and broken glass . . . humiliated. Strangers were gathering around me, staring. I was able to walk out of the restaurant, but on the arm of the manager. Richard had just left me there. Sara sauntered out of there, just like from the party, as if she was some sort of victim."

"Okay, you told me that part already, and I'm glad you weren't more seriously hurt. But I'm more interested with what happened with Richard this afternoon at the office."

Callie nodded. "So, the restaurant manager dropped me off at the emergency room. Everyone there was especially helpful and made sure I was in and out fairly quick, just a few stitches. Hospital security drove me to my car. It was still parked at the restaurant. I drove home to clean-up and change. That made me late for my afternoon appointments. I get to the office to find Richard seeing my patient. This patient, in turn, tells me he wants to switch to Dr. Cortez."

Zane wanted to make sure he understood what Callie was saying. "You feel like Richard stole your patient?"

Again, she nodded. "Yes, mainly because he took the man up on it. Patients play these games all the time. They want what they want when they want it . . . immediate gratification. If they don't get it, then they play the physicians in the practice against each other. Richard knew what had happened. He didn't have to go into details with the man, but he could've explained I was unexpectedly detained and that I'm usually very prompt. He didn't have my back, Zane."

Zane listened intently to the accusation Callie was making. "Did you call him out on it?"

"Yeah, I did. He just said he was so used to covering for me, he didn't think anything of it."

Zane stopped her. "Wait, are you saying Richard threw the problems you had at the Medical Center, concerning your privileges, up in your face? That doesn't sound like him."

"I know, right? But that's exactly what he did. It didn't take long for the conversation to turn around to Sara. He told me I should stop being jealous and try to be more compassionate considering the hardships she's endured in her life."

He didn't want to ask, but Zane felt it was necessary. "It's no excuse to hit you, but are you jealous of her?"

Callie almost became unglued. "Zane, you sound just like Richard. I'll tell you what I told him. This is about her, not me. The one—just one, off the cuff remark I made at her, it was just the final straw. She's been taking jabs at me ever since I met her. I've bent over backwards to be nice to her and make her feel comfortable. And that one comment I made, that's no justification for what she did to me. I've never been so embarrassed and I'm the one with the sutures to the back of the head."

Zane put his arm around her waist and squeezed. He wanted to show he supported her, even though what he was going to say might not seem that way. "Of course, it's not. But I don't think she much appreciated being the catalyst in the cake fiasco at your party either. I know Anderson was the actual target in that, but she was accused of being clumsy or, perhaps, intoxicated. It had to be pretty embarrassing for her, as well."

"Are you taking her side in this, because that's what Richard is doing?"

"Callie, I'm always on your side. And I don't want you to ever forget that . . . just like you are on mine, right?"

She knew Zane was going somewhere with this, because loyalty and commitment had been established in their relationship years ago. "Well, of course. That goes without saying. But what if Richard and I can't work together anymore? What is that going to mean for my career?"

Zane pushed his hands to damper the hypothetical crisis Callie was creating. "Whoa there. You're getting way ahead of yourself. Callie, persons in a relationship will fight at some time—it's human nature. No one is going to see eye-to-eye with another person all the time. Now, in Richard's defense, he really stuck his neck out for you when you found yourself in that situation at the hospital. He went to bat for you. He didn't leave you in the lurch to fend for yourself. That speaks to how deep your friendship goes. And how bad you two are hurting right now does too. You wouldn't hurt if you didn't care. You guys need to take the weekend and cool down. I bet by the time Monday rolls around, clearer heads will prevail. But there's one thing you need to keep in mind."

"What's that?" Callie reluctantly asked.

"Remember a few minutes ago, when I told you I was always on your side—I meant that. That's the way a man gets when he feels strongly for a woman . . . protective like. It doesn't matter how many people try to tell him she's no good for him, he'll defend her to the death. All the reasoning and logic won't do any good. It's not until that final straw you spoke about happens to him. Until it does, not you, not me, not the Queen of England is going to convince him that she's anything less than he sees her to be. Understand?"

"So, I'm just supposed to stand by while she wreaks havoc on his life?"

"Yes, that's exactly what I'm saying. But his life will never be totally wrecked if he's got a friend like you waiting in the wings to help him pick-up the pieces."

Callie let a smile peek through her blue mood. "Zane, you are in my corner, finding the kindest way to tell me to back off. You also helped me to better understand what Richard is feeling right now. You're really a special man, you know that?"

"I love you, too, Callie. Now, I'm going to draw you a bath and get you a glass of wine. It'll help take the edge off your day."

Callie was feeling better. The talk did her a lot of good. Reality came to her. "No wine, remember? I'm on call."

"Then one hot chocolate coming up, just the way you like it, with a big marshmallow on top."

His cell phone rang. "Oh, I need to get this."

The call didn't take long. It ended with Zane saying he'd be right there. Callie asked, "What was that about?"

"Well, it was Cody. I need to go pick him up. He's with Jamie Collins."

That piqued Callie's interest. "Oh, really?"

"Yeah, he's wanting to call on her—date her, I mean. He wants to do it right . . . gentlemanly. I told him he could drive in with me on the weekends. He doesn't make a lot and his truck is pretty unpredictable for highway driving, a clunker. That makes it hard on him, getting a motel room and such. I told him he could stay with us. I hope you don't mind."

A broad smile grew on Callie's face. "Of course, I don't mind. Sometimes, I think you have enough love in that heart for the whole world. Maybe Jamie's lonely nights at *Dickerson's Drug* are over."

After Zane left, Callie sat down in her favorite chair and closed her eyes, relishing the quiet. She wanted to put the day's events behind her, but her mind wouldn't let it go.

The one—just one, off the cuff remark I made at her, it was just the final straw. She's been taking jabs at me ever since I met her.

Oh brother, I knew to Google it, but no, I had to ask.

You've got balls calling me a gold-digging bitch, a stupid ass.

Google it, *gold-digging bitch*

to ask, *a stupid ass*

Callie sat straight up, alarms sounding in her mind. She could feel her heart pounding in her chest. "What in the hell is happening to me?" she mumbled.

Thirty-one

Monday, November 6, 2017 9:35 a.m.

Gus was feeling on top of the world. Normally, a Monday morning wouldn't warrant such a cheerful mood, but this one was different. In fact, he was in such high spirits, he was seriously considering another attempt to stop smoking. Over the weekend, he learned from a co-worker that Dr. Wallace had been fully reinstated at the hospital. It had been a heavy burden weighing on him, the part he'd played in the disciplinary action taken against her. What he had witnessed that day surely didn't warrant that type of smudge on her record, especially so early in her career. Gus liked people, all kinds of people . . . he really did. He wasn't one for churchgoing, but the thought of something that he might have done or said causing harm to another person, that about ate him up inside. He'd learned his lesson for sure. If he came across another situation like he'd witnessed before with Dr. Wallace, he'd just keep it to himself, with the exception of Delores, of course.

The fact that Gus had another work order for the neuro floor didn't bother him, but what surprised him was that it happened to be in the same room. He considered it somewhat odd that another repair was needed in the same dictation room within a month's time, but he'd learned long ago that people tended to be more careless with things that didn't belong to them. This time it wasn't the thermostat, but it was an electrical outlet with a blackened socket. Someone probably overloaded it, he thought to himself. Gus bent down to get a good look at it. The majority of the burn was to the hot slot and the ground hole. He needed to cut the power to the room, but first, he wanted to take the outlet cover off for a look inside. Feeling fortunate enough to have sufficient natural light available to work, Gus pulled out his screwdriver.

That's when he noticed Dr. Wallace had entered the room. For a moment, he thought the encounter might be a confrontation. To his knowledge, his report to administration was supposed to have remained anonymous, but in the hospital, there's always talk . . . always. Gus felt his heart sink when he saw it, the same glazed-over look he'd seen in her eyes before. The joy of the day that he had had only minutes earlier, the one that had put a swagger in his stride, and the one that had sent his hip-riding toolbelt swinging side-to-side, was gone.

Callie Wallace was blocking the door, but Gus wondered if she'd even notice if he tried to skirt by her. He thought better of it. Slowly, he backed to the rear of the room. By the wall, there was a couch—one of those that folded out into a bed. Gus managed to get between it and the wall to crouch down.

The physician was angry, again. There was no mention of the Zane fellow, as before. Her ire was directed at someone named Sara. The physician said the imaginary Sara woman would rue the day she messed with her.

Gus fumbled around his pockets for his cell. He dialed Delores.

Delores was surprised to hear from him at that hour. For years, he dutifully called on his lunch hour to inquire about her day. A call at that time of day was an oddity, indeed. After all, he'd only left the house a couple of hours ago. The first words out of her mouth were to inquire what was wrong.

He kept his voice down, but in reality, anyone in the room would've been able to hear him. But the situation had nothing to do with reality. "It's happening again, Delores. The lady doctor is having another imaginary altercation with somebody named Sara. I don't know anyone by that name, do you?"

Delores inquired if Sara was the woman that worked in the hospital cafeteria—the one who worked in the salad line.

Gus shook his head, peeking up only enough to see

over the top of the couch. "No, no, that's Patsy. She's on vacation, anyway. Wait, hush now. Something is going on. Wallace is rolling around on the floor, throwing punches at, well . . . nothing."

Delores voiced her concern to her husband. The situation he was describing seemed bizarre and potentially dangerous. She wanted to notify the authorities.

"Forget that idea. I'll sound like the one needing a shrink. Wait, now she's straddled with her knees apart. It's like she has her opponent penned. Occasionally, she rears back, as though trying to avoid a swing. Oh no, Delores, Wallace just threatened to kill the imaginary Sara. I can't believe it. I just can't believe it. She always seemed so sweet. How can this be happening?"

Delores's anxiety was rising. The last thing either one of them wanted was for Gus to be caught up in a scandal. She advised her husband to get out of there, even if he had to rush the crazy woman. "Leave now, and then act like nothing happened," she told him. "There is no reason for anyone else to know you were involved."

Gus heard someone outside the room, calling, "Callie, Callie, is that you in there?"

Delores was cut off after Gus whispered, "Honey, I've got to go. Somebody's coming."

Richard had heard Callie's voice and followed it to the dictation room. When he caught sight of her, she was on her feet and dazed.

Gus stayed crouched behind the sofa bed. He felt like he was stuck in a bad late-night movie about an asylum. He watched as Dr. Cortez carefully approached her. He gently shook her and said, "Callie, Callie, it's me, Richard. You seem a little out of it. Are you okay?"

"Yes, I'm fine," the woman flatly managed.

To Gus, her state of mind appeared present, yet confused. He recognized it because his grandson suffered from seizures. It was the state of mind after the seizure called postictal confusion. He wondered for a minute if the doctor had been having a seizure, but it wasn't like anything he'd ever seen.

As the minutes passed, Callie's mind began to clear. "Richard, what are you doing here? Where's Sara?"

"Callie, we're at the hospital. This is the dictation room on the neuro floor. Sara's not here. When I didn't hear from you this morning to report off about the weekend, I got worried. I tried calling you, and even swung by your house. Callie, about the other day, I feel like a heel. You're my best friend, and I'm so sorry."

Callie shook her head, as if trying to clear the cobwebs of her mind. "No, Richard, I'm the one who's sorry. You definitely care for Sara, and I've been butting in where I don't belong. Your relationship is your business, and I was trying to make it mine. Look, can we get out of here? I don't know why, but this place gives me the creeps."

"Okay," Richard said. "But first, a quick hug to seal this forgiveness pact we just made. I want to put this behind us. I was miserable all weekend."

Callie reached out to embrace her friend. "Me too," she admitted.

Gus watched the two leave the room. He stood up, knees and thighs aching and burning from the stooped position. Gus had once asked his son why he didn't take his grandson to Sperling Neurology Group for his care. But his son had insisted on him continuing with the specialist in Dallas. Gus's son also added, despite wanting to hover over every aspect of his son's care, his boy was now a young man. The decisions regarding his care were ultimately his. In retrospect, Gus was relieved. From what he had just witnessed, he was convinced the woman was crazy, and as far as the man, he was running a close second. As far as the Sara person was concerned, Gus just hoped the woman was watching her back.

The cell phone rang. Gus jumped. He looked at the display. It was Delores. "Hey, Delores. Boy, have I had a morning? If you would've called two minutes earlier, those two crazies would've known I was here.

I'll tell you more about it when I get home tonight. Hey, did you pack me a bologna or a liverwurst sandwich for lunch?"

Delores didn't mince words. "Gus, Gus, please stop. I've got to tell you something. The police found our grandson behind the tire shop the other night. Gus, our Fergus is dead."

Thirty-two

Tuesday, November 7, 2017 4:30 p.m.

Rose was frustrated. It didn't seem to matter which line she ever got in . . . it was the wrong one. Now, there in the grocery store, the embedded belief that her line would inevitably be the slowest one rang true, even in the ten items or less line. Rose watched as the one over to her right worked like a well-oiled machine as cart after cart full of food and household items were efficiently checked and bagged. However, the line she was in, it was more archaic—one where the cost of each item was tallied up on an abacus.

Easy now, Rose told herself . . . remember your blood pressure. After all, it was for Callie. Rose regretted that she and her daughter weren't as close as some. She especially envied the relationship her daughter had shared with her late-husband. They'd been close, but Rose and Callie weren't. She recalled one-time she'd even tried to refer to Callie by the affectionate nickname, Corky. The girl had to have been about twelve at the time. She was quick to tell her mother, *that's what my dad calls me, not you*. That remark had cut Rose to the bone, and it still stung today.

Rose knew her daughter was having a hard time of late. When Rose had called Callie, she was in need of a favor. She hated to ask, but her cardiologist wanted her daughter to accompany her to her follow-up appointment on Thursday. Rose half-expected a lecture from the physician on the seriousness of hypertension—a condition the man often referred to as the silent killer. She'd been accused of being noncompliant and he probably wanted Callie there as reinforcement to drive home his point. Although the situation wasn't ideal, Rose was looking forward to spending time with her daughter. She wanted to accent the occasion by bringing along some of Callie's favorite cookies. Actually, the recipe was Marta's, but her good friend and neighbor would never let on that it wasn't Rose's original set of ingredients. But when she went to collect the things she would need, Rose found stone-hard brown sugar. So, there she stood behind *this woman* who was holding up the line, while she held her one item, a sixteen-ounce box of light brown sugar.

The woman was rough looking. Rose guessed her to be in her forties, but the fifties weren't out of the question. Her outfit of sweatpants and a T-shirt did little to flatter her. Rose thought the house slippers she had on her feet did little-to-nothing to dress-up the ensemble. Her hair was pulled back in a tangled ponytail which seemed to be the alternative to brushing it. Her eyes were bloodshot with sagging, dark circles beneath them.

The clerk told her the total of her purchase. The woman pulled out her Lone Star card, telling Rose the woman was on public assistance. When it came time to enter the PIN, her hands shook wildly, causing mis-entries and failed attempts. The frustrated clerk had to reset the machine each time. Her third attempt went through. The woman was told she owed seven dollars and ninety-nine cents. The woman balked, but acquiesced when the clerk explained the state didn't pay for alcohol, the box of wine she intended to purchase. She reached into her bag and fumbled with the trembling wallet, pulling out five and two ones. From the change compartment, she slowly started to count out the change she owed. She caught sight of Rose, looking at her like she was trash, impatiently tapping her foot with each coin that was placed on the counter.

The woman's transaction had taken fifteen minutes. Rose knew her blood pressure was up as evidenced by her throbbing head. She walked out of the store to see the woman at the bus stop. "Hey, you," she shouted at Rose.

Rose stopped to look around to see if the shout-out was truly meant for her. "Me?"

"Yeah, you. You've got some nerve looking at me

like you did in there. I'm a human being. Why can't anyone understand that?"

Rose tried to explain. "Please, don't take it personally. It's just that I'm in a hurry, miss?"

"The name is Jane, Jane Timmons. I used to be like you, proper and such, with somewhere I needed to be. But now, it's all gone . . . my boy, my husband, my career. All I got left to comfort me is this box of wine. I wouldn't wish what's happened to me on my worst enemy, well, with the exception of one person anyway. Not even the likes of you with your nose up in the air."

Rose felt awkward being confronted about her lack of compassion for another human being. "You said you lost your job, is that right? I suppose I could spare a twenty."

The woman held out her hand. Rose placed the bill in it, hoping that would put an end to the unpleasant encounter. She was surprised to hear Jane softly say, "Thank you."

Rose was about to turn around and head for her car, but Jane continued with her story. "I'm supposed to be in Austin in a few days . . . for my hearing, but I can't afford to go. I don't know that I would if I could. The State of Texas Board of Nurse Examiners is going to rule on my substance abuse charge. Does anyone really think I want to be like this? I don't. I had a job—a good job over at the Medical Center. Even if I entered a treatment program, I seriously doubt they'd ever hire me back."

"Do you want help?" Rose asked.

"It doesn't matter. I have no job, no insurance, no money."

"Well, my daughter Callie practices there. Maybe she could help you," Rose offered.

Jane suddenly became agitated. "Callie, Callie Wallace? Is your name Wallace?"

Rose didn't know what she had said to upset the woman. "Yes, it's Rose Wallace. Is there a problem?"

"A problem?" Jane spat. "Your daughter *is* the problem. She ruined my life, that's all."

"My Callie? Are you sure? That doesn't sound like her."

"Oh, yeah, I'm sure that's her. She's the one that reported me. Well, that boyfriend of hers actually did it, but the information came from her. I have to ask you, what kind of doctor, what kind of person, sees me in that condition, and does nothing to help . . . nothing, other than tattle on me? The whole situation was so humiliating. I was publicly chastised, branded with a scarlet A for addict."

Rose was unaware of the situation. Callie had never mentioned it. "Jane, how do you think Callie should've handled it?"

"She could've tried to help me. She could've gone

to the house supervisor and told her I was sick, and she wanted me sent home. I made a mistake—people make mistakes. Callie Wallace makes mistakes, but she gets to have her life—I have nothing."

"You seem pretty angry with my daughter."

"Angry doesn't begin to describe it," Jane huffed. "The only thing, and I mean the only thing that would give me satisfaction is to see her vanish from the face of the earth. There's no justice in this world for someone like me, but if she was extinguished from existence, I would feel vindicated."

"You can't possibly mean that," Rose reasoned.

The bus pulled up. Jane struggled to manage her two bags of groceries and the box of wine. "Oh, Rose, but I do," she said as she prepared to board.

Rose watched her get on. Jane stumbled on one of the steps and some soup cans rolled from her bag. The driver got up to help her on while a man in the front row helped her collect the grocery items. For a moment, Rose thought she should report the threat to the authorities, but after watching the woman, she concluded that the biggest threat the woman presented was to herself.

Standing amid the trail of exhaust that the bus left behind, Rose got lost in her own thoughts. She couldn't believe she'd come face-to-face with a true enemy of Callie's—one harboring such misplaced anger about her situation in her daughter's direction.

It came out of nowhere, the SUV, the engine gunning. A bag-boy gathering stray shopping carts shouted, "Watch out!" He rushed at Rose and pushed her out of the vehicle's path. They were on the ground, dazed. Only the view of the car's rear bumper disappearing by the second was seen across the lot. Concerned onlookers quickly gathered. *You guys okay, do you need some help, I'll get the manager, damn crazy drivers, did anyone get the license plate, I don't think it had plates,* were some of comments Rose vaguely remembered being thrown about. The bag-boy helped Rose up. The palms of her hands were scuffed, skin torn and small rocks superficially clung to her exposed flesh. Her pants were torn at the knees. She found herself standing in the middle of the parking lot . . . the plastic bag containing the brown sugar tightly wound around her wrist.

The vehicle was described by those at the scene as anywhere from steel blue to slate to Aegean to just plain gray. Specifics were lost to the obscurity amid the bus's exhaust. To Rose, it reminded her of Callie's car.

Thirty-three

Thursday, November 9, 2017 11:10 a.m.

Callie was nervous, chewing her lip. She didn't know why. After all, it was her mother's appointment with the cardiologist, not an appointment for her. Of late, Callie had had her full of physician appointments and tests. She rationalized, considering the death of Mr. Murphy, the disciplinary action at the Medical Center, her pre-occupation with her deceased father, and to top it off, the internist ordering an MRI of her brain, it had all been too much, leaving her to feel overwhelmed and her anxiety to crescendo. But despite her reasoning, they were back, the fidgets. She'd named her nervous habits, hating that weak side of herself. They were smothering, much like her mother. Callie had no idea why the cardiologist had insisted she accompany her mother to today's appointment. If the man only knew her mother like she did, no one told Rose Wallace what to do . . . especially Callie.

Callie picked up a magazine of southern recipes and pretended to peruse it as she watched her mother across the waiting room, passing out her baked goods.

She was embarrassed, but part of her was endeared to her mother's generosity . . . to others, anyway. Callie had left her batch in the car, but watching the others eat them, her mouth watered. The appetizing thought was overshadowed by the metallic taste in her mouth. She reached for her lip, the one lanced by her own incisors. She snatched a tissue from the box on a nearby table, pressing it to the cut.

Rose came back to sit with her daughter. Putting her hand to the top of the magazine, she gently pushed it down. "Bit your lip, again, I see."

Callie felt self-conscious. She changed the subject. "It looks like your cookies were a big hit. Got any more?"

"No," Rose said. "They were a pretty ravenous crowd. You should be glad you left yours in the car—this bunch might riot. Besides, you need to nurse that nick."

Callie looked at the tissue, freckled in blood, disgusted with herself. She couldn't talk to her mother about her feelings . . . not ones that really mattered, anyway. "I do appreciate the effort you made—it was sweet. I was surprised to see you made two batches."

Rose acknowledged the compliment. "No one *likes* to come to the doctor, not you, and especially not me. It was the least I could do for you, taking time from your schedule to come with me today. And

I couldn't leave out the rest of the poor schmucks here, waiting to get poked and prodded. You don't think I made the extra batch for your Aunt Clare, do you?"

"No," Callie flatly said. "As far back as I can remember, you have never made or bought her anything."

"Humph," Rose grunted. "That goes both ways, you know, dear. That woman is like a prickly rash that keeps me burning and raw."

Callie knew the topic fired her mother up, but she hadn't brought up Aunt Clare, her mother had. As long as the topic was raised, Callie decided to take another stab at it. "Mother, Mom, is this about the summer of 1995?"

Lips pursed, brow furrowed, Rose tried to contain herself. "Callie, I've told you, I'm not going to discuss this with you."

"Mother, it might help to get it off your chest. I'm not a child anymore."

"Callie, let's not pretend you're interested in helping me unburden my soul. This is about your own curiosities, plain and simple. Why else would you be interested in something that happened over twenty years ago and had nothing to do with you?"

"Wallace, Rose Wallace," the nurse barked out into the waiting room.

The mother jumped up. "Come on, Callie, that's

me." She added, "And not another word about that summer, understand?"

Callie reluctantly agreed before getting up to follow her mother, trailing behind.

Mother and daughter sat quietly in the exam room, waiting for the specialist. The tension between them was palpable. "Mother," Callie started.

Rose cut her off, holding up her index finger. "Ah, ah, I told you not another word on the subject, so drop it."

The two sat in silence until the physician entered the room. "Good afternoon, Mrs. Wallace. Who do you have with you today?"

"This is my daughter, Callie Wallace," Rose replied.

There was a hint of recognition in the physician's face. "Dr. Wallace, the neurologist?"

"Yes, that's me. I understand that you thought it was important for me to accompany my mother to today's appointment."

Rose wanted to get on topic. "Doctor, have you had a chance to review the diary of my blood pressure readings you asked me to keep?"

"Yes, Mrs. Wallace, I have," the cardiologist begrudgingly said.

"And?" Rose inquired.

The specialist was suspicious. "I think you want me to believe these are your actual readings."

Rose interrupted in a panic. “What exactly are you accusing me of?”

The cardiologist felt the need to confront his patient. “Mrs. Wallace, I find it interesting that you jumped to that conclusion, because your blood pressure taken by the nurse this morning was 194/106. This is not consistent with your diary readings which are fairly normal.”

Callie wanted answers. “Mother, have you been lying about your numbers?”

“Phooey,” Rose exclaimed. “Stop being so overdramatic.”

Callie was puzzled by her mother’s nonchalant reply. “What do you mean, overdramatic?”

The man was persistent. “Mrs. Wallace, you’re playing a very dangerous game, here. Your daughter has the right to know you are jeopardizing your own health with this behavior. I use these readings to adjust your medications. If the readings are not accurate, neither is your dosing. What else are you not being honest about?”

“Well,” Rose said in a huff, “I see now why you wanted my daughter here. You wanted some type of reinforcement, to bend me to your will. Now that you’ve humiliated me, are you happy?”

“Mother,” Callie said, “the man needs answers. You’re putting your life at risk walking around with these types of numbers. There's a reason hypertension is called the silent killer. Does he need to hospitalize you to get your blood pressure under control?"

The cardiologist spoke directly to his patient's daughter. "On her last visit, her blood pressure was 192/110. I wanted to put her in the hospital then, but she refused. I'm concerned over the obvious, like myocardial infarction or stroke, but I'm concerned over her kidneys as well."

"Don't you two talk about me like I'm not here," Rose snapped. "It's just stress, that's all. Life can be stressful. Doctor, just change my pills, double the dose, I'll be fine."

"What stress, Mother?" Callie inquired. "Dad left you financially secure. You have friends and an active social calendar. What are you not telling me? Is it Aunt Clare?"

"Oh, Callie, stop reaching. And for your information, I wouldn't waste a bead of sweat on your Aunt Clare. I suppose almost being hit by a car wouldn't qualify as stress to you, does it, young lady?"

"What?" Callie exclaimed. "Mother, when did this happen?"

The cardiologist jumped in. "Mrs. Wallace, did you go to the emergency room?"

Rose was pleased with herself for throwing them off-track. "The day-before-yesterday. A few scrapes, here and there, is all." She held out her scuffed palms as evidence of her encounter. "I was more shaken up than anything."

"Did you call the authorities?" the cardiologist asked.

"No," Rose admitted. "No one saw anything definite, anyway. To think about it now, the incident occurred so fast . . . in a blur. It was probably some careless teenager hopped up on dope."

The cardiologist shook his head. "Mrs. Wallace, I still think hospitalizing you is the best course of action. A well-controlled environment presents the best place to get your blood pressure safely managed."

"Mother, you should listen to the man. You're a ticking time-bomb," Callie added.

Rose was irritated that her attempt to detract from the subject at hand was short-lived. "I'm not going to the hospital, you two, and that's that! Don't think for a minute you can railroad me into doing something I don't want to do. There has to be another way to get my numbers in line."

The cardiologist blew out a frustrated sigh. "Well, Mrs. Wallace, I want to go on the record as saying this is against my better judgement. I suppose I could add a stronger diuretic to your medication regimen, but you're going to have to take potassium with it. It's imperative. Make sure to take it in the morning, or you'll be up all night. Also, how's your diet?"

Callie wasn't going to stay quiet. "Her diet is pretty rich . . . eggs, cheeses, red meats, wine. Boy, does she like the wine."

Rose shot her daughter a dirty look that screamed, *that's enough, blabbermouth.*

The cardiologist sensed the tension between the patient and her daughter. He wasn't about to let the situation play out in the exam room. "Mrs. Wallace, from now on your diet needs to consist of baked fish, chicken, fruits, vegetables, whole grains, and no alcohol, understand?"

Rose simultaneously shrugged and nodded as if she was relenting over the fact that she needed to make a change . . . but she highly doubted she would.

Rose's physician continued. "Dr. Wallace, I would appreciate it if you would take your mother's blood pressure at least every other day and bring it in at her next appointment."

Callie acknowledged the cardiologist's instructions, noticing her mother looking up at the ceiling, disgusted.

"And one more thing, Mrs. Wallace. Keep your stress level at a minimum," he said.

If you only knew, Doctor, Rose thought. *If you only knew.*

Callie and her mother were walking out to the car. A man's voice came from behind them. "Callie Wallace?"

The two turned to see who was calling out. Callie spoke up. "I'm Dr. Callie Wallace, can I help you?"

Little did she know he was a process server. He simultaneously handed her a manila envelope while uttering the words, "Callie Wallace, you have just been served."

Thirty-four

Thursday, November 9, 2017 2:20 p.m.

Gus couldn't just sit around. The mourners and the assuagers down at the church hall stifled him. The family had put his grandson, Floyd Olin Ferguson, in the ground that morning. His was a life taken away too soon. While Delores had tried to console their son, Gus didn't have the words to offer support or the patience to take it. He was angry, plain and simple, with his emotions raw and fragile. The looming question in Gus's mind was, *who could have done this to Fergus?*

Starting school as a boy, little Floyd hadn't given his name much thought. But at the tender age of six, his fellow classmates had proven themselves to be cruel with their endless teasing of the family name that had been handed down through generations. Eager to begin his educational journey, Floyd showed up to school in his Carhartt overalls, carrying his Superman lunch box. It wasn't even lunch time before *Floyd the Fly* was all-a-buzz throughout the classroom. To him, the bzzz, bzzz, bzzz sounds with the children flapping their elbows in the air, was devastating.

Delores was the one that came up with Fergus, short for Ferguson. With the approval of his parents, she went up to the school and spoke to the boy's teacher. After that, the teasing stopped and Fergus was accepted by the other children as one of their own. That was until the seizures started in middle school. Again, the boy was singled-out as different.

Gus was hot. If the family name warranted comparison to a pest, a pest was what they were going to get. That's why he went up to the police station in person. He wanted justice for Fergus. He wanted answers as to what was being done to find the person or persons who left his grandson to rot behind that tire shop . . . and Gus wasn't leaving without them.

The desk sergeant was growing impatient. "Mr. Ferguson, situations such as these take time. I understand the detective on the case has spoken to your son and taken his statement. Leads need to be followed-up. In cases like this one, witnesses tend to get tight-lipped and confidences need to be established. We'll be in touch."

Gus mocked the officer. "*We'll be in touch. We'll be in touch.* That's all I've heard since this happened. I call every day and I'm told the same thing. Maybe you guys think he was a nobody, but he was our boy."

The officer wasn't about to own the insult the man had thrown at him. He wanted to set the record straight. "We're treating this case with the due diligence that we would any other . . . high profile or not. I can assure you of that, Mr. Ferguson."

Gus wasn't convinced. "Well, every time I call, I get the runaround. That's what I'm doing here today. I figured if I came down here, I might get some straight answers. Who is the lead investigator in his case?"

"That would be Detective Monroe. He's got over fifteen years on the force. He's good . . . really good. That's what I've been trying to tell you, but you've got to let him do his job."

"I want to talk to him," Gus demanded.

"If Detective Monroe has any information, he'll be quick to call your son and update him."

Gus slammed his hand on the desk, insisting to be heard. "My son is broken, you get that? He doesn't have the strength or the will to get to the bottom of this, not now, anyway. That's where I come in. I got to fight for him even though he doesn't feel like he has any fight left in him. So, is this Monroe here, or what?"

The desk sergeant tried to be civil, even though someone slamming a hand on his desk rubbed him the wrong way. He knew it was Gus Ferguson who was calling the station everyday—he'd taken the calls. He'd forwarded the grieving man's messages to Detective Monroe, but if the detective hadn't returned his calls, there was little the sergeant could do other than try and reassure the man. “Detective Monroe keeps his own hours, Mr. Ferguson. I can let him know you came by.”

Gus wasn’t about to be shuffled out of the station. There was a door to the right of where the desk sergeant sat. It had a sign on it that read: *authorized personnel only*. Gus made a dash for it, grabbing at the handle, but it was locked. He quickly figured out that access was probably gained by a badge, like at the hospital. Gus started to rapidly hammer at the door with his fist. “Monroe, Monroe, it’s Gus Ferguson! Get out here now, I want to talk to you!”

The desk sergeant was taken off-guard. It took a minute for him to respond to the man’s outburst. He slid out from behind his station and restrained the man. Suddenly, the locked door opened and a plainclothes officer with a holster strapped over his shoulder emerged. “What’s going on out here, Sergeant?”

Gus struggled against the officer’s grip, but it was tight with his arms pinned behind his back. “Are you Monroe?”

“Yes,” the detective replied. “I think I heard somewhere in the raucous you were making that your name is Ferguson. Is that right?”

Gus continued to fight against the hold on him.

"Yeah, I'm Fergus Ferguson's grandpa and I want answers."

The detective didn't see Gus as a real threat. "Sergeant, let him go. Mr. Ferguson, follow me to the back so we can talk. I have some information on my desk that we need to go over."

Gus was relieved to have his arms released. He rolled his shoulders forward and back, and then straightened his shirt. "That's more like it. Maybe now we can get to the bottom of what happened to Fergus."

Gus followed the detective back into the squad room where the underbelly of Sperling's crime was investigated. Several files were sprawled across the investigator's desk. Once the detective took a seat, Gus helped himself to a chair directly across from him. "Detective Monroe, are you any closer to finding out who did this to Fergus?"

"Yes, Mr. Ferguson, we are. But I don't know how well my explanation is going to sit with you. In cases such as these, family members feel a need for retribution—one that fits the significant loss they've encountered."

To the grieving grandfather, the detective was just stating the obvious. "Of course, we do. Sir, what are you not telling me?"

"Mr. Ferguson, we have two guys in lock-up now. Their stories match-up and are consistent with the coroner's findings . . . that Fergus wasn't murdered. It's my understanding that your grandson suffered from a seizure disorder, correct?"

Gus couldn't believe his ears. "What do you mean, he wasn't murdered? He was buried in a shallow grave like an animal."

Monroe knew the finding would be hard for the family to take—it usually was. "Mr. Ferguson, Fergus tested positive for cocaine and alcohol. He was partying with a couple of friends. Because of the epilepsy, that predisposed him to something called Sudden Unexpected Death in Epilepsy or SUDEP. The risk of this is 1 in 1000, but the risk increases when an epileptic does illicit drugs or alcohol. The two friends who were with him knew of his seizure condition. When Fergus started to seize, they thought he was having just another episode, but this time Fergus stopped breathing. They panicked, and not wanting to get hit with a possession charge, chose not to call the authorities. Basically, it comes down to them not thinking clearly. The most these guys are looking at is a year in county jail and a five-hundred-dollar fine for interfering with a corpse. Maybe a little more if we can make a charge of hindering a police investigation stick. I'm sorry, Mr. Ferguson."

Gus just kept shaking his head, wondering how

he didn't recognize the signs that Fergus had a problem. "So, that's it? Fergus's life is over and these guys just get a slap on the wrist. I would've done anything for that boy—he knew the dangers of drugs . . . or I thought he did."

Detective Monroe was sensitive to the man's feelings. "It's not uncommon for the family to feel like they didn't do enough to help the victim, but Fergus wasn't a child. He knew what he was doing and he knew he had a preexisting condition."

Gus nodded, still in disbelief. "I'll tell my son. You don't have to bother. I'll be the one to tell my son that Fergus did this to himself."

With that, Gus stood up. He reached into his shirt pocket and took out a pack of cigarettes. He looked at them with a type of revulsion—a look one might give an unfaithful lover. Gus threw them on the detective's desk.

The gesture confused the detective. "What's with the cigarettes, Mr. Ferguson?"

"I'm not a child either, Detective. I know what I'm doing every time I light-up. I'm just as guilty of putting junk into my body as Fergus. You take those poison sticks, bribe a prisoner, throw them in the trash, smoke them yourself, I don't care. I quit."

Gus wanted out of there. He turned to leave, but bumped right into the man behind him. The man was black with a 9 mm holstered to his ribs. A look of surprise came to Gus's face. "Marcus, what are you doing here? Don't you recognize me? It's me, Gus from the hospital. Hey, what's with the gun?"

Thirty-five

Friday, November 10, 2017 12:05 p.m.

Callie was disappointed she couldn't get in to see Hayden Deutch until Monday of the following week. When she'd called that Thursday after being served, his secretary had said something about him being out of town, but told her she would pencil her in for the upcoming Monday morning. The cause of Mr. Murphy's death was declared adrenal crisis and the wife was out for blood. The hospital had also been named in the suit which wasn't going to earn her any brownie points with Kyle Anderson. Since Callie couldn't do anything about the matter until Monday, she decided to look into something else that was bothering her. That day, she walked into the diner and saw Aunt Clare sitting at a table. To Callie, her aunt appeared to be a fraction of her mother. Not just in looks, but in spirit and wit.

She'd barely sat down before Aunt Clare started in. "Really, Callie, the *Flap 'n Jack*? I thought *Olea's Kitchen* was more your style."

Callie thought back to the disastrous lunch she had there just last week with Richard and Sara.

More than a week would have to pass before Callie would be ready to go back there, but she felt no need to clue her aunt in on the embarrassing situation. "The rich sauces there have really been playing havoc with my weight. The food here is good and nutritious."

"Well, I doubt Fried Fish Friday with Fries is going to help trim that waistline of yours, dear. I do have to say, I'm relieved to know your mother isn't joining us. You know how she can be."

Callie gave a respectful nod, but if her mother knew she was having lunch with Aunt Clare, there'd be no way she would come anyway. "Aunt Clare, you and my mother are sisters. I don't understand why there's so much animosity between the two of you."

"That's because you're an only a child, dear. Of course, you wouldn't understand."

With that, Aunt Clare stopped a waitress walking by. It wasn't the server's station, but that didn't matter to Aunt Clare. "Dear, can you get a rag and wipe our table down. It's all sticky, probably syrup. And bring a dry towel. I don't want to rest my arms in a film of dishwater."

Callie noticed the waitress looking at her in disbelief, but all she could manage was an awkward smile and a shrug of the shoulders.

After the table was cleaned and dried, Aunt Clare

started in again. "I have to say, Callie, I was a little surprised to hear from you. You really have been keeping to yourself since you moved back to town. Last I knew, you were keeping company with some cowboy. I think you could do better than the likes of him, smelling of manure and such. I hear you're in practice with a young man. Is he single?"

Callie gasped at her aunt's straight-forward manner. "Aunt Clare! That cowboy is Zane, and I love him. And for your information, he is a rancher and he doesn't smell of manure. Richard is my partner at Sperling Neurology Group and that is all. Nothing is going on."

Aunt Clare grinned and sent Callie two obvious winks. "Okay, if you say so, dear."

Callie was beginning to better understand her mother's aversion to Clare's company. She was one of those people that affectionately said *dear* and *bless your heart* while simultaneously cutting your life to shreds. Their fish baskets arrived, but Aunt Clare insisted that the hushpuppies be returned to the kitchen. She said they played mayhem with her blood sugar, and as far as Callie's portion, she commented that her niece was getting a little thick in the thighs.

They ate in silence for the next few minutes before Callie decided to take another stab at understanding the relationship between her aunt and her mother.

"You know, Aunt Clare, I was talking to my mother the other day. I was trying to recall something that happened when I was ten, the summer of 1995. When I mentioned it, my mother just clammed up, before changing the subject."

"What is it that you want to know, exactly?"

Callie recalled, "I remember spending most of that summer with my father at Lake Sperling. Mother was gone to the city, a lot. I once asked her if I could come along, and she just about bit my head off. My father said it had something to do with you, but nothing specific comes to mind. All I remember is that he was angry about it."

"So, you want to know why your mother was with me in the Dallas area?"

"Yeah, I guess so. Oh, and why did it bother my father so much?"

Clare took on an air of self-righteousness. "Your mother always had a knack for upsetting everyone in a one-hundred-mile radius. She always had to be the center of attention. As far as your father was concerned, he probably felt like I did, the situation wasn't any of Rose's business."

"And what business was that?" Callie asked.

"I'm talking about sticking your nose in someone else's marriage and not tending to your own . . . that kind of business."

Callie listened intently while munching on a battered fish fillet. "Whose marriage?"

"Well, mine, of course," Clare touted.

The revelation surprised Callie. She began to cough, drawing attention to their table. The coughing continued until she was able to swallow a few sips of water to dampen the reflex.

Clare patted her niece on the back although it served no real purpose. "Bless your heart, child. You were always of the sickly sort."

Callie took offense. "I'll have you know that I just received a clean bill of health. You shocked me, that's all. I never knew you were married."

"Well, dear, where do you think your cousin came from? I still think he would appreciate your father's fishing gear, but I doubt Rose would ever do him any favors. It's not doing anyone any good collecting dust at her house."

"Aunt Clare, some advice, I don't think you should broach the topic. Now, back to your marriage. Your last name is mother's maiden name, and so is my cousin's. I just thought you had him out-of-wedlock. It's fairly common these days. But now that you mention it, I've never heard him talk about his father."

Clare wanted to set the record straight. "Well, that sort of thing wasn't common back then. Your cousin is not a bastard, dear. I took my maiden name back for me and my boy. This was all *after*."

"After what?"

The whole topic flared-up emotions that Clare thought were long buried. "After Rose ran my husband off, that's what. She kept coming to Dallas, interfering with our lives. One night, I came home from work and found a letter that he couldn't take any more of Rose's meddling and he'd taken off. I never saw him again. I didn't even have the chance to tell him I was expecting. Alone, I was having trouble affording the apartment on my salary. So, after the boy was born, we headed back to Sperling."

Callie had questions. "But why would she do that, Aunt Clare? There had to be something motivating her."

"Jealousy, that's what. Now, don't get me wrong, your father was a handsome-enough man, but Tomas made the ladies swoon. I think Rose wanted him for herself. But she didn't get him, neither of us did. She ruined any chance I had at happiness, just so she could have the attention focused on her, even if it was negative in nature. And to top it off, my son was raised in a single-parent home. Your mother, Callie, is the proverbial home-wrecker."

To Callie, her aunt's explanation just didn't make sense. "Aunt Clare, no disrespect intended, but that doesn't sound like my mother at all. She was totally devoted to my father, and if anything, she screams of righteous indignation."

"Oh Callie, naïve Callie, bless your heart. Your mother doesn't belong on that pedestal you have her on."

"I think I see my mother pretty clearly, and that's no pedestal she's on . . . more like a hassock."

Clare couldn't help herself. "Would that be the footstool or a clumpy piece of grass?"

They looked at each other before breaking out in devilish laughter. Callie's phone rang, interrupting them.

The caller was unknown. For a moment, Callie thought about not taking the call, but something in her gut told her to answer it. In the background, Aunt Clare was already mumbling about how rude it was to use the phone at the table. Callie tuned her out.

Callie: Hello?

Sara: It's Sara. I need your help. I'm scared.

Callie could tell she was crying, but she was hesitant to trust her.

Callie: Sara, Sara, tell me what's wrong.

Sara:	I can't really say, but I don't feel like myself. I don't trust my mind. I think I'm in real trouble.
Callie:	Have you tried to call Richard? Do you want me to call him for you?
Sara:	I don't know what I want anymore. What am I supposed to do?
Callie:	Sara, tell me where you are. I can't help you if you . . .

Suddenly, there was no one on the other end of the line. The call had ended.

Callie had a sense of urgency. "Aunt Clare, I need to go. I think a woman I know is in trouble."

"Well, bless her heart. At least she's not getting left high-and-dry for lunch."

Callie took that to mean her aunt didn't want to get stuck with the check. Hurriedly, she dug forty dollars out of her purse and left it on the table before taking off. She was already dialing Richard's number as she rushed out the door.

Thirty-six

Friday, November 10, 2017 1:25 p.m.

It came to Richard in hindsight, he'd just run a red-light. His mind was reeling. When Callie had told him that she thought Sara was in trouble, he didn't know what to think of her reaction. Now, an array of problematic scenarios flashed before his eyes.

Richard glanced at the speedometer. He was going twenty-miles-per-hour over the speed limit. He turned on the car's flashers. Sara's apartment was still a few minutes away, barring any traffic issues. He'd already thought the situation out. If he got pulled over, he'd play the doctor card. Richard had often found it useful in getting his way whether the situation called for it or not. But what troubled him most was what he saw in the rearview mirror. Despite his speed, Callie was hot on his trail. Even though she'd told him she wouldn't butt-in anymore, even though he'd told her he would take care of it, she was positioning herself front-and-center into their relationship . . . again.

Sara's apartment was on the third floor of the apartment building. Richard wasn't about to waste time waiting for the elevator. Instead, he raced up the stairs, taking the steps two at a time. He fumbled with his keys, even though he knew all too well there wasn't time. He opened the door. Hearing Callie not far behind, he remained cautious.

Richard stepped over the threshold. "Anyone here?" he yelled.

Silence.

Callie had made it up the last flight of stairs, out of breath. "Jesus, Richard," she said from out in the hall. "I know you're worried. I'm worried too, but you practically left me in the dust. You could've slowed down for me."

She tried to come in the apartment, but Richard put a stop to it. "Callie, stay there. I want to check out the apartment first. And by-the-way, I asked you not to come. If this turns out to be nothing, and Sara sees you here, there's going to hell to pay, for both you and me. Why don't you just go on back to the office?"

"I'm not just going to leave you here. What if there's real trouble? That's why I called the police and requested a welfare check at this address."

Richard was practically beside himself. "Damn it, Callie! You did what? How do you even know Sara's address?"

Callie felt herself blush. "Internet. I guess I found myself being a little curious, that's all."

Richard couldn't believe how the whole scenario

was unfolding. "Callie, first, you ambush her at the bank, then, you call her a gold-digging bitch in public, and now, you're on her doorstep and have the cops coming."

"But Sara mentioned something about not knowing her mind."

He was losing patience with her. "Sara has a history of depression. I had offered to prescribe her an antidepressant, but she refused. Like so many, Sara feared being stigmatized and saw taking a drug for it as weak. But nothing says stigma like the police showing up at your door. Callie, how could you?"

A depressive state could easily explain the matter, he thought, or something else, but what? Had things gone too far, he wondered.

A man's voice came from the stairwell, "Right this way, officer. It's 302. I'm sure this is just a false alarm, sir."

Richard saw how the situation looked . . . not good. There he was inside his girlfriend's apartment, her not there, maybe missing . . . maybe not, and he just so happened to bring his female partner along.

"Whoa, whoa," the man said, seeing someone standing in the doorway of the Townsend apartment. "Who are you?"

Richard saw the men eyeing him. "I'm Sara Townsend's boyfriend, Richard Cortez. Who are *you*?"

"I own this building. Imagine my surprise when this officer came to my office, concerning Ms. Townsend." He positioned himself to look past Richard, to take a peek inside the apartment. "Jeez, look at that mess. I guess a guy can look the other way to certain flaws when your girl is a looker like Sara."

"When did you last see her?" Richard inquired of the property owner.

"Why, is there a problem?"

The officer wanted to take control of the situation. "I'll ask the questions here. Who are you?" he asked as he pointed to Callie.

"I'm Richard's partner. Sara, Ms. Townsend, called me about an hour ago, upset. She said she didn't know her mind, thought she might be in trouble. I tried to talk to her, but she hung up."

"Did you hear a disturbance, any strange noises in the background?"

"No," Callie responded.

Richard was getting impatient. "Look, can the landlord just answer me?"

"Go ahead," the officer said in agreement.

"Well, let me think about this. Oh, yeah, it was about eight days or so ago. I needed to talk to the tenants on this floor. I had three fuses blow in less than a week. I wanted to see if somebody might know the source of it, but, of course, no one knew anything.

Anyway, I remember talking to her, specifically. I asked her for the November rent, it was due on the first. She said it had slipped her mind. She told me she would write me a check. She didn't invite me in, either. She had me wait in the hall while she wrote it out. Now, I know why."

"Did she seem okay to you?" the officer inquired.

The landlord scratched his chin, trying to recall. "I didn't notice anything strange, if that's what you mean. She's always been a little too much into herself, but the pretty ones usually are. I guess I don't see what the problem is."

Richard felt the need to reiterate the problem. "You see, my partner got this odd call from her. Callie said Sara was crying and sounded distraught."

The property-owner was losing patience. "So, she was upset. My wife, when she was younger, used to cry at a drop of the hat, hormones and all."

The patrolman was taking notes. "Tell me, again, when was the call?"

"A little over an hour ago," Richard replied. "I dashed over here and found the door wasn't locked."

The officer was skeptical. "An hour isn't long. Maybe she was just in a hurry. Have you tried to call her?"

Richard nodded. "I did, but it went to voicemail."

"Did you try her place of employment?" the policeman asked.

"She isn't working today. Yesterday was her birthday, and I took her out for dinner. She told me she took today off, treating herself to a three-day weekend."

The officer continued to scribble in his notebook. "Is that the last time you saw her, last night?"

"Yes, but then I was called away. You see I'm a . . ."

The officer continued to question him. "Tell me, did you see her car downstairs when you pulled up?"

Richard took a minute to think. "No, I don't remember seeing it, now that you mention it."

The public servant pocketed his notebook. "Let's go ahead and look around inside."

The open floor plan of the one-bedroom apartment led them from the small living area to the kitchen. The sink was full of dirty dishes. An open box of cereal sat on the counter and a thin film of grease spatter coated the stove-top. "I don't see a pocketbook," the officer observed. "Let's take a look in the bedroom."

The room was a mess, but it was Sara's usual. Clothes were on the floor, the bed unmade, and a dirty cereal bowl on the end table. "I still don't see a purse," the policeman said. He turned to Richard. "It would be unusual for a woman to leave one behind if she went out. I think you should try her phone again. Let's see if she picks up. This could be nothing more than a misunderstanding."

Richard pulled out his phone and dialed Sara's number. A familiar ringtone came from somewhere beneath the rumpled covers. The landlord began to rummage through the sheets and blankets until he found the device.

Richard took the phone and ended the call. "I don't like the way this is looking. I've never seen Sara without her phone."

The uniformed officer was having trouble seeing the situation as emergent. "I don't think we should panic. She could've just run a quick errand and forgot it. She could've gone out to get a cup of coffee or grab a burger. I think all this situation boils down to is that Ms. Townsend was in a hurry."

"Well, there you go," the landlord concurred. "She probably grabbed her purse, got into her car and is going about her business, not realizing she forgot her phone. I really doubt she'd be very happy to come home and find us rooting through her things. I think we should lock up and go."

Richard shook his head. "You go ahead. I'll risk it. There's a few things I want to check out."

The landlord's friendly demeanor turned official. "Mr. Cortez, I'm not asking, I'm telling you we're leaving. Her name is on the lease, not yours, and I'm going to look after my tenant's rights as I see fit. As far as I know, I could've stumbled on to a domestic situation between you and Ms. Townsend. Maybe, she doesn't want to be found, especially by you. You yourself said she called your partner, not you, and that was just a little over an hour ago. I don't see any emergency here. Now, let's go."

"But, but . . .," Richard mumbled as the man was pushing him towards the door.

"You know what Dandy Don says, 'If all our buts were candied nuts.' Mr. Cortez, this discussion is over," the landlord informed him.

"But it's doctor, not mister. I'm Dr. Richard Cortez," Richard clarified.

The officer was in agreement with the building owner and he wasn't one for pretentiousness. "*Oh, excuse us, Doctor.* Out, Dr. Cortez, out! Everybody out!"

Thirty-seven

Her Final Moments

If she knew it was to be her last day on earth, she would have probably done things differently. But she didn't and she did not.

It wasn't so bad, she reasoned. She could still process thought, but not sure what she ought to be thinking. Another realization, she found herself understanding things she'd never known before . . . open to facts, pertinent or not. She'd heard some people have their life flash before their eyes, but that was not the case. And the more she thought about it, that was probably for the best.

She'd spoken to only a few souls since her arrival. How odd it was, she thought—the absence of breathing. Speech is produced by air passing over the vocal cords and articulated by the mouth and nose. If one is not breathing, how does one speak? The word breath is derived from the Old English word, brǣth. Strange fact for her to know something like that, but it was all strange . . . so strange.

What else did she know? So far, she determined that she had consciousness. She could reason, something that had not come so easily before. But before what? Before, when life was supported through respiration, circulation, and energy to fuel such efforts. This is in contrast to what life was in the absence of such mechanics. Greek origin of machine, mēchano.

To follow this line of logic, she'd been a machine . . . before, not now. Contrary to that line of thinking was the concept of feelings. The whole notion of joy seemed to elude her completely, and happiness, she knew little of it. Anger was a predominant emotion, especially at those who appeared to relish in their bliss. Machines were not to supposed to have feelings. So, could it be, that she had not indeed been a machine?

Let's analyze the situation, she told herself. Feelings originated in the head which housed the brain, a primitive complex of gyri and sulci. Its gyrification interlaced with neurons and their axonal reaches may or may not be conceptualizations of absoluteness. One needs to consider the notion of substance may be no more than a mechanical defect that brings about such conditions as schizophrenia or autism. Let's not forget the miscues of Alzheimer's disease with its plaques and entanglements. The argument thus far supports that the brain itself is a machine prone to defect. Objects without a brain are inanimate whereas those with a brain are fluid and highly prone to misinterpretation.

How cruel to be an organic entity with a brain, she deduced. Origin of the word brain, bregen.

She herself had fallen victim to the machinations of such a primitive device. The most peculiar concepts had come to her before the end. It was difficult for her to determine if they occurred while she was in sleep-mode or booted-up. Some would center around her mother, telling her she was worthless, would never amount to anything, and she should never have been born. Some were around her father, who'd one minute tell her she was daddy's little princess, and then thrash her within an inch of her life the next. The latter would often be accompanied by the stale odor of fermented hops and barley on his breath. She would cry, but it seemed like no one ever heard her. After a time, she didn't even bother with it. The word cry originated from the word, crien.

The whole concept of he/she and father/mother came to mind. An inanimate object wouldn't be saddled with such a label unless done so by a twit afflicted with a defective brain. The concept of gender classification seemed to be reserved to organisms capable of sexual reproduction. Some individuals were offended by such gender designation, albeit a few, and felt the right to assign their own gender or opt for neutrality. The feeling may seem appropriate to these individuals; however, one cannot discount that these feelings may originate from a mechanical defect, such as an engine with a knock. As far as reproductive capacity, karyotyping designates a female as XX and a male as XY. Its concept is as simple as a sewing machine with a needle and a can opener with a blade, each a machine with their respective parts. The origin of the word gender, genderen.

Such arbitrary knowledge that she possessed did little to elucidate the current state she was now in. A spirit, per chance? The concept was intriguing; however, if that was the case, that would introduce into the scenario that there might be a supreme being. She would reject that hypothesis on the grounds that such a divine existence would have heard her cries, including her last, and she was certain that no one did.

So far, she had surmised that her conscientious self, or her mind, was separate from her brain. But that in itself was a problem in that the brain can influence the mind. Descartes coined the phrase, *cogito ergo sum*. It was a concept that had survived the test of time. She pondered if the belief of, 'I think, therefore I exist' was timeless, because the ethereal world in which she found her cognitive self was devoid of time.

To delve further into the perplexing quandary in which she found herself, she began to recall the events that led her into her current situation. She decided she would use empirical evidence—such as would employ the senses and any feeling she thought that would support sound reasoning. Although she could no longer take advantage of such perceptions, she would utilize cognitive analysis in order to come to some sort of conclusion as to why she was lost to another world. Empiric is derived from the Latin word, empīricus.

Her last recollection:

Smell: garlic, yeast, kerosene, roasted beans
Taste: butter, caramelized onions, cheese
Touch: silk, a soft caress, lips kissing
Hearing: music, an accordion, clattering dishes
Sight: a lamp-lit table, duck confit, coffee
Feeling: warmth, fluttering, yearning

She deduced she must have been happy, at least for a moment . . . a rare occurrence for her. But then it came time for her to analyze the moment she was lost to the land of the living.

Smell: disinfectant-like
Taste: salt, mixed with bitter, or was it sour
Touch: an unrelenting hard push to the back of her head, cold and wet
Hearing: muffled, gurgling, gasping

Sight:	blurry, glassy, blue then black
Feeling:	panic, suffocation

She was ready to present her findings.

Conclusion: Sara had died, but she wasn't dead.

Thirty-eight

Monday, November 13, 2017 9:10 a.m.

Zane had extended his stay over the weekend and planned to return to the ranch later that evening. Jamie had gone to visit Cody, so returning him to work on time was not an issue. According to Callie, Jamie had made it back to Sperling without incident, showing up to work that Monday morning, all smiles. The meeting with Hayden Deutch was crucial to Callie's future and Zane wasn't about to miss it. Callie had texted the attorney beforehand to confirm him being with her wasn't going to be a problem. Mr. Deutch clarified that his concerns about not having a loved-one present applied to the initial consultation only, so the would-be client wouldn't hesitate to be forthcoming with him and speak freely. Now, it was time for Callie and her attorney to begin strategizing.

Callie and Zane sat next to each other, across the desk from Hayden Deutch. Zane grabbed her hand in a show of support. Callie surmised what she understood to be the plan of action in the event a lawsuit was filed. "Mr. Deutch, what I remember you saying is that you'd work on my behalf with the malpractice carrier and the plaintiff's attorneys to reach a fair settlement."

The lawyer was somewhat hesitant. "Well, . . ."

The couple just looked at each other. His reluctance confused them. "You got something on your mind, sir?" Zane inquired.

"Well, that was before."

His enigmatic manner had Callie curious. "Before what?"

"Before I spoke to a colleague of mine. Dr. Wallace, let me be frank. The way things stand right now, I think you're at a great disadvantage. The laboratory and pathology results speak for themselves. Mr. Murphy's adrenal glands were atrophied. The increase in catecholamines in the patient's samples was due to extensive use of stimulating adrenergic agents in the attempt to revive him. In his report, the medical examiner cited several studies that show cortisol levels in the postmortem individual does not significantly differ from that of a living person, meaning that it is a valid standard by which to measure a deceased person's cortisol level at the time of death. Mr. Murphy's cortisol level was very low, as was his adrenocorticotropic hormone, but he had a normal level of aldosterone. It also states a specific type of receptor that responds to adrenaline was reduced in number, and that explains why excessive use of adrenaline was ineffective. That led the medical examiner to conclude the cause of death was adrenal crisis related to secondary adrenal insufficiency. Now, with that being said, I don't think we have to throw your entire future on the mercy of the court."

Again, the couple exchanged the confused glance. Callie spoke up. "Mr. Deutch, let's face it, the facts are the facts. I saw the order myself, it read 6 mg instead of 64 mg. The steroid needed to be tapered slowly, instead of such an abrupt reduction. That explains the results you just went over. Whether I mis-typed the order or the error was a result of fatigue, the Murphy family has lost a loved one."

"That is the tragic reality of the situation," Hayden said. "The Murphy family is asking for significant monetary compensation, Dr. Wallace. If you just roll over and let the chips fall where they may, you could be putting your career at risk."

Callie asked, "Is this sum in addition to what the family wants from the hospital?"

"Yes," Hayden replied. "What we need to do is say, okay, you'll accept part of the blame, but a majority of it doesn't lie on your shoulders, but on the hospital's."

Callie wanted to clarify her position. "Mr. Deutch, I feel like the buck stops with me . . . I'm the one ultimately responsible."

Zane felt a need to support Callie's position. "Sir, personal responsibility is a big part of Callie's character. It has been for many years, long before she became a physician. It's one of the things I admire about her."

The lawyer knew that being somewhat seedy was a prerequisite to survival in his chosen profession. The lofty principals his client was spouting made him nauseous. He needed Dr. Wallace to get on board. "Well, while I do find that to be an admirable trait, in this situation, it could prove fatal to your career."

Callie wanted to make sure she understood the lawyer's angle. "So, what you're saying is we need to shift the blame?"

The attorney nodded. "Yes, and a lot of it. More so than what the Murphy family is holding them accountable to."

"What is the hospital's responsibility in this case?" Zane asked.

"Basically, the hospital's responsibility is to hire competent, professional staff to look after the patient during the stay, using evidence-based guidelines, in a safe and effective manner. They are to carry out the physician's orders, question them, if needed, and call the physician when there is a change in the patient's condition, especially if it's felt the change could produce a negative outcome. This mistake slipped through the fingers of a lot of professionals, not just you Dr. Wallace. So, the Murphy family's claim against the hospital is based on whether or not it violated any of these standards. What we need to do is dig deeper."

Zane was eager to help. "Like what? I'll do whatever I can to ease this burden for Callie."

Hayden was thoroughly convinced the two were nothing more than a couple of do-gooders. Made for each other, he thought. "Well, Mr. Atkins, I seriously doubt there is much you can do, personally. What I'm talking about is looking into the personal lives of the staff outside the hospital, contributing factors. We also need to look at the integrity of the hospital's hardware, software, and IT security. For instance, the computerized physician order entry program. Why were there not safeguards in place to prevent such an error? If the dose is not available in the drop-down menu, is there an over-ride option that requires a security code? It's things like that that I'm interested in. Was that the case, Dr. Wallace?"

"I'm not aware of an over-ride security code. When the dose isn't available from the menu list, I type it in the field and the program prompts me if I want to confirm the order. But what do I know? I could've sworn I entered 64 mg instead of 6 mg."

Hayden was beginning to feel a little better about the case. "Good, good, this can work in our favor. You see, that's another thing. Why didn't another staff member, a pharmacist or a nurse, find it strange that this man went from such a high intravenous dose to such a relatively insignificant one?"

Zane chimed in with his own information. "Callie, did you tell him about the doped-up nurse?"

"Zane!" Callie exclaimed, shocked by his insensitivity to the woman's addiction.

Hayden wanted to encourage Zane's straightforward nature. "No, no, Dr. Wallace, Mr. Atkins is right. These are the type of things that affect the staff and bleed into their professional lives. In fact, I know a private eye that would be perfect for this situation."

"But I don't want to inflict more pain and suffering on this woman's life than I already have," Callie said.

Hayden was wondering how in the world he was going to defend this woman. He was surprised she hadn't taken responsibility for original sin. Luckily for him, the boyfriend intervened.

"Callie, you didn't create that woman's problems . . . and you can't fix them," Zane reasoned.

The lawyer backed Zane up. "Your boyfriend makes a lot of sense, Dr. Wallace. You can't afford to shoulder the entire blame here."

Callie wanted some reassurances. "Mr. Deutch, when you talk of private investigators, IT, along with other specialists, and the number of hours you'll clock for this type of trial, it sounds expensive."

"Let's look at the best-case scenario," Hayden

began. "Statistics tell us that when there is strong evidence of negligence, fifty percent of physicians actually win their case."

Zane was willing to chance it, and he wanted Callie to chance it, too. "You see, Callie? What he's saying is that if he can show that a majority of the blame falls with the hospital, you can claim, as a provider, just practicing there endangers your patients and your livelihood—that Mr. Murphy wasn't the only victim in this case, so were you. Isn't that right, Mr. Deutch?"

The attorney was hesitant to commit. "Uhm, yeah, okay."

"All this is well and good, gentlemen, but it still doesn't answer my question about the cost of this endeavor," Callie reiterated.

Hayden wanted to avoid being pinned down to an actual number. Instead, he had more facts. "Dr. Wallace, the average settlement in these cases is somewhere between four-hundred and four-hundred-fifty thousand. Under Texas law, there is a cap on non-economic damages like pain and suffering. However, there is not a cap on economic damages. You're being sued for 5.2 million, an excessive amount. You're only covered up to a million per occurrence with a cumulative amount of two million. If we lose, the insurance company is obligated to pay the set limit. If the damages are seen to be reasonable, you're going to be in some trouble. Once the insurance company pays their obligation, they will most likely not renew your policy, and you would be lucky to find another carrier. If you do, the premiums would be so high you couldn't afford them. But if we take the case before a jury, I feel fairly confident we can get the reward significantly reduced, more in line with similar cases."

Zane posed the obvious question. "Why does the family want so much?"

"I think I know," Callie admitted. "Mr. Murphy was happy with the care I provided, Mrs. Murphy, not so much. We clashed a few times. The Murphys are wealthy. He made his fortune in oil and gas. She expected him to be catered to, although he wasn't like that at all. With his death, the family probably feels they have lost substantial future income. In other words, they want to recoup economic damages."

"There's the possibility that those prices would tank," Zane added. "In the event Mr. Murphy had lived, the family could've faced financial loss if the man had continued to hedge his bets."

Hayden shook his head. "Unfortunately for us, Mr. Murphy's knowledge of that particular market niche resulted in yearly gains of 10-12% over the last ten years. Your scenario, Mr. Atkins, would be almost impossible to prove."

Callie felt defeated. “So, Mr. Deutch, what you’re saying is that this comes down to the almighty dollar?”

Hayden Deutch folded his hands together and put them matter-of-factly on the desk. He leaned into it, looking Callie straight in the eyes and said, “That’s correct, Dr. Wallace. You are absolutely correct.”

Thirty-nine

Late September, 2017

It had been of those days. Richard was supposed to have taken over call that morning but he'd called and told her he'd been held up in Fort Worth, some issue with his mother that required him to extend his stay by a day. It wasn't that she really minded, but that on top of a flat tire and being pulled over by the police for doing forty-two in a thirty-five, her patience was waning. Then came the icing on the cake. The emergency room physician called and told her Clyde Murphy was in Room 2. It appeared that the man's multiple sclerosis was flaring with symptoms that had persisted over twenty-four hours. A word of caution was given to Callie—Mildred Murphy was there and itching for a fight.

Callie arrived at the ER, pulling the man's chart. She quickly scanned it to find the man's chief complaint, but they were numerous: fatigue, double vision, pins and needles sensation to lower extremities, and a weak bladder. Some preliminary blood work had been ordered. She looked over at the closed curtain of the cubicle, wondering how to handle the situation. Not the MS exacerbation, that was going to be easy. It was the antagonistic wife that was going to be a challenge.

Callie felt a headache coming on, but it had to wait. She reluctantly got up from her seat to head to Room 2, but was taken aback by what happened next. The curtain flared open as a male nurse came stumbling out of the patient nook, head first, with such force he lost his footing. His arms extended forward to break his fall. He flew into the front of the nurses' station counter which stopped his momentum cold. He got to his feet, putting his hand up to a bleeding gash to his forehead.

"Get security down here, quick," Callie told the unit clerk.

The curtain for the exam room raked back. Standing there, fuming, was Mildred Murphy. She addressed the dazed nurse. "And don't come back until you know what in the hell you're doing!"

Callie intervened. "What's going on here?"

"I was just trying to get a blood sample from him," the nurse apologetically said. "The guy's vein blew and I was going to have to try again. I told the patient things like this can happen and that I was going to have to stick him again. He was okay with it, but that crazy woman called me incompetent and literally kicked me in the butt, throwing my ass out of the room."

Callie couldn't believe what she was hearing. "The woman assaulted you?"

The crass woman didn't give the nurse a chance to respond. "Assault? Assault? You should see my husband's arm. How about this facility hiring some competent staff? Doesn't he know who we are?"

Callie turned back to the clerk who appeared indifferent to the situation. Working in the ER could do that to those who were often confronted by the unpleasantries of the human condition when stressed. "See that the nurse gets that cut cleaned up. When security comes, have them standby. I'll take it from here."

She motioned for Mrs. Murphy to reenter the cubicle with her and closed the curtain behind them. Callie saw her patient sitting up forty-five degrees on the gurney. "Feeling a little out of sorts, Mr. Murphy? Let me take a look at that arm."

Clyde Murphy held out his arm. "It's just a little bruise, Doc. Mildred has a way of making a mountain out of a molehill. Apologize to that male nurse for me, will ya?"

"Don't apologize for me," Mildred snapped.

Mr. Murphy was usually even-tempered, polite, and easy-going, but he'd had enough. "Damnit Mildred, I feel like shit and I've had enough of your shenanigans! This is about me, not you. Let the staff do their job. Now, shut your damn trap."

Callie noticed the woman fold her arms and turn away like a pouting child. She imagined there was probably no one other than Clyde Murphy who could keep that woman in check. She saw the nurse's blood drawing supplies on the bedside table. "Mr. Murphy, let me see your other arm. I'm usually pretty good at this. Let me see if I can get your blood samples."

She placed a tourniquet on her patient's arm. Callie saw the curmudgeon sneaking a peek at her efforts, but she remained confident. Callie eased the butterfly needle into Mr. Murphy's vessel and took three-color coded vacutainers worth of blood. She slipped the needle out and applied pressure. "There you go. See, that wasn't so bad, was it?"

Clyde Murphy managed a smile, but he knew what was coming. "Nay, Doc, that wasn't bad at all. But this isn't my first rodeo. I know you're going to put me in the hospital, right?"

Callie planned to do just that, but she wanted to hear first-hand the symptoms her patient was exhibiting. She often found when the patient stated their problems aloud, it made them better understand the need for inpatient care. "Tell me what's been going on with you, Mr. Murphy."

"It started a couple of days ago. I started feeling real run down . . . no energy. Then came the prickling in my feet. It felt like fire ants were biting me. I tried to walk it off, but the spasms in my ankles and knees was something fierce, so I got out my walker. Damn, I hate that thing. It makes me feel like an old man. I'd tried to walk with a cane, but I fell. I had to call Mildred to help me up."

Callie half-expected Mrs. Murphy to comment, but the wife remained silent. "You could've broken a hip, or something. You were lucky. Go on," Callie instructed.

"Well, yesterday morning, I was sitting at the kitchen table having a cup of coffee. I picked up the cup and took a sip. But when I went to put it back on the table, things got a little fuzzy, and I missed the damn thing, completely. The cup fell to the floor and busted. I guess the straw that broke the camel's back was when I asked Mildred to drive me up to the office. I had some things I needed to sign off on. She was trying to load me up into the car, but it was just too difficult for her."

"Poppycock!" Mildred exclaimed. "Too difficult for me? That's ridiculous. You pissed on me. You lost control of your bladder, and you pissed on me."

"That's enough out of you, woman," Clyde Murphy huffed.

Callie interceded. "Okay, you two. I think I get the gist of what's going on. I am going to do a brief exam, and run a couple of tests, but you will need to be admitted."

The patient didn't have time to react. There was knocking to the cubicle frame from outside. "Dr. Wallace, it's the unit clerk. Do you have a minute to step out here? It's important."

"Excuse me. This should just take a moment," Callie said. She grabbed the three tubes of blood to have the clerk send them to the lab, and then she stepped out.

The female officer stood behind the clerk. She was stout, fit, and solid. Her hair was pulled back tight, badge to breast, gun to hip. Callie could tell the woman was all business.

Callie addressed the clerk. "What's going on here?"

"This officer would like a few words with Mrs. Murphy. I believe the nurse must have called in a complaint," the clerk reported.

Callie didn't want a scene. "It's paramount that my patient behind this curtain not be stressed. Whatever your business with Mildred Murphy cannot be conducted within earshot of the patient. Is that understood?"

"Ma'am," the officer began, "it's not my intention to be confrontational, but I do have a job to do. I need to speak with Mildred Murphy and it's my understanding that she's on the other side of that curtain.

I'm respectfully requesting that you ask her to step out here. Is that understood?"

Callie's headache was quickly gaining momentum. The pain shot behind her eye as if something was pushing on it from the inside. The grating of the curtain rings against the rod made her wince.

In the cubicle's threshold stood Mildred Murphy. "I'm thoroughly convinced my husband and I are in a facility of imbeciles that believe the spoken word cannot be heard or understood when groups are separated by a single piece of flimsy material. Jean, I understand you are looking for me."

The officer acknowledged her. "Mildred, I understand you're making trouble again."

Callie instinctively backed away. She feared the encounter between the two women might turn ugly.

Mrs. Murphy's addressed the bystanders. "Ladies and gentlemen, for you dimwits who fail to understand the significance of Sperling's finest being called here today, it is a fact that our esteemed police department has assigned Jean to serve as a liaison officer to run interference on the public's behalf against my so-called contentious disposition. And as far as the so-called security guards I see cowering in the corner, perhaps, now that Jean is here, it would be a good time for them to take their nap. What? Can't go night-night without your blankie? Let me help you."

With that, Mildred walked to the six-foot blanket warmer and took out two folded coverlets from the stainless steel and glass appliance. She threw them in the guard's direction. One clumsily unfolded to glide across the floor, the other landed atop a guard's head.

The officer had had enough. Jean grabbed Mildred Murphy's wrist and twisted it behind her back, throwing her up against the counter of the nurses' station. The ruction caused charts and specimens to fall. A vase of flowers was thrown off the top of the counter, resulting in shards of glass and water strewn for yards. A once beautiful arrangement, now a disheveled pile of broken stems and bruised buds. "Mildred Murphy, you're under arrest."

Callie had heard a scream. Suddenly, she realized it had come from her, that her arms were shielding her head.

The woman fumed as the officer cuffed her, the Sperling's socialite reduced to an apprehended suspect. Jane began to recite the Miranda warning, but Mildred Murphy spoke over her. "Jean, spare me the portion of my rights where if I can't afford an attorney, one will be provided for me. I can afford the *best*, and don't you forget that. Don't let anyone here forget that!" she shouted. "I always demand the best. That's why that nurse got what was coming to him.

Disciplinary action is what I call it. Since when is that a crime? And who would dare back up his story against me. Well, it would practically be personal and professional suicide. My reach is far."

Mr. Murphy stood in the opening of the cubicle. The four points of the aluminum-framed walker held him steady enough, although his arms and legs wanted to fail him. They trembled under his weight, but he himself remained a force to be reckoned with despite the hospital gown that was open in the back. "I'll be a witness for that young man, Mildred," Clyde barked. "I'm tired of you throwing your weight around and my money. Hell, if it wasn't for me, you wouldn't have two nickels to rub together."

Mildred was seething. "How dare you, Clyde!"

Mr. Murphy turned to the officer. "You take her in, Jane. I think it's time Mildred experienced some of what she calls disciplinary action. You send somebody up here and I'll provide them with a statement."

Jane took Mrs. Murphy by the arm and began to lead her out of the ER. The socialite was heard saying, "Clyde, you've pissed on me for the last time!"

The man ignored his wife . . . he'd had plenty of practice at it. "Dr. Wallace, I've been through this before. Let's get this show on the road, okay?"

Callie sent the man a smile. She turned to the clerk. "We need to help Mr. Murphy get back to bed.

He'll need a room on the neuro ICU. I have another patient I need to see there, so I'll enter his orders when I get up there."

An aide hurried to Mr. Murphy's side to ensure he didn't fall.

Callie called out to her patient. "I'll see you upstairs, okay?"

Clyde Murphy turned to her. "You got it, Doc," he said, sending her a wink.

Forty

Monday, November 13, 2017 10:40 a.m.

Callie sat across from Richard in his office as he worked on some charts. They were together, but worlds apart, each troubled by what life had dealt them. Callie could tell Richard was worried about Sara. There'd been no word. Callie didn't know how she was going to break the news to him about the meeting with Hayden Deutch. With the case going to trial and the Murphy family so influential, there was sure to be publicity . . . negative publicity. She knew the old saying that there's no such thing as bad publicity didn't apply here. It would steer patients and referrals from the practice. Callie watched her friend, trying to drum up the courage to do what she felt was the right thing.

Richard closed the last of the charts. "You've been quiet."

Callie managed a half-hearted grin. "Yeah, well, I didn't want to disturb your train of thought."

"Is Zane headed back to the ranch?"

Callie nodded, secretly wishing she had gone with him. "Any word on Sara?"

He sighed. "No, and I'm not holding my breath, either."

Callie wasn't following him. "What's that supposed to mean?"

"It means that people like the Murphys get all the attention, while people like Sara seem negligible and barely worth anyone's time."

She wanted to understand, but still didn't. "Can you be more specific . . . nothing from the police?"

"Yesterday morning, I went down to the station to file a missing person's report. The police took my statement, but that was about it. I mean, last night I went back to her apartment building to see if she'd come back—she hadn't. I tried the spare key she'd given me, but that landlord apparently had the lock changed. So, I went and knocked on his door to see if he'd heard anything. An officer had come by to talk to him, asking if Sara had ever filled out a lease application, which she did. It had an emergency contact number listed, but the officer tried it and the line was disconnected. You know what else that landlord told me?"

"No, what?"

"He told the officer that he felt I was making too much of the situation. He showed the officer her apartment, that it was unkept, but nothing out of the ordinary. He also told the officer that it was strange to him that her boyfriend didn't know any of her family. Frankly, I didn't think that was any of the man's business. It was just Sara and I hadn't reached the 'meet-the-family' stage of our relationship."

Callie could sense his frustration. "So, basically, the landlord played down the situation. What's your next move?"

Richard threw the pen he'd been holding across the desk. "Callie, I just don't know. I feel pretty helpless. But never mind me, how did your meeting go with the attorney?"

"About as well as your experience with the police and that landlord. It's just not good news, Richard. But we can talk about it tomorrow."

Richard wasn't about to let it go. "Oh, no you don't. Spill it."

"It's bad, Richard. I just feel like I'm going to pull you down with me."

He wasn't taking her seriously. "That's nonsense, and you know it."

"No, it's pretty much a given. I'm beginning to feel like you'd be better off if you just cut me loose."

Richard had known Callie too long to know she wasn't joking or making a polite gesture. "Callie, remember in medical school, in embryology, Dr. Daniels told me I didn't have what it took to be a doctor. I was sure he had it in for me, determined to flunk me."

"I remember, and he did have it in for you. I don't exactly know why, though."

Richard thought back to those difficult days, trying to push down the hurtful memories. "I like to think it was jealousy, envious of my charisma and good looks."

Callie broke a smile. Richard always had a good sense of humor and a knack for turning on the charm. "I remember that you told him that someday, Dr. Richard Cortez would be a household name. You were determined to be famous."

He couldn't help but smile, thinking how arrogant he'd been in those days. "Humph, I was still young and dumb back then. That was my ego talking. Now, I just want to pay off my student loans. You may not know this, but the scholarships didn't cover it all."

It was time to stop reminiscing and get serious. "Richard, that's my point, exactly. You owe it to yourself and the patients. I'll just weigh you down. I think we need to start thinking about dissolving our partnership."

Richard stayed comfortably in the past. After all, in the past, there were no surprises. "I remember you telling me there was no way you were going to let that guy bully me—that we were going to show him. Slide after slide you went over with me. I was exhausted by the time it was all said and done. And I knew you were, too, but it was all worth it when Dr. Daniels was forced to pass me with a B-."

"The expression on his face was priceless," Callie recalled.

He laughed. "It sure was."

"Well, if I remember right, you weren't humbled for long. I don't even think a week had gone by before you started in again on how famous you were going to be."

"I was sure full of it back then," Richard admitted. "But you stuck by me, grounded me. We've been through thick and thin together, and right now, it's looking pretty thin for the both of us. But it's going to be okay. If, and I mean if, the practice folded, I'd just join in with a group in the city—one where they'd need a young pup like me to carry the brunt of the workload while they go off to their country clubs and sailboats."

Callie thought Richard's loyalty was getting in the way of reality. People like the Murphys had a way of running over the little people with no looking back. They were targeting her, not him. She wanted to present her case again, but Richard's phone rang.

Richard didn't recognize the number, but considering the situation with Sara, he wasn't about to let the call go to voicemail . . . the one that was still full. Richard reluctantly answered it.

Callie watched her friend's face as he took the

news—it sunk. He hung up, appeared to be in shock. "Richard, Richard, what is it? Is it Sara? Tell me, tell me."

At first, Richard didn't say anything. He stood up and took off his lab coat, hanging it on the back of his chair. He grabbed his car keys and started to leave.

Callie could tell he wasn't himself. "Richard, tell me about the call," she demanded. "What's wrong? Where are you going?"

His tone was flat . . . no rage, no fear, no tears. "I'm going to the city morgue to identify Sara's body. Evidently, Kyle Anderson came home from a weekend in Dallas and found her floating in his pool. She's dead, Callie, she's dead."

Keep a straight face, Callie. Show concern. "Anderson's pool, but how?" Callie mumbled aloud.

Richard turned to go, but Callie wasn't about to let him go alone. "Wait up, Richard. I'm going with you. I'll drive. Thick and thin, remember? Thick and thin."

Forty-one

Monday, November 13, 2017 8:40 p.m.

Marcus Davis was getting grief from the Houston authorities. The message was clear—get Kyle Anderson out of lock-up. He wondered how something like this could've happened, especially with Anderson being his only contact within Medical Center organization. Marcus was told too much had been invested to have that beady-eyed, pip-squeak administrator land himself up in the pokey . . . as if Marcus didn't know that already.

Marcus's case was going cold, he knew that, too. Hours of watching surveillance footage and shooting the bull with coworkers, hoping for some gruesome gossip, hadn't gotten him anywhere. He was even beginning to question the link made to the endonasal technique and neurology. When it came to defiling a corpse as those in the morgue had been, Marcus knew the administrator had the knowledge base. Plus, the essential tremor of the man's hands would account for the shoddy technique. But the FBI profiling team felt focusing on the administrator would be a dead-end, because the Bureau felt the behavioral characteristics were more disorganized and impulsive, giving the crime a more blue-collar feel. Even though the administrator could be an ass, Marcus had failed to establish a motive. Anderson's sadism was explained to Marcus as a result of an inferiority complex stemming from his lack of acceptance by his peers and other social groups. It was his way of passing his inadequacies onto the victim. His inability to manage his practice, both financially and medically, would only compound his feelings of ineptness. That resulted in the felony act that led to his incarceration. His lack of social skills, clumsy sexual nature, and white-collar attributes basically excluded him from the suspect list. But Marcus wasn't ready to scratch the man off that list completely.

When it came to his assignment, the undercover operation was on a strictly need-to-know basis. He'd seen Detective Monroe around the squad room, but there'd been no direct interaction between them until he'd run into Gus Ferguson the other day. Marcus thought he'd covered pretty well, but if Monroe was as good as they say, he had to be suspicious about Marcus's actual role in the department. All the department members, with the exception of a couple high-level administrative types, were told that Marcus was just a guest, and they were to extend him every courtesy. Marcus knew the more people who were in on the operation, the more chance of it going south.

He didn't want Detective Monroe to become a need-to-know associate, not if he could help it.

When Marcus had gotten the initial call about the *glitch* in the investigation, he'd just gotten home. He'd worked that day, lifting and pulling patients, and lugging dirty laundry bundles. He felt like the hospital assignment was going to ruin his back. With the physical strain mounting, and trails going cold by the day, Marcus thought disability, at this point, was looking pretty appealing. He walked up to Detective Monroe's desk.

Monroe felt a stare on him. He looked up to see Marcus Davis standing in front of his desk. "Davis, right? If this is about the Ferguson case, it's closed."

Marcus didn't want any attitude. He was tired. "No, I need to talk to you on another matter. Can we talk in private?"

The detective felt put-out, but the captain's orders were, *extend him every courtesy.* "I suppose so. I'm pretty covered up right now, though, so let's make it quick. Is the interrogation room okay?"

A man's voice bellowed from the rear of the building, *I said get me out of here! I want my lawyer!*

Marcus would recognize Anderson's voice anywhere, a ninny's whine.

Another shout came, a different man, *Pipe down, assclown.*

Monroe led Marcus to the interrogation room and closed the door. The detective felt like he owed Marcus an apology. "Sorry about the raucous. He's one of those *entitled* guys. He's been like that ever since I brought him in a couple of hours ago. His lawyer is actually on her way, he just doesn't know it yet. I figured I'd let him stew awhile . . . payback for all the grief he's giving us. Hey, what's with the get-up?"

Marcus looked down at his crumpled work clothes. "They're called scrubs."

"Like the show?" Monroe inquired.

"Yeah, like the show. Look, I'm interested in your newest occupant—the loud one in the back."

Monroe looked on with suspicion. "Anderson? What about him?"

"I need you to let him go," Marcus said.

Monroe couldn't belief his ears. "Uhm, that would be a *no*. Look, I know you have the captain's ear, but this guy is a suspect in a potential homicide."

"You said potential. What is it that you actually know?"

"Caucasian, female, thirty years of age, identified as Sara Townsend of Sperling. She'd been reported missing. The medical examiner is looking into a cause of death as we speak. I plan to hold Mr. Anderson the maximum allowable time to determine whether he was involved or not."

It appeared to Marcus that Monroe wasn't going to volunteer much information without additional prodding. "What's the connection?"

"She was found floating nude in his pool, that's what."

Marcus continued to press the detective. "Anything else? Does he know her?"

"He says he didn't, but he's been saying a lot of things that don't necessarily add up. You see, he was seen arguing with the victim at her place of employment about ten days ago."

The back-and-forth was exhausting Marcus. "About what?"

"At first, he denied it, but Townsend's co-workers confirmed it was a heated discussion. Partially paneled glass cubicles allowed them to see in, but the details of the discussion weren't clear. I pressed him on it, and he finally admitted to going to the bank to see her. He told me some cock-and-bull story about a nine-hundred-dollar shirt that was ruined with berry stains because of her. He said he wanted the woman to reimburse him."

"What was your response?"

"I told him if a man wears a nine-hundred-dollar shirt, he needs to be prepared to lose a nine-hundred-dollar shirt. I also told him I've seen people kill for less."

"Who reported the victim missing?" Marcus asked.

"It was yesterday morning by a Dr. Richard Cortez. The last known contact with her was the Friday prior. The suspect told us he drove to Dallas Thursday evening, left about eight-forty, returning last night. He said he was keyed up from the trip, so he decided to go for a late-night swim. That's when he found the body and called 911. He presented the hotel receipt, stipulating those days. But the problem is that Dallas is only a little more than an hour's drive from Sperling, give or take, depending on the traffic. He could've done this and returned to his hotel without anyone being the wiser. For all we know, he could've killed her before he even left for Dallas, using the weekend trip as a ruse to throw suspicion off himself."

This was proving more difficult than Marcus had originally thought. "Okay, so she was found in his pool. Do you even think the shirt-story will hold water, pardon the pun?"

"That remains to be seen. I asked Mr. Anderson if we would find the shirt in question, and he said he threw it away."

Marcus asked, "Have you established a timeline yet? I mean, how long does the medical examiner think she was in the water?"

"Well, that's where things get a little tricky. The

pool heater was off when Anderson found her, but he swore to us that it was supposed to be on, set to eighty-five degrees. Without the heater, he said the pool stays anywhere from fifty-eight to sixty-five degrees, depending on the ambient temperature. Anderson told us that he doesn't use the pool often this time of year, but he'd found the length of time it takes to warm the pool back up consumes more energy than just leaving it on."

"When did Anderson say was the last time he swam?" Marcus inquired.

"Wednesday evening, just before his trip. Long story short, the coroner told me that he's going to have to look at some other indicators once he got her back to the morgue. The temperature of the pool water last night was fifty-nine degrees. His best guess is two days, at least. Water deaths are tricky. It took us until early this morning just to get the scene secure."

Marcus knew the question would appear bizarre, but he had to know. "Did the coroner mention anything about the victim's nose?"

"Did you say nose?"

Marcus tried to back out of the corner he'd painted himself into. "It's nothing. Forget I said anything."

Monroe was getting more suspicious of the department's guest . . . and his motives. "You can be damned sure I won't, Davis."

Marcus continued to play the devil's advocate. "What about this doctor that reported her missing?"

"A boyfriend . . . dating, at least. The officer that initially looked into the report stated that the landlord was suspicious of the doctor's intentions. But this evening, now that she's dead, he's beating himself up pretty good over the whole situation. He said he wished he'd taken the doctor's concern more seriously."

Marcus could tell Monroe's patience was wearing thin. "What did Anderson say he was doing in Dallas?"

"He said it was business for the hospital. I asked him what kind of business, and he said he met with some contractors about an addition to the hospital. I asked him for names, but that's when he lawyered up."

Marcus thought the alibi plausible. "Could be some validity to that. If I were you, I'd check Anderson's office. Now, this boyfriend, it could be that he was making waves at her apartment building and filing the missing person report to throw suspicion off himself. It could've been a domestic dispute gone bad. Seems to me, a doctor would know best how to throw off the time of death, not a pencil-pushing administrator."

"Nice try, Davis, but I already know the pencil-pushing administrator is trained in neurosurgery. And another thing, I don't need you telling me how to do my job."

Their conversation was interrupted when a burly,

authoritative man entered the room. It was the captain, a suit by his side. A very beautiful suit, at that, Marcus thought. "Monroe, this is Kyle Anderson's attorney. Get his release papers ready. We're letting him go."

Marcus kept a straight-face, but inside he was relieved. Monroe had not become a need-to-know, but his curiosity had to be piqued about Marcus's interest in the case . . . and in Kyle Anderson.

Forty-two

Tuesday, November 14, 2017 10:15 a.m.

The next morning, Marcus had a whole cartload of laundry bundles to throw down the chute in the utility room. The repeated twisting and turning motion triggered an attack to his back. The pain was stabbing, radiating down his left leg to his big toe. His face spoke to the pain as his hands went to the sway of his back to support it. He needed to see a doctor, but not one in Sperling. He decided on his next break he would phone his family physician in Houston to see what could be done until he was off assignment. Marcus was startled when a noise came from the corner of the room, behind a cafeteria rack filled with used breakfast trays awaiting pick-up.

There it was again. “Psst, psst!”

This raised Marcus’s curiosity. “Who’s there? You best come on out.”

A man stuck his head out from behind the rack. “It’s me, Marcus . . . Gus, Gus Ferguson.”

“Gus, what are you doing back there?” Marcus asked, relieved.

The maintenance man still stood behind the rack

as if it really obscured his presence in the room. He spoke in a whisper. "I don't want to blow your cover, but I have something to report."

Marcus thought the man was acting strange, too cloak and dagger for his taste. "You do?"

"Yeah, I do. I want you to look at this."

Marcus watched as Gus carefully stepped out from behind the rack and lifted the lid off one of the food trays. He picked a half-eaten sausage patty off the plate.

"Here, Marcus, smell this."

Before Marcus knew what was happening, Gus had shoved the sausage patty up under his nose. Instinctively, he raised his hand to bat away the remnants of the hours-old cold pork patty. "Hey, man, get that out of my face."

They both watched as the patty took air and landed on the floor across the room.

Frustrated, Marcus asked, "Gus, what's this about?"

Gus spoke as if in code, but it wasn't. "You know, at the station . . . *the undercover operation*."

Marcus pretended to go along. "Oh, yeah, yeah. Look, Gus, we need to be more discreet."

"Okay, but I wanted to tell you that I got a bead on a pressing matter. The situation, it's a real doozy."

"The situation?"

"The black-market meat. It's Patsy, right?"

"Patsy?"

Gus's eyes grew big and round. "You mean it's bigger than Patsy?"

The man's reaction made Marcus feel like he needed to make a correction. "Gus, tell me what you know, but not here . . . the men's room around the corner. You go first, and I'll meet you there."

"Roger Dodger," Gus said.

"*Okay?*" Marcus mumbled, wondering what he'd gotten himself into.

He watched as Gus left for the rendezvous point. Marcus wanted to think of Gus as a simpleton, but the man was such a nice guy, naïve was the only word that came to mind in describing him. Marcus needed a moment, something to make the supposed meat scam work to his advantage and keep Gus out of his hair. But then another spasm hit that sent Marcus to his knees. He hated to, but Marcus was probably going to have to report sick after the farce restroom meeting. He needed to be placed in a cushier job, something closer to Anderson to keep an eye on him. But first, he needed to talk to Gus about the supposed meat-scam *plaguing* the hospital.

It took a few minutes, but Marcus was able to get to his feet. What scenario could he concoct in his head about a meat-product, he wondered. It's going to be okay, Marcus, he told himself . . . not really certain he believed it.

Marcus met back up with Gus, checking the stalls to make sure the coast was clear. Marcus had no idea who Patty was, but planned to use open-ended questions to draw information out of Gus while making him feel an integral part of the hospital dragnet. "Okay, Gus, it looks all clear. Start by telling me what you know about Patsy."

Gus was enthusiastic, animated with his explanation. "I think the power has gone to her head."

"Power?"

"Yeah, she used to work in salads, but then got promoted to Director of Nutritional Services. In my day, we just called it a cafeteria manager. Anyway, I think it has her head all swelled-up. She was no sooner promoted before she took yet another vacation down to the coast."

"What coast are we talking about, Gus?"

"Texas coast, the Gulf of Mexico. Suspicious, huh?"

Marcus thought his idea of what warrants suspicion and Gus's were entirely two different things. "Last I knew, going on vacation hardly warrants suspicion."

"Not ordinarily," Gus buoyantly suggested while waving his index finger in the air. "But do you know who she went to see on this supposed vacation?"

"No, who?"

"Her brother, that's who."

Marcus pleaded ignorance, looking confused.

"Her brother—the one who owns a food distributorship."

"Gus, I have to admit, you have me a bit baffled. How does this equate to black-market meat?"

"The way I hear it, the old vendor contracts were terminated and replaced with, guess what?"

"Those with her brother's company?"

"Yeah, yeah," the spirited maintenance man confirmed. "Food complaints are at an all-time high. Rumor has it that the meat is U.S. Utility Grade."

"I don't believe I've ever heard of that," Marcus said. "But that's just rumor, right?"

"You know, the type they use to make hot dogs and dog food," Gus seriously replied.

"Well, Gus, you know the saying, *one man's meat is another man's poison*."

Gus became practically hysterical and started to pace. "Are you kidding, poisoned? What do you know? What do you know?"

Marcus patted Gus on the back. "Easy, Gus, easy. Keep it down. I didn't literally mean poisoned . . . I meant, oh, never mind."

Gus kept going over it in his head. "Who knew, Patsy . . . a poisoner?"

Marcus felt like he'd made the situation with Gus worse, instead of better. He faced Gus, placing a hand on each of Gus's shoulders and looked him square in the eye. "Gus, listen to me. No one is poisoning anyone at this hospital. I just meant it's stereotypical to think of hospital food as bad, not tasting good. It doesn't mean that there's anything heinous going on in the cafeteria or with the meals it puts out."

Gus was unnerved, losing his cool like he did. He tried to cover. "Oh, yeah, sure, I know Patsy isn't poisoning anyone . . . that concept is utterly ridiculous. The change in food vendor, that's what I heard," the flustered man said.

Marcus saw this as an opportunity to keep Gus busy and out of harm's way. "Actually, Gus, I think you might be on to something."

Gus suddenly felt like the prized pig at the county fair. He just knew that he'd be an integral part of Marcus's investigation.

Marcus continued, "Gus, you have brought some pivotal information to the table. From what you said, you *heard* about the food contracts between the hospital and Patsy's brother, but what we need is evidence . . . hard evidence. Do you think you can get your hands on one of those contracts?"

Gus stood up straight, sucked in his gut, thrusted his chest forward, and proceeded to salute Marcus.

"I'm on it, sir!"

With that, Gus was gone. Now, Marcus stood alone in the men's room, his back aching and his head throbbing. The man's theatrics had made Marcus hang his head, slowly shaking it with disbelief. *Oh, brother*, he thought.

Forty-three

Tuesday, November 14, 2017 11:25 p.m.

"Corky, Corky, wake-up."

Callie got up on her elbows and looked over at the digital clock. It was late, almost half-past eleven. She blew out a long breath through puckered lips, annoyed that she needed to accept the inevitable. In actuality, these occurrences would always come right after she'd gone to sleep, although the feeling was one of being asleep for hours. One other thing she realized about these episodes, falling back to sleep afterwards was almost impossible.

"Corky, you there?"

"Coming, Dad," she said as she leaned over to turn on the bedside lamp. Again, he sat on the edge of the bed, wearing his signature fishing vest and bucket hat with hooks dangling.

"Corky, you're looking tired. Are you getting enough rest?"

"Dad, lately, I've been having a hard time of it. As far as my sleep, I was finally getting some rest until . . ."

The apparition interrupted her. "You don't sound glad to see me, Corky?"

"Oh, Dad, of course I am, but I'm a living being, and I need my sleep. You're the one eternally at rest. Can't you visit at four in the afternoon?"

He avoided the question. Instead, he had one of his own. "These hard times, have you talked to your mother about your troubles?"

"She knows a bit of them, but not in detail."

"Why not?"

"You know Mother. She's always been so quick to pick up on my faults and readily reminds me of them on a regular basis. What I need now is support."

"Is this about *the mistake*, Corky?"

"Yeah, Dad, and it was a pretty big one. I'm being taken to court and my future is looking pretty shaky right now."

"Oh, I see. Perhaps, I did come at a bad time. Maybe, I should go."

Callie shook her head and waved her hands, indicating that the fatherly illusion had it all wrong. "Dad, no, I'm sorry. Please, don't leave. It's never a bad time for a visit from you. Did you have something in mind, or is this strictly a social call?"

"Oh, I just remembered something and thought you might get a kick out of it. You see, I was talking with the guys and . . ."

Now, it was Callie's turn to interrupt. "Wait, wait, just a minute. You were talking to the guys? Who are the guys?"

"Sure, Corky. Social convention *up there* isn't so different than it is on earth. A few guys meet up, start up a card game, or something like that, and talk about old times. My best friend is Vinnie . . . an artiste."

Callie was trying to imagine such a thing. "So, you're saying you sit around and shoot-the-bull with these guys? Is it like when you and Raul Gutierrez went for coffee in the mornings, down at the donut shop?"

"Well, the term *sitting* is relative, but yeah."

"Okay, I think I can wrap my head around that. I guess I interrupted you . . . go on."

"Now, where was I?"

"You don't remember, Dad?"

"Oh, yeah, yeah. So, I was telling the guys about a time I took you fishing at Lake Sperling. It was springtime."

"Which springtime would that be, Dad? There were so many."

"Now, don't be ugly, Corky."

Callie felt like a scolded child. "Sorry, Dad," she said apologetically.

"Anyway, it was the spring of '96, you were eleven going on twelve. I made this incredible catch—a rainbow trout. Do you know the odds of catching a rainbow trout in that lake? Around here, they're mostly found in the streams. Forget the math. Let me just say, the chances were slim . . . real slim. So, I'm standing up in the boat, holding up my catch, and I ask you to grab the camera and snap some pictures. I heard the shutter click plenty, and I thought you'd get at least one good shot, but . . ."

Callie didn't care for the story. She remembered the outcome. "But I forgot to take the lens cap off, and without the pictures, in your words, *this yarn will be nothing more than another. . . well, just another fish story.* Yes, Dad, I remember."

"Well, the guys got a hoot out of it, Corky. It was twenty years ago. Can't you laugh about it, even today?"

"No, Dad, I can't. It's kind of like I was saying about Mother. Now is not a good time to throw my mistakes up in my face, I feel bad enough. Who are these guys, anyway?"

"Well, there's Vinnie—he was a painter. Oh, and I think you know Mr. Murphy . . . oil and gas was his game."

Callie's head trip was getting out of hand. "You were cutting-up with Mr. Murphy? Does he know what his family is doing to me?"

"Well, don't be getting upset. To tell you the truth, I tend to favor Vinnie, interesting fella. Mr. Murphy sort of hangs around—a third wheel you might say. Vinnie and I humor him."

Callie was beginning to wonder if she should change her diet, limiting spicy foods, caffeine, and alcohol. These visits with her father were becoming more disturbing.

"Now that you mention it, Corky, I don't think Mr. Murphy cared for his family. From what he's told me, some of them might be going southbound, if you know what I mean."

To Callie, that was an understatement. "His wife is awful. Once, she literally booted a male nurse out of her husband's room. She'd grabbed his arm, forced him to the door, and planted her foot right on his derriere."

"Sounds like she is literally a pain in the . . ."

"Dad!"

"Well, according to Mr. Murphy, his wife kicked his own mother out of their house. She was living in the mother-in-law's quarters. His wife wanted to use the space for her own personal art collection, so she put Mr. Murphy's mother in a nursing home while he was gone on a business trip."

"That doesn't surprise me," Callie stated matter-of-factly. "She's turned both Richard and me into the Texas physician licensing board for refusing to prescribe her benzodiazepines. She calls them her *nerve pills*. She's not even our patient."

"Sounds to me like it's those around her that need the anti-anxiety pills more than her."

"Exactly! You know, Dad, it's funny to me that you hang around such an eclectic group of men. I guess what I mean is, you've always been about fishing."

"No, not really."

"What do you mean?"

"We all have a certain degree in common. You see, I tell the story of the rainbow trout caught in the spring. The artiste tells us that he painted a picture called *Fishing in the Spring*. Then, Mr. Murphy chimes in that his wife bought that painting stolen and forged a certificate of authenticity. If you don't believe me, you can ask Pauly, he was there. He said the painting was already done by the time he moved in with Vinnie at The Yellow House. Anyway, it's supposed to be the centerpiece of Mrs. Murphy's private collection."

The story was making Callie dizzy. "Wait, Dad, back up. Pauly? The Yellow House? Do you mean Paul Gauguin? Dad, does Vinnie have one ear?"

"Well, yeah, he does, but we try not to judge him. Now Pauly, he was initially a money man. He and Mr. Murphy talk profit margins. They're kind of uptight, like . . ."

"You mean like me, don't you, Dad?"

"Come on, Corky, the rainbow trout story was funny, admit it."

Callie's head was swimming. "Okay Dad, whatever

you say, but it sure wasn't as *funny* as the one you just told me."

Callie heard the heater pop on and took a quick look around. The house was quiet except for the heater's hum. But when she turned back, her father was gone. "No more spicy food . . . definitely, no more spicy food," she mumbled aloud.

Forty-four

Wednesday, November 15, 2017 09:20 a.m.

Jamie often found herself humming. Something about birds singing in the trees, sunsets, beaches, or something of the sort. Ever since Jamie Collins had met Cody, the most *apropos* word she would use to describe her life was 'perfect'. Hardly a day would go by without someone asking her if she'd lost weight, had a new haircut, or if she'd been working out. They just knew there had to be some logical explanation to the woman's vim and vigor.

But that morning, she was feeling overwhelmed, underappreciated, and to be quite honest, a little lonely. Cody's weekend visit to Sperling was still two days off. There were dozens of refill requests on the answering machine, a subpoena had arrived for a copy of Mr. Murphy's medical record, and the afternoon schedule was double-booked. For one reason or another, with one of the physicians being out, it made rescheduling the patients an absolute nightmare for the nurse. And to top it off, the accountant who handled the practice's books was calling about a loan repayment schedule he'd received from First National

Bank for equipment. He wanted to know what type of equipment, if he had to set up a depreciation schedule, the interest rate, the total amount of the loan, and the life of the loan, basically, its terms and conditions. Jamie grumbled that that sort of thing wasn't her job—she was a nurse.

And then there was the matter of her employers, the doctors. Just the thought of how they'd been acting lately made her jaw clench and her teeth grind. Jamie knew going in that office nurses weren't the highest paid, but the working conditions were an improvement from the hospital and its pressures. Generally, working with Dr. Wallace and Dr. Cortez had been a pleasure, treating her with courtesy and respect. They both genuinely seemed grateful for her efforts. And if it hadn't been for Dr. Wallace's boyfriend, she never would've met Cody. But these last few days, the tensions were rising, each taking turns snapping at each other. Both of the physicians had been blindsided by tragedy . . . and it showed. Dr. Cortez had lost his girlfriend under suspicious circumstances, and the lawsuit brought against Dr. Wallace had tongues in Sperling wagging. The worst was yesterday. Every spare moment Dr. Cortez had, and there weren't many, he was on the phone trying to get information on Sara. It was causing a back-up and patients were complaining. It didn't help that the Tuesday morning newspaper headline featured the mysterious death of Sara Townsend, and as Jamie recalled, the article mentioned Dr. Cortez several times. And Dr. Wallace hadn't expected the lawsuit brought against her to be so high-profile. It just wasn't local news. News agencies from across the country were calling the office, trying to get a quote. It was all becoming too much. Jamie wondered if the practice could survive the weight of it all, because Jamie herself felt like she might buckle if just one more thing went wrong.

The nurse looked up to see a man standing at the reception window. Jamie didn't get up from the desk, but shouted out, "Can I help you?"

The man stuck his head through the window's opening to keep the conversation more civilized. "I'm looking for a Jamie Collins. I was given this address."

Jamie wondered who the man was and what he wanted. For a brief moment a panic ensued at the thought of being summoned to appear in court. Jamie anxiously got up from her chair and approached the window. She swallowed hard. "I'm Jamie Collins."

That's when the man lifted the bouquet of roses, a dozen long-stemmed, yellow buds. "These are for you. Have a good day."

Jamie took the vase from the man as he delivered them through the reception window. They were beautiful, and the vase was decorated with a bow tied with yellow, brown, and orange ribbons, bringing an autumnal feel to it. She took the card that had her name boldly printed on the outside of the envelope and opened it. It read, *I love you, Jamie* and it was signed Cody.

The delivery man was gone. She was alone in the office, grinning ear-to-ear. No man had ever sent her flowers before and no man, other than her father, had ever told her that he loved her. The experience was absolutely magical to her. Jamie was floating on air, but came down long enough to dial Cody's number, putting him on speaker. For the simple couple, the conversation was lovesick banter. For the bystander, a nauseating exchange, to say the least.

"Hello, beautiful," he said.

Jamie was feeling overwhelmed. "Cody, the flowers are beautiful. I don't know what to say."

"Say you love me, Jamie. I'll understand if you can't say those words, yet. I won't like it, but I'll understand."

"I do love you, Cody. Probably more than . . ."

Cody was full of anticipation. "More than what, Jamie?"

"I was going to say, probably more than you love me."

"I don't think that's possible, Jamie."

"I dream about you every night," she admitted.

"I dream of you, both night and day. Shoot, I practically severed my hand off working some cattle the other day—it was the daydreaming of you that had my head in the clouds."

The thought of Cody getting hurt pained her. "Oh, Cody, you have to be more careful. My heart aches being away from you like this. I miss your kiss . . . your touch."

"Jamie, you need to be strong. Friday night isn't that far off. But I know, a week away from you seems like years."

"It doesn't have to be like this forever, does it, Cody?"

"No, my love. I don't think my heart could stand it."

Jamie felt the cold stare on her. She looked up to see Dr. Cortez standing over her. She felt herself blush, wondering how long he'd been standing there and how much he'd heard.

Cody's voice could be heard on the other end of the line. "Jamie? Jamie, are you there?"

She was struck with a sense of urgency. "Cody, I love you, but I got to go. Bye."

She felt bad about how abruptly she'd ended the call. She would explain it to Cody later. But right now, Dr. Cortez looked in a foul mood.

"Jamie, we don't pay you to gush over the phone

with your boyfriend. I see the answering machine is blinking, so I assume you have plenty of work to do to keep you occupied. But first, I need you to get me the number of the funeral home. I guess I need to start making some arrangements for Sara. It doesn't look like any of her *family* is going to step-up, but we don't know for sure, because the bungling police can't seem to find any of them."

Jamie had never seen that side of Dr. Cortez before—one of hostile sarcasm. It frightened her. Her response was soft, but squeaky. "Yes, sir."

"Oh, and one more thing," he growled. "Move those flowers back to the breakroom. You may not be aware of this, but some of our patients have allergies."

Jamie nodded to indicate she understood. She was afraid to speak, fearing her voice would crack. She was fighting back the tears as it was. She watched as her boss went into his office and slammed the door.

Jamie let a few minutes pass before she knocked on Dr. Cortez's office door, a sticky note with the funeral home's number on it in hand.

"Come in," he said.

"Here's the number of *Eternal Rest*."

Dr. Cortez barely looked at her before snatching the piece of paper from her hand. "Thank you, Jamie," he said curtly. "That'll be all."

Jamie knew there was something she needed to

tell him, but she was nervous and didn't want to get yelled at. "Dr. Cortez, the accountant called and he wanted to speak with you or Dr. Wallace about . . . about . . ."

"About what, Jamie?" Richard demanded.

Jamie bowed her head, letting her face fall in her hands. She started to cry and ran out of the office, saying, "I don't know. I can't remember."

The pressure was getting to him. Richard hadn't wanted to admit it, but that was a fact. It seemed that everywhere he turned, he was confronted by curious busy-bodies who wanted the inside scoop on the high-profile lawsuit or his girlfriend's mysterious death. But Jamie running out of his office bawling was proof-enough—he was stressed and he took it out on her, acting like a jerk. He got up and ran after her. "Jamie, Jamie, look, I'm sorry."

Forty-five

Wednesday, November 15, 2017 10:40 a.m.

The mid-November morning hadn't gone well. First the run-in with Jamie, now the battle of wills. Richard didn't trust the man sitting across from him, knowing the detective didn't have his best interest at heart. Richard wasn't going to be intimidated. They were staring each other down, each trying to get a read on the other. The true intention of Detective Monroe's visit to his office hadn't been established. He was fishing for something, but Richard hadn't exactly figured that out yet. The physician knew he had to tread lightly.

"Dr. Cortez, I asked you when you last saw Sara Townsend," the detective repeated.

"The last I knew of Sara was when my partner informed me that she'd called her, sounding distressed."

"But I asked you when you last *saw* her, physically laid eyes on her."

Richard was agitated. All he wanted were answers from the police . . . not conjuring up more questions. "But what does it matter? If she was physically able to call Dr. Wallace, that was prior to her demise. Dr.

Wallace came to find me when she couldn't reach me by phone. I'd been doing a consult, thinking it would go to voicemail, but I forgot my mailbox was full. After she told me what happened, that's when I went looking for Sara."

"What I'm wondering, Dr. Cortez, is why you're evading the question? You just keep circling back to the call between Ms. Townsend and Dr. Wallace. If this is going to take all day, we're going to have to take this discussion down to the station."

It took everything Richard had not to lose his temper, but he knew to do so would only work to his detriment. "Do you know what I'm wondering, Detective? I'm wondering why you came to my office today? You asked to see me, implying that you had information for me regarding Sara's death and what happened to her. Instead, this feels more like an interrogation. Next, you'll be asking if Sara and I had problems."

Detective Monroe remained stone-faced. "Did you?"

"No!" Richard loudly exclaimed.

Monroe wasn't fazed by the man's outburst. "So, you're not going to tell me the last time you saw her?"

"Maybe, when you tell me why you're questioning me like I'm some sort of suspect."

The detective laid it on the line. "Because it's possible Sara Townsend was murdered."

That wasn't a slip of the tongue. The detective purposefully put the information out there to gauge the physician's response to the news. It was one of shock, but was it an act or was it genuine, Monroe wondered.

The detective continued. "We've failed to establish a solid link between Ms. Townsend and Mr. Anderson. However, . . ."

Richard interrupted, a sarcastic tone to his voice. "Wait, wait, let me guess. There is an indirect link to Sara and Kyle Anderson, and that link is me."

Monroe cocked his head to the realization. "You said it, not me. The way I see it, the animosity between this office and the administration at the Medical Center is pretty much common knowledge. That, on top of the fact that the hospital has been drawn into the Murphy malpractice case, has to have strained the relationship even further."

The physician, again, mocked the detective's logic. "What, so kill Sara Townsend and place her in Anderson's pool? That's ridiculous. You're out of line, Monroe. What you and so many others have failed to see about Sara was the fact that she'd led a hard life. Sure, she wasn't what you'd call book-smart or refined, but she was determined to live the best possible life on her own terms . . . not yours, not mine. Have you guys even tried to contact her mother? If she's in the state's prison system, surely, the police can track her down."

"If it was only so easy," the detective explained. "The victim's mother was released from prison two years ago. She violated the conditions of her parole, so it's been revoked. The authorities have been unable to locate her. The theory is, and it's just that . . . a theory, mind you, that the family is sheltering her somewhere off the grid and that's why we haven't been able to locate a single-one of them."

The story only made Richard more adamant in his defense of Sara's behavior. "Do you see my point, then? What chance does a child have growing up in that sort of family?"

"Tell me something, Doctor. Are you aware of the statistic that about eighty percent of individuals from low-income homes are unable to swim? A co-worker of Sara's told me Sara was deathly afraid of the water. Makes a person ask what she was doing in a pool, especially this time of year."

Richard was exasperated. "Detective, this whole situation is puzzling. Sara and I only began dating early autumn, and with the holidays approaching, it would be highly unlikely that swimming would even enter into the conversation. In fact, I know very little of this situation with Sara other than what I've been told. The only thing I seem to know for sure is that Sara just couldn't seem to catch a break."

Monroe wasn't sure what to make of the guy. "Are you some sort of champion of all the down-trodden or is it Sara Townsend's situation in particular that has you so impassioned?"

The comment angered Richard. He hit back. "Tell me, Detective, what has made you so callous and cynical? Is it the day-to-day dealings with society's failings, or are these the toxic results of a cold and indifferent mother?"

The jab hit a little too close to home. Detective Monroe felt the blow, but he couldn't let it show. "Are you done, now? It's time you tell me about the last time you saw Sara Townsend alive."

"I want to know how Sara died," Richard demanded.

"I'm usually not one to haggle for information, Dr. Cortez, but in this case, I'll play. I mean, after all, you are a physician and I don't think it would be that difficult for you to get your hands on a copy of her death certificate. It was drowning."

The detective, again, tried to judge the physician's response, but the man's affect was flat. He wondered if the physician had dealt with death on such a regular basis that the specifics didn't seem to faze him.

"It's my understanding that drowning homicides

are difficult to prove, if that indeed is your intention. No indication that she just fell in?" Richard inquired.

"No," the detective replied. "The victim was found in a place she wouldn't ordinarily have been. I mean, Anderson wasn't exactly hosting a pool party that weekend, was he?"

Richard tried to explain. "I guess I was just trying to look for a plausible explanation. I don't want to think this, but is there any chance Sara and Kyle knew each other intimately? I mean, I just didn't know her for that long. Everybody has a history, right?"

Monroe had no intention of answering the man's question. "Your turn," the detective said.

"What?"

"I want to hear about the last time you saw Sara alive."

Richard was still hesitant. "It's kind of personal."

The detective reminded him of the deal they'd made. "There's no one here but you and me, so tell me what you know."

"Fair enough. Last Thursday, it was Sara's birthday. She'd turned thirty, so it was some sort of milestone for her. I don't know about you, but it seems like certain people, women especially, start to think that their youthful life is something of the past and that it's all downhill from there. Anyway, she likes . . . I mean she liked to go to what she called fancy restaurants, getting all dolled-up. So, I took her to this French bistro that Callie likes, but of course, I didn't tell Sara that fact. When it came to my partner, Sara had quite a few insecurities. The fact that their birthdays were only a couple of weeks apart, I felt like I was walking a really fine line."

The detective wanted clarification. "This bistro, is it the one on the square?"

"Yes, anyway, we had a nice dinner, even though I'd take a good burger any day. Afterwards, we took a stroll around the square and talked. I was on call and really couldn't commit to a lengthy evening."

"What did you talk about?" Monroe inquired.

"The future, mostly. I think it was the first time I ever heard her be so positive about what the future held for her . . . for us."

"Anything mentioned about her plans for the weekend? Perhaps, she had a little too much to drink?"

Richard shook his head. "No, nothing like that. She was really up, pretty optimistic. I don't know if you can understand how hard it is for someone from Sara's background to have hope . . . to believe in something or someone."

The detective was finally beginning to see a common connection. "Would someone understanding what it's like to come from a troubled home be someone like you, Dr. Cortez? Is that why you've been so sympathetic to Ms. Townsend's circumstance?"

"Yes, Detective, Sara would be someone *just like me*."

Monroe was curious. "Tell me, Doctor . . . do you swim?"

Forty-six

Thursday, November 16, 2017 11:55 a.m.

It was a rare November day. When the hostess of *La Pomme d' Amour* asked if the two women wanted to eat alfresco, they took advantage of it. It was sixty-eight degrees and beautiful. The high was to reach seventy-two before a cold front was due to cross later in the day, bringing icy conditions.

"Marta, I can't believe this day," Rose said as she looked up to admire the clear, blue sky overhead. "Your idea to go to lunch was just what I needed. Callie raves about this place."

"Rose, I know how worried you've been about her. For an hour, this will take your mind off your troubles."

Rose wanted to relax, really, she did. "Marta, why is it that some mothers and daughters are so close and then some, like Callie and I, well, it feels like there's a chasm between us."

Marta shook her head. "I don't know the answer to that. I only hear from my son Raul four to five times a year. He's married to one of those high-society types in Connecticut. Do you know they've been married six years and not one grandchild? I think when they're born, the parents have all these expectations, but then inevitably get disappointed. You know what I'm saying . . . our hopes and dreams are not theirs."

Contemplating what her friend had just told her, Rose said, "In my case, Marta, I think it is Callie that is disappointed in me. Marta, did you hear me?"

Marta had been looking at a young couple that were seated by the door to the inside dining room. They were in love, it was obvious. "I'm sorry, Rose. I guess I couldn't keep my eyes off the two over there. The ones getting ready to leave. The way they were looking at each other, it took me back. There's nothing like young love and the way it makes you feel."

Rose turned to where Marta had been looking. The man had put down a tip and was helping his date with her chair. Their longing to be close was apparent. "They are a cute couple. Tell me, Marta, was it like that for you and Raul?"

Marta leaned in. "Rose, don't tell Raul this, but he wasn't my first . . . *in that way*. I'd told him I'd never been with a man, but in reality, that wasn't true. Even now, the thought of that man takes my breath away, but not in a good way. Anyway, it wasn't like Raul knew the difference."

A waitress appeared at their table with a bottle of Perrier and two glasses of ice. "Welcome ladies, my name is Colette and I'll be your server today. Can I offer you something else to drink besides water?"

Rose and Marta looked at each other with mischievous eyes.

"Shall we dare?" Rose playfully asked.

Marta giggled, consumed with guilty pleasure. "Let's do it."

Rose was careful with her pronunciation. "We'll have a bottle of Zind-Humbrecht Gewurztraminer, 2016, please."

"Very good, Madame," Colette replied. "May I show you a menu today or would you care to hear the special?"

Marta eagerly chimed in. "I'd like to hear the special."

"It is a *prix fixe* menu that includes a mixed salad or onion soup, followed by a chicken and mushroom crepe, a cheese course, and crème brûlée or carrot cake for dessert."

"That sounds decadent," Rose said with a devilish grin. "I'll take the special, with the salad and crème brûlée."

"Me, too," Marta echoed.

The women watched the waitress walk off with their order, pleased with their selection, but each of them cognizant of the elephant in the room. Marta felt compelled to get the topic out in the open. "Rose, is it Dallas and Tomas that's weighing so heavily on you?"

Rose nodded. "Callie brought it up, again, the summer of 1995. She suspects I'm hiding something from her, which I am. It was right before she was served those papers, in fact. I've been thinking of telling her. If I don't, how am I supposed to support her through this Murphy fiasco, if she doesn't completely trust me?"

Marta quickly looked around to see if anyone was within earshot. She was adamant. "Rose, you can't. We vowed to take this secret to our graves."

Rose wasn't one to break her word. "I know, I know. But Callie isn't a little girl anymore. She would keep our confidence."

"No, Rose, no. Even in her wildest imagination, she couldn't possibly picture you in such a scenario. So, let's leave it at that. Besides, there's more to it than just your relationship with your daughter at stake."

It was Marta's cautionary words that brought Rose back to the reality that silence was essential. But then there was something else. Something that Rose caught sight of out of the corner of her eye, across the street. It was the Timmons woman, pushing a grocery cart full of *stuff*.

Colette returned to the table with the bottle of wine and two glasses. She stripped off the foil that encased the neck of the bottle, then dislodged the cork, careful not to let a stray fragment fall into the wine. She poured each of the women a taste. They both smiled as the spicy, peppery ambrosia spilt over their tongues. The pleasant experience that had just begun as Colette filled their glasses half-full was about to go awry.

Rose glanced across the street, in hopes that the Timmons woman had moved on. Instead, her heart began to race as she saw her heading straight towards them. The only thing that separated the two women and the outside sidewalk was a waist-high rod iron fence. Rose tried to pretend she didn't see her, but it only took a second for their eyes to connect. The vagrant continued her trajectory, basket in tow.

Marta noticed that Rose was distracted. She followed her friend's line-of-sight to see the familiar woman. "Oh, no. Has she really sunk this low?" Marta mumbled aloud.

"You know her?" Rose asked.

"Unfortunately, yes," Marta confessed. "She was let go from the hospital. She has *problems*."

Rose figured the encounter was inevitable, but wanted to be wrong. "Oh, I hope she's not coming over here, surely not."

"She's making a beeline straight for us," Marta

acknowledged. "Maybe, we should move to a table inside."

The homeless woman was just a few feet away. Rose spoke the obvious. "It's too late."

Jane's mood was that of a bitter wisenheimer. "Marta, how's the mop and bucket?"

Marta was uncomfortable. "They're fine, Jane. I am, as well . . . thanks for asking," she said sarcastically.

The drifter smirked, looking around the chic restaurant grounds. "I can see that, Marta. I would think that you'd have better taste in the company you keep, though. You better watch your back before her daughter does to you what she did to me."

Marta noticed how Jane jerked her head in Rose's direction. She wasn't about to let such a dig at Rose's daughter go unchallenged. "Jane, I'm sorry for the difficulties you're experiencing, and for what it's worth, the hospital isn't the same without you. However, your current situation is of your own making. Until you stop seeing yourself as a victim, you're not going to be able to make the positive changes necessary to get your life back on track."

Jane didn't appreciate the housekeeper's self-righteous attitude. After all, she was sitting in a posh restaurant, drinking French wine. Jane had been on her way to the mission for a free lunch when she'd caught sight of the two. Her tone was harsh . . . and loud.

"Victim? Victim? I am a victim. I'm a victim of every sorry-ass individual who ever trampled all over my life, leaving me broken and alone."

Colette heard the disturbance and came rushing up to the table. "Ladies, is there a problem here? May I suggest we move you into the dining room for the remainder of the meal. I understand my manager is reporting this intrusion to the police."

The waitress began helping the patrons collect their belongings, moving with a sense of urgency and offering no additional options other than what she'd proposed. Rose and Marta obediently followed the woman without objection. Once inside, Colette closed the back door to the restaurant and locked it, shutting out the wild ramblings of the homeless woman outside. On the way to their new table, Rose stopped in her tracks, noticing no one was carrying the bottle of wine. She informed Colette, who reluctantly went back out to get it. The waitress was relieved to see that the transient was gone . . . but so was the wine from the Alsace region of France. Colette caught sight of the woman, a block down, taking a swig.

Forty-seven

Thirty-seven Years Earlier

Marta spat in the toilet, hoping the urge to retch wouldn't resurface. It was the dry heaves, but gagging just the same. She tried to keep the coughs and sputtering to a minimum, muffling what noise there was with the hum of an overhead bathroom fan. She told herself it was just nerves, nothing more. Part of her wanted to run home like a little girl, a part of her curious to the mysteries of the sexual realm that still eluded her. Marta knew Jackson Kendall was far more experienced than her. After all, he was twenty-six, and as far as Marta was concerned, the guy was worldly. And here she was, held-up in the bathroom of the man's apartment, trying to figure out her next move.

At eighteen, Marta's virginity was intact. She knew he knew. How could he not? Whether it was her clumsy caress, too much tongue . . . too little tongue, or her yanking her hand away as he placed it to his bulging crotch, her body language screamed amateur. She went over to the sink to rinse her mouth out. Looking up at the mirror, she saw water dripping off her chin and a complexion pale with fright. The diamond pendant he'd given her only a week ago fell delicately to her chest. It reminded her of what her mother had once said, sometimes a gift is not a gift, it's an obligation.

She knew the stone was real, just like the man's corvette, and his high-rise apartment in the upscale Highland Park region of Dallas. Marta was from Sperling, the sticks. She knew nothing of the city . . . or its fast-lane. The brilliance of the pear cut piece entranced her, taking her back to her first encounter with Jackson Kendall.

She'd dreamed of the excitement of the big city, and once graduated, Marta was on the first bus to Dallas. She landed up there with a couple of girlfriends. They pooled their money and rented an apartment, but needing jobs. One of her girlfriends got a job at the mall, working for a chain retailer. The other got a job at a convenience store, the nightshift. The other two told her that it could be dangerous, but she wanted the shift pay. For herself, Marta worked in an upscale tobacco shop, specializing in imported cigars. That's where she met him, when he asked for a box of Cedrus Belicoso Fino. He told her he was in pharmaceuticals. She was pretty naïve. It never occurred to her to question it. She was caught up in the thrill of it all. One of the first things that caught her attention was how most people would react when she told them who she was dating, the hesitation. Marta chalked it up to the man's importance, and their envy of her significance to him. One of her girlfriends had the guts to tell her the diamond necklace she was wearing was paid for with blood money. It was through a friend of a friend, that kind of thing, so she didn't want to believe it.

A knock came to the bathroom door. "Marta, you doing okay in there?"

"I'm fine, Jackson. Just a little embarrassed, is all. I guess the wine went down the wrong pipe. I'll be out in a minute."

But last night was proof enough. He was taking her home after the movies when he suddenly slammed on the brakes as he pulled the car to the curb. Marta saw the frightened look on the boy's face. He couldn't have been more than fifteen, at the most. He took off running. Jackson reached over her to the glove compartment. The lid fell open as he popped the latch. The handgun sat inside. Marta had never even seen a gun except on a policeman's hip, but there it was, just a couple of feet away. Jackson grabbed it and started to get out of the car. He told her to stay put, but she didn't and afterwards wished that she would have.

The chase was on. The boy had a head start, but Jackson was gaining. They darted in and out between buildings until the boy made a fatal mistake. He made a split-second decision and entered a dollar store in hopes the crowd would deter Jackson. But it didn't. Jackson followed him in, dragging him out by the back of his shirt. The boy's legs came along, an afterthought as the back of his sneakers scraped the payment. Jackson's words to the onlookers, *mind your own fucking business, or you'll wish you had.*

Marta caught up with him in time to see Jackson dragging the boy down an alley. The boy's pleas fell on deaf ears. The piercing cries went weak, then silent. Marta couldn't be sure, but she thought the word for what she saw was pistol-whipping. Jackson seemed to be on auto-pilot until the boy's body became lifeless.

He looked up to see her standing at the top of the alleyway. Jackson walked towards her, a smug stride. He came up to her and kissed her hard on the mouth. His only explanation to her was, *he had it coming.* He put his arm around her, firmly directing her away from the scene. Marta took a quick glance back over her shoulder. The boy still wasn't moving.

She heard him from the other side of the door. Marta grabbed the edge of the sink, frozen in fear. "Marta, I've tried to be patient. Don't be a tease. A man has needs. You have to understand that."

Marta hadn't intended to keep their date that night, but she was frightened about how Jackson would handle rejection—not well, she surmised. She'd already told her roommates she had to go back to Sperling because of a family emergency. Marta planned to be consistent with her lie. She didn't want Jackson to be suspicious. She needed to sound convincing.

He'd been aggressive with her ever since she'd arrived that night. It was if she'd seen his true nature the evening before, so there was no longer the need for polished charm and flattery. It was what she feared, she knew too much. But he wanted her, and to get out of the untenable situation, she was going to make sure he got what he wanted.

Marta didn't want his hands on her any longer than necessary. She began to undress, wrapping his monogrammed towel around her. She held her head high despite, wearing only his towel and his necklace, being stamped as his possession. Jackson was there when Marta opened the door. She let the towel drop and stood in the doorway like a treasured hood ornament to an expensive car.

Jackson liked what he saw. "Now, that's more like it. No more games."

"No more games," Marta confirmed with a disingenuous smile.

Marta fought every urge to cover herself. She let him touch her. She'd read about foreplay, but it would only prolong what she didn't want. "Take me to bed," she said.

She'd gone over it and over it, the *things* to say to expedite the encounter. Marta knew the experience would take her virginity, but it was the lead-out of the horrible situation she found herself in. If she had second thoughts, all she had to do was envision the boy's body in the alley. She would let the criminal take her and then find a way to break the news to him that a situation beyond her control would take her back home. It would be a situation that he couldn't bully, thrash, or kill.

His mouth was all over her. She thought in a panic, what were the *things* she'd rehearsed? Oh yeah, *stick it to me, Jackson, give it to me, ram me.*

Marta felt the pressure between her legs, heard the grunting. She'd heard men like to hear their names called out. *Oh, Jackson. Oh, Jackson, you're all man.*

It was working, he was going at her with a voracious appetite. She didn't want to say it, that word, blah. She'd made up her mind. After tonight, she'd only be with a man she loved. That man would be her real first. It was time. She needed to get that awful word out. *I have to have it now, Jackson. Give me your jism.*

Marta was almost brought to tears with relief when it was over. But there was something she hadn't expected, a glitch in her plan . . . the sight of the stained sheet. She saw Jackson take note of it, but she had to see it through.

"Were you a virgin, Marta?"

"Jackson, it was everything I thought it would be. It was fabulous. You were great, you made it so special."

The man was so caught up in his own ego, Marta thought he might actually start strutting around.

She knew it was now or never. "I do hate to mention this, though, but I'm going to have to go back home tomorrow. I hope that won't present a problem."

"Home? But we're just getting to know each other a little better. You're not skipping out on me, are you, baby?"

"No, nothing like that, Jackson, I swear. You see, my mother needs me. She has cancer."

"Cancer?"

"Yeah, it's breast cancer. She's in a bad way."

Forty-eight

Friday, November 17, 2017 10:35 a.m.

The storm had blown off, but the air was heavy and cold, skies overcast and gray. Bleak was the word that came to mind. The day weighed on the shoulders of the sparse few that had gathered, particularly Richard. Perhaps it was the obscure sheen of ice on the black top that resulted in such a meager showing that Friday morning, or it may have been the picture that Richard had painted of Sara's life— one fraught with hardship, turmoil, and loneliness that said it all. Besides she and Richard, only a handful of people were in the tiny chapel, making it look exactly like it was . . . small. *It's all for the best, Richard. A good Sara is a dead Sara, Callie thought.*

Sara's coffin was all-consuming in the crossing before the altar. Prior to the service, there was an open casket. But when Richard observed that the paltry showing of onlookers seemed to be gawking instead of paying their genuine respect, he had it closed. He called those in the pews to come forward to join him in prayer. It seemed more communal than just two people scattered on the right-hand side of the aisle, four on the other. Richard stood stoic, a somber proxy for her troubled family no one could seem to find, despite the fact that he'd only known Sara for six weeks. The whole situation was sad . . . really sad.

After reading some verses from scripture, Richard informed the small group that, due to the weather, the graveside portion of the service was cancelled, but announced a meal was being served in the adjacent room for the mourners.

Callie happened to look around to notice the awkward glances between those present, as if they were wondering if anyone was actually going to stay. Despite all the trouble Sara had brought to her life, she felt compelled to intervene on Richard's behalf. "Everyone, I know each of us have our own reasons for attending Sara Townsend's service today, despite the weather. But I was hoping that while we are all here anyway, we could fix a plate and share those stories over some good food and a cup of hot coffee."

A couple of women looked unsure and seemed to be edging their way to the door while putting on their jackets. What Callie did next, she did for Richard. She begged, "Please, please, stay for just a little while."

The two women were about out the door when guilt washed over them. They felt self-conscious and looked around the chapel at those that remained. They shared a quick glance as if in agreement to stay, taking off their coats.

Callie came up the rear as the small group sheepishly lumbered into the make-shift dining hall. She was taken aback when she finally entered the room. There had to be enough food there to feed fifty people. It was sad . . . really sad.

Each of them had filled their plate, sitting at a large round table. It was so large that an empty seat was left between them. When Callie approached the table, she did a quick count. There'd been six of them, initially, but now the count was down to five. "Where did the other woman go, the one in the blue coat?"

"I saw her sneak out the side door," a young woman at the table said.

Callie addressed her. "Hi, my name is Callie Wallace. And you are?"

"My name is Minnie. I worked with Sara at the bank. I mean, not directly. You see, I work in the basement—I'm a proof operator. The loan department is on the fourth floor."

Callie had a flash-back to her encounter with Sara at the bank. She regretted ever having gone to the bank to see her that day. "Well, your paths must have crossed at some point?"

"Yes, ma'am,"

Callie took the young twenty-something lady to

be respectful. "Minnie, would you mind sharing your experience with us?"

"It was in the ladies' room, the one in the basement. It was about a half hour before I got off. She was crying, said none of the other women in her department liked her. She said it was her birthday, but no one had even said a word, no card, no cake, no nothing. She did perk up a bit when she mentioned having dinner plans at a really posh restaurant later that night."

The two middle-aged women who'd been trying to leave earlier exchanged a knowing look. Callie wondered if they were from the loan department. She recalled her own surprise party and all the well-wishers that had come out to celebrate with her, including Sara.

Minnie continued. "But she teared up again. She said the only birthday card she'd received was one from her insurance agent that wished her a happy birthday and thanked her for her business. I felt bad. I didn't know what to do, so I offered to go out with her for a quick drink after work. I didn't think she'd actually take me up on it, but she did. We went out, but it was weird. We didn't have anything to talk about other than some small talk about the bank. That's the last I saw of her, well, uhm . . . until today."

"Oh," was all Callie could manage to say.

The middle-aged women, one fair complected, the other darker and raven-haired, looked at each other, wondering if they should share their experiences with the group. Finally, the dark-haired woman cleared her throat and spoke. "We worked with Sara in the loan department. I wouldn't necessarily describe her as the friendly type."

The fair-skinned woman backed her up. "I should say not. One of the last times we saw Sara was late Thursday afternoon. She was going on and on about some dinner plans she had at *La Pomme d' Amour* with some doctor. If that was the guy conducting the service this morning, he didn't seem all that great to me."

Callie took offense, but she didn't want to alienate the woman. "Richard does have a lot of positive qualities, but I guess you have to get to know him first. Had Sara never introduced him to any of her co-workers?"

The fair-skinned woman answered. "Not that I'm aware of. But the way she bragged about him was endless. After a while, a person really tires of it. And from what I saw this morning, he just seems like your average Joe to me."

The raven-haired woman put her two-cents worth in. "I'd never met him either. Sara did mention she'd planned to do whatever it took to get this guy to the altar, and I mean whatever, and when she did, she was going to tell our supervisor to go to hell."

The only man at the table appeared eager to speak.

Callie provided the opportunity. "You're from Sara's apartment, right?"

"Yeah, look, is Dr. Cortez around?"

"I'm sure he's around here, somewhere," Callie replied. "Perhaps, he's finishing up with the funeral director."

The man was adamant. "Well, I want to talk to him. I owe him one big apology. I feel like such a heel, the way I treated him and all."

The fair-skinned woman's interest was piqued. "It may not be any of my business, but may I ask what this is in reference to?"

"I was Sara Townsend's landlord. Dr. Cortez had come by her place to see about her. When I caught him in her apartment, and her not being there, I made him leave. He was trying to tell me something was wrong, and I wouldn't listen. If I'd just given him the benefit of the doubt . . . I feel partly to blame."

Callie was reassuring. "You shouldn't think like that. I can't be certain, but to the best of my knowledge, the police haven't publicly indicated if Sara's death was an accident or not."

"I got a lot of guilt. I do feel partially responsible . . . and nobody is going to convince me otherwise, understand? Maybe I should try to go find Dr. Cortez," the landlord insisted.

That was enough to trigger the rest of the antsy group to disband, their plates barely touched.

Callie went outside in the hopes of finding Richard. She caught up with him just in time to see him shaking hands with the landlord. Then the landlord took off. Richard sat on the steps of the funeral home, burying his face in his hands.

Wrapping her coat tightly across her chest, Callie took a seat beside her friend. "It's cold out."

"Is it? I hadn't noticed."

"Where have you been?" Callie inquired.

"I accompanied Sara to her final resting place. Talk about cold, she's resting in the ground . . . the cold, hard ground."

"Richard, try not to think like that."

"I can't help it. She had no one . . . no one."

"She had you."

"Callie?"

"Yeah?"

"Can we just sit here . . . just sit? Let's not talk. Sometimes, just being there is enough, okay?"

"Okay," Callie replied.

Ding!

It was Callie's phone, a text from Jamie to call the accountant.

"Anything important?" Richard asked.

"Nay, nothing that can't wait," she said, pocketing her phone.

Forty-nine

Friday, November 17, 2017 5:10 p.m.

Marcus had caught wind that Kyle Anderson's home had been searched and drove straight to the station after work. He was caught off guard when he entered the squad room. Instead of plain-clothes and uniformed officers going about their usual routine, he saw law enforcement personnel dressed as an elf, a candy cane, Tom Turkey, a cornucopia, a pilgrim, and a reindeer. The mood was festive and light, all except Detective Monroe sitting at his desk with his sleeves rolled up and a scowl on his face.

"Where's your costume, Monroe?" Marcus jokingly asked.

"Very funny, Davis. What's up?"

"Wait, first things first," Marcus replied. "I know, you're Scrooge, right?"

The detective wasn't in the mood. "Sperling's *Lights on the Square Parade* is tonight, officially kicking off the holiday season. Officers intermingle with parade participants to keep an eye on the crowd, make sure it proceeds in an orderly fashion, and keep things family friendly. It never fails, every year some punk tries to ruin everyone's good time. Now, what can I do for you?"

"I wanted to know if anything came from the search of Kyle Anderson's home."

Frustrated, Monroe threw his pen down on his desk. His voice was loud enough to quiet the squad room. "You've got some nerve, Davis. You strut in here like you own the place with your smug big-city attitude and we're all supposed to lay out the red-carpet for you, all the while turning a blind-eye to your motives. The Townsend case is *my* case and I would appreciate it if you would keep your *nose* out of it."

Marcus felt a little self-conscious being called out in front of everyone. He quickly glanced over in the direction of the captain's office, but the door remained shut. He didn't even know why he'd done it. Marcus wasn't a trainee anymore and the thought of Monroe's superior having to intervene on his behalf was emasculating. "I'm sorry you feel that way, Detective."

Marcus's glance in the direction of the captain's office didn't go unnoticed by the detective. He stood up from his desk. His attitude remained hostile. "Don't be looking for the captain to get you out of this situation—this is between me and you."

"He's gone, isn't he? That's why you chose this opportunity to pick your fight," Marcus challenged.

"Doesn't matter whether the captain is here or not. This has been a long-time coming," Monroe chided.

Marcus tensed up as those in the squad room started chanting, *fight*, *fight*. So much for the holiday spirit, he thought. "I think we should talk . . . in private."

Monroe came out from behind his desk, emboldened by the chant, but he didn't give into it. "Let's do it—the interrogation room." That was followed by the room vocalizing their disappointment that a physical altercation hadn't materialized.

Marcus closed the door after entering the cold room. Monroe had already taken a seat, his body posture signaling his mind was closed off. "Look, Detective, I get why you're upset, but you know the drill."

"Davis, don't lecture me on protocol. The fact of the matter is that I'm not going to disclose information to you on an on-going investigation when I have no clue regarding your intentions, knowing that if I did, it might ultimately hurt my case."

"You didn't have an issue talking to me the other day," Marcus reminded him.

"That was before I found out you'd been snooping around the Floyd Ferguson crime scene behind my back. Stay out of my way, Davis. I mean it."

Marcus was steamed. He picked up one of the metal chairs around the interrogation table and flung it backwards, up against the wall. "That's a shit excuse and you know it! I was just asked if I knew the guy, and that was it. I wasn't withholding anything relevant from that case, so why don't you cut out the bullshit? I know local law enforcement and outsiders don't always get along, but you've been ordered to cooperate."

Now Monroe was on his feet. If the situation was going to come to blows, the detective wasn't going to be caught sitting on his ass. "I'm telling you right now, Davis, if you want any more information from me, you're going to have to come clean. Otherwise, this conversation is over."

Marcus had his suspicions about the detective's behavior. When an investigation hits a wall, like his Medical Center case, nerves are raw and tempers flare from nothing more than sheer frustration. He put his hands up as if to surrender. "Okay, what do you want to know?"

Monroe relished his small victory. "Are you with the feds and what exactly is your interest in Kyle Anderson?"

Marcus sat down, a gesture of cooperation. "I'm out of the FBI field office in Houston. We've been working a case of interstate organ trade. A couple of bodies from the hospital morgue at the Medical Center had brain tissue samples crudely extracted. A young South Korean student doing a rotation there landed up dead. Her family has some diplomatic connections, making some noise, so I was sent to find out if there was any connection."

"So, you think Anderson is somehow involved?" Monroe inquired.

"There was a couple of things I wanted to follow up on, but I've come up with zip. Look, the other day, when I was trying to throw suspicion off Anderson in the Townsend case, it wasn't like I was trying to get a murderer out of jail. One thing I do know about the man is that he's no murderer. He's more like a poindexter with a big chip on his shoulder."

Monroe's stern demeanor cracked, thinking of the comparison the visiting agent had just made. "Well, I think that might actually be something we agree on."

Marcus was expecting tit-for-tat. "Okay, your turn."

"We've failed to turn up any concrete connection between Anderson and the victim. All we found in the house search was nothing more than a bunch of ostentatious crap, things like a monogrammed Waterford Crystal bar set, a commercial grade kitchen, but no food in the house, and a set of high-end golf clubs. I understand he fancies himself quite the golfer. I went out to the club where he's a member, asking around about him. He's a high-handicapper and the pro out there described him as a duffer. He strikes me as a guy who's always wanted to be somebody, a major player, but instead, he's a poindexter, like you said, and a loner. The victim died from drowning, but as far as it being accidental or a homicide, the autopsy was inconclusive. All it turned up, of any significance, was stomach contents with undigested raisins. How am I supposed to make a case with damn raisins?"

"The neighbors didn't hear anything? Any surveillance footage?"

Shaking his head, Monroe replied, "I spoke to the neighbors. They say the place stays quiet—no parties, no barbeques. They don't understand why he keeps such a large home when it's just him"

"Appearances," Marcus said.

"Exactly," Monroe confirmed.

"Did you have a chance to talk to the boyfriend?" asked Marcus.

"Yeah," the detective said. "From what I could gather, their brief relationship was cemented in the fact that they both were from troubled homes. He was on call that night they went to dinner, like he said. Friday morning, he had back to back procedures at the hospital with a consult at noon."

Marcus thought Monroe's investigation was going about as well as his was, nowhere. "So, what is supposed to be the significance of the raisins?"

"According to the medical examiner, studies

support that about five percent of people have recognizable food contents in their stomach after death. The percentage goes up to nineteen percent four hours after death. So, it's almost five times more likely the victim consumed raisins up to four hours before her death. Dr. Wallace reports a phone call . . ."

Marcus stood up. "Dr. Callie Wallace?"

"Yeah, anyway, she receives this call from Ms. Townsend between noon and one on Friday that goes dead. That would lead me to believe that she consumed raisins somewhere between eight and nine that morning, give or take an hour. That's if she died soon after the phone call."

Marcus started to pace. "All that and it just sounds like she had raisin bran for breakfast."

"Yeah, I know," Monroe said, watching the agent walk back and forth. "But the only cereal we found in her apartment was some multi-colored kiddie cereal, the one with the rabbit. I tell you, it's frustrating as hell. And to top it off, I was called to a homicide last night of a homeless man down in the warehouse district. The poor slob died from trauma to the brain, from the nose. A bloody awl was found a few feet from him. We think it's the murder weapon. Know anything about that?"

Marcus couldn't believe his ears, a stroke of luck. "Monroe, I need to see that file, no joke, everything you got," he said in an official tone.

The detective was having trouble getting a read on the agent and his sudden restless mood. "Okay, okay, Agent Davis. Is that what has you so worked up?"

Marcus shook his head. "No, but don't get me wrong. The homeless man, that might be the break I've been looking for. It was your mention of Dr. Wallace. Unless you have something to back up this supposed call, she may not be the credible witness you might think."

The detective didn't know what to make of the information, but he wasn't going to dismiss it. "Davis, let me get you that file. Oh, and about earlier, the case, it's just been getting to me. I hope you can understand. In fact, my brother is DEA. According to him, it's not local police and the feds that have such a problem getting along. It's when one government agency goes up against another that the gloves come off."

Marcus knew there was a lot of truth to what the detective had said. "Monroe, forget it. Maybe, we just might be able to help each other out," he declared.

Fifty

Friday, November 17, 2017 7:00 p.m.

If Hollywood wanted to entrance movie goers with small-town America, the ticket-holder could rest assured that the hamlet would model a town such as Sperling. In the center of the town square sat the county courthouse. From its roof, ascending tall toward the sky, was the domed-topped clock tower. The clock kept impeccable time. It served as the mainstay by which all community events in Sperling began and ended. Quaint shops lined the square, storefronts proudly touting American flags that gently unfurled to a brisk breeze off the lake. The slow-paced, lazy North Texas town had a certain allure whether it was the latest drama being performed at the Playhouse, the outdoor concerts, or a tour of the local brewing company. But that night, the businesses were quiet. With a little less than a week to Thanksgiving, the grand clock chimed seven times, and the *Lights on the Square Parade* was underway.

Callie and Zane held hands as they tried to make their way, zigzagging through the crowd. She knew she should've come earlier to get them a good spot to watch the parade, but she waited for Zane to drive in. She was also trying to convince Richard to come out and see it, thinking it would be a good distraction for him, but he'd volunteered for call that weekend—something to keep his mind busy, he'd said. He'd reasoned that, if an emergency were to occur, it would be too difficult to navigate the hordes of people and the traffic to get to the hospital in a timely manner. Deep down, she knew her colleague was right, but as far as her friend was concerned, she didn't think it was good for him to spend too much time alone.

Despite the couple's attempts to navigate the crowd, it was still difficult to get a clear view. Between the shoulder-to-shoulder line of people on the front row, Callie was able to see the lead vehicle. It was a tractor decked out in lights, pulling a flat-bed trailer with a choir of youngsters in shiny, burnt orange robes singing a harvest song.

Callie felt someone bump-up against her. She turned to see a woman in her late fifties who seemed to recognize her. "Excuse me, young lady. Lately, I've been all-thumbs. Hey, wait, I know you. You're that lady doctor—the one that everybody's been talking about. Do you remember me? We met at the Fourth of July festivities, right down here on the square. My husband introduced us."

"I'm sorry, but I don't," Callie replied.

Zane felt like he needed to intervene. “Is there a problem here?”

Not much ever left Delores Ferguson with a loss for words, but in this circumstance, she felt flabbergasted. “Oh, no, no. My, you’re handsome. Dr. Wallace, is this your fella?”

Callie wasn’t sure about the woman who apparently knew her name. “This is Zane Atkins, but you’re going to have to refresh my memory. You are?”

“My name is Delores Ferguson. My husband works at the Medical Center. I think you know him, Gus Ferguson? He works in maintenance. I didn’t mean to interrupt your night out, but I did want to tell you how bad I feel about the legal troubles hanging over your head.”

Zane felt a need to protect Callie. “Mrs. Ferguson, we’re just trying to have a good time. I don’t think Dr. Wallace wants to go into any on-going issues, legal or otherwise, okay?”

“Well, I didn’t mean any harm, Mr. Atkins. Really, all I wanted to do was offer her our support. Dr. Wallace, Gus and I are in your corner.”

Callie smiled at the generous gesture. “Thank you, Mrs. Ferguson, it means a lot. Is your husband not here, tonight?”

Delores took a quick look around. Distracted, she mumbled, “Oh, he’s around here, somewhere. He said something about getting some hot chocolate, but I thought he'd be back by now." Then she got off-topic, someone catching her eye. "What in the world is *she* doing here?"

"Who?" Callie asked.

Delores pointed to about thirty degrees to her left. "*She* is such a busy-body. Always in everybody's business. I can see her husband's not here, probably can't bear to show his face. I wonder who's that woman with Marta?"

Callie's eyes followed the trajectory of the woman's finger. Her line of sight came to rest on a familiar face. "Mrs. Ferguson, that's Rose Wallace. She's my mother."

"Oh, no," Marta said.

"What is it?" Rose asked.

"It's not a what, but a who. It's that Delores Ferguson. She's right over there with Callie, see? That woman gets on my last nerve."

Rose caught sight of her daughter. "Humph, I guess Callie couldn't think to include me in her holiday outing. She's with her boyfriend. I suppose I'd be nothing more than a third wheel. Is the Ferguson woman the one next to them?"

"Yeah, that's her."

"What's your beef with her, Marta?"

"I work with her husband at the Medical Center, not in the same department, of course. His name is Gus. We used to take smoke breaks together, but he's quit and told me his wife quit as well. She keeps telling people I'm a gossip, and who knows what else. If I didn't know any better, I think Gus talks a little bit too much about me to his wife. You know, to light the flame of jealousy and fan it a bit. That's where I think her resentment of me originated . . . nothing more than jealousy."

Rose thought back. "Well, Marta, you've kept my secret all these years, and for that, I'm eternally grateful. Frankly, I don't know where my family would be today without you. And you know all too well what vicious emotions jealousy provokes."

Marta soberly nodded in agreement.

Rose perked up at the sight of her favorite float. "Here it comes, Marta. It's the Winter Wonderland float sponsored by First National. Have you ever seen such blend of shades—white, silver, blue, and gray hues against a dark sky with twinkling lights? It amazes me every year. I don't think I'll ever tire of it."

Marta's mood was somber. "Rose, speaking of First National, has Callie ever mentioned a Sara Townsend to you?"

Rose was caught up in the pageantry of the

procession, barely listening. “Hmm, I don’t think so, why?”

Marta’s mood persisted. “No reason. Just forget I ever said anything.” Then, the woman had a sudden turn in her tone . . . an anxious one. “Rose, don’t look! Quick, turn around! That woman with the grocery cart is headed our way—the one who stole our wine.”

But it was too late. Their eyes locked. Rose looked at Jane Timmons with pity, thinking of the cold Sperling nights and if the woman had anywhere to go. Suddenly, Jane changed her direction as if Rose’s compassionate stare was too much for her to bear.

The line at the concession stand was long and moving at a snail’s pace. The night sky was clear, resulting in plummeting temperatures. Marcus wanted coffee to take the chill off. Thankfully, the roads were dry, he thought. The icy conditions had cleared, and he wanted to see for himself what the brouhaha was all about. From a distance, he heard the marching band playing *Joy to the World* while the crowd cheered.

Instinctively, Marcus brushed his right upper arm when he felt some sort of nip sensation. He looked back over his shoulder. When nothing was there, he turned back facing forward in line—it hadn’t moved.

Suddenly, there it was again, like a pebble hitting him. This time he took a more careful look. At first, he didn't see anything, but there was just a familiar call. "Psst, Marcus, over here."

Marcus knew right away it was Gus Ferguson. He let his head drop in defeat, knowing the man wasn't just going to go away. He saw Gus in the shadows, behind a tree. Marcus regrettably got out of line, noticing how the person behind him quickly occupied the vacated spot. He made his way through some pine trash to converse, supposedly incognito. "Gus, I thought you'd be out enjoying the parade."

Gus spoke in a whisper. "Oh, I just come for Delores. She likes this sort of thing. But guys like us are always on duty. Isn't that right?" The comment was followed by a couple of winks.

The whole situation with Gus Ferguson made Marcus nervous. The man probably didn't know it, but he had enough information to blow his cover at the Medical Center. "What's with the winks, Gus?"

"Just part of it, isn't it?"

Marcus didn't want to play these games, but he knew he had to go along, at least for a little while longer. "Part of what?"

"The meat scam investigation, the black-market meats. I been meaning to tell you I've had trouble getting into Patsy's office when she's not there. Who would think getting access to her files would be like breaking into Fort Knox . . . like a fortress? I almost had an opportunity this afternoon, but my radio went off. I had another work order for the dictation room on the neuro floor. Can you believe it? That's three now in a matter of weeks. It has something to do with the fluorescent ballast. I'll get to it sometime next week. How is it going with you? Any new information for me?"

Marcus had trouble keeping up with Gus's train of thought. Marcus lowered his voice to barely above a whisper. "I have it from a very reliable source that this racket is big . . . bigger than any of us initially thought."

Gus was having trouble believing it. "Bigger than Patsy?"

With sad eyes, Marcus confirmed it. "Way bigger . . . way bigger. Tell me, Gus, what do you know about Dr. Callie Wallace?"

When confronted with the question, Gus panicked. "Sorry, Marcus, I got to go. I think I hear Delores calling me."

Fifty-one

Sunday, November 19, 2017 11:10 p.m.

Callie thought back on the weekend and how wonderfully everything had gone. It seemed like such a long time since she felt so carefree. Zane had left an hour-and-a-half ago for the ranch and had sent his obligatory text that he'd arrived safely. It was getting harder—the goodbyes. She'd picked up on his not-so-subtle comment about the strength of his parents' marriage that had afforded them the ability to build a strong family and grow old together. It was weighing on her—what she'd do in the event Zane proposed. Her life was a mess, but when she was with Zane, everything felt like it was going to be okay. She knew that feeling. It was one she had as a little girl and Daddy had the ability to make all things magically *better*. It'd be just like Zane to want to rescue her from all of life's struggles, but Callie had no intention of saddling him with her problems . . . and the Murphy lawsuit, it was a huge problem. Besides, Zane had his own troubles. He and his sister had been grappling with the fact that it was getting harder and harder to manage their parents' needs in the shift-like manner they had been using. It was his parents that had brought it up . . . *kids, we think it's time we go to one of those assisted living places*.

But that dilemma was for another day. She was to take over call from Richard at seven in the morning. She climbed into bed, hoping sleep would come easy. But she had no sooner closed her eyes before she heard, "Hey, Corky, are you awake?"

To that question, Callie felt her shoulder muscles stiffen up, and instead of opening her eyes, she squeezed them tightly shut. She didn't know why her deceased father was lurking around in her subconscious, but what was the alternative to these surreal dreams that seemed to border on an aberration, not sleep? She didn't hear anything else and thought that, maybe, the idea of her father was fleeting. Relieved, she opened her eyes, but there he sat. The look on her face said it all.

"Well, a howdy-do to you, too, Corky. I thought the days of you playing opossum were over. Girl, you're making me feel about as welcome as an ant at a picnic."

Reluctantly, Callie engaged the familiar specter. "Dad, it's not like I don't enjoy these talks, but on some level, they seem very unnatural, and frankly, not in my best interest."

Insulted, he replied, "Since when is your old man

'not in your best interest'? I've been looking out for your best interest since before you were born, young lady."

Being called young lady by her parents had never been a good thing. Callie tried to back-pedal to explain what she'd meant. "Dad, do you know what I almost went out and did?"

Her father shook his head in ignorance.

"Based on the latest head-trip I had in which you were the star, I went over to Mrs. Murphy's house in the hopes of finding some stolen painting. Do you realize how reckless that would've been for me to do?"

"No, Corky, but I bet you're going to tell me."

"You bet I am. I'm being sued by the Murphy's. They are a very powerful family, and they are suing me for medical malpractice, alleging I contributed to the death of the family patriarch. Here, you go on and on about hanging out with him and *the guys*, talking about fishing and stolen art. On a whim, I went to the FBI's National Stolen Art File and typed in *Fishing in the Spring* into the search box. The painting had indeed been stolen from the Art Institute of Chicago. So, what do I do? I go over to the Murphy estate, parked out front, thinking of ways I could gain entry into the house."

"Did you find it?" her father asked.

Callie was matter-of-fact with her response. "No,

I didn't find it, because I came to my senses and got the hell out of there." She became more emotional, frustrated. "Dad, I love you, but you're driving me crazy."

"Corky, I don't think you should bring H-E-double hockey sticks into . . ."

Callie was just about at her wits end. She cut him off mid-sentence. "Dad, can you just stop? I don't want to hear anything more about that stupid painting. You just don't get it, do you? My credibility is in question here. If I'd been found out deliberately misrepresenting myself, I would've tanked any case Mr. Deutch is trying to build for me."

"Oh, how is Hayden? I haven't heard from him in years."

"Dad, you've been dead for years."

"Corky, I've told you before, I died, but I'm not dead. Anyway, I always thought his type of fishing was just showy. It's freshwater fishing that is the true sport."

"Dad, can we stay on topic? What I'm trying to tell you is that if, and I mean a big if, Mrs. Murphy is complicit in stolen art, that is immaterial to the malpractice case against me. If I would've been caught over there, the only worthwhile thing my medical degree would be useful for is wrapping fish in."

The fisherman scoffed. "Corky, don't you think you're being a bit dramatic?"

"No, Dad, I do not."

"Well, I didn't know that what we discussed needed to be deemed appropriate. Tell me, Corky, what would you like to discuss?"

Callie felt strange bringing this up. "I have been wondering one thing. Have you ever met a man by the name of Kyle Anderson?"

Callie's father ruminated over the question a minute or so before responding, "Hmm, Kyle Anderson, the name doesn't ring a bell. Why do you ask?"

She was even more reluctant to elaborate. "Oh, it's nothing. It's just something I heard is all . . . something I heard in passing—that you knew that Kyle Anderson was too mean to die."

"Corky, one thing I know for sure these days is that no one is too mean to die. Now, I've told you before you have a parasite in your waters. What I mean by that is somebody is messing with you."

"Dad, if you're implying that I have an enemy out there somewhere, I think you are way off base. If anything, I'm probably too nice—a trait that hasn't always worked in my favor."

"Too nice, huh? Corky, that's not what Sara Townsend said."

Callie's heart started to race, and her breaths came short and quick. The fact that her father mentioned the woman's name was disturbing. She was hesitant to ask, but she did anyway. "Dad, have you met her?"

"The meeting was brief. It was kind of like you said, *in passing*. Did you know the poor dear was murdered?"

"Dad, this is important. Did she say who killed her?"

"Corky, before I answer that, can you tell me if this is a safe topic for us to discuss, or one of those forbidden ones you mentioned earlier?"

"Dad, that isn't funny. Now isn't the time for your saucy sense of humor. Now, did Sara Townsend tell you who killed her, yes or no?"

"Yes."

Callie was waiting for him to elaborate, but he kept quiet. Frustrated, she pushed him for an answer. "Who, Dad, who?"

"Well, it's complicated, Corky. You see, this parasite . . ."

Callie was losing patience with her father's ridiculous riddles. "Dad, I can't take any more of your fishing metaphors. Give me a name. Who's responsible for Sara Townsend's death?"

"She said it was you, Corky."

Callie sat straight up in bed in a panic, two fists full of hair in her hands, the sheets soaked in sweat. As she suspected, she was alone in the room.

Fifty-two

Monday, November 20, 2017 12:10 p.m.

Monday was sheet day. Delores stripped the bed, and with the dirty linens wadded up in her arms, she proceeded across the house to the laundry room. But in her jaunt to the washing machine, something stopped her in her tracks. Over the top of the rumpled bedding, she saw the back of someone's head. The person was sitting in Gus's thinking chair. She wasn't sure what to do—an intruder was in the house. She thought about screaming, but when she opened her mouth, nothing came out but a wheeze. Delores started to back away. She figured that if she could get to the kitchen, she could run out the back door.

"Delores?" the man uttered.

Then came the scream. She threw the laundry up in the air and darted for the kitchen. She was just about out the back door when she heard her husband scolding her. "For Pete's sake, Delores, what's got into you?"

It took Delores a few minutes to get her wits about her, but when she did, she gave it right back to Gus. "Old man, you scared the bejesus out of me. What in the world are you doing home in the middle of the day?"

Gus started to pick the sheets and the pillowcases up off the floor. "Is it a crime for a man to come home for lunch?"

Delores was flabbergasted, fanning herself with her hands. "It is when you haven't come home for lunch in ten years."

Gus didn't want to fight. He did what any man would do that had been married any length of time and wanted to stay that way—he apologized. "Look, Delores, I'm sorry. I guess I should've called and let you know I was coming."

That seemed to appease her, but then she became alarmed. "Oh, Gus, have you been fired? Why else would you be home in the middle of the day? What did you do?"

"No, Delores, it's nothing of the sort."

Fear and dread had overcome her. "Oh, then it's something worse. Gus, do you have the cancer? I knew I should've thrown out that microwave the very day you brought it home."

"Delores, calm down. I don't have cancer . . . not that I know of anyway. And for the last time, the microwave doesn't give you cancer, but cigarettes sure can. By the way, that's how I knew it was you behind me. All those years of smoking, you still wheeze when you get excited. You haven't been sneaking smokes while I'm at work, have you?"

"No, I haven't. You know what the doctor said. She said it could take several months before we start seeing some of the ill-effects of smoking start to reverse themselves. She told us that it's what we don't see that is already being repaired. Is that why you're here, to check up on me?"

Gus thought about it a minute, telling Delores that that was the actual reason he'd come home for lunch. But he knew it was wrong. He didn't want to come clean as to the real reason, but he knew Delores wasn't about to let it go. He was a creature of habit, and, well, Delores knew him better than anybody. "I had some thinking to do."

"Is that why you were sitting in your thinking chair?"

"Yeah."

"I tell you what, Gus. You hand me those sheets and I'll go throw them in the washer. You go and get situated in your thinking chair. I'll be there in a minute, and you can tell me what's got you so troubled."

Gus obediently handed the laundry to his wife, but then he scratched the back of his head and shuffled his feet. "Gosh, Delores, this is a work problem. It's a little complicated."

Delores had gone into the utility room off the

kitchen, preparing the load. She called out to her husband, "You go on to your thinking chair. I'll be right there. In all our years as man and wife, there hasn't been one thing we couldn't figure out if we put our heads together."

Gus did as he was told, and it wasn't long before Delores came in. She pulled up a chair and took a seat next to her husband. "Okay, Gus, lay it on me. What's the problem?"

He was hesitant, but he began to explain the situation. "Well, okay, so I've had these work orders to the same room on the same floor in just a matter of weeks, a thermostat, an outlet, and now a ballast. The room is just for physician dictation. So, I'm talking to this guy who works on that floor part-time about how odd the situation seemed. I think he's a speech therapist. Anyway, he said there's been two occasions that he knew of where the circuit breaker for that room had flipped. Instead of calling maintenance, he just flipped it back. He showed me which one it was, and sure enough, that was the breaker for that room. So, in the breaker panel, I threw an amp meter on the hotwire for that circuit, and something is pulling too many amps. I didn't see anything in that room that would account for it, just the standard stuff."

After listening intently, Delores gestured with confidence. "So, the real problem here is that you don't want to look like you don't know what you're doing, right?"

"Oh, jeez, Delores, do you have to put it that way?"

"Do you know what it sounds like to me?"

Gus couldn't believe he was about to ask the question. "What?"

"It seems to me that if one person at that hospital felt so inclined to do a DIY without calling maintenance, then why wouldn't someone else feel so inclined to jimmy rig something?"

"Delores, are you suggesting that someone has tied into that circuit as a kind of do-it-yourself project?"

"That's exactly what I'm saying, Gus. If I were you, I'd get back to that hospital, back to that room, and examine every nook and cranny of wall space, making sure there's not a wire or cord coming out that shouldn't be there. Open every cabinet, pull out every drawer and look back in there with a flashlight, and look for grommets in the countertops with cables fed through them or conduit housing."

Gus felt inspired by how Delores was attacking the problem with such energy. That's when it hit him. "Delores, I think you're on to something. What I need to be looking for is a junction box. But for someone to mess around with the hospital's electricity, to be able to read a circuit diagram, that would take a really smart person."

Delores just smiled. “Honey, hospitals are full of smart people. I ought to know, my husband works at one.”

She’d made his day. He felt himself choking up. “I love you, Delores.”

She patted his hand and looked him straight in the eye. “I love you, too, Gus. Now, have you had lunch?”

Gus’s creative juices were flowing. He couldn’t wait to get back to the hospital to attack the problem head on. “No, I left the lunch you packed me in the breakroom refrigerator. I’ll grab it when I have time. But right now, I need to get back to work.”

Delores got up from her chair and said, “Are you sure? I could whip you up a grilled-cheese sandwich. It’d only take a minute.”

Gus pecked his wife on the cheek. “Delores, you’re the best, but duty calls.”

Fifty-three

Monday, November 20, 2017 2:20 p.m.

Callie sat in Richard's office in silence. She watched him gently run his finger along the edges of a frame that held some photo booth pictures. They were of Sara and Richard, some kissing, some just acting silly—they were happy. His eyes were sorrowful, but a hint of a smile was on his lips as if he was replaying a fond moment he'd shared with Sara in his mind.

It was the holidays—the harbinger of stress. Thanksgiving was approaching, office visits were down, and emergency calls were up. People tended to overindulge, and that, combined with family stressors, often landed an overweight, hypertensive person in a hospital bed. That afternoon, the lull in the appointment schedule gave them time to talk . . . or not.

Callie planned to spend Thanksgiving at the ranch with Zane's family. Jamie and Cody would be there as well. It was going to be a memorable Thanksgiving for the Atkins' family as Zane and his sister planned to move their parents to an assisted living apartment in the city the following day. They had insisted on it and were supposedly excited about the next stage of their lives, looking on it as an adventure. As far as anyone knew, it could be the last holiday they'd all celebrate together in the family home. Richard would cover call that day. Callie would pick it up on Friday morning at seven.

The thought of Richard by himself on the holiday brought tears to her eyes. "Richard, do you think there's any way you could go with me to the Atkins's ranch for Thanksgiving? I don't think you should be alone."

Richard shook his head. "Who would cover our patients? Besides, it's just one day. When you get back Friday morning, I plan to leave for Fort Worth to see my mother."

"Well, I do have the number of that neurologist from Dallas who goes around doing relief work. Perhaps, he could cover for the day?"

Richard was adamant. "Callie, no. What could he really know about our practice or our patients? I don't know about you, but I don't think I could relax, all the time wondering what could possibly go wrong. Look, I know you're worried about me, but I'll be fine."

"When you go to Fort Worth, will your brothers be there?"

"Honestly, Callie, I don't know. Ever since I can remember, those two have been in and out of trouble. It seems the only constant in my mother's life has been me, and lately, much of my time has been spent here in Sperling. It's not like she could ever count on my old man—the deadbeat. No one has heard from him in years. Last any of us knew, he was in Dallas."

Callie's phone rang. It was the hospital. She took the call, and before all was said and done, she'd told the caller she'd be right there.

"I've got to go," Callie said. "It's Mrs. Tarrington."

"The old woman who's always showing up in the emergency room, thinking she is having a stroke?"

"Yes, that's her. She's been admitted to the hospital for a bladder suspension, but when her supposed neurological symptoms presented, the admitting physician insisted she be transferred to the neuro floor and one of us consult. Apparently, he didn't think the urology floor was equipped to handle her condition . . . called it too unstable."

Richard was doubtful. "So, is she really having a stroke, or do you think it's another migraine?"

Callie cracked a smile at the thought of how many times both of them had been called up to the emergency room, only to find the elderly woman had a headache. "That remains to be seen. I don't have another patient until four, but I'll try to be back by then."

"Don't worry. I have things covered here," Richard said.

Callie was just about to walk out of Richard's office

when a frustrated Jamie came up and blocked the exit. "Look, you two. I've taken call after call from that accountant, and now, he's threatening to quit if one of you doesn't call him right back."

Callie tapped her forehead with the tips of her fingers. She said, "Oh, Jamie, I completely forgot."

Richard waved her on. "You go ahead to the hospital. I'll give him a call."

Jamie was reluctant to believe the matter was really going to be handled. "Promise?"

With a reassuring nod, Richard told her, "Jamie, I promise."

Marcus took an opportunity to leave the floor, making a beeline for the cafeteria. At lunch, he'd used restraint when it came to the dessert line, but his resistance was waning. There was a sweet potato pie with his name on it. That's when he thought he heard his name. "Psst, psst, Marcus, over here."

He stood in in the middle of the hospital lobby, visitors passing every which way around him. Looking over to his right, he saw Gus peeking out behind a popcorn trolley. Marcus tried to act like he hadn't seen the man, but Gus had him in his sights.

Gus's stride was long and quick. Marcus was

having trouble keeping up with him, trailing behind to watch the man's tool belt repeatedly bounce on his hips. Marcus had followed him up the stairs, exiting the staircase on the neuro floor. Just being on that floor again caused Marcus's back to ache. The journey appeared to end outside the dictation room.

Marcus only had a few minutes left on his break. "Gus, I really appreciate all you've done. But I've got something pretty urgent to handle for the new head nurse, uhm . . . uhm, down in the lab."

Gus was just about to bust at the seams with excitement. "Trust me, Marcus, *this* is urgent."

"This? Where physicians dictate to the electronic medical record?"

"Marcus, behind this door is the evidence to break your case wide open. I've already decided, I don't want any of the credit. The kudos can all go to you."

Marcus wasn't sure what case Gus was referring to, but he knew it wasn't *his* case. "Is there black-market meat behind that door, Gus?"

"No," Gus said flatly.

Marcus didn't like the fact that Gus seemed to want him to play a guessing game as to what he'd found. "Are there food contracts in there—the ones with Patsy's brother?"

"Nope."

Marcus was trying very hard not to lose his temper,

but trying to keep it together had his back muscles tied up in knots. He had to put an end to the game Gus was playing. "Gus, open the door . . . now. Show me what you have to show me . . . now."

Somewhat offended by Marcus's stern tone, Gus said, "Okay, okay, don't get your skivvies in a wad."

Using his badge to access the room, Gus held the door open for Marcus. Marcus was shocked at the condition of the room. It was trashed—every cabinet was open, every drawer pulled off its track, contents strung across the floor. "Gus, what is this? This place is a mess. You know if the head nurse sees this, she going to have your hide."

Gus wasn't fazed by Marcus's reaction. "It was all Delores's idea. Delores is my wife. Have you two met?"

Marcus was having to count to ten to keep from exploding. "No, Gus, I can't say I've had the pleasure. So, what am I supposed to be seeing here?"

Gus pointed to a cabinet beneath the countertop. "It's under here. You need to bend down. It's way back in there."

Marcus supported his back with his hands as he stooped over to look deep inside the cabinet. "What is it?" Marcus asked. "It seems to be on."

"The machine in the middle is an amplifier, but I don't know about the other two," Gus replied.

Marcus was confused. "It doesn't seem to be currently in use, but I'm wondering why the power lights are on. And another thing, the amplifier doesn't seem to be part of the computer system. That would be something more like an audio interface."

"Exactly!" Gus exclaimed. "This is what's been pulling so many amps, resulting in flipped breakers and fried wires. See that silver box off to the right?"

"Yeah," Marcus grunted.

"That's a junction box—someone has tied into this circuit."

Marcus needed to get going. It seemed Gus had stumbled onto something strange, but he didn't have a lot of time to throw ideas out with Gus. "First things, first. Let's power this thing down."

Gus complied while Marcus stuck his head out the door. He saw Dr. Wallace coming down the hall. He mumbled to himself, "Why does it have to be her? Why does this stuff always have to happen to me?"

He knew he had to bite the bullet. Marcus had managed to avoid a confrontation with Dr. Wallace up until now, but he needed help and he needed it quick. "Hey, Dr. Wallace, I've been meaning to talk to you. Do you have a minute?"

Callie knew this day would eventually come. "Hello, Marcus. I haven't seen much of you lately. For a while there, I thought you might be avoiding me."

"Dr. Wallace, about that incident. It was just like you said, nothing more than a misunderstanding. I guess the situation had both of us a little rattled. I've straightened the whole matter out with Human Resources and Mr. Anderson. No hard feelings?"

Callie was glad to have the air cleared, but she hadn't received any official notification that the matter had been resolved. "No, none. Consider the matter forgotten. What can I do for you, Marcus?"

"Well, I was hoping you could look at something in this room. A friend of mine pointed it out to me and I don't know quite what to make of it."

"Okay, I don't know for certain I can help you, but I'm willing to give it a try."

Marcus knocked on the door for Gus to let them in, but Callie accessed it with her ID. She followed Marcus into the dictation room, astonished to see how things were strewn around.

Gus picked up on the physician's bewildered look. "Ma'am, sorry for the mess. It was Delores's idea."

Marcus needed everyone to stay on track. He was needing to get back to work and quick. "Never mind Gus, Dr. Wallace. The machines are down here."

Callie bent over, but quickly came to stand up straight.

"One is an amplifier, but do you know what the other two are?" Marcus asked.

"Yes, Marcus, I do. One is a waveform generator, the other, an oscilloscope unit."

"An oscilloscope? Is it something that belongs in here?" Gus inquired.

"It measures the speed of sound through air," Callie replied. "The equipment does seem a bit dated, however. Newer models have the waveform generator built-in. None of this should be in here, not in any capacity that I can think of, anyway."

Gus pressed her. "If you know, you can tell us, Doc. We won't tell. It's okay. Marcus, here, he's with the law . . . undercover."

Suddenly, Gus realized what he'd said. Immediately, he placed his hands over his mouth, eyes bugging.

Callie looked at her once accuser. "Is that true, Marcus?"

"I would appreciate your discretion, Dr. Wallace," Marcus replied.

"You got it, Marcus. Now if you gentlemen will excuse me, I have a patient to see."

After the physician left the room, the look Marcus gave to Gus was one of shooting daggers. Gus had wanted to explain his slip-up, but Marcus wasn't having any of it. He was steamed. He stormed out. But before he did, his incensed mood was exposed. "What a mess, Gus . . . what a damn mess!"

Fifty-four

Wednesday, November 22, 2017 09:40 a.m.

Callie heard her mother banging around in the kitchen, literally. Slamming pans and cupboard doors sent a loud and clear message . . . her mother was pissed. Callie knew she should've broken the news that she planned to celebrate Thanksgiving at the Atkins ranch before now, but it never seemed like a good time.

Rose came into the living room with a tray of tea and slices of pound cake. She let the weight of the tray fall free the last half-inch or so to hit the coffee table, clattering cups in their saucers.

Callie winced. "Mother, I said I was sorry."

Rose didn't want to talk about it. "Tea?"

"Is it Earl Grey?"

"Is there any other kind?" Rose snapped.

Callie recalled one Christmas in which she gifted her mother a variety of Chinese teas. The disappointment in her mother's face was evident, followed by some comment about regifting it to someone at the homeless shelter, or possibly, Aunt Clare.

Her mother handed her a cup of tea, along with a

slice of cake. Callie wasn't hungry, but dared not upset her mother any further.

"Callie, you know this Thanksgiving is my turn. You and Zane were with the Atkins's family last year. Marta and Raul are expecting three for dinner."

"Mother, what am I supposed to do, tell Zane to skip such a symbolic holiday dinner to appease you? He thinks I'm emotionally unavailable most of the time, anyway."

"*I know how he feels*," Rose mumbled under her breath.

Callie was having trouble keeping the conversation civil. "Well, I'm here now and look how things are going. Oh, remind me to take your blood pressure before I go."

Rose was indignant. "I'm just saying this wouldn't be an issue if your father was still alive. You would've invited him to the Atkins's ranch. And never mind my blood pressure. It's high, damn it, it's high! Besides, if I go ahead and die, at least I won't be putting you out anymore."

There it was . . . the guilt trip. "Mother, even if I'd invited you out to the Atkins's ranch, I doubt you would've come anyway. You've never really got along with Zane's mother . . . not like with Marta. I swear, you two are as thick as thieves."

"So, what, I'm not supposed to have any friends?"

Rose huffed. "It just kills me we're not closer, especially after all I've done for you."

August 7, 1995

Dearest Rosa,

I'm not one for letter writing, but your bull-headedness has forced my hand. It would be better for all involved if you would just give in to the passion we share. I knew it the first time I saw you, wanting you. Clare is a poor substitute, but it has kept you close. You can go to the police if you want, but we both know those protective orders don't mean shit. Every year, so many women file protective orders, and every year, so many women die. I've learned over the last few months that Clare means little to you. I've fantasized about taking a skillet to her head, just to shut her the hell up, but I realized it would do little to motivate you.

It may surprise you that I was in Sperling the other day. I followed that gringo husband of yours to the coffee shop and then to that cushy office of his. He lunched at Rotary. I approached him after he came out and asked him directions to the YMCA. Don't believe me, just ask him. I had a hatchet tucked in the back of my pants, under a jacket. I could've put it in his head, and this would all be over, but I want you to come to me willingly.

I spent that afternoon at Sperling Elementary. I spoke to a Mrs. Grayson. She will be little Callie's teacher this next year. Nice lady. She was getting her classroom ready for school that starts in two weeks. I told her I was family and gave her a fifty to help with supplies for the classroom. Precious girl, that Callie. It would be a shame if anything was to happen to her, but I make seed for you every day, Rosa, in my loins. You can have as many bebés as you want. It wouldn't be long before Callie was just a memory.

Love forever, Tomas

"What about Richard?" Rose inquired. "I suppose you're leaving him high-and-dry for the holiday as well. He could go with me to the Gutierrez's. I know they wouldn't mind."

Callie couldn't even imagine bringing that up to Richard. "Thanks anyway, Mother, but I think Richard needs a little space and it might be awkward for him. Friday morning, right after I get back into town, he plans to go see his mother."

Rose grabbed herself a slice of cake. "Where are Richard's parents from?"

"Well, they are not together. His mother still lives in the same apartment Richard grew up in . . . that's in Fort Worth. But last he knew his father was in Dallas."

Cough, cough, cough

Callie looked over to see her mother hacking, her face beet red, and eyes tearing. She took the cup of tea from her mother's hands and put it down on the coffee table. "Mother, Mother, are you okay?"

Rose was able to wave her daughter off. She took a few deep breaths before she could speak. "I'm okay, dear, really. I guess the cake tried to go down the wrong way."

But the disturbing thought lingered in Rose's mind . . . *Dr. Richard Cortez . . . Dallas . . . Tomas Cortez.*

"Are you sure you're okay, Mother?"

"Yes, I'm sure. Stop fussing, Callie! It was nothing more than an unpleasant fit."

Callie reached for her mother's cup. "Here, take back your tea. Small sips, okay?" Callie noticed a red envelope. "Hey Mother, what's this on the table?"

Rose saw the holiday greeting Callie was holding. "Oh, that's from your Aunt Clare. It's her annual Christmas letter to the family. Can you believe her? Tomorrow is only Thanksgiving. But that's your Aunt Clare—me first. Just bragging is all—bombastic bluster. There's a photo in the envelope of her and your cousin, Tommy. My stars, that boy of hers is a little old to be taking Christmas pictures with mommy dearest. He has to be about twenty-one or so by now."

Callie looked in the envelope and found the picture. "Wow, I can't believe Tommy's that old already. Where did the time go? He's fairly handsome, I'll say that for him. You know what? Look here, Mother. See his forehead, the shape of the eyes, and the prominent bridge of the nose . . . I think they call it a Roman nose. You know who he reminds me of? I think he looks a lot like Richard."

That's when the tea cup fell to the floor and shattered beyond repair. Callie looked at her mother, but this time she was pale and clammy, eyes glazed over. She appeared not to notice she'd dropped her cup, but her words were clear. "Callie, Mother doesn't feel very well. I'll get the mess. Perhaps, you should go. Have a safe trip to the ranch. I'll give you a call sometime tomorrow, okay?"

Callie thought her mother was acting strange. "Mother, are you okay? You don't look so well. Do I need to take you to the emergency room?"

Rose didn't look at her daughter, but straight ahead as if she was watching a bad movie play out that only she could see. "Callie, stop asking me that, just go. I'll call you tomorrow, okay?"

Callie was hesitant to leave her mother in her current state. She got up from the couch and started for the kitchen. "I'll just get the broom and dustpan to clean up this mess first."

That's when her mother lost it. "Callie, just go, now!"

"Okay, okay," Callie relented, feeling pushed out the door. She went over to the chair where she'd left her handbag. She dug for her keys and made her way to the door. Before going, Callie took a quick look over her shoulder at her mother who continued to stare off into space. Frustrated, she gently closed the front door behind her.

Fifty-five

Thursday, November 23, 2017 Thanksgiving

Callie and Zane walked hand-in-hand down one of the ranch's many tree-lined paths on that crisp afternoon, leaves crunching beneath their feet. The nip in the air was refreshing as both of them had had their fill, and then some, to a point of being uncomfortable. Callie had a feeling that the stroll was much more than an exercise to aid digestion. She knew Zane and Zane had something on his mind. She knew he'd ordinarily be inside, watching the Dallas Cowboy game with his family. A chill ran up her spine at the thought of him proposing, not knowing how she'd respond.

"I love this place in the fall," Zane pointed out as he took in a lung-full of fresh air.

Callie agreed. "It is beautiful and serene. When I'm here, I feel like I don't have a care in the world. If it was only true."

"You barely said two words over dinner, Callie."

"Zane, I didn't mean to be such a wet-blanket at your family's holiday celebration, especially the last one to be celebrated in the family home. The place won't be the same without your folks."

Zane seemed to take offense at Callie's comment. "It's not like they'll never be back. My sister and I have already talked it over. We plan to bring them back here for all the major family events. They're really looking forward to the move. My dad will have regular access to physical therapy and strength training. My mom is looking forward to someone else doing all the cooking and cleaning. Both are excited about making new friends their own age."

Callie was shocked by his attitude. "Zane, I didn't mean that you and your sister plan to put your parents in a home and throw away the key. I'm sorry if it came across that way. I can't help but feel like you're a little put out with me. I do have a lot on my plate right now. I'm sorry I can't be as optimistic about my future as your parents, but I'm doing my best. Can you tell me why we're out here? I know you'd rather be watching the football game."

The leaves rustled around them, cattle were calling out in the fields, the horses were neighing, and the doves were cooing as if they sensed what was about to come. To Callie, it felt like she was caught in a glass bubble that was about to shatter.

Zane looked her square in the eye. "You're right, Callie. I'm angry with you."

Callie was stunned by his words. Zane had always been able to control his temper with her, but today, the very way he carried himself, she knew it would be different. She began to tear up, but became defensive. "Are you saying I'm somehow to blame for what's going on in my life right now?"

Her tears didn't detract him. He had to get it out. Zane had kept his feelings bottled up for too long now. "No, that's not what I'm saying. I'm angry because I love you more than you love me."

It was like Callie had taken a shot to the gut. She felt like she might be sick. Her voice was weak. "That's not true."

But Callie's denial only strengthened his conviction. "You're selfish, Callie. You keep all your pain and your grief to yourself. You won't let me in. When all is said and done, you spend more time with Richard than you do with me. You cry over Richard. You cry over Richard's girlfriend. Even when your father died, Richard was your consoler."

Callie couldn't believe her ears. She never saw this coming. "Is this what has you upset? You're jealous of Richard?"

The allegation had Zane steaming. "I am not jealous of Richard! You're not hearing what I'm trying to tell you. You keep me at a safe distance . . . at arm's length. I'm not part of your day-to-day life. I'm no more to you than your weekend activity."

Callie wanted to state her case. "Our living

arrangements are more a matter of practicality, not choice. I'm a neurologist. I practice my field at the nearest medical center. You're a rancher. You make a living at your family ranch, an hour away. I know it's not ideal, but I thought it was working."

"It's not working, Callie, at least, not for me."

His words seem to knock the wind out of her. Callie hadn't seen it coming. She felt foolish, thinking Zane was close to proposing, when in fact, he'd planned to end things with her after all their years together. She could barely speak. "I just thought . . . I just thought we'd marry someday."

His tone was as sharp as ever. "How, Callie? How are we supposed to have a marriage, be united as one, when you don't even let me in? You don't allow me to help shoulder your pain. The day I stayed behind to go with you to Hayden Deutch's office, I practically had to insist. The Sunday night before, you were ready to shuffle me out the door, as usual."

Callie was lightheaded, feeling lost. "I just thought we'd wait . . ."

He stopped her before she could finish. "Wait . . . wait . . . wait for what, Callie? Wait until you got out of medical school? I did that. Wait until everything is perfect? That day will never come. Wait until I'm no longer a rancher? Wait for you to figure out Sperling isn't the same hometown you remembered? Wait for the Murphy family to come to their senses? All I've been doing is waiting. Tell me, Callie, how well is your life working out for you? Frankly, I just can't do this anymore. And another thing, your ten-year plan has long since expired!"

She didn't want to ask, but felt it necessary. "Do you hate me, Zane? Because that's the way it sounds."

He'd gotten it out. It was a relief to Zane. But the real question was where would they go from there. "That's frustration you hear, Callie, not hate. I love you. I want a life with you. But in a couple of hours you're going to head back to Sperling. Tomorrow, I'm going to say goodbye to a life I've known with my parents, and I'm going to have to do it alone. That's not what I call having a life together."

Callie contemplated what two more hours of confrontation with Zane would be like. She couldn't bear it. She couldn't bear to think of a life without Zane. Callie didn't know what to do. She didn't know how to fix such an unfixable problem. Her strength was gone. Her voice was hardly above a whisper. "Maybe, I should just go ahead and leave."

Zane gave into the idea, broken himself. "Maybe, you should."

Rose and Marta lazily glided on the porch swing,

watching the sun go down. With a blanket over their laps, sipping wine, they were as comfortable as two old friends could be with each other. It was a peaceful evening except for the occasional expletive coming from the house as Raul watched the Cowboys get pummeled by the San Diego Chargers.

Rose was wondering if she'd ever eat again. "Marta, you outdid yourself. Honestly, I don't know how you do it. That was an excellent meal."

Her neighbor smiled, relieved to be off her feet after twelve hours. "It feels good to be appreciated, Rose. It seems like Raul just takes my cooking for granted. And that boy of mine, he hasn't been home in three years. It's that uppity wife of his that's the problem."

"I remember when you and Raul moved in. Your son was a toddler then, and I'd just had Callie. Remember how we used to joke around that maybe someday they'd fall in love and marry?"

"Humph," Marta grumbled. "If only that had been the case . . . that daughter-in-law of mine." She shook her head in frustration before returning to remember old times. "We were so young back then. I often wonder if we knew what the future had in store for us if we would've done things differently. You really had me worried yesterday, Rose."

Rose sighed. "It just seems like no matter how

much time passes that ugly business with Tomas Cortez keeps rearing its ugly head. Do you really think Callie won't put two-and-two together?"

Her friend was adamant. "Rose, you did the right thing sending Callie away like you did. You might've let something slip. After you called, it took me awhile to get you settled down. But remember, it's imperative that *no one* finds out the part we played in Tomas's disappearance. We had no choice. What else were you going to do?"

Rose knew an iron-hearted deportment was a necessity to live with their secret. She refilled their glasses as if the wine could numb the unpleasant memories. "His threats—they never stopped. I don't even think Clare knew Tomas had children. If she did—she never told me. But that was Clare's problem, never questioning any of the man's motives."

Marta remembered it like it was yesterday. "That summer, I hardly saw you. I didn't work outside the home back then, so I would know. Your husband and Callie were practically on their own, spending a good deal of time at the lake. If I remember right, it was early-to-mid August and I'd gone out back to empty the trash. You were in your backyard, crying on the porch."

Having been caught so vulnerable made Rose uneasy, still to that day. "When you called over the fence to see if there was anything you could do, I was mortified. I mean, I knew you in a friendly neighbor sort of way, but we weren't particularly close. The tears, they just wouldn't stop. That was the day I really marked as the start of our friendship."

Marta agreed, grimacing at the thought of the pain her friend had endured. "I felt so bad for you. You were just sobbing. And on the surface, your family looked so ideal. I remember asking you if you could turn to your husband, but you felt you couldn't."

"I was at my wits end. This man was obsessed with me and I felt like I had no recourse. When I was at home, I was a nervous wreck over what might be behind every corner. Tomas even sent a few 'love letters' to the house. I don't know what I would've said to my husband if he'd intercepted one of them."

Marta topped off their glasses before continuing the story. "When I came across you that day, you were about to sacrifice yourself to that animal . . . for your family. I knew I needed to do *something*."

Rose was curious. "Marta, how did you ever come to know someone like *him*?"

"Look, I know you don't have a good word to say about Clare, and I get that with all you were put through, but I know what it's like to grow up in a small town like Sperling, yearning for the excitement of the city and all its possibilities. I do think it's better you don't know the details, but needless to say, I was naïve and landed up in a situation that was way over my head."

Rose realized something was out of place. "Wait . . . wait . . . wait, Marta. All this time we've been out here, after a big meal, with the wine, you haven't lit up once."

The neighbor was proud of herself, and justifiably so. "I quit. My friend Gus Ferguson convinced me to give it up. Do you know him?"

Rose couldn't recall anyone by that name, a look of doubt on her face.

"Are you sure? He's married to Delores."

Rose shook off the odd question and clinked her friend's glass. "That's wonderful, Marta! I'm so proud of you. I guess I've been so caught up with my own issues, it took me this long to notice."

"That's okay, Rose. Think nothing of it. Actually, it was when all this ugly business started, that's when I started to smoke . . . to calm my nerves."

Rose felt a twinge of guilt to her friend's admission. "I guess Tomas drove many of us to our bad habits."

Marta was curious. "How has your blood pressure been?"

Rose tried to play the situation down. "It's like you said, my friend. I do think it's better you don't know the details. But when it comes to that man, he must have been especially fond of you, though."

"Enough to kill Tomas Cortez when I asked him to do it," Marta admitted.

The porch light suddenly popped on. The sun was down. The wine bottle empty. The Cowboys had lost. Thanksgiving was over. Rose and Marta's secret had survived another day.

Fifty-six

Friday, November 24, 2017 09:45 a.m.

The trip back to Sperling had been a blur, leaving Callie to wonder if what happened with Zane yesterday was real. She'd already made rounds and came back to the office. She didn't want to go back to an empty house. Callie didn't really need to be at the office—she just didn't know what else to do. She sat there numb. Her plan was to give Zane a few days to cool off. Then, they'd talk and work things out . . . hopefully.

Callie felt alone. She hadn't spoken to her mother since their last strange encounter the other day. Her mother had told her she would call . . . but she never did. Richard had left town a couple of hours ago. She was on the outs with Zane who'd been a constant in her life ever since she could remember. She even doubted anyone else was in the whole office building that morning. Callie thought about doing some Black Friday shopping, but in her current state of mind, she feared the loneliness would follow her even in the midst of the plethora of bargain hunters.

The office phone rang and the preoccupied Callie

jumped in her chair. For a moment, she thought about letting the machine pick it up, but she was desperate for some type of distraction, even if it stemmed from a robocall. Being alone with only her thoughts was too overwhelming. She answered the phone. It was the accountant, Jim Cohen, and he was steamed.

"Honestly, I don't know how that practice stays afloat. Has anyone over there ever heard of fiduciary responsibility?"

Callie was rethinking her decision to answer the phone. "Hello to you, too, Jim. I'm fine. Thanks for asking. Are you having a nice holiday? Well, yes, it's been lovely."

"Dr. Wallace, joke if you will, and why you think my manner is not particularly cordial, I do have a job to do—one I take quite seriously."

"I'm sorry, Jim. Didn't Richard call you back?"

"Yes, he did, but he said he was going to fax me a copy of the loan agreement, and he didn't. Do you know how much time and frustration has gone into just this one issue? If I don't get it today, you can find yourself another guy. I'm having surgery on Monday and I'm going to be out-of-pocket for at least six weeks. I don't want the year closing out with this type of loose end."

"Jim, I'm sorry to hear you're having problems. Nothing serious, I hope."

"Never mind my health concerns, Dr. Wallace. Just get the loan agreement to me . . . and today."

"What loan agreement?"

"The loan for the medical equipment—the one taken out early last month. Dr. Cortez knows about it."

"Is it for the EEG machine? If it is, we haven't taken delivery of it, as far as I know."

"Dr. Wallace, the bank doesn't care if you're in possession of the equipment. They just want their loan repaid. I'm losing patience here."

Callie gave the man a blow-by-blow of her movements. "Okay, okay, Jim. Let's see. Right now, I'm walking from my office to Richard's. Just about there . . . just about there, okay, I'm here. Let me see what I can find. Hold on just a minute. This office of his is a mess."

Callie cradled the cordless receiver between her chin and shoulder as she started to go through Richard's desk. "Uhm, paper clips, credit card receipts, medical journal, building lease, some type of instruction manual, troubleshooting guide. Wait, this hanging file is unmarked, but something is in it. Let me take a look."

A shout-out came from the waiting room, *anyone here . . . the lights were on.*

"Hold on, Jim. I've got someone up front."

Callie unlocked the door that separated the waiting room from Jamie's work area. She opened it to find Marcus Davis.

The accountant could be heard on the other end of the line. "Hello . . . hello? Dr. Wallace, are you there?"

"Jim, I'm going to have to call you back. I've got someone here. I promise, I'll call you back within the hour."

The accountant's irritation escalated with yet another delay. "You just better hope you do, and trust me, I'll be true to my word. If I don't get it today, you can find yourself another guy."

Callie heard the line go dead, and put the receiver down. She addressed her visitor, feeling the need to explain. "Temperamental accountant. He gets like this around the year-end. What can I do for you, Marcus?"

"Oh, I was just driving by and saw your car out front. Are you here alone?"

"Yeah, the office is closed until Monday. I have call. Richard just took off for Fort Worth to see his mother."

"I see. About the other day, it's imperative that my cover stay intact. The case I'm working at the Medical Center is touchy, to say the least. I would appreciate you staying tight-lipped about it, telling no one, including Dr. Cortez."

Callie was suspicious, moving back towards Richard's office to continue her search. "Marcus, I told you I would be discreet, and I can assure you I have been. Is there anything else on your mind?"

It was awkward, but Marcus needed to know. "Dr. Wallace, while at the hospital, I couldn't help but hear the rumors regarding your mental state. But when we had that run-in the other day, to me you seemed direct, lucid, purposeful, knowledgeable. It just doesn't make sense."

Callie wanted to laugh it off, but she couldn't. Marcus's real role at the hospital hadn't been determined, but she knew he wouldn't be asking if he didn't need to know. "Marcus, I underwent physical and mental testing to determine if my health was sound. At first, I was reluctant, but actually, I'm glad I went through with it. I'm healthy, and Dr. Lambert, the psychiatrist, signed off on my emotional wellbeing. I have his report if you need to see it."

Marcus didn't think Dr. Wallace was who he was looking for, because she just didn't seem to fit the profile—someone who would defile a corpse for a brain sample, and more recently, taking a sample while the subject was still alive. But something was out of place. "No, no, that won't be necessary. But tell me, is this your office?"

Callie sat behind the desk going through stacks

of papers and file folders. "No, it's Dr. Cortez's. I guess he had his hands full over the holiday. Oh, look, there's Mr. Patterson's chemistry panel. He was looking for that. I'm sorry, Marcus, but if there's not anything else, I have my hands full looking for this loan agreement. Half of these folders are not even labeled."

"No, that was it. Thanks for your time. I'll see my way out. Happy Thanksgiving."

Callie didn't look up, but diligently continued her search. "Happy Thanksgiving to you," she said.

Marcus was walking to his car. He was having trouble shaking the gut feeling he'd come to depend on over the years. Something just didn't fit, but what? He unlocked his car and got in. Was it something about Dr. Wallace, something he saw in the office, something that was said? That's it, he thought to himself . . . something said. Maybe it was that Dr. Lambert. Did his name ring a bell? No, that wasn't it. And the psyche ward, that wasn't anywhere he'd looked. Mental note to self: check-out the patients and staff files on the psyche ward. He sat in his car, beating his hands against the steering wheel in frustration. It was there, on the tip of his brain, but what?

Then it came, the file. Dr. Tohias Ricardo Cortez, DOB 6-18-1984. Siblings: Armando Cortez, incarcerated at Clements Unit, Amarillo, Texas. Mateo Cortez, incarcerated at Huntsville Unit, Huntsville,

Texas. Father: Tomas Cortez, missing, presumed dead. Mother: deceased, suicide.

Marcus reached under his seat for his gun, got out of the car, and rushed back in the building. He ran through the empty foyer, his sneakers squeaking against the freshly waxed floor, echoing throughout. He threw open the doors to the Neurology Group office and darted towards the back. “Dr. Wallace, Callie?”

Silence

He readied his gun before going back into Cortez’s office. No one was there. But something was different. A binder was broken open on the floor and its loose-leaf sheets were strung all over. Marcus did a quick search of the closets, the bathrooms, but nothing. The woman’s SUV was still out front, parked next to his beater. He made sure he was alone before going to get a pair of gloves from a box at the nurses’ station. Marcus then stooped down and started picking up the sheets, one-by-one, carefully putting them into an unused trash can liner. He just about finished the task when an old-fashioned ringtone was heard coming from somewhere in the office. He stood up and tried to follow the sound. It was coming from under the desk. He bent down and picked up the cell phone. The display read, *Mother*.

Marcus thought the word use odd. Most people

would use a much more affectionate, *Mom*. He answered the call. "Hello?"

"Who is this?" the woman snorted.

"This is Agent Marcus Davis, FBI."

The woman came across as apologetic. "I'm sorry. I must have dialed the wrong number. I was trying to reach my daughter."

"Wait, wait, don't hang up," Marcus said. "Would you be trying to reach Callie Wallace?"

The woman's voice had a nervous lilt to it. "Why isn't Callie answering her phone? What's going on?"

"I take it you're her mother. Your name would be?"

"Rose Wallace, and I want a straight answer."

"I've found her phone, and while I believe there's no need for concern, I'd ask you to call around to your daughter's inner circle to report back if they hear from her today, but let's keep it low-key. No need to incite a panic. If you hear anything, you can reach me back at this number."

Nervous was springing into hysterics. "The FBI has my daughter's phone and you tell me not to worry?"

Marcus wished he could believe what he'd just told the woman. He was hoping this was some sort of false alarm. He wondered, could the physician really have been taken in just the short time he sat out in his car, no more than fifteen minutes? "Just do as I asked, Mrs. Wallace. I'll be looking forward to hearing back from you." Marcus hung up. He had work to do.

It came only after a minute or so, the group text from Rose Wallace. It read:

911-anyone who hears from Callie Wallace, call me right back.

It must have been to each listing in the mother's contacts, because he saw it included such places as the local market, the dry cleaner, and the gym. The problem was that it also included the suspect. His head sunk when he realized what the mother had just done . . . tipping off the perp. He turned the phone to vibrate with the intention of only taking a call from Mrs. Wallace or, of course, Richard Cortez.

Fifty-seven

Friday, November 24, 2017 3:50 p.m.

Dr. Douglas Lambert sat in the interrogation room down at the Sperling police station. Agent Davis and Detective Monroe showed up on his doorstep about two hours ago, making demands. He was incensed that the holiday with his family was being interrupted. They'd all gathered around the television as his alma mater, Texas Christian University, was playing the Baylor Bears, and it was looking like TCU might have a shot at the Big 12 title. A colleague of his was on-call, not him. He demanded that that doctor be called, but when the threat of an arrest was made, he knew the lawmen meant business.

It was Davis that explained the scene down at Sperling Neurology Group. Dr. Callie Wallace was missing and the mix-matched collection of scientific notes could possibly hold the key to her whereabouts. The Bureau man mentioned words like *in vivo*, *ex vivo*, *in situ*, *chromosome 19, sine wave, calcium channel receptor, strong priors,* and *diagnostic markers for mental illness* had caught the doctor's attention, but this together with reference to Callie Wallace and Sara Townsend, *henceforth referred to as Subject A and Subject B, respectively* had him on high alert. It was told to Douglas Lambert that time was of the essence and his 'dicking around' wouldn't be tolerated.

"Anything?" the detective asked.

"Gentlemen, do you want it fast or do you want it right?" the psychiatrist snapped. "These notes are handwritten and I'm still unsure if we have the pages in the correct sequence. Besides, there is some genetic engineering involved and I'm not exactly up-to-speed on this type of technique. One thing is clear, the guy is crazy."

"*Crazy*?" Marcus inquired. "This is your specialty and all you can come up with is *crazy*?"

"Let me put it this way," Lambert began, "there's delusions of grandeur written all over this thing, perhaps a bipolar. For one thing, he seems to believe he's actually conducting a bona fide study with just two subjects, and the ethical implications, well, the whole thing is reprehensible. Tell me, what makes you think this man took Dr. Wallace?"

"I hit *69 on the office phone and got the number of the accountant. He admitted that he'd grown impatient, and instead of waiting for Dr. Wallace to find the copy of the loan agreement and call him back, he phoned Dr. Cortez's cell phone and told him Dr. Wallace was rummaging through his desk to find it.

The accountant had wanted Dr. Cortez to call his partner to tell her exactly where it was, but instead told me the physician was put out, spouted some gibberish intermixed with anger and profanity. Now, Dr. Lambert, while all this might seem interesting to you, we need you to interpret for us what's in front of you. We need to know what we're getting into."

The doctor took off his reading glasses and put them on the table. "The two women received an injection of a modified adeno-associated virus, specifically type 2."

Now Monroe had a question. "What's his endgame? Was he trying to see if they got sick or what?"

"Actually, this specific virus has low pathogenicity in humans. It was used as a delivery method of a gene sequence to be integrated into chromosome 19. The gene product is a signaling protein that would target a receptor found only to the central nervous system, or CNS. Once activated, they'd be prone to hallucinations."

Monroe was smart, but he was already confused. "Signaling what? Brain proteins?"

The psychiatrist wanted to make himself clear. "Think of the virus as a carrier pigeon delivering a message. A sender wants to deliver a note, a piece of information, to a particular receiver. The modified virus is the pigeon, the note is the code for the signaling protein, and the receiver is a brain receptor that will be activated when the signaling protein arrives."

Marcus had spent several months at the hospital. He wasn't aware the physician was having that sort of issue. "Callie Wallace has been having hallucinations? Townsend, too?"

"Yes, according to the notes, but Dr. Wallace didn't divulge any of that to me. Dr. Cortez was using ultrasonic noise, high-frequency sounds. In the presence of generated ultrasound, cellular calcium levels are altered by which a person is not just prone to have a hallucination, but ripe for one. When the ultrasound is turned off, the calcium level or electrical balance of the cell goes back to its previous state. He was experimenting with varying frequencies, stipulating that as a variable to whether the subject could recall the hallucination or not."

Marcus remembered the equipment Gus Ferguson had found in the physician dictation room, but didn't elaborate. "So, what you're saying is that these hallucinations would only be limited to where ultrasound equipment might be, like the hospital?"

Lambert shrugged his shoulders. "Well, yes and no. I see what you're getting at, making ultrasound use exclusive to medicine. However, it can be all around us and we wouldn't even be aware of it. Ultrasound is sound above human hearing. In the past, it was used in auto-focusing of cameras, but that's been replaced with infrared signals. Today, you see it in something as simple as a home jewelry cleaner, or security systems, pest control, commercial dishwashers in restaurants, in the industrial sector to locate minute leaks that otherwise would go undetected, and in the food industry for processes such as homogenization or meat tenderization."

"So, these women go out, and at any time, could become vulnerable to these sound waves?" Monroe asked.

"That's correct. While they could randomly come upon it, the Methods Section of this paper lists equipment physically located within twenty-four yards of the subject's awake or sleep-state. This makes me think equipment could be in the home environment."

"What would these hallucinations be like?" Marcus asked.

Lambert knew the answer would be difficult to explain. "According to entries in the scientific journal, there has to be video and audio bugs in proximity to where the equipment was found. But that is not the real issue. Studies are telling us that, whether the hallucination is auditory, visual, or both, the experience is wrapped around a person's core belief system or what the individual determines to be true, their perception. In the case of Dr. Wallace, I happen to know that she has experienced guilt over being away to study medicine when her father died . . . not being able to help him or tell him goodbye."

Monroe needed to know. "Doctor, there is an ongoing investigation into the death of Sara Townsend. Is it possible that Dr. Cortez killed her?"

"The scientific log, and I use the term loosely, states that it was discovered that Subject B needed to be excluded from the study because of an undisclosed aberrant condition. It was later revealed that the subject had been, in fact, a victim of repetitive shaking as an infant that resulted in behavioral problems, learning disabilities, and self-esteem issues later in life. Long story short, the woman's brain was damaged goods."

Marcus couldn't believe what he was hearing. "So, that's it . . . he just kills her? But I asked Monroe about any unusual findings to her nose. He said there wasn't any."

"There wasn't," the detective reiterated. "But *needed to be excluded* isn't something that's going to hold-up in court. What's the issue with the nose, anyway?"

"That was how Dr. Cortez was obtaining his brain samples," Lambert explained. "It goes back to Egyptian mummification practices to remove the brain through the nose, using a hook. Actually, the method of brain access is used in practice today, such as removing pituitary tumors. It's called a transsphenoidal approach. Dr. Cortez would need objective data, control subjects, to support his hypothesis. My guess is that the brain tissue was reduced to a single-cell suspension for study. He would need a place to conduct this kind of work, a centrifuge, for example. There're also different microscopic images of neurons. But in the case of Sara Townsend, her results would be considered tainted because of her past history, so I can see him not harvesting a sample."

Marcus started to pace, his anxiety rising. "Dr. Lambert, if Dr. Cortez realized his unethical study involving human subjects had been discovered, what frame of mind would he be in? I mean, if he is holding Dr. Wallace, is she in any immediate danger? The two are supposed to be friends."

"Let me assure you of one thing, Agent Davis," the psychiatrist said. "Dr. Cortez is no friend of Callie Wallace. The man will become desperate, pressed to bring the study to a conclusion, and the only way that can happen is obtaining the brain sample from Subject A."

Monroe stood up in a panic. "Holy shit, he's going to kill her! We need to think, Marcus. Where could he be holding her? He'd need access to medical equipment. Is there a place at the hospital, a wing not in use, anything?"

Marcus sensed the urgency. "No, almost every

square inch of the place is utilized and heavily trafficked. If not, surveillance cameras are in place. Monroe, our man is disorganized and impulsive. That homeless man that was murdered, is there anything nearby there that fits what we're looking for?"

Monroe's phone went off, a text from the head waiter of *La Pomme d' Amour.* It would have to wait.

Monroe was racking his brain, knowing the urgency of the matter. It came to him in an instant, snapping his fingers. "Old man Dickerson used to have a wholesale medical supply company down there. It's my understanding that it never really turned a profit, so the son shut it down. I can't be certain what he might've done with the inventory, because when the son took over, most of the equipment was pretty outdated."

Marcus already had his coat on. "Let's go."

Fifty-eight

Friday, November 24, 2017, Dickerson Wholesale

She was freezing. The wind was blowing. She knew that because of how it whistled through every minute crack of the once solid storehouse. The earthy, musty smell told her there was mold nearby. Callie's eyes darted in every direction, a limited scope. She tried to move, but it was hopeless. Even her head was held tightly in place. She could only surmise it was restraints, and strong ones, that held her immobilized. There was some natural light, although dim. It was either overcast or near sunset, hours scrapped from her memory. She could hear him nearby. A fraction of light that he worked by bled in her direction. The source of the electricity was unknown as the weathered building must have been without utilities for some time.

He didn't flinch, looking down at her . . . he didn't care enough to. His eyes said it all. Warm and brown replaced with cool disdain as if inanimate oculars. She was immaterial, a mouse that had jumped the maze. "Well, there's my sleepy head. I saw what a little pill could do to you, so I knew an injection would be more than enough. That's the problem with that drug, the half-life is so long. I thought you'd never wake up. A text came in about you while you were out—one from that whore mother of yours. Seems people are looking for you."

The reference escaped her. Her nerves were on edge, despite her groggy state. The man beside her, Richard, a stranger. "Is that all you have to say, you bastard?"

A mocking howl bellowed across the building. "Really, Callie, profanity? Such a foul mouth for someone so virtuous. You with your syrupy sap, sap, sap."

"That's unfair and you know it. I'm the victim in this scenario—your perverted science. You violated me. You made me trust you. You must feel nothing but absolute contempt for me."

"Contempt, contempt? You're the nails on my chalkboard. You're the dog muck stuck on my shoe. You're the drop of water in my hot oil pan. You're that jagged knife in my gut, twisting around with its gnarled barbs."

Callie felt herself shrinking back as he derided her with his weaponized words. Somehow, she felt the strength to say what she didn't want to believe. "You're the parasite in my waters."

Richard didn't know what to make of the accusation. "A bit over-dramatic, don't you think?"

She continued. "No, I don't. You see, from what I was able to read of your research journal, with the ultrasound frequency you used at the hospital, I can't remember any of those episodes. Tell me Richard, did you murder Mr. Murphy? Because if you were the one to change his dosage, you knew all too well what would happen. You could've done it, using my password for the computerized order entry. I mean, you had it written right there on the top of page one. Oh, and let's not forget how you *suggested* to Kyle Anderson that I undergo all those tests. You knew I'd share the results with you. What better way to monitor the progress of your research?"

He was amused at her guessing game. "Oh, come on, Callie, enough with the wild assertions. Isn't the real question whether you went back and altered the dosage, without remembering? You don't know much of the hallucinogenic state, do you? You should really catch up on some of your reading. I mean, really, how could the impeccable, faultless Callie Wallace do something like that, even in an altered state? I'm the screw-up, right? Yes, Callie, to answer your question, it was me, and it was fun as hell to watch you spin out of control. I'll have you know my work was going along seamlessly until that damn Korean girl caught me in the morgue. She threatened to tattle, the little brat. I had to do something."

"You did *something*, all right. You injected Sara and me under the auspices of giving us a flu vaccine. How could you do something so twisted? Is this why Sara is dead?"

Richard's condescending manner was obvious. "Callie, Callie, Callie, don't you know research costs money? Once the bank approved my loan, it was only right to include Sara in the study . . . such a simpleton, that one. Boy, her insecurities were off the charts. Put that up against a suggestion that you harbored unrequited romantic interest in me, and her claws came out. But as always, you were right. When I confronted her with the possibility of her being traumatically shaken at a very young age, she confirmed it. She had to go."

Callie didn't want to cry. She choked it down, but felt a tear escape across her temple. "But how? You were booked solid up until the time she disappeared."

"Callie, don't waste your tears on Sara. Trust me, she wouldn't do it for you. You see, appearances can be deceiving. It was shortly after I began experimenting with her, she called me with some frantic message, before the mailbox was full, thinking she was going crazy. I took the message, transferred it to my tablet and modified it using a voice recording app and played it, using a burner phone. That's what I called you with that Friday. But she was long-since dead, killed the evening before. What I hadn't counted on was you leading some type of humanitarian charge on Sara's behalf. I was able to plant her phone back at the apartment, but thanks to you, the lock to her apartment was changed before I had an opportunity to get my equipment out."

Callie couldn't wrap her head around it. "But at Kyle Anderson's pool?"

"Look, Anderson had given Sara a lot of shit over that shirt. So, after Thursday night's dinner, I proposed a little naughty fun. I suggested we go over his place and skinny dip. At first, she didn't want to go, told me she couldn't swim. I reassured her we'd stay in the shallow end . . . have sex, but needed to keep the noise at a bare minimum . . . get it? It would be daring, not getting caught. I knew Anderson had left for a long weekend. What is it that they say about the best-laid plans? Anyway, she eventually got into the idea. She even suggested leaving our underwear behind for him to find, a slap in the face. Basically, I pinned her in a corner and held her head under the water until she stopped resisting. Humph, now that I think about it, that was the first time since I'd met her that she stayed quiet for so long. That's why I never emptied my voicemail. I couldn't take another one of her damn ridiculous messages."

Callie remembered, *there was a parasite in the water*

that year, forcing the fish to shallow water. Ultimately, the fish were oxygen deprived and died. "I believed in you. How can you be so callous?"

"That's your trouble, Callie. You believe too much. I thought the jig was up when you asked Sara about the Japanese Maple in the front of the bank, its foliage."

Callie thought back to Sara's response, *who cares? It's just a tree.*

"Oh, come on, Callie. You're the smart one. Mary Scott?"

Callie drew a blank, and her expression showed it.

"I suppose I need to draw you a picture. I asked Sara to spend the weekend with me, but at my condo, not out-of-town. She was such an easy lay. That Saturday night, I logged into the system and saw you had an admission. I told Sara I was going to get us some take-out, but I went to the hospital first. They were understaffed, as usual. After I hit the mute button on her monitoring equipment, a syringe was attached to the sampling port. It was partially filled with heparinized saline and topped off with air. It was driven into the woman's arterial line with a high-pressure syringe pump, and violà, retrograde cerebral air embolism. The whole thing took less than 5 minutes, in-and-out. Don't worry, she didn't suffer . . . much."

She knew the confessions would come with a price,

her silence. If death was inevitable, Callie needed to know why. He could've chosen anyone else to practice his obscene science, *anyone else*. "Why me, Richard? You were supposed to be my friend."

His patronizing demeanor went dead serious. "You can't possibly understand. My mother was such a beautiful woman."

"Was?"

"Yes, she killed herself one week after I left for Southern Methodist University. She left a note saying her intention was to wait until after I left home, way on the road to success just like I'd promised her I would be. She died a broken woman, and her death broke me. It seems only fair your mother should suffer the same fate."

Callie didn't know the deranged man beside her. "What on earth does my mother have to do with anything? Don't drag her into this insanity."

"Really, Callie, I don't think you're in any position to make demands," he said followed by a hedonistic chuckle. "It was a quirk, really. While I was an undergraduate in Dallas, the Dead Letter Office of the United States Postal Service forwarded a letter to me—one that I didn't recognize. It had been undeliverable because of insufficient postage. I did recognize the sender, my father. Evidently, with the crude handwriting, Tomas was inadvertently taken as Tohias. It was addressed to a Rose Wallace of Sperling. I read it, of course, and learned who the woman was that destroyed my family home. When we were assigned that project in medical school, the realization was almost instant . . . it hung in my gut. Do you know what it was like, sucking up to you, day after day, to gain your trust? It was sickening, really."

Callie reflected on what her Aunt Clare had said, referring to her sister as a homewrecker. "Richard, I know my mother, and something isn't right. You have to believe me. We can clear this up. Besides, the way you tell it, my mother should be tied to this litter, not me. You're confused. We can talk this out."

"Wow, what a way to throw your own mother under the bus, Callie. But let me make myself clear. My mother always told me that nothing hurts a parent like seeing their child suffer. She took a beating for me more than once, you know. Don't get me wrong, I thought about it, taking your mother out myself. I almost did it one day. Remember when I borrowed your car? I'd told you I had a flat and was waiting for the auto club. But some Good Samaritan intervened. You need to trust me, though. This is will pain her far more."

"So, your answer is to destroy my life, and then take it, all for my mother to watch?"

"My name will go down in the history books. That would show my father. Who knows? He still could be out there somewhere, the son-of-a-bitch."

She knew no reputable journal would publish his work. "The way I understand it, your father didn't care enough for his own family, much less anyone else's. Looking at you now, I see the family resemblance."

That was the grain of salt in Richard's open wound—his raw nerve exposed. "That's the difference between you and me, Callie. You're so compassionate, so caring . . . so weak. Good science takes sacrifice."

A cacophonous buzzer went off.

"Speaking of, there's the sterilizer," he said. "It's time to collect your sample, Callie. It will be the pièce de résistance of my research. You should feel proud. And for your information, the only mistake I've made was using awls. Do you know how expensive they are? The other day, I picked up an ice pick for next to nothing at the dollar store. I'll go get it. Now, don't go anywhere. I'll be right back."

The man's sybaritic laugh sent chills up her spine. Callie started to hyperventilate, but it was more from anger than panic. She screamed out, "You know what, Richard? Dr. Daniels was right, you don't have what it takes to be a doctor!"

Fifty-nine

Friday, November 24, 2017, Dickerson Wholesale

The old area of Sperling hardly saw any foot traffic, but that day, it appeared deserted. The lawmen parked the car half a block away to avoid suspicion, deciding to walk in. There was only about twenty minutes of daylight left, and a cool drizzle started to fall which quickened their pace. There was no doubt the Dickerson warehouse had seen better days. The windows at eye level were boarded up, but not the upper rows of clerestory windows. Some were busted out, some were not, but mineral and dirt deposits dulled them. The pitched metal roof made access seem almost impossible.

As the two men started to approach the building, Marcus asked, “You got a first name?”

The detective watched his step, careful not to trip over a heavy-duty extension cord that ran along the blacktop, back into an adjacent building. “Looks like someone is siphoning power. Do you think it’s Cortez?”

Marcus thought the theory plausible. “Maybe. You ignoring my question?”

"I guess I don't see the relevance of it, that's all."

"We're about to go into a dangerous situation, someone's life on the line. Seems to me like I ought to know the name of the man whose back I'm covering," Marcus explained.

You know what, Richard? Dr. Daniels was right, you don't have what it takes to be a doctor!

"Holy shit!" Monroe exclaimed. "Did you hear that? I'm going back to the car to call for back-up."

"Wait," Marcus urgently whispered. "That's her—she's in there, but you heard Lambert, the man is desperate. Hell, he practically snatched the woman right under my nose."

"Is that supposed to be funny?" Monroe inquired, not amused.

"What?"

"Forget it," Monroe acquiesced. "Look, we need a plan. We could rush him, but with a building this size, he could get to Dr. Wallace before we could take him out. Another idea is to pull that plug. If that's Cortez's only electrical source, that would stop him in his tracks. He might come out here and check the connection and we could grab him then, but frankly, I think the guy's too smart for that. He might sense a set-up. I'm sorry, Marcus, but I think we need to call in the Hostage Negotiation Team. You need to look for a way for us to see inside. I'm going to call this in."

The detective turned the northwest corner of the building, but quickly drew back. “Damn!”

“What is it?” Marcus asked.

“It’s some guy, a rodeo-type. I don’t think he saw me. He was looking down at a tablet.”

Marcus peeked around the corner. The man had a side door open. He called inside.

Come on, Callie. Enough with the games already. Come on out—let’s talk. It looks dangerous down here.

Marcus rushed to the extension cord and pulled the connection apart. The situation had turned critical. If they were going in handicapped, he wanted Cortez to be too. “Let’s go, Monroe.”

The detective was hot on the agent’s heels, a hint of embarrassment to his voice. “Marcus, before we go in there, it’s Marion. My name is Marion Monroe.”

Marcus let the information sink in, the significance of it all, before he let out a muffled snort. “Come on, friend, hurry up. We’ve got a job to do, and I want to go home.”

She could see Richard coming at her through the corner of her eye. He wore a procedural headlamp and was holding an ice pick, a pair of grasping forceps, and a container that amounted to nothing more than a denture cup. It came to her, *but do you know how the*

parasite enters your body? I'll tell you, it's through the nose. Unpleasant, right?

But Callie's name being called out stopped Richard in his tracks. It was Zane. That's when it all went black except for the headlamp he wore, but he quickly shut it off.

Callie called out, knowing it could be the last words she spoke. "Zane, be careful. It's Richard, he has a weapon. He changed Clyde Murphy's dose and it killed him. Sara, too. He drowned her. I'm back here, tied down. He wants to kill me. I'm so sorry, Zane. Please forgive me."

She'd said what needed to be said and prepared herself for the pick to come down on her, but it didn't happen. There was silence, a deafening silence. She lay in the dark, praying for her eyes to adjust. A stool fell over to the far left of her, followed by a faint expletive. She wondered if Richard was still beside her. "Richard?" she whispered.

Silence

Only a hint of residual sunlight shone at the horizon as the sun crept beneath it. Marcus and Monroe entered the warehouse, closing the door behind them. Marcus informed the detective that Zane was the name of Callie's boyfriend, but neither could venture a guess what had brought him there. They agreed to split up, one to the left, one to the right—their guns drawn.

"Cortez!" Monroe screamed out. "There's no getting out of this."

Silence

Marcus liked the idea of drawing the man out. If they could elicit a response from him, they could follow his voice. "Cortez, we know about your mother. I bet your crazy-ass drove her to kill herself."

Richard took pause, *Marcus from the hospital*? "You shut the fuck-up, Marcus! This doesn't concern you. And if you mention my mother again, I'll cut your dick off with a popsicle stick."

Bingo, Marcus thought. "Like to see you try, *T-o-b-i-a-s*."

Marcus wasn't sure, but he thought he heard angry grunts. He continued his blind advance.

Callie's heart was pounding, but when she felt the hand slip over her mouth, she heard it booming in her ears. He came in close to her, she felt his breath on her cheek. "Callie, it's Zane," he murmured. "I'm going to take my hand away, so no more than a whisper, okay?"

"Zane, he has me restrained. Start with my wrists. If my hands are loose, I can help with the other ties.

Say you forgive me, please, I just need to hear it. I've been such a fool."

Zane began to feel his way down her arm. The restraint was leather, buckled in place. He started to work it lose. "Callie, you're not the only one that needs forgiving, but let's sort that out later."

With her hands freed, Callie began to help Zane with the head immobilizer. To her, no doubt, the cruelest of her shackles—one meant to stabilize her head so he could extract his sample. She knew he'd planned to keep her conscious, a demoralizing act to mock her privileged life. Once the waist restraint was removed, Callie sat up. "Zane, you get the left ankle, I'll get the right," she whispered.

Fumbling around in the dark, she felt for the buckle. The shadow creeping up behind Zane caught her eye, but it was too late. The silhouette of the ice pick came down to his back, Zane calling out in pain as he dropped to his knees. The contours of a mad man left standing.

Callie quickly finished the work Zane had started and took a standing position on the gurney. There was no time to think. She would have no running start, her adrenaline had to be her momentum. In gymnastics, the move was called an Arabian flip. She flung herself off the cart, turning high in the vast darkness over Richard. Her landing was spotless, behind her

Judas. Callie turned and snatched the headlamp off his head. She flipped it on, aiming the beam at Richard's deranged face. That's when the muzzle flash came and a shot rang out across the warehouse. The weight of Richard's body took him swiftly to the ground. Callie heard his final words, *Madre, eres tan hermosa*. Whether Richard, himself, had experienced a vision or it was some trickery of a bullet-mangled brain, the man's last thought was of his mother, *Mother, you are so beautiful*.

Sixty

Sunday, November 26, 2017 5:10 p.m.

Callie and her mother sat in Zane's hospital room. They were expecting Detective Monroe any minute to brief them. Zane was in good spirits, considering the chest tube that was in place. His lung had collapsed as a result of the puncture, but the thoracic specialist didn't foresee any further complications.

They were all on edge, awaiting what further peril Richard had left for them to deal with. Rose didn't want to have that talk with Callie, but she knew it was necessary. She pulled two dated envelopes from her purse and broached the subject. "Callie, I can't begin to understand what you might be feeling right now. I hope you know how much you're loved and that we're here to support you. I don't want to put any more on your plate than you're already dealing with, but it's time. It's time we talked about the summer of 1995."

Zane felt the need to shield Callie from anymore heartache. "Rose, is something twenty-two years ago really relevant right now? Maybe it can wait for another time?"

The mother was unyielding. "Zane, there are things a parent just doesn't tell a child, but Callie isn't a child anymore. It's time she knew the truth. Callie, I want you to read these letters. Note the sender in the upper left-hand corner."

Callie took the antiquated envelopes from her mother and read the return address, "Tomas Cortez, Dallas, Texas. Richard's father?"

Rose nodded. "Honestly, I hadn't made the connection until you were over the other day."

Callie recalled how her Aunt Clare had insinuated that her mother was the reason for her failed marriage. Callie thought the worst, taking one of the letters out to read. She read the first few lines before she couldn't keep her feelings to herself. "Mother, did you have an affair?"

"No, Callie, no," Rose insisted. "It was nothing like that—keep reading."

Callie wasn't sure what to believe. She continued to read, until she finally said, "This man sounds insane."

Rose confirmed her daughter's suspicions. "Not only insane, but dangerous as well. Read the other letter, Callie."

She got the other letter out. Callie's mouth fell open when she got to the point where the man said that Rose's unrequited love would cost her daughter her life—that he was losing patience.

Callie thought it, but didn't want to ask. "Mother, did you know Tomas and Teresa Cortez had three sons?"

Rose knew Callie had to have questions. "Dear, there's another child."

Callie dropped the letters. Her hands rushed to cover a gaping mouth.

She couldn't believe her ears. It took her awhile to find her words. "For Pete's sake, Mother, are you saying my cousin, Tommy, is Richard's half-brother?"

Rose had tears flowing down her cheeks. "I'm afraid so, but I don't want the boy told. Why have this grief put at his door? His life is just getting started."

Callie needed to know more. "So, this man's sick infatuation with you just stopped? What became of him?"

This was the part Rose dreaded. She didn't want to lie if it wasn't absolutely necessary. She knew it was Marta that had forged the letter Clare had found. Rose knew how Clare felt, so the letter was structured in a way to confirm it, making it more believable to her sister. "Callie, I can honestly say, I don't know where Tomas landed up. All I know for sure is that the letters stopped."

There was a knock on the door and Detective Monroe popped his head in. "Is it a good time?"

All eyes were on the detective as he took a seat. "I'm sure you have questions. Some of them, we may never know the answer. Going through his condo, interviews with people who knew him from college, the one common theme that keeps rearing its ugly head was his contempt for the Wallace family. Apparently, he bided his time, the adage that revenge is best served cold, that sort of thing."

"Revenge for what?" Callie asked him. "I never did anything to him that would warrant such cruelty."

The detective knew it would be hard for her to hear. "It's not anything you did, per se. Coming from what appeared to be an idealistic family, living in Hometown, America. These are things Richard never had. And in his mind, he didn't have that because of you, Mrs. Wallace."

Rose panicked at the sound of her name. When she'd told Callie and Zane about Tomas, she hoped that it would just stay in the family. She couldn't let the *entire* truth come out. She had to protect Marta just like Marta had protected her and her family. "His father was married to my sister for a brief time. It's my understanding that he left her."

The detective continued. "But it wasn't her that Tomas Cortez had designs on, was it, Mrs. Wallace?"

Rose could barely speak. "How did you know?"

Monroe wouldn't give specifics. "We found a letter his father had written to you in Richard's belongings."

Zane wondered how Sara fitted into the equation. "What was his motive with Sara Townsend?"

Monroe thought the question was reasonable. "He saw her as malleable with very little family to speak of—a pawn if you will. There was no one to question her behavior. Before the incident at the warehouse, I'd received a text from the head waiter at *La Pomme d' Amour.* He listed the items on the couple's dinner ticket that night which included duck confit with pickled raisins, making her time of death more conclusive and consistent with what Cortez had told Dr. Wallace. I have to admit, Dr. Cortez fooled me when he said, *what, so kill Sara Townsend and place her in Anderson's pool?* His statement indicated to me that he thought she was killed outside the water while I knew she died from drowning. He played me."

Callie knew how close she'd come to losing Zane, but there were others not so lucky. "What about the Murphy chart and my password?"

"I do have some good news. IT experts have verified that that particular order was modified only thirty minutes after it was originally put in. That, in conjunction with Dr. Cortez in possession of your password and evidence to show malicious intent towards you, puts a really big hole in Mrs. Murphy's lawsuit—one she's unlikely to win. Also, there's Dr. Lambert's expert opinion that a person's hallucinogenic state is what that person believes to be true. The tapered dosage that is true to you is 64 mg, not 6 mg."

Callie felt some relief, but she wondered what had become of justice. "It's seems so unfair that Richard will never have to pay for what he did to Sara and me, not to mention that Korean student or Mary Scott."

Monroe thought about the homeless man—a population too often forgotten. He'd gone to explain to the Scott family what had become of their loved one. They were still trying to make sense of it . . . in a state of shock. One thing for sure, Anderson would have to answer for the CT scan results that he withheld from them.

But when it came to Richard Cortez's so-called science, that was another story. He remembered Gus Ferguson and when he had to explain the limitations of the law. "Now, don't get me wrong, murder is murder and kidnapping . . . kidnapping, but Dr. Wallace, your type of case would've presented a conundrum for the district attorney. In the past, unethical human experimentations have occurred without prosecution. In general, society doesn't expect criminal behavior from researchers. To punish a culpable researcher, whether intentional or not, might deter other research efforts. With what Richard Cortez did to you, the district attorney's hands would've been tied to a charge of assault and battery, and depraved indifference."

Zane had never heard the term before. "What is depraved indifference?"

"It's engaging in reckless conduct with grave risk to life, or possibly, the death of another," the detective explained.

The whole situation frustrated Zane. "But what is Callie to do now? Where is she to practice medicine and not inadvertently be exposed to ultrasound? How long will she be symptomatic? This whole thing is insane!"

Callie didn't give the detective an opportunity to respond. "I've already spoken to Dr. Lambert. He's prescribed for me a low-dose calcium channel blocker, targeting N-type channels. He plans to start controlled studies on me in his office next week. We believe, with continued use, the blocker will impede further hallucinations in the presence of extraneous ultrasound."

"Callie, that's great," Zane said with relief.

What happened next caught everyone in the room by surprise. Callie had been foolish, so much time blindly trusting Richard. But one thing was true . . . her love for Zane. Callie got down on one knee. "Zane, you are my world, and somewhere along the way, I lost sight of that. What I've learned is that no plan can ever prepare you for what surprises life can bring, good or bad. We need to trust in those who love us to handle what comes our way, whatever that may be. I trust you, implicitly, and though I may not deserve it, can you put your trust in me? Zane, what I'm saying is, I want to marry you."

Everyone waited with bated breath for Zane's response. But the look on his face wasn't one a person would expect . . . it was dread. "Callie, there's something I've been meaning to tell you."

Callie's hopeful expression sank. She got to her feet. "Okay?"

"It's about how I found you the other day. I don't need people making me out to be some kind of hero, when I'm not. You see, the night I took you up to the hospital when that lady died, I know you called me Richard. You denied it, but I knew what I'd heard. Honestly, I didn't know what to make of it, or how you were behaving. I believed the worse, that there was somebody else and that somebody might be Richard. I had to know, so when you were asleep, I installed a spyware app on your phone. It became hidden after installation, so you'd have no way of knowing. The other day, after your mother sent out that text, I actually found the agent carrying your phone around, not you. I just thought you should know."

Callie was caught off guard, but her resolve was strong. "Zane, you cared enough to *do something* about my behavior even when I didn't. I knew something wasn't right, but instead of addressing the issue, I denied it. I even went as far as trying to beat the psychological exams, and when it came to the hallucinations I'd been having, I kept that from Dr. Lambert. I lied by omission. Zane, you are my life, and I won't make another decision that puts our relationship at risk. So, I'm going to ask you again, will you marry me?"

His smile said it all. "Well, when you put it that way, what took you so long? I'd love to marry you, Callie, but I do have one condition, though."

Callie wasn't about to let anything get in their way. "Lay it on me."

Zane explained. "You know what family means to me. I must insist that Mother Rose comes with us. There's plenty of room in that big old house. Not to mention our kids will need their Nana."

Callie glanced over at her mother who looked stunned by the offer. "Mom, what do you say?"

Rose cleared her throat, trying not to cry. The word *Mom* didn't go unnoticed. "I think that would be a wonderful idea. But what about your practice?"

"I'm going to try and sell it. I'm not going to be specializing in neurology any more. I plan to concentrate my practice on rural medicine. I'm leaving Sperling and going to open an office in Hoffen."

No one was taken more by surprise by what had just transpired than Detective Monroe. "Where's Hoffen?"

Callie was glad to explain. "It's a small German community, a hop-skip-and-a-jump from the Atkins' ranch, with about twenty-five-hundred people."

Sixty-one

Monday, January 1, 2018 3:30 p.m.

It had been a grand New Year's Day, and a long time coming, some would say. Earlier that afternoon, Callie and Zane had exchanged vows. Rose was the Matron of Honor. Zane's father stood up for his son. Callie wanted to honor Gus Ferguson for his role in uncovering the hidden ultrasound equipment at the hospital. People were having trouble deciding who was beaming more, the bride, or Gus Ferguson walking her down the aisle. Delores was crying her eyes out, her camera clicking away with each step taken.

The Atkins' home was full of family and friends, celebrating the union of the two they held dear. The couple exchanged gifts. Zane gave his bride a shingle to hang outside her new office in Hoffen. It read: Dr. Callie Atkins. She'd sold the practice in Sperling to the traveling relief specialist from Dallas. Callie got Zane a customized saddle he'd been eyeing at the local leatherworks shop. Marcus Davis had driven up for the occasion. He and Marion Monroe were in the corner, cutting up. Most likely at the expense of Kyle Anderson, but perhaps, that someone named Marion could be such a deadeye with a gun. Jamie and Cody were snuggled on the couch as if they were making future plans of their own.

In an upstairs bedroom, away from the reception crowd, two friends were saying *see you later.* They refused to say goodbye. Rose had sold her house in Sperling.

"The neighborhood just isn't the same without you, Rose, but the new neighbors seem nice," Marta said, trying to sound positive. "But change is good, right? I know you were looking forward to getting closer with Callie. How's that going?"

"Callie still has to deal with the fallout from the loan Richard took out with First National, but she and her attorney are going into mediation with them in a couple of weeks. She's been able to recoup part of the money by selling some of the equipment he'd bought."

"I saw her home was for sale," Marta commented.

"Maybe someday it will sell, but there haven't been a lot of offers, considering. That asshole had equipment on a timer up in her closet, tiny cameras and listening bugs planted every which way to Sunday. I heard the Townsend apartment was the same."

"But she's doing okay?"

"Marta, she's practically a new woman. The medication has kept her symptom free. I couldn't have asked for more. Do you know Callie asked me to call her Corky? But I told her that was something she'd shared with her father and we should work on finding something special just between us. I think I'm going to show her how to make those cookies she likes so much. Did I ever thank you for that recipe?" Rose's voice cracked. She was choking up.

Marta moved closer to her friend on the bed. "Now, Rose don't cry."

Rose couldn't seem to help it. She missed her special talks with Marta. They had shared so much.

Marta tried to remain upbeat, but she, herself, was feeling the loss. "You know what? It won't be long before you're making those cookies for your grandchildren. You're going to have to bring them to visit Aunt Marta and Uncle Raul. But how about you tell me what's really bothering you? Is it your blood pressure?"

Rose wiped a tear off her cheek, but she felt proud of her numbers. "I'll have you know, Marta, my pressure this morning was 138/84. How about that, huh? That was with the stress of the pending nuptials and everything."

Marta was glad to hear it. "Rose, that's wonderful. It had to be a relief to get the burden of Tomas off your chest. I can only assume it was an important factor in mending your relationship with Callie. But come on, Rose. I know you. Something else is on your mind. What is it?"

Rose blew out a heavy sigh. "Lately, I been thinking a lot about what we did to Tomas Cortez. I have some guilt. I feel like I'm responsible for taking a life. But there's no one I can talk to about this, except you."

Marta couldn't believe her ears. "Guilty? That man threatened your daughter. We wouldn't be here celebrating today if we hadn't done something. He didn't care how many lives he ruined. I don't want to hear you talking like that, Rose."

Rose perked up. "I can't help how I feel, but you know what I did? I took some of the money from the house sale and put it to good use. I feel like I might actually be *saving* a life."

Sperling

Flurries batted around in the air. Jane Timmons hugged the south wall of the mission shelter, trying to block the north wind. The shelter would unlock its doors in thirty minutes and she wanted to make sure she got a bed for the night.

Most people turned away when they saw her coming, but a well-dressed woman approached her. "Hello, I've been asking around for someone named Jane. I was told she might be here. Are you Jane Timmons?"

Jane was leery. "Who wants to know?"

The woman handed Jane her card. "My name is Janice Miller. I'm with Hope House, the rehabilitation and assistance center. I'm the trustee of a donation that has been made on the behalf of Jane Timmons. Do you have any identification?"

Jane couldn't believe what she was hearing. Her first thought was that it might be some cruel joke. But she began to dig through her cart to find a tattered wallet with little money. It contained her driver's license. She opened it and showed the woman.

"Very good," the woman said, extending her hand. "Come with me, Jane. Let's start putting your life back together, okay?"

THE END